Contents

Hero of Rome

Book 9
in
The Sword of Cartimandua series
By
Griff Hosker

Hero of Rome

A CIP catalogue record for this title is available from the British Library.

Map of Northern Britannia in 122 A.D.

Prologue

Senator Julius Demetrius waited, patiently, outside the Principia of the First Germanica Legion fortress at Castra Vetera in Germania Inferior. Having been summoned by Emperor Hadrian, Julius had ridden hard to reach this tenuously defended frontier of the Empire. The land he had ridden through had reminded the former cavalryman of his time in that other dangerous northern outpost, Britannia, but Germania appeared to be populated by far more forests. Every Roman soldier remembered the disaster of the Teutonberger forest and travelled through this dangerous land with every sense alert to danger. When he reached the fortress he noticed that the legionaries of the First Germanica had the hard lean look he had seen amongst the now-disbanded Ninth legion; you could take a legionary and put him anywhere and he would look the same, tough and resilient. As he heard the clatter of hooves outside, the former senator saw a troop of auxiliary cavalry trot into the fortress. That was the difference between legionaries and auxiliaries, the auxiliaries always managed to look exotic, even when they wore standard Roman armour. Some had distinctive shields or weapons whilst others used a variety of saddlecloths but each had a standard which marked them distinctly on the battlefield. Now that he knew where he was being posted Julius was looking forward to returning to Britannia and seeing Livius and his latest ala.

The ancient clerk shuffled out of the office, his inky fingers absentmindedly marking his bald pate as he scratched it. "The Emperor will see you now." The other waiting officers clambered forward but his stridently high voice squeaked, "All in good time gentlemen; the Emperor knows that you are waiting."

After the noise and energy in the outer office, the interior felt remarkably calm. Hadrian was standing at a calfskin map pinned to the wall of the fortress office. Without turning Hadrian pointed his vine staff at the province of Britannia and said, "No matter what my so-called advisers say about the precarious nature of this frontier it is nothing compared with the problems of Britannia. At least here we have a river as a natural barrier and an enemy which, thankfully, does not use boats." He turned to clasp Julius' forearm. "Good to see you old friend. How was the journey?"

"I should have come by boat; I think it would have been more comfortable."

Hadrian laughed. "I know the older you get the harder the saddle appears and the more unforgiving the horses." He unrolled a smaller calfskin map on the table. "Now we have little time to waste." He pointed at the map. "Our protégé Lucius has done well. He had the intelligence to have his clerk draw a map of the region and the salient features. It seems to the Decurion Princeps, and I agree with him, that this strip of land north of the Stanegate would be perfect for our *limes*. There is a steep cliff to the north for much of it and there is a river at both its eastern and western extremities. I want you to go to Britannia and liaise with the new Governor, Quintus Pompeius Falco. I need the two of you to build me a line of defences from coast to coast."

Julius leaned over the table to inspect the map. It had been some time since he had had cause to look at a map of the province he had served in as a young man. "As I recall that looks like the best site. "He pointed to a place further north on the map. "It is narrower here. It would require fewer fortifications. I recall that Agricola built some forts here."

"Yes that would make life easier but the land north of the Stanegate is too unstable at the moment. From the reports I have received, the natives on both sides of the Stanegate are becoming restless, Governor Bradua did not perform as well as I would have hoped." Bradua was the former Governor and Lucius had sent reports back to the Emperor reporting on his mistakes. "The two of you will have to build the defences and control the natives at the same time." He looked intently at Julius. "I realise that I am not making your job any easier. As soon as we have secured this frontier I intend to visit the province and see at first-hand what it is like."

Julius shrugged. "We both know, Emperor, that the lot of the soldier is never easy."

Hadrian slapped Julius on the back. "Good man! I knew I could rely on you. It is reassuring that I can give the task to two such sound and reliable men. By the way, do you know Falco?"

Julius smiled, "Actually we were at military school together. I think I spent more time with him than my brother Scipio."

"That is even better. Now then do you have any questions? I will be sailing to the province just as soon as this frontier is stable but I realise that the two of you will have to make decisions without direct reference to me."

"Well I won't have a problem working with Quintus but I know that the Prefects of the legions are sometimes a little prickly about their men. What authority will I have?"

Hadrian handed over a letter. "Here is your authority. You act in my name. I trust you Julius and know that the power will not be abused." He peered curiously at Julius. "How do you intend to use the legions then?"

"It seems to me that, if the tribes are restless, it would be unwise to take a legion from a region further south for it would weaken our tenuous hold on the other Britannic frontiers; far better to use a vexillation from each of the legions and have them responsible for their own section of the frontier. It appears to be about ninety miles of frontier, which means thirty miles of building for each vexillation. They can build their own forts and the auxiliaries can protect them."

"Good. I have ordered more auxiliary units to be dispatched to the north of the province. I assume that you and Falco will see to their deployment?"

"That will be a crucial deployment. It is a difficult frontier to police."

"I know Julius which is the reason I am sending my two best Legates."

Chapter 1

Faolan surveyed the seas to the east. For his tribe, the Ebdani, the wild waters were a constant source of speculation as well as a supply of slaves. The traders who ventured this far west told them tales of the Romani who had conquered the tribes of Albion. That was not the cause of their speculation for peoples had conquered and departed before, leaving little trace of their passing on the land but these, they were told were different; for they built in stone and they left their indelible mark upon the land. It was said that their homes were warmed by the earth in the winters and they could make water move uphill. Even the wise women of their tribe could not explain that phenomenon. They also made mighty weapons which were the cause of Faolan's interest. He had risen through his clan to be the leader and now eyed the throne of the tribe with a hidden and secret desire. His cousin Corentine was the king and far too powerful for him to be assaulted but if Faolan could obtain those weapons of the Romani then he might be able to seize the crown from his popular cousin. He had tried, in vain, to persuade his cousin to invade the rich, ripe lands of Britannia but Corentine worried that his neighbours, the Voluntii would use the opportunity to invade and steal their land while they were fleecing the now tamed Brigantes and Carvetii of the west. The land itself was important but more important was the holy site which they controlled; Si an Bhru was so old that even the tales about it were shrouded in mystery. It was also the largest stone building on the whole island. Whoever controlled the monument controlled the priests of the ancestors and they controlled the people.

"Lord?"

"What is it Loegaire?" His chief bodyguard and oathsworn warrior was far older than Faolan but devoted to his lord. The veteran Ebdani had fought all over Hibernia with Faolan's father and now devoted his life to the service of the young prince.

"The day is ending."

Faolan sighed, his men feared him but they also feared saying the wrong thing which meant it took all day to get a simple answer to a simple question. "And?"

"The High Priestess said that we were to arrive before the sun had set."

Loegaire was a huge bull of a warrior and as loyal as they came but he had a mortal fear of witches and the priestesses of the Mother. Faolan doubted that they had as much power as they suggested and had only agreed to the meeting as a means of improving his chances of kingship. "Fear not. We will reach the shrine in time. It is but a short way away. Come."

The thirty warriors, the only mounted warriors in the Ebdani, kicked their short ponies to follow their leader over the spongy turf. They were all lightly armed and none wore armour for they were safe within their own lands. Faolan's reputation as a puissant warrior meant that few would dare to raid their cattle or steal their women. It was one of the reasons Corentine allowed his obvious rival to live, he was insurance against anyone else taking his throne.

Sceanbh was old, even by the standards of the priests and druids of Mona from whence she had come, sixty years earlier having fled the Roman war machine. She had harboured a hatred for the Romans ever since. She had been frustrated for most of her life by warriors who preferred to war amongst themselves rather than taking on the might that was Rome. Her frustration had ended when the daughter of her fellow priestess Fainch had moved from Britannia to Manavia. Morwenna had used some of the Keltoi as her bodyguards and this had encouraged the old priestess to recruit more. She had identified Faolan as a tool she could use to foster an invasion of Britannia. Brynna, one of Morwenna's daughters had brought messages from the island to Sceanbh, messages which had been calculated to induce Keltoi warriors to take up the challenge of fighting the Romans.

She watched the warriors as they trotted towards her. She was not offended that Faolan had chosen to delay his arrival, she was well aware of his attitude towards her and her priestesses; it mattered little. He was a tool with which she would gain her revenge on the Romans. She had chosen Faolan from the other leaders for his cunning and his aptitude with a blade. She needed a powerful warrior and he fitted the picture she had in her mind. She knew of his desire to be king and that would be the key to her manipulation of this erstwhile king. She watched Faolan leading his men and saw that he had all the qualities which would make men and women follow him. He was taller than most of his men and, to an old woman's eyes, handsome. His dark beard and jet black hair framed a powerful face. But it was his eyes which were the most disturbing feature; they were a cold hard blue which both mesmerised and terrified all who peered into the translucent pools.

She knew that she had little time left before she joined her sisters with the Mother and so speed was of the essence. She entered the low passageway to the chamber she used as her home. She smiled as she saw the warriors with Faolan look fearfully at the ring of standing stones which surrounded the outside of the enormous rock-lined tomb. She marvelled that men, who feared no living creature, could not face the dead. The lamp which burned in the chamber gave off an eerie yellow light and reflected on the pile of yellowing bones in the corner. Sceanbh had created the effect to inspire awe. Most men would refuse to enter this place of the dead and Faolan's reaction would tell her much about the man she had chosen to be her champion. The bones were so old that millennia had passed since they were interred and the old women did not fear the dead.

The princeling's face showed no emotion as he stooped to enter the small and claustrophobic chamber. Sceanbh gestured for him to sit on the stone which passed for a seat. She offered him neither food nor drink but held his gaze. Faolan had expected such a test and he stared back intently. The dead and their priests did not frighten him. Eventually, apparently satisfied, the old woman nodded. "You desire to be king."

The bald statement was unexpected and Faolan, for once, was taken aback. He quickly recovered his composure and shrugged. "I am related to the king but he lives and I am a loyal warrior to my liege lord."

"But you would be king and I can give you an opportunity to achieve your aim."

Faolan suspected a trap but he could not see who had set it. Sceanbh was known to be unconcerned about worldly matters so the question remained; who was setting the trap, if this was a trap? He kept silent and watched, now with more interest, the emaciated skin and bones which stared back at him, rheumy blue eyes boring deeply into him. "The king grows fat and will not go to war. How will you become king?" There was no answer for Faolan knew that the old woman would get to the point eventually and he was a patient man. "Suppose you had a weapon of legend and suppose that you could attain glory; would that not enable you to become king?"

"A weapon? Where is there such a weapon of legend?" Faolan wracked his memory for the stories of mystical blades but he could not recall any of the many.

The old woman smiled for she knew now that she had intrigued this would be king. "In Britannia, across the water, there is the sword of the Brigantes, The Sword of Cartimandua."

Faolan's interest was piqued. He had indeed heard of the weapon and knew that it had won many a lost battle for the one who wielded it. All swords had powers, every warrior knew this but the sword of the Brigante was even older than the oldest weapon wielded by the many kings of Hibernia. It was said that it had travelled from the south, from the lands of the Gauls when the Celtic peoples who had lived there had conquered Albion and Hibernia. "I heard that the sword had been lost when the Queen disappeared."

"No, it still exists and is worn by a Roman."

"Then how would I get my hands on such a weapon?"

"The lands of Roman Britannia are no longer secure. The Votadini defeated them and they have taken the vaunted legions back to Rome. It is a plum which is ripe for the picking. You would gain much honour and fame." She smiled as she saw that her seed had been successfully planted.

Faolan's face filled with suspicion as he wondered at the source of this remarkable intelligence. "How do you know this? You never leave the safety of this shrine."

She laughed a cackling laugh which made Faolan shiver in the dark bone lined tomb. "I may not leave but others come and go. Believe me Faolan, warrior of the Ebdani, if you land in Britannia with enough warriors then there will be nought to stop you. Not only will you achieve the sword but slaves and gold, for the Romans and their puppets, the Brigante, are rich beyond belief."

Faolan began to consider the prospect. There were many swords which would follow him in a quest to gain treasure. The slaves alone which could be captured would pay for the raid and make him rich. He also knew that the land of the Britons was a richer land than that of the Keltoi; the Romans had brought much prosperity. The thought came to him that, even if he did not gain the sword, he would gain enough riches to enlarge his army and enable him to take the throne by force. His eyes narrowed and he leaned forward. "I cannot believe that you are doing this because you wish to do me good. What is in this for you?"

"You are wise Faolan. You see my mind. What I want from you is a promise. When you become king you will make Si an Bhru the centre of worship and study protected by your warriors and you will continue to raid and steal from Britannia until the Romans are driven from its shores."

Faolan considered the offer. What did it matter to him if the priests and priestesses gained power, it would not affect him if he were king. As to the raids on Britannia, that was already an idea growing in the greedy mind of the Ebdani prince. "I will do so if you will endorse my raid as a war for the Mother."

"I was right to choose you, Faolan, Prince of the Ebdani. It will be done and when you have enough warriors you can travel to Manavia where there is already an army of Keltoi warriors there, waiting to serve with you."

Faolan looked at her in surprise. "You have already planned this?"

"The Mother, in her wisdom, has worked towards this since the Romans desecrated the holy groves of Mona."

Morwenna's second daughter, Caronwyn had not only her mother's hair and eyes but also the fierce determination to be revenged on those who had killed her Grandmother. While Brynna had been in Hibernia enlisting the help of the warriors there, she had been sent to the land of the Brigantes to foster dissent and rebellion. Morwenna knew, too well, that the land around the old capital of Brigantia, Stanwyck, was filled with staunchly pro-Roman Brigantes but, further south, there were those who resented the last fifty years of Roman rule and wanted a return to the time of Cartimandua when Rome had protected their borders but they had ruled their own land. Most hated was the tax demanded by Rome. The roads they had built brought prosperity but the trades of Mamucium and Eboracum did not like the fact that there were so many ways to take tax from them.

Caronwyn had found a bed with one of the sisters in a small hamlet just north of Eboracum. She had disguised her stunning hair with a dull linen hat and she kept her gaze towards the ground. She and the priestess of the Mother with whom she was staying spent their days at the market listening to the complaints of those who came to sell their goods. Morwenna had been quite emphatic about her daughter's mission. She was to find someone with money and power, someone who was willing to act as a leader against the Roman invaders. They had spent three weeks so far and Caronwyn was beginning to doubt that they would find anyone who fitted the precise requirements of her mother.

The Priestess was a widow called Morag. Her husband had died in the earlier rebellion led by Morwenna and Decius Sallustius. Rather than making her hate Morwenna, it had driven her to hate the Romans. She was delighted to have been given the mission and worshipped Morwenna as the embodiment of the Mother on earth. After another fruitless foray into the Forum, they trudged back up the Northern road to the hovel they shared. They ate well for Morwenna had provided gold for food and clothes. To the other customers, they looked to be a mother and daughter eking out their last coins when the reality was they were haggling as it enabled them to stay longer without drawing attention to themselves.

As they walked back to their lodgings they discussed, as they had each day, the people they had met. They needed to choose their leader soon. "There was one trader who seemed a little more belligerent and vocal than the others."

Caronwyn nodded, "Yes Morag, the fat man with the thinning hair. I have not seen him before."

"Neither have I." She hesitated, wondering if she ought to question the plan devised by the High Priestess. "I am not sure how we will be able to speak with these traders for we are little more than slaves to them."

11

"Fear not Morag. We will seek employment with the one we wish to entice. We both have skills which would be valuable. We will return on the morrow and if this man is there we will seek employment with him." She shrugged. "Time is not important. If this man is not suitable for our purposes then we shall leave and seek another."

Antoninus Brutus had quickly learned that, to do business with the Romans, one had to become Roman. He had changed his family name to a Roman one and affected the Roman style of dress. His farm in the valley to the north of Eboracum had mosaics and a bathhouse but Antoninus was still the son of the Brigante chief, Tadgh, below the skin. He despised the Romans; having brought civilisation they had greatly benefited the Brigante but now that they were bleeding them dry with their ever-increasing taxes, many businessmen like Antoninus felt that they should go. His son, Gaius, was even more vociferous. He wanted to fight against the Romans. The blood of the Brigante ran deeply in his veins and he yearned for the chance to wield a sword as his grandfather had. The Roman soldiers he had encountered had not seemed the vaunted, invincible killing machine that the rest of the province feared. The ones he had seen were lying in the streets of the vicus, puking their insides out having drunk too much unwatered wine.

Father and son spent each evening firing each other up with fantasies about life in Britannia without the burdensome yoke of Rome rule. "Their legions have left and the ones who remain are the leftover warriors from the defeated parts of the Empire."

Antoninus was a little more cautious than his son. "Perhaps but they have managed to put down each rebellion my son." His son was his only reminder of the wife who had died in the last harsh winter, taken by the coughing sickness. He cherished the handsome young warrior and did not want to lose him as well. He wondered if it was time to take another wife or at least a mistress for the farm. Antoninus was very successful; the farm was more than profitable but it was the sale of stone from his quarry which really made him rich. The Romans could not get enough of the rocks his grandfather had hated. Now it was Brigante who wished to emulate their conquerors and build stone-built villas but Antoninus had a contract with Eboracum. He could make far more gold from his countrymen than the parsimonious Romans who made money from Antoninus' profit.

"Could we not begin to prepare for the day when the Romans leave? The barbarians from the north are raiding along the Tinea and Dunum. Perhaps we should do as some of the farmers further north and arm our own men." The farm and quarry had many slaves but also skilled freemen. They were mainly the remnants of the old clan which had been ruled by Antoninus' grandfather. Gaius knew that many of the younger ones also wished to use the weapons of the tribe. "We are making enough profit and it would ensure that, if there were more raids then we could defend what we have."

The businessman was proud of his son. His father and grandfather would also have been proud. He was intelligent and what he had said made sense. Rather than putting the profit into the banks of Eboracum which charged exorbitant amounts, he would invest in arms and training. "We will return to Eboracum tomorrow my son. I will try to negotiate a better contract with the Romans and you can find out where we can acquire weapons."

Gaius' face beamed like a room suddenly lit by a fresh lamp. "I already know. In the vicus, there are some men who served in the Roman army and they sell old weapons captured from our people."

Caronwyn and Morag waited by the Forum for the angry man they had seen the previous day. He had spoken angrily to those who were his peers but Brynna had noticed that he had changed his tone whenever an official chanced by. He was a duplicitous man and in that character trait lay her hope. Morag had asked around and discovered that he was very rich but, more importantly, descended from a chief and, as such, could command respect in any rebellion. Morwenna had made it clear to her daughter that they merely needed to fan the flames of rebellion rather than take part and lead. She had learned, to her cost, the dangers of such action and the rebellion was only one part of her plan for Morwenna and her daughters were still intent upon bringing death and destruction to Macro the son and half brother they all loathed.

When Antoninus entered the busy market place, Caronwyn noticed the handsome young man with him. She took an instant decision. "Morag. You follow the older fat man and I will watch the young man with him." Morag glanced at the handsome young man and a half-smile played around the edge of her mouth. Morwenna's daughter had an eye for a buck.

"Yes, my lady. I will return here."

Antoninus headed towards the fortress and the invisible Morag shuffled along behind. Caronwyn was intrigued for her prey moved purposefully away from the market towards the seedier and less reputable parts of the vicus. She was not intimidated by the potential danger; she carried a knife and her mother's bodyguards had taught her how to use the weapon. It would be a foolish man who tried to take advantage of the stunningly beautiful red head. She kept to the shadows as he moved around the vicus. He was behaving furtively and she wondered where he was heading. He was taller and younger than most of the others in the area and she was able to keep far enough back to avoid detection. It was obvious that he had reached his destination when he looked all around him to see if anyone was watching. He disappeared inside. It seemed to Caronwyn that he would never come out but eventually he did, a huge grin on his face and he almost ran past Caronwyn to head back to the market. The witch's daughter had a dilemma; she was desperate to know what had pleased the young man so much in a visit to a grubby hut tucked away far from prying official Roman eyes. In her mind, she had assumed it was a whorehouse which would explain his joy but not the short time he had spent within the building. She could find out later. She hurried back to the market where she saw Morag. Morag gestured with her eyes and she saw that the young man was reunited with the angry man. The two of them looked pleased and, arms around each other's shoulders, they headed for a tavern.

"I have found out who they are my lady. The younger man is Gaius Brutus, the son of the angry man, Antoninus Brutus."

"You have done well Morag. We will have to visit a house in the vicus later but I think that we will seek employment with the two of them."

"There is no lady of the house. She died last year."

"Did she? That bodes well. You can cook?" Although phrased as a question Caronwyn implied that Morag would cook for the two of them. Morag nodded. "Good, then we present ourselves as a mother and daughter who have come from the north, fleeing the barbarians who killed our family. I will play the tearful and distraught girl."

The tavern was crowded with men who had successfully concluded their business and were celebrating. Caronwyn knew that there would be no women in the vicus and their appearance would attract attention. They slipped into the crowded room and made their way to the barrel of a man who was obviously the owner. The room hushed as the two of them entered. Caronwyn had already rubbed herbs under her eyes to make them weep. The owner began to make his way towards them. "Out!"

"Oh sir, take pity on a widow and her daughter. Have you no work for two hard-working unfortunates such as us? My mother is a good cook and I am a diligent worker." The hood over her head prevented the tavern keeper from getting a good view of the girl but he could see that the older one was a hag who would not be able to earn a little extra for him as his workers had to serve drinks and entertain the customers.

"Go, before I have you thrown out!"

Caronwyn and Morag left, having done their work; they had seen all the eyes, including their two targets, watching and listening. Once outside Caronwyn began to make herself look more attractive, lowering her hood and pinching her cheeks. They waited patiently for their targets to emerge. The other traders and visitors who left assiduously avoided them which suited Caronwyn. As soon as she saw Gaius leave she prostrated herself before the two men. "Oh please sir, take pity on a widow and her only child!" Her green eyes flickered beneath her long lashes and Gaius felt himself become aroused.

Antoninus was about to wave them away, much as the tavern keeper had done when Gaius said, "We need a cook father. The slop the slaves serve is not fit for our pigs."

15

Antoninus was not convinced. "I will go to the slave market and buy a better one then."

Morag held her hands out in supplication. "Sir, we are free, we will work for seven nights for no pay and if you do not like my food we will leave and you can then buy yourself a slave. What have you to lose? All we need is a roof under which to sleep and food."

Gaius turned to his father. "What have we to lose? If the hag cannot cook then we throw her out."

Antoninus shrugged. "Very well." He pointed to their cart. "Get aboard the cart you have three days and nights to impress me!"

Caronwyn nodded gratefully. "Do not worry sir. You will not regret your decision." She had succeeded in the first part of her plan. Now she would need to work on the young man and find out what the curious hovel contained. That would have to wait until she next visited the vicus. It was important that they spend the next three days impressing Antoninus and, once established in the home, they could begin to manipulate the two men.

Morag had not lied, her food was excellent, and within two days Antoninus had decided that they would be an asset to his home. He could begin to entertain the other minor chiefs who had also turned to trade. His home was the most impressive one outside of Eboracum but hitherto he had been unable to invite others there because of the paucity of the food. Now he saw an opportunity to build his power base.

For his part, Gaius was besotted with the lovely Caronwyn. Once ensconced in the villa she had discarded the dirty and dishevelled look she had adopted and used every wile taught to her by her mother to enhance her beauty and attraction. The herbs and perfumes she used to improve nature's bounty proved too much for Gaius. His eyes followed her around the room and his body told him that he wanted her. Had she been a slave then he would have taken her the first day but she was free. He approached his father to ask his advice.

Antoninus smiled; he remembered when he had been a lusty youth and he understood the young man's attraction. He too had felt his slightly more ancient loins stir when the lovely auburn-haired vision served their food making what was delicious seem like ambrosia. "You will have to woo and court her." He shrugged apologetically. "It is the way of women. They need to be assured of your continued affection. Speak kindly to her, take her for walks, and bring her flowers. You are a fine young man and she will soon do your bidding."

So Gaius began his courtship. Caronwyn for her part knew how to play the virgin and she fluttered her long eyelashes and giggled at every inanity which came from the Brigante mouth. Inside she was cheering for she knew that within a few days he would be under her spell and she would be able to create her own rebellion.

Chapter 2

Julius Demetrius felt strange as he stepped from the boat at Eboracum this was not just down to the crossing from Germania which had been rougher than the seas in the Mare Nostrum. The main reason was it had been many years since he had left the shores of Britannia. It smelled and felt very different even from Germania Inferior which he had just left and a world away from his villa at Surrentum. It was, somehow, greener. He couldn't explain it. More importantly, it felt like coming home. As he stepped from the bireme he regretted, not for the first time since he had left Rome, that he had not brought Hercules and his own ship, *'The Swan'*. It was somehow reassuring to have the old sea captain looking after him. He decided that he would send a message back to Ostia and have the old man bring the ship here. It struck the senator that travelling by ship would save much pain from the backs of saddles. He left instructions for his baggage to be sent to the fortress; his Imperial warrant ensured that there would be no thefts.

As he walked through the vicus, he noted the changes in the old legionary fortress. The vicus was enormous and seemed to spread over a large area. The fortress itself now had dressed stone replacing the wooden palisade he remembered. The towers looked solid and, unlike Rome itself, bristled with ballistae and scorpions. This was a frontier fortress. The sentries were auxiliaries this time and he wondered when the Sixth legion would arrive. Hadrian had ordered it to leave Vetera but Julius was certain that the Emperor would wait until the province had settled down a little more before the reliable force was despatched to police yet another frontier. The sentries recognised the senatorial purple and, almost before he had flashed his warrant, had allowed him speedy entry.

The Prefect, Octavius Saturninus, had been expecting the Senator for a few days. He was wary of the politician for he knew him to be an intimate of the Emperor, a friend of the new Governor and, more importantly, he knew the area well having served as a cavalryman. He was unusually impressed when he met the man for the first time. He looked far younger than his real age and did not affect the mannerisms of a courtly man. His first words put the nervous Camp Prefect at his ease. "Sorry to have to put you out Camp Prefect. I know that having your own quarters is a perk of the posting and I promise I won't be a nuisance for too long; when the Governor returns, I shall head north to Coriosopitum."

Octavius was taken aback, how did this newly arrived visitor know that the Governor was inspecting the frontier? Julius saw his look and smiled. "I am no magician Prefect. The Emperor told me that the Governor would not be in residence for our task is not in Eboracum but north where we intend to build some *limes*."

The Prefect sighed with relief. "And about time too sir. We have had too many raids in the past few years and not just from the north but across the sea."

Julius leaned forward. "I had not heard that report. Whence do these raiders come?"

"From the icy lands north of Germania. They have fast boats and they raid for slaves and booty. The fleet is too thinly spread to stop them. You may not have heard because the last Governor thought it merely an inconvenience."

Bradua again! "You did not share his views I take it?"

The Prefect was a military man and not a politician but he felt, instinctively, that he was speaking to another man with a strategic brain. "The raids made the people worried and that means less productive. Also, we had to react to the raids ...."

"But you would have had men closer to the coast to prevent them?"

"Just so." The Prefect was right Julius Demetrius knew his stuff.

"The Ala we despatched is it still based at Morbium?"

"No the Decurion Princeps moved it to Coriosopitum to be closer to the Votadini and Selgovae." He looked keenly at the Legate. "You know him I believe?"

Julius smiled at the diplomatically phrased question. The real question was, *'is this one of your favourites?'* "Lucius is a good friend and I served with him but, to put your mind at rest, I have no self-interest in the officer. He is to be promoted to Prefect rather than appointing one from Rome."

"That makes a change; a sensible appointment." Realising that he might have spoken out of turn he blushed and held up his hand. "Sorry sir, that just came out."

"Don't worry about it Prefect. You will soon learn that I did not take to politics and duplicity. I still prefer those who speak the truth and their mind. And now..." He stood and spread his hands, "I assume there are quarters for me?"

Relieved the Prefect stood, "With the Governor still on his travels his quarters are available."

"Excellent. Lead on."

Governor Falco was impressed with his frontier troops. He had been worried about the lack of a legion this close to the frontier but, having spent a month travelling the Stanegate, he knew that the auxiliary soldiers based there were sound troops who were well led. He was worried about the strength of the opposition to Roman rule. In Moesia, where he had been governor, and in Rome where he had received his orders, he had been led to believe that Britannia was a conquered province and people. He now knew that to be false. He could not understand why a succession of Emperors had taken away good legions to fight abroad. Had the province been peaceful there may have been a reason but he was under no illusions, this was a war zone. He looked at the officer next to him, Decurion Princeps Livius Lucullus Sallustius. He had been told of the man's exploits before he arrived, the way he had thwarted an invasion, his time as an Explorate, his adventures in Aquitania and a vague rumour about Capreae and Emperor Hadrian but nothing had prepared him for the modesty of the man. He had waved away the compliments for his exploits and pointed out that it was the ala and their officers which deserved the credit.

"Yet I understand that when you took command there was resentment from some of the former officers? And you have had to recruit most of the men in the ala as the numbers were so depleted?"

"There were a couple of officers who took exception to the new role but the majority of troopers performed as well as any men I have ever commanded." The Governor admired the loyalty of the commander to his men, it spoke well of him.

Pompeius looked over his shoulder at the column of men who followed them. They looked confident and alert. Although they had not seen any problems the Governor knew that they would be able to deal with any attack or ambush. "Decurion Princeps if you were me how would you use the ala?"

"Good question. I served in Britannia with Marcus' Horse and the Prefect then knew that we would only need the one thousand troopers together in a major battle. The best way to use us would be to divide it into turmae and give a specific area for a pair to patrol. We could easily join together should the occasion demand but we could cover a greater area." He waved his arm at the men following. "While we are together then barbarians could easily slip over the frontier and create chaos."

A mischievous smile appeared on the Governor's face. "Sorry Decurion Princeps for tying down your whole command."

Behind them, Cassius hid the laugh behind his hand. He wanted to see how his friend and leader got out of that one. "No sir. It is important that we are together now for this tour. It would not do to have a new Governor killed or captured and besides it makes a statement to the tribes hereabouts that we are still a force to be reckoned with. They have few cavalry themselves and we are warriors whom they respect and fear." He spoke proudly but without bravado, stating the facts.

"It is what I heard and fear not we will be heading back to Morbium tomorrow. Once there I will return to Eboracum and meet with the other Legate, Julius Demetrius. A friend of yours I believe."

"Oh yes, sir. And he served in Marcus' Horse so he knows how we ought to be used. I am pleased that the Emperor has appointed two such Legates."

From another officer, he would have thought that this was flattery but he had spoken with the Emperor before he left and knew that Lucius Sallustius was that rare bird, a warrior who led well and was modest. "I agree with your assessment but I feel that Coriosopitum is too far east for your ala to be truly effective. I would suggest somewhere closer to the centre of the Stanegate."

Livius thought about it for a while and then said, "Perhaps closer to Vindolanda. There are a few sites, as I recall where we

21

might be based although, as I said earlier, I intend to split the ala up into eight sections and spread them further apart. In the last couple of years, the problems have not been with full invasions but incursions by warbands. My troopers are quite adept at building smaller camps and using them as a base but I will do as you suggest and build a fort closer to Vindolanda."

"It was only a suggestion Decurion Princeps. I am no cavalryman and this country is certainly different from Moesia. Here I am the novice."

"And it was a good suggestion. When we patrolled against the Votadini we spent too long just travelling to our patrol points. This is more efficient."

Macro and Marcus were riding together at the rear of the column. They shared a turma although, with the death last year of the traitor Spartianus, Livius had made it clear that they would both be promoted soon. Despite the fact that they were both young even the older troopers respected them. In Macro's case it was because he was the best fighter in the ala and in Marcus' case it was because he wielded the Sword of Cartimandua and could master any horse, no matter how wild. He now had two turmae who had sworn a blood oath to protect the sword and its bearer. Marcus felt honoured with the accolade.

"What do you think of this Governor then Macro?"

"He couldn't be any worse than the last one. He was about as much use as a one-legged man in an arse-kicking contest."

"A little crudely put but I get your drift. The important thing is that Livius seems to approve."

Macro nodded, "And that says it all." Both young men felt the same about Livius. He was the model of leadership to which they both aspired. Although both their fathers had been great warriors and great leaders they only knew of them through the words of others. In Livius' case, they were able to witness his wisdom and skill. "You or me for the hunting today?"

Each day one of the two young officers had taken a couple of men and hunted the food for their evening meal. While most legionaries and auxiliaries survived on a diet of porridge the men of the ala had grown used to fine food. "You if you like. I am not as familiar with this part of the country as you."

Macro laughed as he gestured for the two troopers to join him. "You are getting lazy brother. I'll save the deer's heart for you, build up your strength."

That evening the ala feasted well on the fresh venison which was superbly roasted by the ala's cooks. As the decurions sat with the Governor and the Decurion Princeps around the blazing fire, Livius looked over at Pompeius who nodded. They had agreed that he would brief the ala on their new role.

"Gentlemen I hope you have enjoyed your feast and thank you Decurion Macro, once again your hunting skills have helped us eat like kings." While the other decurions cheered Macro looked at Marcus. He had been called Decurion; was this Livius' way of promoting him and what about Marcus? They both paid rapt attention to every word. "It may well be the last such feast for the Governor and I have decided that the ala will serve the province best by patrolling a larger area. Tomorrow Cassius will escort the Governor to Morbium while the remainder of the ala will build a new fort on the frontier, north of the Stanegate. Once our headquarters is built then pairs of turmae will be allocated a section of the frontier where the turmae will build their own camp and patrol the immediate area." He waited while the murmur of questions and comments rippled through the assembly. When it died down he continued, "The clerk, quartermaster and cooks will be based at our new fort as will the weapon trainer and horse master Decurions Macro and Marcus and me." The two newly promoted Decurions grinned as the news sank in, they had been promoted, and the other decurions slapped them on their backs. "You will need to liaise with the clerk and the Quartermaster to ensure you have sufficient supplies. You will have to be self-sufficient in such things as guards, food and forage."

The Governor took it all in. It was a mark of the leader that the decurions felt like a team and, indeed, almost a family. He had noticed the easy way they had with each other. He would have thought that discipline would have suffered but, if anything, it improved and they were a well-drilled and efficient team. If this could be replicated then his task might be easier. He was looking forward to meeting the new Legate for they had an enormous job. In his experience, the moment you started building a barrier then the local tribes took instant offence. Once they began building, they would also begin fighting and it looked like this ala would be the only mobile strike force until the reinforcements reached Britannia from the mainland Empire.

Livius held up his hand for silence. "This is a new phase for us and a difficult one. I know that all of you will meet this new challenge for, gentlemen, you will be operating on your own, making your own decisions." He gestured at Cassius, Metellus, Rufius and the two young decurions, "We Explorates know how to do this and if you need any advice then these officers are your mentors. Enjoy the feast." As the decurions crowded around the five Explorates, Livius and the Governor retired to the headquarters tent.

"One thing Governor, I would like to hire and train some troopers to act as guards for the main fort. At Corio and Morbium we were able to use the auxiliaries nearby but it seems a waste to tie down cavalrymen to guard a fort."

"Excellent idea. I realise that the men with the money will squeal but the Emperor has faith in you and a need for this frontier. Go ahead." He poured Livius a beaker of the Gaulish wine they had taken to sharing at night. "You have a close relationship with your men."

Livius understood the question. It had been asked before. "That is because they are family. The two brothers, Macro and Marcus are sons of former decurions of the ala. We still keep in touch with those officers who have retired and remember those who fell." He looked apologetically at the Governor, "The decurions feel more like brothers than inferiors."

"Do not apologise, for it is to be commended. The difficulty is replicating it."

"Oh, that can be done. We have built this ala on the model of the first one Marcus' Horse which grew from the Second Pannonians who rescued Cartimandua and her sword."

Pompeius looked intrigued. "I have heard the legend. Was she as beautiful as they say?"

"I was not with the ala while she lived but Gaius, Marcus and Macro's father said that she was."

"I wonder what happened to that sword. Perhaps it never really existed. The stories told of it are too incredible to be true and seem the stuff of legend."

Livius smiled. "Oh it does exist and the legends are true." He stood, "Would you like to see it?"

For the first time, Pompeius Falco showed real surprise. "You have it? It is here?"

Livius went to the tent's entrance and shouted, "Marcus, bring the sword!" Returning to face the Governor he continued. "The sword is the heirloom of the Brigante and Decurion Marcus is the second son of the heir of Cartimandua. His elder brother farms and it is the warrior who wields the weapon." He lowered his voice. "Many of the men took a blood oath to protect Marcus and the sword. I know that it is not an Imperial policy but many of the men are Brigante and it makes them even more passionate and loyal about the ala." There was a cough outside. "Come in Marcus."

The Governor knew fine weapons but even he had never seen such a glorious sword. It looked unlike anything Roman with its long-tapered blade and its jewelled hilt. The craftsmanship was exquisite from the runnel for the blood through the well-shaped guard through to the jewelled hilt and pommel. He looked longingly at it and Livius, smiling, nodded to Marcus. "Would you like to hold it, sir?" With an almost childlike grin, Falco nodded and Marcus handed it to him. "It is lighter than it looks is it not sir? The blade is sharp enough to shave with."

Falco swung it in his hand. "It is indeed a fabulous weapon. Are the legends true then Decurion Princeps?"

"Which ones, for there are many?"

"You know, the sword has never been defeated in battle. It heals any wounds and a light shines from it."

Livius and Marcus smiled. Livius gestured for Marcus to explain. "It is true that it has never been in a battle which we lost and even when used in a skirmish we are successful. As for the healing and the light they are not true but when we fight on a sunlit day and the light is right the steel of the blade seems to shine brighter than other swords so perhaps the light part is true. One legend which is true is that it binds men together. When the sword is unsheathed in battle the men fight as though double the number."

"If only we could forge more like this."

Livius shook his head. "The legend is that the sword came from Gaul and is ancient. Certainly, we have never seen its like. It can also create problems for its owner for every barbarian who has ever heard of it desires it and seems willing to throw their life away just to gain it. Marcus' father believes that the only reason the Brigante have not openly revolted is because the sword fights for Rome. If it were ever lost then problems might ensue."

Handing the sword back Falco said, seriously, "Then you must make sure that the sword never leaves your side."

"Don't worry sir. My men and I guard it with our lives."

Prince Faolan stood before the assembled warriors of the Ebdani and raised his sword in the air. "And I swear that I will kill the warrior who wields the Sword of Cartimandua and return it to Si an Bhru from where it was taken. Any warrior who wishes to follow me will share in the honour."

There was a huge roar of approbation and Corentine narrowed his eyes. His cousin was indeed cunning. He did not know what the old witch Sceanbh had had to do with it but he was certain that the sword of the Brigante had never resided in Hibernia. His cousin was up to something but the King could not see what. He was worried that many of his finest warriors would leave on this foolhardy quest to Britannia. Pragmatic as every the wily ruler began to work out how he could use this to his advantage. With his biggest rival away he could recruit newer, more loyal warriors to be his bodyguards. He would also question Sceanbh and discover what the plot was for he had not stayed in power for so long without being careful and overly suspicious. He stood, the decision made and held up his hands. "We applaud our cousin and his quest. If he and any of those who wish to undertake this perilous journey return, we will welcome them once more to the family of the Ebdani."

The cousins exchanged a look of pure hatred. Faolan had to admire his cousin; while allowing him to leave he was telling all of the assembly that this was not Ebdani business. He could absolve himself of all responsibility while still enjoying the glory of the success and a share of any plunder. Faolan would throw any plunder into the sea rather than share it with his cousin. He nodded back to his cousin. "We will return cousin with great glory, great riches and even greater honour."

As Faolan left the hall Corentine was disturbed by the huge number of warriors who followed. He knew that he should have allowed his men to raid their neighbours and that would have assuaged their blood lust but now it was too late. He would need to begin to build his own army to thwart his young cousin's obvious ambitions.

Sceanbh also smiled as Faolan left. Her life would soon end but she had fulfilled her duty to Morwenna and the Mother. Rome would be attacked. Corentine did not know that the sisters had already spread the word of the quest to seek the sword and hundreds of warriors were heading from all corners of Hibernia to join in this quest for glory and riches.

By the time Faolan was ready to embark on the fifty or so boats they had organised for the short crossing to Manavia, there were almost twelve hundred warriors gathered from the four corners of the island. Every landless prince and warrior had been drawn by the lure of adventure and plunder. Watching them arrive in ones, twos and sometimes tens Faolan knew that it had only needed a small pebble to be pushed for this avalanche to start. Everyone knew that Roman Britannia was weaker than in the days of Julius Agricola but they also knew that it would take a large warband to survive. Faolan's biggest problem was stopping the blood feuds and old tribal enmities from flaring up. Loegaire had to kill two particularly belligerent warriors and Faolan himself sent back ten warriors who had a blood feud with each other. As they left he knew that it would be a matter of hours before most of them were dead, killed in a pointless bloodbath. The culling had the desired effect; no-one questioned his leadership and there were no more outbreaks of old fights and feuds. Leaving Loegaire to oversee the loading of the boats Faolan and his bodyguard set sail in the most seaworthy of the ships.

Morwenna stood with Brynna watching the ragged fleet as it edged its way to the port. Forewarned by her daughter, Morwenna now understood the nature of the pragmatic man who was heading her way. She was no longer the stunning beauty of a few years ago and now had to rely more on intelligence than pure animal attraction. Smiling at her beautiful daughter the witch with the grey flecked hair knew that she could leave the attraction to her daughters. Caronwyn was in Eboracum with the most dangerous of missions, Brynna had successfully recruited her warriors and Eilwen was busily preparing the young priestesses who would flood the land of the Brigante with their particularly subversive religion. Ever the realist, Morwenna now knew that she was the spider, spinning her webs and waiting for her victims to be brought to her. She now knew where she and her mother had gone wrong, they had tried to lead from the front too often and it was unnecessary. There were others who could be fodder for the Roman Ballistae and crosses.

She turned to her daughter. "Bring him to me when he lands."

Brynna nodded as her mother left. She knew that it was now down to the careful staging arranged for the benefit of the warriors who would be arriving soon. She wanted them to be in awe of her and her power which meant dressing the room and making it as ethereal as possible. Heavy scents and candles would fill the air. The half-darkness would create fearful shapes and shadows and, out of the midst of this would appear, as though by magic, Morwenna the Red Witch Queen of Mona. Even though she had seen it many times Brynna still found herself getting a thrill of anticipation at the thought and dreamed of the day when she would do as her mother had done and command the world.

Chapter 3

As they headed north from the Stanegate Cassius rode his mount so that he was riding next to Livius and would not be overheard by the troopers. "Sir?"

Livius smiled; Cassius was just what he needed, the faithful gainsayer who would ask questions, just like a young child, until he was satisfied that he understood. Cassius had fired regular questions since they had left the Governor and his escort. "Yes Cassius what can I do for you?"

"This strategy of dividing up the ala; is there no alternative?"

"It is how we operated when we were Explorates Cassius." He needed Cassius to make the same connections he had made when devising the strategy.

"Yes I know sir but we were only a handful then and, well, we knew what we were doing."

"Ah. That is it. Well firstly Cassius we are the only cavalry here at the moment and so we are the handful. Would you have us in one place, perhaps forty miles from a problem? By the time we arrived, it would all be over." Cassius could see the wisdom there; he was not happy but he would live with it. He bit his tongue to prevent himself from asking the question he had meant to ask. Livius knew his second in command and answered it anyway. "You are worried about the decurions are you not and the lack of experience amongst the whole ala?"

Cassius sighed with relief. "Yes sir. I mean most of them are new and have not the experience."

"You mean like Marcus and Macro?"

Quickly Cassius replied. "Oh no sir. They are good officers and they will lead their men well, I am not worried about those two."

"But they are the youngest and they are new are they not? Both only recently promoted." Livius almost hated himself for playing with his loyal and faithful friend.

"Yes sir, but…"

"But they served with us and you know them, that is the idea in your head is it not?" There was a silence as Cassius took in the painful truth. He did not know the new officers. The ala had been

thrown into the melting pot quickly and promotions had had to
be made. Livius put his hand on Cassius' arm. "They are good
officers and we promoted them because they showed, as we did,
the potential for leadership. They will make mistakes, as we did,
which is why I am putting you, Metellus, Rufius, Macro and
Marcus as one of the turma in five of the pairs. That way the five
of you can pass on your experience. I will keep the least
experienced, Graccus with me. That will just leave Calgus and
Spurius. They are the most experienced of the others." he
paused. "Satisfied?"

Grinning Cassius replied, "Yes sir. Sorry I am an old
woman."

"No you are right to question my judgement and as my
adjutant, you need to know my reasoning. Now, "he waved his
arm at the land through which they were travelling, "what do you
think of the site I have chosen?"

Cassius looked at the land which rose towards the north and
the barbarian's lands. They had travelled steadily north-west
from Coriosopitum. They had forded the Tinea and passed what
Cassius had thought was a perfect site for a fort, a knoll above
the Tinea. Livius had pointed out that it was too close to Corio
and they needed somewhere closer to the middle. Now, ten miles
further on Cassius could see that Livius had thought this through
well. The land to the north fell sharply away leaving them with
an uninterrupted view of both the river crossing and the Votadini
border. "Just up there is it?" His soldier's eye had picked out the
high point which had enough flat land for construction. Livius
nodded. "Should be about right then sir. There are enough small
trees to provide wood for the buildings. I can see enough stones
lying on the surface to give us some foundations and there is
water close by." He rubbed his chin thoughtfully. "The grazing
looks to be good but this is high up. We may struggle when the
snows come."

"Those were my worries too. Still we will cross that bridge
when we get to it. Come let us begin to build our fort."

The ala set to with a will. Every trooper was accustomed to
building a camp each day but this one would be a little more
permanent. That meant that they worked harder knowing that
they would not have to repeat it the following day. With one

turma on guard the rest set to digging the double ditch and piling the spoil to make the ramp. Inside, Septimus and his cooks erected the tent whilst Julius Frontinus, the ala clerk. fussed to ensure that everything was as it should be. Where there was, for a while, chaos and disorder, soon the shape of the camp became clearer. As soon as the stakes were buried in the rampart it looked like every identical Roman camp being built by soldiers the Empire over.

Cassius noticed the sun beginning to set. "Sir, I don't think we will get the gates finished tonight."

"You are right. Get the cooks to prepare the food and use the four carts we brought as temporary gates. Make sure the horses are picketed and well guarded. We would look stupid if the horse thieves set us afoot." The Votadini envied the Roman mounts and would risk anything to get hold of cavalry mounts.

"Sir." Cassius bustled away, happy now that they had walls around them.

Macro and Marcus had not had time to hunt and Septimus was forced to use dried meat for the evening meal. Although not as good as their normal fare it filled the hungry bellies of the exhausted men. He had already spotted the stones he would use to build his bread oven and even seen the hollow, just outside the fort, which he would use to site the necessary fire risk.

That evening, as the decurions sat in what would become the command tent until the Principia could be built, they listened as Livius outlined his plans. "You will all have three nights here in the fort until it has been completed and then, I am afraid you will be away from Septimus and his fine food." The cook was within hearing distance and he saluted Livius with his ladle. "This will not be temporary, this is the future." He waved to Julius who had been hovering nearby. He brought out a beautifully marked map which he had been preparing for months. He spread it on the floor and stood with a pointer waiting for Livius to speak. "We are here at er... "he struggled for a name for the fort and looking at the ground to the south had a sudden inspiration, "Rocky Point. Rufius and Antoninus will take the eastern end, towards Coriosopitum, Drusus and Macro will take the next section followed by myself and Graccus, Calgus and Spurius will be further west, then Marcus and Lucius, Metellus and Cicero and finally Cassius and Decius. You will each have friends on both flanks. Rufius and Cassius will have forts whilst the rest of you will have two turmae. You need to build your own camps and operate from them. You will all have a box of land to patrol from the Stanegate to the south, your friends east and west and the barbarians to the north. Keep in touch with your fellows." He stopped and looked at them all to make the point. "If you do not see your neighbours for more than a day then assume they have been killed and send a rider back to me."

They all looked at each other; it was a sombre and uncompromising message their leader had delivered. The ala was really on the wild frontier now. Rufius raised his hand, "Sir. What if we find trouble?"

"Good question. We need to stop incursions from the north and prevent raids on the Stanegate. You will all have at least fifty men each and you should be able to stop them. Anything larger and one turma shadows while the other spreads the word to the others. You all know where the others will be, find them and then we can gather quickly. The Governor is sending us a century of auxiliaries raised amongst the Brigante to act as guards for Rocky Point and that means that I will not be tied here and," he smiled, "Julius will have his protection."

Sniffing Julius rolled up the map. "Quite right too!" As he strode his way back to his tent the decurions burst out laughing. Cassius caught Livius' eye and nodded. The decurions would do.

"You and the Emperor were right about young Livius." Falco suddenly realised that he had criticised the Emperor by implication and began to bluster. "What I mean…"

Julius smiled and held up his hand. "Pompeius if we are going to worry over every nuance and word in our conversations then we will get nowhere." He leaned forward. "We have to trust each other implicitly or we shall fail."

"You are right Julius. I spent too long in Rome worrying if the hand that offered friendship would stab me in the back."

"This is the frontier and believe me there are enough of our enemies around to do that. So, you have assessed the line of the limes?"

"Yes and I concur with all of you. Has the Sixth arrived yet?"

"No, we will have to use the Twentieth and the Second Augusta to make a start." He stood and went to the map. I suggest that the Twentieth starts on the west coast and the Second in the middle. When the Sixth eventually arrives, they can fill in at the east, they will be arriving from that direction anyway. Did you summon the vexillations of the Second and the Twentieth?"

Falco laughed, "Aye although the Prefects were none too happy to have to lose a cohort each."

"I would have preferred two cohorts from each. The task is not an easy one. As soon as we begin to build this wall the barbarians will make life very difficult. I served in the north with Agricola and we lost more men to ambushes than in battle. The barbarians are very adept at hiding."

"Which is where the auxiliaries come in."

"Precisely. The Emperor has ordered at least four new units to Britannia including a mixed cohort of Gauls."

"Excellent for we do lack horses."

"Fortunately, there is a remount stud not far from here close to Morbium run by an ex-trooper so we will never run short."

"Another of your old comrades eh?" Julius shrugged. "You are almost a secret society."

Julius laughed. "You may be right. If you go into the vicus you will find that the Saddle, which is the best tavern in the province, is also run by an ex-trooper called Horse. None of them wished to move far from the ala. Pompeius. I shall head north and await the first of the vexillations. If you set up the Twentieth you can then get back to the problems of running the province."

"I think I would prefer your job working with those boys of yours. They do eat well."

"A lesson we learned years ago, a well-fed ala works better. Oh did you get the report about the raids from across the Mare Germania?"

"No. This is the first I have heard."

"I thought so. Your predecessor suppressed it. Apparently, they are raiding the east coast and taking slaves. I will have Livius allocate two turmae to patrolling the coast. Until the Gauls arrive that is our only option."

"I think I will have the Batavians build some signal towers on the coast. The cliffs look like they have clear line of sight."

"This is where it starts, Pompeius. Let us hope we can make some progress before the Emperor arrives or we may find ourselves without a job."

"I think that would be the least of our worries old friend."

Morwenna did not impress Faolan as much as she had wished. A sceptic and a rationalist he was not taken in by the smoke and lighting which were supposed to make him fearful of the magic she supposedly controlled. If he did not fear the dead in Si an Bhru then why should this faded beauty frighten him? He was, however, impressed with her mind, which she used more than her charms once she realised that she would have to try a different approach with this warrior. It was an unpleasant awakening for the Queen that she could no longer make warriors do her bidding just because she wished it. This one would require persuasion and reason.

"My daughter tells me you have brought many men."

"I have many men to command but only as long as your promises of plunder are true and not a trap to lure me to my death."

She liked this man who would not be led on by dreams of glory. He wanted power; she knew that much from her daughter and Sceanbh and the Sword was the means by which he could achieve that. "I see we are both after the same thing Faolan." She took out a calfskin map. "Here," she pointed to the land around the west of Britannia, "is the part of Britannia which is poorly defended. There is a fort here," she pointed at Glanibanta, "which houses a couple of centuries of auxiliaries. Once taken, it will secure your retreat, give you a quick victory and, more importantly, provide you with more arms and weapons."

Faolan nodded. She was not trying to trick him and he began to trust her; everything she had said made sense. "No plunder here then?"

"Very little, beyond arms and a few horses. The Roman soldiers do not eat well. The trade comes up the east coast. The Romans have gathered their forces here," she pointed to the land north of the Stanegate, "but here at Eboracum is where their treasure is. There are warehouses filled with valuable goods and the Brigante now keep their gold there, in the fort."

Faolan looked satisfied. "And the Sword? What of that treasure?"

Morwenna hesitated. "It was here, at Morbium, the last I heard but it may be in the hands of a young cavalryman, Macro, who serves with the Second Sallustian Wing around Coriosopitum. The sword was, for many years, at a farm south of the Dunum and not far from Morbium. The parents of the wielder of the sword, Gaius and Ailis, have a heavily fortified farmhouse there. If they were attacked then the sword would return to defend the homestead."

"Ah, not quite as simple as the old hag suggested then?" The sneer in his voice was intended to be insulting and Morwenna had to take it, for it was the truth.

"We never said it would be easy but Faolan, who would be king of the Ebdani, if you take Eboracum then the Sword will come for you. The cavalry of the sword is the one they use to put down invasions and raids. If you plunder then, believe me, they will come, do not doubt that for a moment."

"And the legions?"

"There are but two. One of them is here at Deva," she pointed at a place on the map, "and the other far to the south of the country. The cavalry would reach you before the legions."

"I was told there would be more warriors for me here?" he posed it as a question as he had not seen any evidence yet.

"There are five hundred of my personal bodyguard and they are yours to command." She saw that he was considering his actions. "The Brigante and Carvetii do not like the Romans. If you have success there are many who would join you."

"Farmers and field hands," He scoffed.

Morwenna put her hand on his. "Farmers and field hands who can die for you, leaving your warriors alive to take your treasure back to Hibernia."

She was a ruthless woman, consigning those who would fight for her to an ignominious and pointless death. Faolan had already decided that he would take the risk. As far as he could see there was little risk for him. He would make sure he was mounted and, if he thought he would be trapped, he would flee home. He would have a huge army and once he had plundered Eboracum he intended to travel west and let the sword follow him. The old Witch Queen had a shrewd head upon her shoulders. He knew she had an ulterior motive but it mattered little to him. All he wanted was to be king and this would deliver him the crown but he had to ask the question. "What will you get out of this?"

Her eyes hardened and her voice became steely. "When you have begun the rebellion, the people will rise and the Romans will be defeated. I will be able to return to my land and rule in the traditional way and not with the false ideas of Rome. When you have the sword then I will be revenged upon those whom I hate the most."

Those were motives the warrior could understand, self-interest and revenge. At last, he trusted her. "You will have your invasion."

Smiling Morwenna kissed him on the lips. She was a little hurt and offended when he did not respond. Usually, men took the kiss as an invitation; it was another sign that age was catching up with her and it would be her intelligence which ruled from now on and not her looks. "Come we will find Idwal and he will select your warriors for the sooner you begin your task the better."

He looked at her curiously. "And why would that be?"

"My spies tell me that the new Emperor in Rome is interested in Britannia. Once he arrives then we will have to tread warily for he will bring legions. If we can strike before he comes he may well decided that this province is not worth the deaths and withdraw."

For the first time Faolan saw beyond Hibernia. Everyone knew that Britannia was a richer land than his poor homeland. Who was to say what might happen if the Romans left? Perhaps he could claim a mightier kingdom here, beyond the waters of home. "Let us see your warriors then."

Caronwyn played the part of servant well and, when Antoninus entertained the rich and powerful the discreet and subtle servant hovered invisibly in the background. She heard all that was said for the men around the table dismissed her firstly as

a servant and second as a woman. The men believed that neither
of those states had the capability to understand what they were
planning. The biggest problem Caronwyn had was that, apart
from Antoninus and Gaius she did not know their names, they
did not use them. Perhaps that was part of their secrecy and their
security. It mattered little in the grand scheme of things. As long
as they revolted then her work was done. The problem was that
they were worse than village gossips; they talked a good
rebellion but did not get as far as the planning stage.

It was early in spring and Morag had done them proud
serving new spring lamb with carefully cultivated spring
vegetables, good beer and fine wine. The ten men around the
table were looking very pleased with themselves. Gaius kept
glancing lasciviously at Caronwyn but she could control that.
Once in their cups their tongues and plans ran a little freer.

"When was the last time you saw a Roman soldier father?"

"You mean apart from the ones in the fort at Eboracum?" The
nods of approbation from his peers gave Antoninus satisfaction;
he loved his son but he should know his place.

Undeterred and aware that Caronwyn was in the room
clearing the detritus of supper away he continued. "Precisely.
There are but three or four hundred and where are the rest?" he
answered the rhetorical question himself. "Far to the north trying
to stem the tide of invading Picts." To the Brigante anyone from
the north was a Pict, a blue painted terror who had ravished and
rampaged through their land since the earliest times of the
Brigante. Some of the men around the table looked at the young
man anew. He was making sense.

"But we are not warriors."

Gaius leaned forward addressing the others rather than his
father. "But we have warriors. Since I acquired those weapons
we bought in Eboracum I have been training our men." He
looked meaningfully around the table. "Some of those who are
your sons and followers have also joined us and are becoming
warriors too. When we get more weapons they too can be
trained. By the summer we will have an army."

One of Antoninus' neighbours asked his host. "Where did the
weapons come from?"

"I paid for them and my son bought them at the vicus." He pointed the finger around the table. "However I will no longer bear the burden alone. If you want your men armed and trained then you will provide the money and my son will provide the weapons and the training." There was a buzz of conversation as pairs of the diners discussed the problem. Antoninus smiled and gave a subtle nod to Gaius who raised his beaker in a toast. When the buzz died down Antoninus looked at each man in turn as they nodded their agreement. "So we are agreed, you will each fund the training and equipping of your own men under the command of my son Gaius."

"Agreed."

"To help the secrecy and to give the venture a Brigante name Gaius will be known as Venutius." This brought smiles and cheers from all those around the table. Caronwyn was puzzled. Why choose that name? Antoninus answered her as he went on, "It is right that the last free King of the Brigante, Venutius, betrayed by the wicked and traitorous whore, Cartimandua, should give his name to this enterprise which will see the land of the Brigantes returned to the Brigante people and the rightful heir to Venutius will rule." Although they all cheered none of them could, as Caronwyn was able to do, see that the next King of the Brigante would be Gaius, the son of their host. He had made an implied connection, obviously false, to the last royal family and no-one had gainsaid him, and he would rule the north of Britannia. His ambitions ran high indeed.

Later that night Gaius came, slightly drunk, to the barn where Morag and Caronwyn slept. The witch's daughter had been expecting the visit and went outside with him her cloak wrapped tightly around her to keep out the sharp spring air. "I saw you watching and listening, you little vixen."

"I understood nothing." The innocence in her voice disappointed Gaius who had hoped that she would have been impressed enough to open her legs for him.

He looked around as though expecting his father to be listening. "My father is arming the men of the vale and I am to command them. When the time is ripe the Romans will be driven from this land." He leaned in towards her his breath heavy with the sweet, stale smell of beer and wine. "And I shall rule. Would you be my Queen?"

Still playing the part she kissed him quickly on the lips. "Be your wife! Of course! Why should we wait until you are king?"

Gaius had not thought it through; his offer was a metaphorical one. He had no intention of marrying a servant, no matter how beautiful and he began to backtrack on his words. "We would need to wait until I was king and you could be presented as a fitting Queen but before then we could..."

Caronwyn saw the pathetically clumsy attempt at seduction and played the innocent virgin well. "Oh no Gaius you would not want a Queen who was soiled. Better to have a pure Queen you could present to the Brigante. But Gaius, have you fought in a war?

"Fought in a war? Of course not; what a stupid and inane question. What has that to do with being my Queen?"

"If you have not fought in a war then how will you know how to lead an army in battle? I would not wish you to die in your first battle." Gaius' desires evaporated as the cold reality settled in. While he was the best warrior in the land he did not know how to fight. Caronwyn went on. "I am sure there are, what do you call them, ah yes, mercenaries who would advise you. All you would need to do would be to find one. Perhaps the place in Eboracum where you buy your weapons? They might know of someone." She played the innocent well enough and the idea was securely planted in the young, would be Roman killer's mind. Although he said nothing she knew that he would seek out such a man and then take the credit with his father. It mattered little to Caronwyn; Gaius was merely a piece being used in a larger game.

She decided to leave him with an enticement to do as she had bidden him. She leaned in to him and touched his lips with hers, her tongue darted in like a tiny snake and Gaius became aroused. She put her hand between his legs and squeezed his enlarged member. Stepping back, she said, "When you have killed your first Roman then come to me and I will reward you even more."

The Fist had been one of the troopers in Livius' ala. He, and the corrupt decurion Aelius Spartianus, had bullied and cowed the men before the arrival of Livius. Once he had seen his leader suffer death by bastinado, the huge trooper had decided that his days in the ala were numbered and he and another three or four of his ilk had deserted. Whilst they could exist in Eboracum selling stolen weapons and armour the fact was The Fist was a huge unmistakeable man. He could be recognised. In addition, his bullying had meant that many men knew him and would turn him over to the authorities in an instant. So he had a solitary existence in the forests preying on those merchants heading to the coast. It was a meagre existence but occasionally his cronies from Eboracum would get wind of a merchant travelling along the Roman road and they would ambush him. The result was that they were doing quite well and certainly earning more than when they had been auxiliaries.

When Gaius had first approached them for weapons they realised that they had found a gold mine, for he paid whatever they asked of him. Now, as they met not far from the vicus, The Fist formulated his ideas. "This Brigante will keep coming for more and more weapons and eventually we will run out of the crap we have been selling him. We need a more regular supply. How about the fort? Is the Quartermaster there amenable to a bribe?"

Lucius, the leader of the others shook his head. "The old one was but this new Prefect got rid of him and the current one is a list man. Always checking his inventory."

"So we need to get weapons before they reach the fort."

"Not so easy. They generally come in by boat up the river and guards escort the wagons into the fort."

The Fist grinned, remembering the fort at Coriosopitum and the way the Romans had used boats to supply it there. "Then we take the boat south of Eboracum before it docks. The sailors won't be expecting trouble so close to the port. We wait in a boat and board them." The five others in the gang looked dubious. Robbing wagons on solid ground was one thing but hijacking a cargo on a ship was another. "Listen, you spineless jackals how many men on a boat? Four maybe five. Are they warriors? No. Are they used to being robbed in a river, where they can't run? No. All we need to do is find out when a shipment is due. Lucius, any contacts in the fort?"

"Yes, there are a couple of lads who bring us stuff to sell. I should be able to find out."

"Good and next time this Brigante comes to see you arrange for me to meet him. Tell him I am a chief or something. These barbarians are impressed by titles and fancy sounding names."

Caronwyn and Morwenna would have said that The Mother had arranged the presence of The Fist and his unique knowledge of the auxilia. Livius would have just said that the Parcae were having a game. Whichever had the true version events began to move when Gaius returned to buy more weapons. He had become adept at slipping through the seedier side of the vicus and entering the hovel unseen. As on his previous visits he was made welcome. They had even taken to buying some rough wine to give a semblance of hospitality.

Gaius had no time for such pleasantries and he waved the beaker away. "I need more and better weapons. The ones we have are second rate, not as good as Roman weaponry. Can you organise that or shall I go elsewhere?"

Lucius almost laughed at the palpable bluff. There was no other game in town, if he did not get his weapons from them, he would not get any weapons. "No my lord, we can accommodate you but a larger and better order will take time and cost more."

"That isn't a problem. I can get the funds you require but there is one more thing, I need a warrior, a mercenary, someone who has fought with or against the Romans." He looked at the four of them; they looked to be ex-soldiers. Perhaps they might be the ones he was seeking.

Lucius held back the smile. This was easier than he had expected. "There is someone who might be able to help but he could not meet you here." He leaned to Gaius conspiratorially. "He is a wanted man but he sounds just like the man you need. He fought the barbarians as a Roman and he has also fought against Romans. He is a powerful warrior. Return tomorrow at this time and we will take you to him."

Gaius almost ran back to the farm to tell Caronwyn his news but, as he rode back, he reflected that he ought to distance himself from the serving wench. Soon he could be a Prince leading warriors into battle and he would be able to choose a partner more fitting his status. The wench would do as a toy to be played with and to amuse him. He would tell his father the news and accept the paternal approbation he knew he would receive.

Chapter 4

When Faolan met Idwal he was neither impressed nor drawn to the dour Manavian. The man wore his amulets with an arrogance which Faolan did not like. He spoke to Faolan as though he were a child, new to war. For his part, Idwal resented being asked to baby mind a warrior who had yet to fight in a real war. Faolan quickly let Morwenna know that he would take her men but not her leader. Surprisingly that suited everyone for Idwal did not wish to be associated with failure and Morwenna had grown to value the safety which the powerful warrior brought with his presence. Faolan began to believe that all of his victories would be as easy.

The last words Morwenna spoke to him, as he boarded the ship which would cross the short passage of water were, aptly, prophetic. "Do not underestimate the men of the Roman cavalry who ride beneath the dragon standard and be wary of the one who wields the sword. He may appear little more than a boy but he has fought in many battles. I tell you this because I want you to succeed and you need to prepare yourself as much as you can. Do not fail me."

After he had assured her of both his fidelity and reliability he rid himself of the island of intrigue. Now that he was within smelling distance of the Roman world he began to become excited. The men he commanded did not constitute an army; he knew that it was a pack of wild dogs, barely controlled and certainly not on a leash. The only army he had which he could truly rely upon was his personal bodyguard, led by the invaluable and ever faithful, Loegaire. Those fifty warriors were the ones in whom he could trust but, once he was in the Roman heartland he could let loose his dogs of war. He had two aims, to gather as much treasure as he could and to secure the sword. One of Idwal's men, Angus, had served in the land of the lakes and Faolan attached him to his bodyguard. It made sense to have as much intelligence as possible. He had been more impressed by Angus than Idwal. Firstly, because Angus was a quiet unassuming warrior, and secondly because he was older. Faolan did not feel that he had to constantly prove himself with the younger Idwal.

"There is only one fort I believe? Morwenna said there were but two centuries there."

"Aye, a little wooden affair at the head of the lake. You could just take a different route and avoid the conflict altogether."

Faolan looked at the gnarled warrior. He was obviously past his prime and looking for an easy life. He obviously thought that he would live longer serving with a cautious Faolan! "No, I wish to fight the Romans. I understand that the soldiers have a room in the fort where they keep their coins?"

"I have heard this but as I have never captured one I cannot comment." Angus wondered where he had gathered this intelligence. Faolan had been well briefed by the resourceful Morwenna.

"We will both find out then will we not when we have razed this little outpost to the ground?"

Once they were ashore they quickly crossed the narrow pass which led to the fertile land. The ships had been too small to take horses and Faolan told Loegaire to have his men find some at the earliest opportunity. Faolan wanted to be able to get out of trouble faster than he got into it and being mounted would certainly facilitate that. On the second day, Angus took Faolan and three of his trusted men to scout the fort. Faolan was surprised; Angus had said that it was a pitifully small affair but to Faolan it looked substantial. There was a double ditch and a rampart topped with sharp stakes. Towers flanked the four gates and the walls were manned with sentries. He could also see the deadly bolt throwers mentioned by Morwenna. As they returned to the warband Faolan asked him about other forts.

"The stone ones are much bigger than this. There is one at Morbium. I would avoid that for the garrison is experienced and it has a river as a barrier. The other one is at Cataractonium but that is only a wooden one like this one at Glanibanta."

"And Eboracum?"

"The biggest fortress I have ever seen." Angus wondered at the ambition of this Hibernian who did not have nearly enough men to take the mighty bastion of the north.

Faolan found himself readjusting his ideas. He might be able to take these smaller forts with a sudden night attack but Eboracum, when they came to that particular hurdle would require a different plan. He gathered the leaders of his warbands around him. He had one group led by one of Morwenna's men, a surly silent warrior who commanded the respect of Morwenna's five hundred men, two groups, both opportunists from other parts of Hibernia. They each had four hundred men and the bulk of his warband, the six hundred warriors from Ebdani would be led by Loegaire. "We wait until moonset and each one of you will attack your allocated side on my signal. One warband will each attack a wall."

Angus spat, "There will be spikes, and the Romans call them lillia, in the bottom of the ditches. I would have your first men carry bundles of wood and throw them in."

Faolan could see that Angus would be a valuable asset. "Good. See to it. Now prepare your men. Tonight we begin our quest for plunder and riches. We will see just how good these vaunted Romans are." Morwenna's men apart, the other Hibernian warriors were keen to test themselves against this race which had conquered their neighbours with such apparent ease.

That night, the heavily armed warriors spread through the fellside and woods which lined the fort. As they had neared it Faolan saw that those attacking from the south would have the hardest role for they would have to come through the lake which was within fifty paces of the walls. It also meant the ditch on that side was, perforce, shallow. Faolan took the northern gate, for the forest afforded the best cover. He had few archers but the ones he had were, along with the slingers evenly spread out. They needed to take out the sentries as silently as possible. Faolan nodded to Loegaire who gestured for the men to crawl on their bellies towards the ditch.

Inside the sparsely defended fort, the Gallic sentries, who were on the walls, thanked the Allfather that they had drawn this assignment; no fighting, plenty of game and fishing and local women who could not get enough of the exotic Gauls. Far better to be here, than their brothers up at Vindolanda, where the protection of your manhood was a daily event. The only drawback was the sentry duty but it was a small price to pay for this cherished posting. The sentries glanced towards the forest and saw what they expected to see, bushes moving in the slight breeze and the snort of the wild pigs their officers like to hunt. The first that they knew of an attack was when four sentries crashed to the ground; the other eight made the mistake of looking at each other and failing, for a few moments to raise the alarm. The delay cost three more their lives but at last, the oldest sentry yelled, "Attack! To arms!" His warning was timely but he never lived to see the result as two arrows pierced his neck.

With a roar the Irish warriors raced forward, hurling their faggots into the ditch and then springing over the trap to the walls. The largest men in each warband put their backs to the walls and the lightest warriors leapt onto their cupped hands to be thrown over the walls. The garrison, which had just been enjoying a restful sleep, were taken aback as it appeared to rain painted howling warriors. Before they could even ascend the walls to fight the attackers, the gates were opened and the barbarians flooded in. The massacre, for it was never a battle, nor even a skirmish, lasted but a few minutes. The one hundred and sixty defenders died to a man, outnumbered as they were, by at least, ten to one.

Faolan was the last to enter as the last of the Gauls was being despatched. Loegaire came over to him. "Just two men dead, three wounded and a couple of the boys hurt their ankles when they landed. There are horses!"

"Excellent. How many?"

"Five."

"Good, then we at least can ride." He pulled his lieutenant to one side as the Irish stripped the bodies of anything which was of any value. "I am told that the Roman soldiers are given somewhere below ground to bury their gold. Find it and bring it to me."

Faolan strolled through the ground which was slippery with blood and gore. The Principia was the place where the Romans would put their maps and other valuable documents. He had hated his education as a young man but now his ability to read might stand them in good stead. He hoped that there might also be lists showing where the other Roman forces were based but the Gods would have to be seriously on his side for that eventuality to happen. He sat on the only chair in the office and scanned the maps and the lists. His Latin was rudimentary but he managed to translate most of the information. By the time the door opened and Loegaire slipped in he had deduced that he already had most of the information to be garnered from the fort.

Loegaire took the amphora he had uncovered from beneath his cloak. "You were right. It was buried near the back of this room. You could see where the earth was fresh."

"Put this in the strongbox I brought with us. Is there a cart?" The warrior nodded. "Good. Put the gold and my weapons in the cart and have two trusted men assigned as drivers. That will leave a horse for both of us and another for Angus, he seems a dependable warrior. And now I will sleep." He nodded to the mayhem going on outside. Make sure too many of them don't kill each other and that I am not disturbed. We leave at daybreak."

Macro and Marcus sat at the heads of their turmae. Although they had been separated when Macro undertook his mission to the north this was a more permanent parting; the frontier was increasingly hazardous. Who knew when they would again share the pleasures of hunting; when would they have someone in whom they could confide anything? "Take care, brother."

"You too Macro, and listen," he lowered his voice. "Don't let her prey on your mind."

"Who?" Macro asked innocently but the narrowing of his eyes told Marcus that his brother was fully aware of his nemesis.

"You know who. The witch who was your mother."

"My mother is your mother Marcus and she lives at home with our father Gaius."

Marcus looked at his brother for the hint of a lie in his eyes but he could see nothing. "Good! And try not to get yourself captured again. Metellus may not be there to save you; he will be fifty miles away."

"Huh! That was the one and only time. And you take care of that sword."

The turma heard the last statement and roared, "Sword brothers!"

Marcus laughed. "See I have got over sixty men to protect the sword."

Just then they heard the sound of a buccina and every trooper went on the alert. They were close to Votadini country and who knew when a warband would raid. It was with some relief that they saw the small column of legionary cavalry trot into sight, headed by Julius Demetrius. Next to him rode Gaius Saturninus the Decurion Marcus had met when Macro was in the land of the Votadini.

Livius rode to meet the senator and they embraced. "I am pleased that we have found you before the ala split up."

"Why has something happened?" Livius wondered if there had been a revolt in the southern half of the province.

Julius laughed and Livius noted the ironical smile of the face of Gaius Saturninus. "No, it is just that you may need to readjust your instructions. The Emperor has confirmed you as Prefect of this ala."

The decurions and troopers closest heard the Legate's words and a huge roar erupted. As others asked what had been said the cheer rippled throughout the camp.

"Well, I ..." never an ambitious man, unlike his dead brother, Livius reddened and stammered.

"It is deserved Livius and now that you are of the noble class no-one can gainsay you. It means that you will have to have a Decurion Princeps promoted and a decurion to replace you. I am going to Coriosopitum to begin work on the limes. The other reason I came here is that the legionary vexillations will be here soon." His voice became very serious. "The barbarians will not like the building of a solid frontier. You and your troopers can expect more action in the next few weeks." He pointed at the fort. "A century of auxiliaries raised around Morbium are on their way here now. They were recruited from those who were unable to join the ala so they will be loyal warriors. And now I shall return to Coriosopitum," he looked ruefully at the wooden fort, "where they do, at least, have baths and stone walls."

As they rode away the decurions all clambered around the new Prefect. "Thank you but I don't think it will change the way things are run at the moment."

Julius, the clerk, sniffed. "That is all you know! No more gallivanting for you Prefect."

"And who is to be the Decurion Princeps?" As one of the youngest decurions and most recently promoted, Marcus knew that he could ask the question without prejudice and without others thinking he was seeking the post for himself.

"Give me time to think lads."

From the back, Metellus' voice sounded, "What's to think about? It is Cassius or I will show my arse in Eboracum's Forum."

Everyone laughed and Livius nodded. "You could at least have allowed me to come up with that decision. Well, Decurion Princeps, if you could delay your departure for a short time we will discuss the ala. The rest of you have a mission and remember the Legate's words. This is now a war zone. Be careful out there."

Tole, King of the Selgovae, was still smarting from his humiliation at the hands of the Roman auxiliaries when they had stolen away from the barbarian conclave; although his ally, Lugubelenus had suffered more loss of prestige and status, Tole was young enough and sensitive enough to feel aggrieved that Roman spies had discovered their invasion plans and caused them to be aborted. The young king had wanted a war to show off his newly acquired power and keen army; the Roman army would have made a perfect opponent, for a victory of any size would have led to an enlargement of his kingdom. He had already taken over the lands to the west and assimilated the tribes, who had lived there, within his growing kingdom. East was too problematic as Lugubelenus was a powerful and suspicious king and, more importantly, a successful leader having destroyed the Ninth some years earlier. Northwards lay painted, unpredictable and belligerent tribes who lurked dangerously behind the two mighty rivers; all of which just left Tole with the land to the south, the land of the Carvetii, Brigante and Rome. He had sent out small scouting warbands to identify the weaker parts of the frontier. He would not waste time with allies he would find a vulnerable part and take it. Already he knew that the fortress at Luguvalium was heavily defended and his scouts were now heading for the land between Luguvalium and the high land which split the country in two.

It was one of these warbands which spotted Macro and Drusus as they headed north towards the huge forest which ran all the way to the heart of the Votadini heart land. Luarch, the leader, was wary for they were close to the disputed land between that of the Selgovae and the Votadini. Formerly Carvetii land, that buffer tribe had disappeared leaving the ownership a matter of arms. Luarch had but thirty men with him and the column was too big to take on but he was intrigued by their behaviour for they appeared to be about to camp for the night. He sent two of his men north to circle around the column while he and the bulk of his scouts watched as the Romans quickly dug a ditch and built a camp with stakes and a rudimentary gate. The barbarian was impressed. He began to fear that they had been seen when three of the Romans left the camp and rode hard west, towards their hidden position. He was relieved when they skirted the woods. He signalled for two men to follow them and then resumed his watch. The Selgovae were a patient tribe and his new king would not appreciate garbled misinformation. Better to wait and return with accurate information than risk the king's ire.

When the troopers returned he saw that they had been hunting and had a wild pig across the saddle. He heard the cheer from in the camp as the troopers saw Macro return with the kill and then the Selgovae scouts had to suffer the smell of roast pig wafting across the fields making their hunger even more acute. The next day the hungry and morose scouts watched the Romans. He had heard that they built and demolished their camps on a daily basis but when he watched he saw that they left the camp as it was and headed north. Waiting until they were out of sight Luarch led his men to the camp. Everything was laid out as though they intended to return. This was important news for the king. The scouts quickly ransacked the camp for anything they could take back with them. Spare javelins, shields and cloaks were all taken as well as the remains of the pig. As quickly as they had arrived the scavengers left and headed north west to report to their king.

When Macro and Drusus returned to the wrecked and ransacked camp the two young decurions were angrier with themselves rather than the enemy. They should have left a guard and they both knew that; but hindsight is always accurate. "We have learned a lesson here, Drusus and, more importantly, discovered that we have been discovered. I will ride back to Rocky Point and report to the Prefect."

Drusus sighed with relief for he had been dreading the dressing down he knew would ensue. "But you will be reprimanded, Macro, will you not?"

"I know but I feel more responsible. I have been brought up in the ways of the ala and it has been drilled into me that you either take down a camp or guard it and I did neither." He smiled ruefully at his companion, "The next cock up and you can take the blame."

When Livius saw the lone rider approaching the fort, now with gates and one tower, he knew that it did not bode well. When he saw that it was Macro he knew that there would be a good reason for the journey. Livius frowned when the sentry waved him through with a smile. As Macro dismounted Livius went up to the sentry and asked, quietly, "Why did you not stop the rider and ask his business?"

The sentry made the mistake of grinning and then, when he saw the dark look on the Prefect's face, stammered his answer, "Sorry sir but it is Decurion Macro. Everyone knows Decurion Macro."

"Even if it is Emperor Hadrian himself, you stop them and ask their business and check the password."

The trooper looked confused. "But sir I don't know Emperor Hadrian. I have never seen him."

Exasperated Livius gave up. "Just ask everyone. Clear?"

"Sir!"

When Livius reached Macro, he was not in the best of humours and Macro's report did not improve it. "Sir. I have to report that the barbarians know we are here. They have ransacked our newly built camp."

"Casualties?"

Macro looked even more uncomfortable. "Sir there was no-one in the camp. We were on patrol."

The silence was even more painful than a torrent of words. "So when I said the words war zone and be careful were you not listening or merely assuming that the mighty and invincible

Macro would ride his luck again?" The young Decurion had the sense not to reply. "I am disappointed in you Decurion. You have been lucky. It could have been far worse and resulted in deaths. What would you have done if the barbarians had waited for you to return? You would have been ambushed in your own camp! Think on that. Now return to your command and try to find those barbarians. It would be useful to know which tribe now knows we are building up here."

Macro rode back to the camp with a silent anger. This was the first time he had had a dressing down from anyone and he had not enjoyed it. The fact that he knew it was deserved made it even worse. He wondered if he needed Marcus as a touchstone to keep him focussed for he knew that, had Marcus been with him, they would have left a guard. Perhaps he was too young to be a decurion and should have remained as training sergeant. He resolved to make better decisions in the future.

"And they did not take the fort down?"

"No sire!"

"You have done well Luarch. Return and this time take with you, eighty men. If the Romans are foolish enough to go into the forest you may be able to ambush them. When the scout had left Tole summoned his council and told them Luarch's news. "Let us push further south. If there is one fort being built there may be others. Perhaps the Romans are coming to us."

"Was it just cavalry sire?"

"This one was, about sixty men. Are they scouting or preparing an invasion? Let us assume it is the latter. Call the army to arms."

One of the older men, a confederate of Tole's father, Aindreas ventured, "But sire the men are gathering in their crops. If they rot in the fields then we may starve this winter."

Tole was tempted to roar an answer at the whitebeard but he had learned discretion. "Make it known that the king wishes every woman, child and whitebeard to gather in the crops. All of the people will have to shoulder the burden eh? I will leave you in charge of that Steward and I know that you will work diligently so that we do not starve this winter." The Steward walked out red faced. He had been outwitted by the young king who was rapidly learning how to get his own way in all things.

Tole then took his lieutenant to one side. "Macklin, I want you to take a mounted warband. Go to Luguvalium but do not let them see you. Ride east until you reach Luarch. Check this Stanegate of theirs and see if there is traffic upon it and any other sign of war. The Romans are up to something and I want to know what."

The land through which Metellus and Cicero had been assigned was not good cavalry country. The wide river which traversed it had boggy, treacherous ground on each bank and when it did become narrow, the land around it rose sharply, with savage rocks. The thick woodland had few paths and was perfect ambush country. His only consolation was that the patrol further east had even worse country with sheer cliffs and a huge stretch of water; Marcus and Livius would need their wits about them. He only had fifty men with him as he had left ten to finish the camp, prepare a meal and then guard it; his first day of patrol he wanted to see the type of country he had to deal with.

Cicero was one of the newly promoted men. He was a little older than Macro and Marcus but had the same enthusiasm. His men, most of whom were older, looked on him fondly and gave him no trouble. Part of that stemmed from the fact that his brother had been a trooper in the ala until he had been murdered when The Fist and his companions had deserted. As The Fist had been one of the turma they had felt responsible for his death and tried to make it up by looking after his younger brother. Metellus knew that the boy had much to learn but he had the potential to be a good officer; he listened to the other decurions and carried out his orders punctiliously. When on sentry duty he ensured that none of his men were slacking. The only thing which Metellus did not know about him was how he would react in combat. Because Metellus and Macro had spent some time away from the ala they had not been there when they had fought their skirmishes with the barbarians. It was one reason why Livius had placed the calm and experienced Metellus with the younger novice.

His experienced eye picked out the trail which skirted the thick forest to their left. The land rose steadily and was like the boss on a shield; the horizon constantly dipped away. He turned to Cicero, "You take the lead, ride in single file and I will bring up the rear."

The keen young officer scanned the skyline, "Do you see something?"

"No Cicero but I do not like blind summits, you never know what is over the rise. You have keen young eyes and you may see something quicker than the older men of your turma. Be cautious and if you see anything then withdraw towards me. I will stay at the rear to make it easier to react to problems."

"Sir!" The keen young decurion galloped to the head of the turma, shouting orders as he did so. Metellus shook his head. He was just like Marcus and Macro when they first joined. The long line stretched out a long way once the orders had been given. Metellus was playing the percentages. If there were enemies around then they would only have the opportunity to attack a few of the troopers and Metellus would be able to react quickly. He saw the head of the column was just fifty paces or so from the summit.

Suddenly the trooper behind Cicero pitched to the ground and even from that distance, Metellus could see the arrow sticking out from his side. To his horror, he saw Cicero plunge into the woods with his turma behind. Metellus roared, "Hold your positions." Turning to the signifier he said, "Sound recall." As the buccina's strident notes rang out Metellus kicked his horse on, and, with sword at the ready led his turma to the body of the trooper. To Metellus' relief, he saw Cicero's turma beginning to emerge from the woods. The empty saddles confirmed his worst fears. "Form a defensive line." The twenty-five men of his turma formed a half-circle around the trooper lying on the ground as the signifier, who was also the capsarius of the turma saw to his injuries. As the survivors of the turma emerged from the woods Metellus ordered them behind his own men. He could see a mixture of anger and shame on their faces. Recriminations could come later. He turned to his chosen man, Lepidus, "Hold the men here I will take six men and seek the survivors."

Lepidus began to protest, "Sir!"

Metellus was in no mood for an argument. "Obey orders
Lepidus." He angrily gestured at the wounded men being
attended to by the capsarius. "This is the result of not following
orders. You six," he pointed at the nearest six men. "Dismount,
swords and shields only, leave your cloaks and follow me."

Metellus stepped into the forest. The trees were mighty oaks
and sycamores with a few elms. The trunks of some of them
were large enough to hide two men and Metellus cursed the
impetuous decurion who had led his men into an obvious trap.
He heard a noise and held up his hand, he saw the wounded man
lying on the ground. "You take this man back and then follow
us." The man's horse had been hamstrung and was lying close
by. Metellus took his sword and quickly dispatched the beast. He
hated the suffering of animals. Ahead he could hear the sounds
of blades clashing. He gestured his men forward. The six he had
chosen were experienced men and Metellus was pleased as they
readjusted their shields and tightened their grip on their swords.
When he saw the flash of cloth he waved his five men left and
right to surround his enemies. There was a small clearing and in
the middle, he saw Cicero and one of his men standing over the
body of one of their companions. Eight Selgovae surrounded
them advancing purposefully with axes at the ready. Their rapt
attention was on these three victims and did not see the six
troopers launch themselves at their unprotected backs. Metellus
was in no mood for mercy and the eight of them fell to eight
sword blows.

Cicero began to speak, "Sorry sir."

"There is no time for that." He turned to one of his men.
"You lead the decurion and his men back to the edge of the
woods. I will finish up here."

Without waiting to see his orders being carried out Metellus
led his four men deeper into the woods. It soon became obvious
that this was the furthest point the turma had reached and
Metellus turned them around. By this time his eyes were
accustomed to the gloom and he saw the first trooper he had sent
back returning. The man held up his hand in warning and pointed
north. Metellus trusted his men enough to obey the instruction
and he led his patrol in the direction indicated. They found six
men standing over a wounded trooper. The weapons in their

hands, daggers and knives showed that they were torturing him for information. The five troopers leapt forward. One of them tripped over a branch and the Selgovae saw their opponents. The leader was a tall man who quickly picked up his axe and shield and headed for the red-crested Metellus. Roaring a war cry he hurled himself at the Roman. Metellus stood his ground and watched the axe as it arced towards him. At the last minute, he moved his shoulders to the side and watched the blade as it slid harmlessly off his shield to thud into the ground. The problem with axes was that their momentum always gave their opponent an opportunity to strike while the axeman was vulnerable and Metellus took his opportunity. He slashed his sword, not at the warrior's body as he was expecting but at the back of his knees. As the tendons were ripped open the man fell to the ground and Metellus hit him hard on the back of the head with the flat of his sword. He had his prisoner. The rest were all dead and Metellus nodded his thanks to the keen-eyed trooper. "Right lads. Back to the open but watch out for any others. You two bring this barbarian with us."

There were four cloaked bodies lying on the ground by the time Metellus and the patrol returned. He looked up at Cicero. "Are they all accounted for?" The ala never left a dead man on the battlefield. Cicero nodded. "Right Decurion, lead the patrol back to the fort. Put the bodies on the spare mounts."

Lepidus said, "Sir, we don't have enough."

"Well put two on a mount. It isn't as though we are going far is it?" He realised that he had snapped his answer and Lepidus was only reporting. "Sorry Lepidus. You are right and it is not your fault."

Lepidus smiled, Metellus was a good officer most would not have worried that they had offended their men with a thoughtless comment but Metellus was a thinker and his men liked that.

"Make sure the barbarian does not bleed to death as we have some questions for him."

The men left to guard the camp had done an effective job and the ditches were littered with crudely fashioned lillia and the gate was in place. They looked in shock as the battered remains of turma thirteen arrived. The senior trooper in the fort took charge and immediately stoked the fire under the bubbling cauldron.

The broth which was for their evening meal would now be used as medicine for those who were wounded. Metellus nodded his approval as he rode through the gate. "Decurion make sure there are sentries and be alert; this may have been a scouting party or it could be a warband. We will find out. Lepidus, bring the barbarian here."

The warrior was dragged by two of the biggest men in the turma. His hands were tied but he kept trying to bite and kick them with his good leg. Lepidus smacked the flat of his sword against the warrior's teeth smashing them and making his mouth a bloody mess. Metellus gestured for him to be spread-eagled on the wheel of the cart they had used to bring their tents. Once he was satisfied that the man could not move he took out his sword. "You are going to die, you know that already Selgovae. It is the manner of your death which is in your hands. I can give you a swift warrior's death if you cooperate but if not I will make sure that, in the afterlife, you have neither eyes to see nor hands to hold a weapon and your enemies will be able to pleasure themselves with you for all eternity. Will you answer my questions?"

The answer was a bloody mouthful of teeth and gore spat at Metellus who, fortunately, was out of range. Cicero had given the sentries their orders and was standing behind Metellus wondering how this experienced officer would deal with the prisoner. "Ah, I see we have an honourable barbarian." He walked over to the freshly stoked fire and brought out a brand which he held in his left hand. Without preamble, he walked up to the barbarian and hacked off the fingers and thumb of his left hand with a swift slash of his blade. He then thrust the burning brand to cauterize the wound. The barbarian was tough and did not utter a sound but the facial muscles showed the agony he was suffering.

"Now you can still wield a sword but that will change unless I get an answer to my questions." He waited while the prisoner sullenly stared at him. "Are you a scout or part of a warband?" There was no reply. "Before I slice off your whole right hand, I will ask a different question. How many men were with you?"

The question seemed harmless to the troopers and they wondered if the decurion was losing it but the warrior coughed and said, "Three handfuls."

Cicero looked at Metellus with a confused expression. "Fifteen men." To Lepidus, he said, "Find out how many bodies we left in the woods." When Lepidus went to ask the men who had accompanied Metellus the decurion put the brand back into the fire and the barbarian seemed to sigh with relief. "So you were a scouting party and what were you to do once you had seen us?"

The barbarian looked confused. The loss of blood was making him light headed and he had given them some information. He could not work out if giving more information would make his crime worse. He did not want to wander the afterlife unable to defend himself. He had killed many men and some of them were not killed in battle. He shrugged, "The king asked me to return to Caerlaverock when you were found."

Metellus had found out more than he had hoped. "The king knew we were here?"

The barbarian laughed, "One of your little forts was found and destroyed by my brother. He knows you are here and he is coming for you."

Metellus nodded and walked behind the barbarian. He put the point of the sword to the neck of the wounded warrior and said, as he sank it into the jugular, "Go to the Allfather. It seems that we have not escaped notice for long."

"What did he mean little fort?"

Metellus waved his arm around the camp. "A little fort, one such as ours. Some of our comrades have not been as lucky as we." Putting his arm around Cicero he led him out of the camp through the gate. "Cicero you will be a good officer but today you got your men killed. Your men trusted you and they followed you when they knew it was a mistake. You have all of their lives in your hand. Why did you disobey my orders?"

Cicero looked almost tearful. "When Aelius was hit I just wanted the men who had done that. I didn't think."

"That is the trouble with being an officer. You always have to think. You will be in a similar situation again, of that I have no doubt. I hope that next time you are able to think before you act for if not then your turma will suffer." He looked west. "I am going to report this to the Decurion Princeps. Until I return you are in charge. Burn the barbarian outside the camp. We will honour our dead tonight when I return. Keep a good watch. I will not be long."

Cicero looked amazed. "You trust me? After that?"

Metellus smiled grimly, "If we were all punished after we made a mistake there would be no one to command the ala. Do not dwell on it but learn from it."

Cassius was disturbed by Metellus' report. "I don't like this. Which of the patrols was hit? Tomorrow I want you to ride east and see if Marcus and Lucius have suffered any assaults. Pass the news along to them and they can send the news to the Prefect, although he may already know." He looked carefully at Metellus. "Cicero?"

"Made a mistake, we have all done it. I don't think he will do it again but I have to say sir that this country is a bastard for horses. You are better off on foot."

"I know. The sooner the mixed cohort gets here the better."

Chapter 5

The meeting between The Fist and the one who would be prince of the Brigantes went well for both parties. The Fist had grown tired of his lonely existence out in the forests preying on lonely travellers and the offer of a paid job as a military adviser suited him. He also saw the opportunity to become even richer by selling the weapons he and his crew had stolen from the trader who had suddenly found himself boarded just ten miles from Eboracum. The burning boat did nothing to suggest anything other than a robbery, especially as the crew's bodies, when washed ashore had all had their throats slit. The Fist cared not, as long as they couldn't be identified.

For Gaius' part he was very impressed with this knotted and scarred mountain of a warrior. He already had a vision of the men with The Fist forming his bodyguard and making him invincible. "So what do I call you?"

The Fist grinned and the look was disconcerting as a couple of teeth were missing. "I think General will suit."

Gaius was less than happy with that but, as the ultimate prize was the crown it was a small price to pay. "Very well, General and how about your rates of pay?"

The ex-trooper frowned. He had not thought this through. Had Aelius Spartianus been there he would have known the price immediately. He gave himself time to think. "First things first. You will continue to buy your weapons from us at the price stated?"

Gaius nodded irritably. "Of course! As many weapons as you can get your hands on."

"You have a big army then?" The Fist was intrigued about the force involved.

"We have a thousand training at the moment but I have hopes that the number will increase."

"In that case, we will continue to supply you with arms and I will take half of the booty and plunder we capture from the Romans, including slaves." He wondered if he had gone too far with such an outrageous demand.

Gaius shrugged. "I am not interested in plunder or slaves. All I want is the crown of the Brigante and to be able to rule this land of my father." Gaius had easily believed his own lie that he was the rightful heir to the throne. All of the other young men in the newly formed army had bought into the fantasy as well. The Fist regretted not asking for all of the plunder but this was his first solo deal and he was pleased with the result.

"Excellent. We have a deal." He looked curiously at Gaius. "How will you keep this army a secret? A thousand men are hard enough to hide but more than that will be impossible."

Gaius tapped the side of his nose. "There are many forests north of Eboracum, far beyond the few Roman roads and soldiers. We have cleared a large training ground. We could hide ten thousand men there if we had them."

The deal was becoming sweeter by the minute. The deserter would no longer be alone and he would have a thousand men to order around. Aelius Spartianus would be proud of him.

Faolan had finally crossed the high part of this land. He had expected more settlements but his guide had explained that they were isolated. On reflection that had suited the Irish prince for it meant they had captured many slaves and much livestock. He had already sent large quantities back to Manavia where Morwenna had promised him that she would act as a broker and sell it. Loegaire had suggested that she might cheat him but Faolan had pointed out that all the gold they had collected was not to be brokered or shared. In anticipation of a rapid retreat he had sent fifty warriors to the high pass to build a barrier should they find themselves pursued, he wanted to be able to escape from this island with as much gold as possible. This was an easy war but, once they neared Eboracum he knew it would become more difficult.

One night, as they camped less than thirty miles from Morbium, Faolan held a meeting with Angus and Loegaire. He had come to trust this warrior of Manavia for he spoke the truth and was not afraid of arguing with the Irish prince. Faolan knew it was what he needed. "The sword we seek is close to Morbium. Morwenna said it was in a fortified farm."

"Aye, I know the place." Angus glanced over at Faolan. "It is close enough to the fort to have reinforcements over there in less than half a day."

"How many men at Morbium?"

"Probably a cohort." Faolan had a blank look. "About a thousand men."

Faolan did the calculation in his head. He did not have enough men yet to take on that number. So far the rebels who would flock to his banner had been noticeably absent. "If we caused trouble south of Morbium would they send troops then?"

Angus chewed on a piece of mutton bone as he debated the answer. "They wouldn't send a thousand. They have to defend the river so they would probably send five hundred men but then they would send men north from Cataractonium and Eboracum."

"Which are much further away?"

"Aye, considerably."

Faolan was a risk taker; he knew that if he could draw five hundred men into an ambush, he would gain a considerably large cache of weapons and it would leave him free to rampage and plunder at will. He already had a large amount of gold and precious objects; the province was, indeed, as rich as he had been led to believe. "Which is the largest force we could come against?"

Angus was intrigued by the Irishman's questions. He was a planner and that was no bad thing. "There are no legions within a hundred miles so it would be either an ala of cavalry and there's only one or a cohort of infantry. Either way, it is about a thousand men."

"That's it! Unless they pool their soldiers, we will outnumber any force that can be sent to attack us unless they empty their forts in which case they would lay themselves open for further attack. Which is the biggest settlement south of Morbium?"

"Easy. That would be Stanwyck, the old capital. The Romans took down the defences but the people moved back around it. It is a very prosperous town. Good cattle country and the people are happy because Morbium is half a day away which affords them protection."

"Then we head for Stanwyck. I want to reach there towards dusk. That way they will be busy eating and if we fire their homes then it will be seen from Morbium."

"And they will send soldiers to reach it by morning." Angus nodded admiringly. "Good plan. It might just work."

"And then I can head for this fortified villa and claim my sword."

Julius Longinus hummed his way around the Principia. He hated to be disorganised and disrupted. He also preferred order; now that the Decurion Princeps had been promoted to Prefect he had order in his world again. He could check lists, stores, and standing orders instantly without waiting for the officer in charge to return from a patrol. As he entered the office Livius was thinking the exact opposite. He hated being confined to the wooden oblong that was the fort. Like Cassius, when he had had to suffer all the clerical work, he hated lists and ordering supplies. Julius and the Quartermaster managed to do much of the tedious work but the Prefect still needed to authorise everything and now he had the problem of two of his forts and patrols being attacked. They would need more remounts and he would have to organise some recruits. At least the eighty guards who had arrived earlier in the day had relieved him of one headache. He had feared an attack on the vulnerable Rocky Point. With just ten men to guard it, they would have struggled. Unlike the smaller forts, Rocky Point had many of the characteristics of a major fort, supplies for a year, a water supply and most importantly as far as the troopers were concerned, a safe underground room in which to keep their savings.

He sighed as he entered. "What joyous work have you for me this morning Julius?"

The clerk ignored the sarcasm. The Roman Empire could not survive without clerks and clerical work. "You need to request more weapons. Many were taken in that first attack and we require twenty recruits." His tone became accusing. "We still haven't replaced those eight deserters."

"I know I will do it now."

The clerk pushed over a request already written out. "Just put your seal there."

"You know Julius my life would be much easier if I gave you the seal. Sort of cut out the middleman."

For the first time, Livius realised that he had shocked the clerk. "Don't even jest about such matters! Why that it is tantamount to treason! I have never heard such a suggestion. Take the seal indeed!" He thrust a document wallet at him. "Here are the latest dispatches from Eboracum."

Smiling at the old man's outrage Livius began opening and reading the documents. "It looks as though the first legionary vexillation has reached Eboracum. The Governor says they will be heading for Coriosopitum in the next few days." He put the document to one side and began to read the next. He suddenly sat bolt upright. "This can't be good." He stood and went to the map on the wall.

"More bad news, Prefect?"

"Potentially disastrous. The Prefect at Luguvalium reports that the garrison at Glanibanta has been slaughtered. It appears there is an army loose in the land of the lakes. He wants me to help."

Julius came over to the map. "Those four turmae are the closest."

"Yes, Julius but it begs the question who is it? Who is rampaging this close to our forts? An army that could destroy a fort and a garrison could not have slipped past Luguvalium nor us which means it has come either from the west or the south. The south is unlikely as the vexillation from Deva is on its way north which leaves the west and that can mean only one thing." Julius looked expectantly at the Prefect. "Morwenna, the Witch Queen, is up to her tricks again." He looked at the dispositions on the map. "Write out an order for Cassius to take the four western turmae to investigate the fort and a second one warning Marcus that he is now the westernmost outpost, he is the new flank. This would be a bad time for those in the east to raid our shores for we would be hard pushed to stop them."

Julius looked at the map closely. "We are very thinly stretched Prefect."

"Yes, Julius we may yet have to put you on a horse."

"The day that happens I shall pack my bags and head back to Aquae Sulis!"

Of all the Brigantes settlements, Stanwyckhad flourished well under the benevolence of Roman rule. They were close to the main road and their goods had a ready market in Eboracum. The garrison at Morbium meant that they were rarely raided and the elders had become complacent. The gate on the palisade was rarely closed and there was no town watch during the hours of darkness. Indeed, many of the more affluent inhabitants had taken to building fine stone villas away from the noise and stench of the busy town. The only security they had was the twenty or so ex-soldiers who had chosen Stanwyck as their retirement home and had small farms just outside the palisaded walls, far from the more expensive homes.

When Faolan's men fell upon the town in the early hours of the morning, it was as though wolves had been allowed into the sheep pen. Faolan's orders had been clear; his men were to slaughter all the men and old people but to capture the children and women as slaves. He knew he had enough men to outnumber the townspeople and he had threatened the leaders of the smaller warbands he was using with death if any potential slaves were killed. Faolan was already calculating that he could soon return home. He could make enough with this one raid to buy Hibernia for his scouts had told him that there were hundreds of women and children in the town. He realised that he did not have to risk failure by attacking the heavily fortified fortress of Eboracum. Sceanbh had been correct, Britannia was indeed a rich heifer waiting to be milked. He could return as many times as it took to replenish his finances. His losses had been negligible and his successes, incredible.

The opposition, inevitably, came from the veterans. All of their farms were in the same place, just south of the old hill fort, well away from the Brigantes. As soon as they heard the screams and the clash of blade on blade they reached for their weapons. Marius Spurius had been an optio in the Ninth legion; now almost fifty, he was still fit and he roared his orders. "Shield wall! I know some of you nancy boys were horse shaggers but even you know how to keep a fucking shield next to your mates!"

The old members of Marcus' Horse grinned at the banter. One of them shouted out, "Better watch out lads, we all know that the Ninth preferred men to horses!"

"Forward!"

The double line, with Marius in the centre, moved towards the walls of the hill fort. Over the years the glacis had been eroded and they easily mounted it to reach the top. The inhabitants of Stanwyck who had not been killed or captured were fleeing across the open centre of the old hill fort towards them. The ridges and ditches were allowing the Irish to catch up with those who fell and they were killed or captured depending upon their sex and age. The old instincts of the veterans took over and they jogged forwards, breathing heavier than in times past but keeping a straight line. The first survivors from the slaughter saw them with their shields and spears, easily recognisable as Romans and ran to the sides, crying their gratitude as they kept running south. The veterans had bought them time to escape the horror of the knife in the dark.

The leader of the Irish warband, Conan, was not enjoying the slaughter. He had come to Britannia for honour and glory. So far all they had slaughtered were fat old farmers and traders. His sword had yet to strike a shield! Suddenly, before the rampaging, disorganised mercenaries appeared a phantom, a line of Roman soldiers. As they trudged forwards from the mist they appeared like ghosts from the past. The first Hibernian warriors fell to the javelins of the veterans. Marius' voice roared, "Throw!" and twenty javelins flew through the air. The Irish were spread out but even so, silhouetted against the sun rise and being but fifteen paces from the Romans, eighteen of the weapons found their mark. Enraged the barbarian raiders recklessly charged the Roman line. The front rank was composed of all ex legionaries and auxiliary infantry and they locked shields to make a solid barrier. The troopers behind knew what to do and they braced themselves with their shields pushing against the front rank of veterans. To the attackers, it was like hitting a stone wall. They bounced back in shock to be hacked down to a man by the veterans who still remembered their training.

Marius risked a glance around and nodded proudly. Not a man had fallen. He was in no doubt that they would all die that day but they would die with honour intact. These raiders would remember the last stand of the veteran Romans.

Appalled at the slaughter of his men Conan yelled, in Gaelic, "Halt!" Most heard and obeyed but three of the younger warriors carried on their advance and were cut down, too, as they came close to the killing machine who had once been legionaries. Conan could now see that there were but a handful of these Romans and they could be outflanked. "You ten, round that side, you ten round the other." The twenty men ran to their positions.

Marius could see what was coming. If they stood their ground they would be slaughtered, better to take the initiative. "Wedge!" Both infantry and cavalry knew the wedge formation and, with Marius as their point, they made a dagger shape. The rear rank had ten men in it and, as Marius roared, "Run!" the tight wedge hurled itself to cover the fifteen paces which separated them from the Irish mob. Any more would have been too much for the old men but they hit the line and killed those in the front rank pushing inexorably on. Their impetus brought them close to Conan who marked Marius as the leader. Here was his chance for glory. As the man in front of him was gutted by Marius' gladius Conan stepped forward, his huge sword arcing down towards the optio's head. He had never fought Romans and Marius used that to his advantage. He let the blow come and then deflected the blade along his shield to slide harmlessly into the turf. In one motion he stabbed upwards and Conan felt the razor-sharp blade slide along his side, cutting through to his ribs. He dropped to his knees and Marius smashed him in his face with the boss of his shield. Trampling over the body the wedge continued forwards.

Time is no friend to old warriors and the twenty years since they had last fought in anger took its toll. Those on the right of the wedge were facing an enemy who could attack with impunity as their shields were on their other arms. The men were picked off one by one. Almost in an instant, the cohesion of the wedge disappeared and the Romans found themselves each fighting three opponents. Despite killing two of the three, inevitably the third killed the veteran. The Irish could not understand why the old men died with smiles on their faces. The last to go was Marius who was struck from behind with a ring of bodies around him. The last stand of the Ninth and Marcus' Horse had not been in vain; a stream of refugees fled south to alert the neighbouring towns that there were raiders in the vicinity.

Over in the town the flames could be seen flickering as the wooden buildings quickly caught alight. Faolan was pleased with the assault until he came upon Conan and the decimated warband. Conan had come to and was having his side dressed by one of his men.

"What happened here?" Faolan's tone implied that there was something Conan could have done.

Angus spoke up quickly, "These are veterans of the legion. These are the warriors you should fear."

"But the fort when we attacked them, they died so easily."

"Yes Prince but we surprised those men. These heard the noise and had time to prepare. Man for man they will defeat any you send against them. You need to outnumber them and surround them."

Faolan looked in dismay at the corpses littering the field. The circle of dead Romans seemed very small indeed. "So the Romans south of us will know we are here?"

Angus pointed to the north where the flames and black smoke were rising, liked a mountain, high into the sky. "And to the north. You had best prepare your defences."

The Irish warrior bit back the snappy reply that was in his head, the old adviser was right. He looked at the old fortifications of the hill fort. "We can pull the men behind those ramparts and they will have to climb up to us."

"Good plan but I would have your men hide to gain the surprise. They will expect you to have fled and not be waiting for them."

Faolan nodded at the sound advice. He glanced at Conan and the wounded warriors. "Conan, take the slaves, the plunder and the booty back to Manavia. Use your bodyguard." He looked intently at the red-haired old chief. "It is vital that the captives and the plunder get to Manavia. Understand?" Conan tried to struggle to his feet. Faolan snarled disparagingly, ignoring the bravery of the warrior who had fought for his Prince. "You will be no use in a battle. Take one of the captured horses and then you will not slow down your escape." He dismissed his chief from his mind, as the tired warrior limped away, and the Prince turned to Loegaire. "Get the men behind the ramparts. Make sure we have stones and arrows to hand. No-one attacks the Romans until I give the order." He looked at Angus. "Anything else?"

"I'd feed your men if I were you. Hungry men don't fight so well and these Romans will not be surprised. They will be expecting to fight today."

The fire was recognised for the danger it was both in Morbium and at Gaius' farm. The Prefect at Morbium immediately mobilised six centuries to investigate and sent a messenger both to Coriosopitum and Eboracum. It might be nothing but the Prefect knew that they lived in parlous times. Gaius too understood the significance. "Decius, take your mother, your family and the women to Morbium. You will be safe there."

Decius shook his head. "I am not leaving you alone with the few men we have. You take the women and I will defend the home."

Gaius took his young heir to one side. "Decius, I have the wasting sickness." He had been dreading telling his son but the time now seemed appropriate. He had come to terms with his fate but he knew his eldest would not.

Decius recoiled. "But you can't...."

Gaius smiled, "Your mother and I kept it from you. We both know there is nothing that we can do about it and we are prepared but if I am going to die soon at least let me die defending your heritage." Decius looked distraught and Gaius embraced him. "It is for the best. If I survive then all well and good but if not then tell your brothers that I love all of you and I am as proud of all three of you as any father who walked this land."

Holding back the tears Decius went to gather the wagons and horses. Ailis came over. "You told him then?"

"Aye. I didn't want to but if things go badly..."

"I will be at your side anyway."

Gaius held her at arm's length. "No, you shall not! You are a healthy woman and I would not deprive my children of both parents. You will leave and you will live. The boys will need your advice and comfort. I will not take no for an answer."

Ailis almost recoiled at the tone but she could see the sense and she nodded, the emotion too much for her to risk an answer. She stood on tiptoe to kiss her husband. "You are the finest man I ever knew."

"And I am grateful for the day we raided the Caledonian camp and I found the woman of my heart."

By the time Decius had organised his wagons Ailis was under control. As they heard hooves clattering along the lane every man's hands went to his weapons but were relieved to see Old Sergeant Cato with a string of horses. He dismounted and gave the string to Decius. "You will move faster with these."

Decius looked at the former trooper. "You are staying?"

"Aye. My farm is harder to defend but your father and I have more chance here." Gaius nodded his thanks. "And Decius, in front of these witnesses, I would like to say that should anything happen to me, my horse farm is yours and your family's." Gaius clasped Cato's arm and the grey-haired horse whisperer shrugged. "Who else would I leave it to?"

"Decius, go now. It is some time since we saw the flames."

The tearful column headed up the road towards Morbium passing as it did so the auxiliaries marching south. Decius' family were all in tears and the auxiliaries wondered why the whole farm was not being evacuated. The centurion halted the column close to the farm gates. They knew each other well. "Not leaving then Gaius?"

"It may be nothing in which case leaving would invite destruction and we have spent too long building this farm up. If it is trouble then I would like to try to stop it."

"Good luck then."

"We'll have food ready if you find it is just a field fire."

Looking at the black smoke the centurion shook his head. "That is the fire of burning buildings. I think things just went from bad to worse."

"We will just have to pray to the Allfather."

"And I hope that this time he listens."

Chapter 6

First Spear left Gaius' farm wondering why someone would risk his life for a few stones and scrubby piece of land. He would have high tailed it to Morbium the moment he had first seen the fire. He had been a soldier for twenty years and, next year, when he retired, he would take the land he would be rewarded with for his service to Rome and sell it! All he wanted out of retirement was a tavern and plenty of good food, more than just his porridge and bread. He knew that he either had too many men or not enough. If this was a raid then any force large enough to burn Stanwyck could take his vexillation. He was not convinced about the quality of the auxiliaries he commanded. He thought back twenty years to his arrival in Britannia and then the men had been tougher and more resilient. The newer recruits took the salary but did not want the hardship.

He glanced over his shoulder and noticed some of those at the back lagging behind. "Optio, take your vine staff and hurry those lazy bastards at the back. If this is a field fire then I would like to be back before mealtime."

Once they crested the rise a half-mile from Stanwyck, First Spear could see that it was not a field fire. The town was a smouldering ruin and there was no sign of life. The huddled corpses in front of the gate told him that there would be few survivors. "Optio, take six men and scout the wall." As his second in command trotted off First Spear turned to the column behind. "Form three lines!" Although the land was a little broken with some undergrowth the auxiliaries found the task easier than a legion would have done. Accustomed to fighting in a looser formation, the vexillation presented a front of one hundred and sixty men. The front rank was already preparing their spears for they were the assault troops. Most of them thought that they would be burying bodies rather than fighting as there were carrion crows and magpies already plucking at the eyes of the already stiffening bodies. By the time the line reached the bodies the optio had returned. He shook his head. "No-one left alive sir. Looks like barbarians but they aren't Selgovae, Brigante or Votadini."

First Spear rubbed his grizzled chin. He wondered if it was raiders from the sea again. There was little use in speculating. "Any sign of the whoever it was that was responsible for this?"

"No sir. But they went in that direction." He pointed south towards the old hill fort.

"Take the second century and form a skirmish line. The last thing we need is to walk into an ambush." Within a short time the third rank had shrunk by half and the skirmishers went forward in an extended line. They were just below the crest of the first ramp when they were attacked. A thousand men erupted over the crest, a shock onslaught on the surprised eighty men. Before First Spear could issue an order two more warbands came at the line from the left and right flanks. "Close ranks! Optio retreat!" His huge voice boomed across the battlefield but few in the Second Century heard it for they were already dead. The ones who could, ran as fast as they were able for the safety and security of the line.

"Prepare pila!" As the survivors dived beneath the shield of the front rank First Spear shouted. "Front rank! Release! Fall back!" After they had thrown their missiles, the front rank became the third rank. The skirmishers squirmed through to join the shorter second line. "Front rank! Release! Fall back!" This time the front rank was just one hundred men in length but the spears had done their job and the barbarians were warier now. "Keeping time, fall back!"

The centurion at the rear did an about face and the third rank followed suit. They began to march back through the still burning town. As soon as the Romans began to move back the barbarians charged again. "Front rank release! Fall back!" The shorter line became the second rank and First Spear wondered if the barbarians would keep up their pursuit. They had but two more volleys of spears and already the arrows of the enemy were picking off one or two of the auxiliaries. He glanced over his shoulder and saw that the gates of the town were less than a hundred paces away. He turned and shouted, "Lucius take the rear rank in column, secure the gates." Without waiting to see his order obeyed he continued, "Front rank release. About turn, double-time in column." They had the element of surprise and the barbarians sheltered behind their shields expecting the same measured retreat. As soon as he reached the gate the men were ordered into line with those who had retreated first forming the front rank. They still had two javelins left. First Spear walked over to the centurion. "Lucius, give those who try to get through the gate a volley. They will find another way I know but I want you to buy me some time so that I can prepare a line further back." Lucius looked confused. "I want a fighting retreat to Gaius' farm. It is the only place we can make a stand. But do not take risks."

As they trotted up the road at double time the barbarians tried to rush the gate. Twenty spears found some victims and they halted. Some of the braver ones climbed the smoking palisade and rushed at the auxiliaries. Rather than risk their valuable pila the ones who made the Roman line were killed by gladii. The next two rushes were more concerted and Lucius glanced over his shoulder; he could not see the First Spear. "Last section, release javelins! About turn and double time." The column ran in a column of four up the road. Lucius joined the last man who plunged to the ground with an arrow in his back. The centurion felt a prick on his leg and knew that he had been hit but he carried on with gritted teeth. He found himself hurdling bodies as the men in front of him were picked off. He caught a glimpse of red uniforms ahead and knew that First Spear had his ambush. He sensed rather than heard the warrior behind him and he stopped, crouched and turned in one fluid motion. The surprised barbarian sliced his axe through fresh air and Lucius ripped open his unprotected gut. He could see that barbarians were less than thirty paces away and he rose to his feet and ran as fast as he could for the protection of First Spear's line. He was relieved to see that the remnants of his men had formed the third line as the arrow struck him on the shoulder. This was not the pinprick of his leg and he collapsed in a heap. He heard First Spear shout, "Capsarius," and then "well done Lucius. Front rank release!"

As he lay with his wound being tended the centurion could see that they were stopped with a wood on one side and a wall on the other. The enemy could advance but they would lose many men while doing so. Equally the survivors could not stay where they were. He looked up at First Spear who was busily organising the defence. "How far?"

"I think we are about two miles away."

"That sounds too far."

First Spear shrugged. "Maybe they'll get fed up of losing men and wait until night. When you are bandaged I want you to take the wounded and head up to the farm. Tell Gaius we are coming and get a message to Morbium. I think this is more than just a raid."

Nodding Lucius said, "What is your plan?"

"Exactly the same, leapfrog back with as many as I can. Now go! May the Allfather be with you."

The centurion was shocked to see that he had fifty men with him some wounded more than others. He had seen the bodies of his men littering the field and a glance over his shoulder told him that First Spear was defending the line with just over two centuries. He hurried the men on as quickly as he could for he knew that soon the survivors would be upon his heels. The wound in his shoulder was still oozing blood and he hoped that he would not pass out before he reached the farm. He saw one of his men seated at the side and he dragged him to his feet. "Come on soldier. These barbarians will have your bollocks as a trophy."

"What's the point we are all as good as dead anyway?"

"There's dead and there is torture. While you breathe you move." He dragged him to his feet. "Move soldier, enough good men have died already today." Lucius had to admit that this uphill section was hard on legs which were weakened by the exertions of the run. It was with some relief that Lucius saw the barred gates of the farm loom large in front of him. Someone inside must have seen them for they swung open and Gaius raced out with some of his men to help the wounded. Lucius was impressed that the old soldier did not bother to ask questions which suited Lucius as he had not the breath to speak.

Once the gate was barred shut Gaius came over and helped Lucius towards the house. The centurion shook his head. "There will be more men coming. And we need to send a message to Morbium. It is a large warband. More than a thousand."

Gaius took it in quickly. He grabbed one of his young farm workers. "Aelraed, get a horse and ride to Morbium. Tell the Prefect that this is a large warband and his men have been badly mauled." The boy looked confused. "Just repeat my words and he will understand." Gaius grabbed his own bow and shouted, "Cato, get archers on the wall and prepare to support First Spear."

Gaius had twenty armed men in the farm and they quickly manned the walls. Lucius gathered as many men still capable of fighting as he could and dressed them in two lines behind the gate. "When First Spear gets here he will be hard-pressed by an enemy close on his heels. We open the gates and I want a volley over the heads of our men and then form a shield wall on each side of the gate. They bought us time let us return the favour."

They all heard the clamour of battle long before they saw anything. Gaius was in the tower above the gate and he shouted down a commentary. "They are about four hundred paces from the gate, unbar it. Archers shoot as soon as you can see a target. Centurion, there are few survivors."

Lucius hefted his shield so that it was tight against his wounded shoulder. The pain helped him to focus. Suddenly he heard Gaius shout, "Open the gate!" The men at the gate quickly swung it open. The sight which greeted them shocked the Centurion. There were less than fifty survivors and they were all covered in blood and gore, whose, it was hard to tell.

"Forward! Release!" Above their heads they heard the flight of arrows as their own javelins thudded into the eager barbarians. Lucius stepped forward as did his men and they locked their shields. The auxiliaries flooded through the gate while First Spear, his helmet now gone and blood dripping from a scalp wound, walked slowly backwards. Lucius could see that his shield was badly hacked in places but he still moved purposefully. As Gaius' arrows took out any that approached one warrior took his axe above his head and ran hard for First Spear. Despite the arrows which struck him he continued to run at the brave auxiliary. First Spear waited and then plunged his sword forward taking the warrior through the throat. The barbarians halted as their champion fell and the last of the auxiliaries stepped through the gate to the sanctuary of the farm.

First Spear looked at Lucius and Gaius. "Thank you, gentlemen. That was a close-run thing. A few more paces and they would have had us."

Later, after they had been fed and watered, the three of them joined Cato at the gate to work out their options. "I don't think we will get any help from Morbium."

"You are right there Gaius which means we are left to ourselves for our defence." They glanced around at the pitiful remains of the six centuries. Many of the soldiers had succumbed to wounds and they were left with a total of ninety men who could fight whilst outside there were around a thousand barbarians. "I think all we can do is make it too expensive for them to kill us. We have already bloodied their nose. If the Governor can send men from Eboracum…"

Gaius shook his head. "He will want more intelligence than our first message. No First Spear you are right. It is up to us. I wish we knew what their leader was thinking."

Faolan was less than happy. He had lost far more men than he had expected. The fight at Glanibanta had convinced him that the Roman soldier was not a worthy opponent. The events of the morning had proved him wrong. He knew that this was the farm of the sword and he was now close enough to almost taste it. With the sword and the plunder already collected, he could return to Hibernia and claim his throne. Looking at the fortified farm that was easier said than done. Already they had lost twenty warriors trying to attack the walls. He had to admit it was well made with ditches lined with lillia and ramparts lined with deadly archers. They had a day in which to reduce the defenders for, after that, relief would probably be on its way. He called a meeting of Angus and Loegaire. Hopefully their experience would find a solution.

"The time has come!" Caronwyn embraced her young Brigante prince. "There is a rebellion."

All of Eboracum was aghast at the news. Stanwick's population had been massacred; the few survivors brought tales of terrible warriors wielding axes slaughtering innocents in their beds. The fact that the Governor had no troops to send emboldened the would-be rebels.

"I will see my father and see what he says."

Caronwyn looked at him with undisguised scorn. "And I thought you were a man. When you said you wanted to throw off the Roman yoke then you were a man. Now you are just a frightened little boy who has to ask his father's permission." Gaius Brutus brought back his hand to strike the red haired beauty but he stopped as the knife was placed at his throat. "You would die choking on your own blood if you struck me. Go and ask your father but remember, the longer you wait, the less chance you have of success."

The young man, quite shocked at the threat of violence from what he had seen as a subservient girl, fled and Caronwyn laughed. He was pathetic. It did not matter if he was successful or not, as long as he struck it would make others believe in the possibility of change. That was the message her mother had given her. She sought out Morag. "Come we can leave."

Morag looked surprised. "They will fight?"

"I believe so but it is important that we return to Manavia for I have important information for my mother and we can do no more here."

As they left she would have been gratified that her words had stung Gaius Brutus into action. He had bearded his father. "Now is the time father! If the Romans had power they would have sent a force to punish these barbarians. They have not. Do we wait to be slaughtered in our beds too? Or do we seize power? My men are ready. There are two thousand warriors willing to fight the Romans and if we capture Eboracum then we are halfway to victory."

Reluctantly the trader agreed. He was torn between ridding Britannia of the Romans and losing his son in war. If they failed then they would lose everything including their lives. It was a gamble and Antoninus was not a gambler. He had to have some insurance. "My son I agree and give you my blessing if you will agree to one condition."

The young warrior, now grown into a man with a man's body looked sceptically at his father. "What condition?"

"Wear this." He took, from a wooden box, a helmet. It gleamed and shone in the firelight. Gaius Brutus' eyes widened with joy. "I had it made when you began your training. It is a helmet fit for a warrior."

Taking it almost reverently from the box the warrior looked at it from all sides. It was a thing of beauty made from a single sheet of metal, there were neither seams to rupture nor edges to catch blades. It covered the whole head and yet the eyepieces had been cleverly made to enable to the wearer to see well and not run the risk of a deflected arrow. When he put it on, Antoninus breathed a sigh of relief. His son was unrecognisable in the anonymous yet startling helm. If things went awry as long as his son escaped the battlefield, their part in the revolt would remain a secret and if his son died, well that would be the end of the old man's world anyway and he would take the poison he had paid Morag to brew.

"I will wear it with pleasure father." He was pleased with the helmet for it marked him as different. When he and his 'General' went into battle, it would be as warriors, and not rag-tag brigands.

Angus had had enough of this raid. Had he not promised Morwenna to stay until the end, he would have left with Conan and the slaves. This Faolan was like a dog with a bone. The best of the beast had been picked clean and yet he insisted on chewing the remains. Already some of the Irish had drifted off to brigandage and robbery, had they been in a regular army it would have been called desertion but here it was down to each man to choose. Their casualties were increasing and Angus feared what would happen if they came upon an organised force which was expecting them. Hit and run was the way of the raider and they had tarried too long in this land of roads and organisation.

"How long to break into the farmhouse?"

Angus shook his head in disbelief. Faolan was determined to get into the farm at all costs. "Why? We would lose many men if we did so."

"There is something in the farm I want."

"The Sword? I am not sure it is there. They would have used it as a rallying cry."

Faolan agreed with Angus but he remembered Morwenna's words. The farm was the home of the sword-bearer. If he slaughtered all in the farm then the sword would follow him no matter where he went. Like Angus, he was ready to leave but he had one more throw of the dice left. "How long for us to break in and not lose too many men?"

Angus sighed. He would need to come up with a good plan which would facilitate their departure. His eye was caught by the huge stand of trees. "Chop down that tree and make a ram. Attack them tonight when the men are rested and then use fire arrows to set the place alight. I would not want to be here this time tomorrow for even the slow armoured Romans will have sent reinforcements by then."

Faolan agreed with the Manavian and set Loegaire to chopping down the tree. "Rest those not engaged in cutting down the tree and make sure they are fed for when the tree is down then we will end this. Those cutting down the tree can rest when we attack." They had plenty of food looted from Stanwyck and Faolan wanted to travel lightly and quickly when they left."

Inside the farm, a heated debate was taking place. "I am not throwing you out First Spear; I am offering you a chance to save you and most of your men."

The centurion was an honourable man and he did not want to abandon this brave old soldier and his men. "What makes you think we can escape undetected?"

Cato pointed towards the Hibernians, clearly visible from the tower upon which they stood. "We can see that they are to the south. They have not encircled us," he shrugged. "Either they are incompetent or fear being attacked by relief from Morbium. The way north is clear."

"In which case why cannot we all leave?"

Gaius shook his head. "They would see that we had deserted the walls. Do not worry, First Spear, I will ask for volunteers." He gestured at the litters with the wounded. "It is their only chance and, to be honest, I am being selfish. If you get to Morbium then there are more men to protect my family and they are more valuable to me than these stones." He lowered his voice. "Cato and I have said our goodbyes. It is time to meet my comrades and the Allfather."

First Spear could see the sincerity and recognised the wisdom. He nodded. "I promise you I will protect your family for as long as I live." He clasped his arm and then descended. He turned to Lucius. "Gather the men and prepare them. We are leaving."

Within a short time Lucius had all the men readied. First Spear looked on in amazement as every one of Gaius' men refused to leave, knowing that they were going to die. "You had better go. I can hear chopping in the woods so they are planning something. When they realise you have left they may depart themselves."

First Spear shook his head, "You know that is not true. But we will honour you. Come Lucius let us get the men moving."

"Sorry sir but I am staying." Before First Spear could say anything Lucius lifted up his armour to show the wound. "I am finding it hard to breathe. This is a death wound. I would slow you up and I would like to die honourably, with my sword in my hand amongst these brave fellows."

First Spear understood and he clasped his arm. "May the Allfather be with you."

The ramparts seemed deserted and sparsely guarded by the twenty odd men who manned it. The auxiliaries ghosted silently northwards leaving only the buried comrades who had fallen and those who were about to fall. Gaius looked at Lucius. "Well Centurion it looks like we will be greeting the Allfather together."

"For my part, I am honoured to be in such illustrious company as two of the men who rode with Marcus' Horse. My story will now be told alongside yours but my name will live on."

"Your comrades will tell of your bravery Centurion and that is our reward; it is good to know that those who fought with us will remember us and in that we live forever; just as I remember those who fell before me, and await me, Ulpius, Decius, Macro and Marcus."

Suddenly the air was filled with flaming arrows which descended like fiery rain. At the same time, they heard the roar as a hand-picked band of warriors threw themselves and their ram at the gate. Even had First Spear and his men remained they could have done little. Every man was forced to hold his shield above his head to protect himself from the arrows which allowed those with the ram the freedom from attack. The gate was a strong one but, at the second attempt it burst open and the frustrated warriors burst in, eager to wreak revenge on those who had stood in their way. As they filled the courtyard they were bemused. Where were the defenders? They were answered by the arrows which poured on their unprotected backs. Had Faolan left his archers to continue their deadly torrent then the defenders would have been less effective but, having seen the gate open, he had ordered all of his men through the gate.

"Stay on the ramparts. It is our only hope."

The Brigante defenders kept firing at the barbarians who were largely unarmoured. Had they had unlimited ammunition they could have held out for longer but as the quivers emptied the attackers were able to climb the rickety ladders to the ramparts. The first few who made it were dispatched easily, they were isolated, but as more and more men made the ramparts the outnumbered defenders fell. None asked for quarter for they knew they would be given none and they fought on despite the life-sapping wounds they endured. They fought in double trust, first as the oathsworn of Gaius and secondly to protect their families now sheltering in Morbium. The more of these barbarians they killed the better the chance of survival their families had.

It was fitting that the last three were Gaius, Lucius and Cato. One glance at Lucius told Gaius that the brave Centurion had but minutes to live. The savage slash across his stomach showed his intestines which rippled out to hang like a strange armour. Saluting with his sword the brave centurion hurled himself at the three warriors who were advancing on them. The four crashed to the ground ten paces below. Lucius and two of them lay dead and the third had a broken back. Gaius and Cato stood back to back. The warriors who advanced had to do so in a single file for the walkway was narrow. Below, Faolan hurled his curses as warrior after warrior fell to the two calm old men who were buying time for First Spear. It was only a matter of time before they would fall for Cato, although a trooper was not a swordsman and, inevitably he fell. As in life, he died without fuss, silently but with a sword in hand. Gaius knew that he was alone as the body slid down his back. Now surrounded, he smiled and roared out his challenge. "Come on you whoresons

and meet the steel of the last warrior who fought for
Cartimandua!" Oblivious to the blows he took he hacked his way
forward, discarding the shield which was chopped to shreds.
Taking his pugeo out, he still advanced despite the deep cuts
which were slowly sapping his life's blood from his body.
Finally, one of those standing below, with Faolan, took the
opportunity to hurl a spear which embedded itself in his side, the
impetus of the missile throwing the lifeless body over the
palisade to lie untidily across the discarded ram.

The silence which fell over the bloody battleground seemed
unreal and supernatural. As Faolan glanced around he saw that
there was but one auxiliary and the rest were farmers. They had
been held up by old men and boys! That thought made him
wonder about the treasure of the sword. They would not have
fought that hard if they were defending but stones. "Search the
farm, dig up the ground. I want all the treasure and weapons you
can find." As his men set to, eager to gather plunder, Faolan
turned to Loegaire. "Prepare our horses and my guards. If the
Romans return I want to be able to escape quickly."

"And the sword?"

"If it is not here then our destruction of this place will make it
follow us. I would prefer to fight them on ground of my
choosing in the west." He gave a wry smile, "I think we have
outlived our welcome here and we have enough now for the
throne."

"Aye we do."

When Decius and Ailis saw the remnants of the cohort
bringing their wounded through the gates they knew the worst.
Their father and husband had joined the Allfather, meeting again
Gaelwyn, Decius, Macro, Marcus and Ulpius. They had mixed
emotions for they knew that it was the death he had sought but
they were sad for themselves and their loss. It was they who
were left to mourn. As First Spear entered and saw them he and
his signifier stood to attention and saluted. It was as fitting an
end as could have been wished.

Chapter 7

Fortunately for Eboracum, Hadrian had made a wise choice in his Governor for Falco was both calm was level headed; he was not a man to panic when the refugees began flooding through the gates of the legionary fortress. Already warned by the messenger from Morbium, he had delayed the legionary vexillation's departure. The erection of the *limes* was not urgent but a raid in the heartland was. He sent a rider to Coriosopitum to requisition some of the cavalry. Although he knew they were stretched he also knew that the mixed Gallic cohort should have arrived at the frontier alleviating some of the paucity of resources at the frontier. He also commandeered every vessel in port and their cargo. The captains bleated but Falco wanted to ensure that they could survive a siege. Finally, he had ordered a cohort of the Second Augusta to be sent to Eboracum as a reserve in case of events worsening. He tried to cover every eventuality

When Julius received the message from his fellow Legate, he rode directly to Rocky Point to deliver the request in person. He hoped that Hercules and '*The Swan*' would arrive soon for he wanted to be able to travel between the frontier and the Governor both quickly and safely. As soon as Livius saw Julius enter he knew that there was trouble. The Legate knew Livius too well to beat around the bush. "We have an uprising of the Brigante close to Eboracum. And there is worse news there are Irish raiders at Stanwyck and Morbium and the Governor has requested your cavalry."

Eboracum was a fortress and had been attacked before; Livius felt that it would be safe but Stanwyck? It was a peaceful settlement and, to make matters worse, close to Gaius and Ailis. Livius looked around at the half-built fort. "I know we need to help the Dunum valley but what about the *limes*? What about the Selgovae? If we pull out then they will pour across the frontier and the problem will be even worse."

"I said I wanted your cavalry. You will stay here."

"On my own! I think you seriously overestimate my abilities, Julius."

Julius laughed. "No not on your own. The Gallic auxiliaries are here. They arrived in Coriosopitum yesterday. Their Prefect died on the way. I want you to take temporary command of them until this trouble is sorted. You can billet their horsemen in your forts and the infantry here."

"Who will command my men?"

"Cassius I assume."

Livius shook his head. "He and three turmae are off to Glanibanta to check on the garrison there."

"Send a message to him and tell him to head directly to Morbium. Rufius can take charge until then." Julius could see Livius biting back his anger. "I know what you are thinking Livius. You do all this work and then have to leave it halfway through well I am sorry but the barbarians just aren't cooperating. Had this been in a few months' time we would have had legionaries up here and the Gallic cohort would have been trained but this is the reality and there is nothing we can do about it."

Livius' shoulders sagged and he sighed, "You are right and I know it. I just wish Rome knew it." He turned to Julius Longinus who had been hearing every word, "Write out the..."

"I am already begun."

Livius smiled at the Legate. "You see you could cut out the middleman and save so much time." As they left the Principia, Livius asked, "Do you think we can hold on sir?"

"I don't know Livius. This attack has come from nowhere. The Selgovae were to be expected, especially after Metellus' report but not Glanibanta, that was a shock. There are few forts in the west and now that side of the country is open to raids across the frontier for the Prefect at Luguvalium will be stretched beyond belief."

"You know what I fear the most?"

"Morwenna."

"Exactly and knowing how she feels about her son perhaps I ought to retain Macro here."

The two of them left the fort and peered northwards across the magnificent yet bleak and empty land which rolled northwards. "Would he thank you for it?" Livius shook his head. "Would he obey or would he desert to be with his brother?

Perhaps you could leave both brothers here and protect them too?"

"Enough sir. I can see where you are going and besides it may not be Morwenna."

"The reports did suggest Hibernians and it is known that she used those as her bodyguards. "

"If this is some plot of Morwenna's then I know that the next focus of their attack will be Gaius' farm. I hope they escaped to Morbium in time."

"Gaius was always a canny warrior. He will be safe; of that, I have no doubt."

The Fist was not sure that the 'army' he commanded was ready for revolution. The two thousand young warriors were well armed and trained to fight efficiently and they were keen to fight but, having seen many recruits in his career, these did not appear to have the backbone to carry a campaign through to its conclusion. He was preparing for flight, he had already hidden his gold and had the best horse in the army. When things went awry, as he knew they would then he would escape. He had heard that Manavia was recruiting mercenaries such as he and he knew that Rome's influence would never extend to the realm of the Witch Queen. He would do as requested, he would advise but he would assiduously avoid any fighting. The whelps of Brutus' army would do the fighting, the bleeding and the dying.

"Well, General, our army is ready and we can attack."

The Fist fixed the young armoured warrior with his steely stare. "Where would you suggest we attack?"

"Eboracum of course!"

"It is a fortress and not easy to assail."

"Which is the reason we employ you, as a military adviser. What is the speediest way to capture the fortress?"

The Fist was tempted to say 'with real troops' but he bit his tongue. "You need to be subtle. A frontal attack will result in too many casualties. The gates are their weaknesses. They are open during the day. If you could send small groups of men with hidden weapons into the vicus they should be able to overpower the guards and the entrance could be rushed. There are probably only five hundred soldiers in the fortress. If you are lucky then you should not have to suffer too many casualties."

Gaius' face lit up with pleasure. The plan seemed eminently plausible. "Excellent. You have earned your pay already." He turned to summon his four young nobles who thought themselves the next generation of Brigante leaders. The Fist turned away in disgust. This young whelp reminded him of every arrogant Roman youth who had arrived to command men twice their age and with twice their experience. Regardless of the outcome of the rebellion he and his men would be leaving. He rode towards the tent which housed his confederates.

The five of them were lounging outside awaiting instructions. "Do we fight?"

In answer the deserter who had chosen the wrong moment to say the wrong thing was kicked, hard, between the legs. "Don't be a soft bugger all your life. Have a day off! No, we do not fucking fight. I want you to pack all our plunder on the backs of the pack horses. Pack food and tents. Once we leave for Eboracum I want the four of you to lag behind and take the first opportunity you can, to head west. Avoid the Dunum and mark the trail. Travel due west but south of Stanwyck. There is an old trail we can use. I will find you."

"Where are we going?" The Fist noticed that the tone had become far more respectful and his men feared an attack on them.

"Eventually Manavia but first we get as far away from here as we can. These soft buggers don't seem to realise that, even if they beat the auxiliaries, the legions will come and they will all end up on crosses."

"Why are you going with them then?"

The Fist put his face close to the small weasel-faced ex trooper. "To buy you ladies time to get my treasure well away from here!"

The sentries were on high alert. The rumours were racing around the fort but all of them had one thing in common, two groups of auxiliaries had been badly handled by some barbarians; one of them massacred to a man. Every one of the sentries scanned every face to see if they were foreigners. It was with some relief when the drunken Brigante youths wandered up to the Porta Praetorium. The guards smiled, drunks they could handle. Behind them, they could see their mates all laughing at them. Obviously, they were celebrating a coming of age.

The optio wandered over to them. "Now come on lads. You know you aren't supposed to be here. You could get in trouble." One of them looked as though he was going to vomit. "Hey, none of that! If you can't hold your ale get home." He put his arm around the boy to steer him away. He looked down in amazed shock at the knife which suddenly ripped open his guts. The four sentries were equally surprised to be attacked and killed by the drunks.

With a roar, the party of celebratory youths raced through the open gate, their cloaks discarded to reveal armour and shields. A mounted warrior whose face was hidden behind a visor galloped up and roared, "Today Brigantia is free!" and led the mob into the open fort.

Governor Falco did not panic. He turned to the centurion who had returned to the fortress with the vexillation of the newly arrived Sixth Legion. "Centurion, form your cohort in front of the Praetorium."

Quintus Licinius Broccus was a twenty-year veteran and he nodded his acknowledgement and strode off. He was already annoyed at having to leave his pleasant little billet with his Batavian slave girl. The fact that he had had to march twenty miles north to be summoned back had merely added to his ire. These barbarians would pay for fucking with the legion.

The Fist waited outside the fortress walls and watched his acolyte lead his brave but foolhardy warriors forward. He had seen the standard of the Sixth and knew that whatever happened, the rebels would die. The legion did not lose. None of the rebel army cared what the deserter did for they were now doing what their ancestors had done; they were fighting for their country, and they were winning. He turned his horse around and kicked hard. With luck, he could rejoin his men before the rebels had all been slaughtered and the sweep for others began.

The Brigante rebels were ecstatic; many had not expected to breach the gates but now all fell before them. The auxiliaries they met were disorientated and confused and easily despatched.

The vaunted Roman Army was a myth and these young warriors would prove it. Gaius was almost orgasmic with excitement. He had killed his first enemies. Five auxiliaries had fallen to his blade. Behind him were a thousand young bloods. How could they lose?

The vexillation of the Sixth was but a thousand strong but all of them had at least ten years experience and many of them had double that. They watched the young unarmoured warriors rushing at them and began to work out what time they would eat supper. First Spear checked his chin strap and began to estimate the distance to the enemy. They were not warriors; he could see their inexperience and their youth, they were little more than boys but that would not save them. He waited until the front rank was but thirty paces away and then he roared. "Front rank release.!" A heartbeat later and he shouted, "Second rank release!" Finally, he roared, "Rear rank release!"

Gaius Brutus could not believe what happened in a few moments. His thousand warriors became a heaving, bleeding, dying mass with the few hundred survivors vomiting over their dead friends. As the Roman line tightened the young nobility of the Brigante fled but to no avail. The legionaries double-timed forward and scythed down the retreating, fleeing unarmoured would be warriors. The gate they had breached proved to be their undoing as it was soon clogged by a mass of fleeing humanity who were ruthlessly slaughtered by gladii well used to this sort of butchery. The only survivor was Gaius Brutus who, with urine dripping down his leg, kicked his horse westwards towards his home and safety.

First Spear just spat and said, "Tossers!"

The Decurions and their turmae wondered why they had been summoned so hastily to Rocky Point. When Rufius saw Julius Demetrius present he had a premonition that it would not be good news. Livius took them into the Principia to give them their orders.

"There are raiders in the south around Morbium." He glanced at the two brothers whose faces were impassive. "The Governor has no idea how large the force is but it may have destroyed a garrison at Glanibanta before ransacking Stanwyck." Marcus and

Macro exchanged a nervous glance. Morbium was one thing but Stanwyck was too close to home, literally. "The Decurion Princeps and four turmae are investigating the raid at Glanibanta but Decurion Rufius will lead you to Morbium to either act as support or to pursue and destroy these raiders."

Julius held up his hand to interrupt and stepped forward. "I know that this information is a little vague but you need to know that the Emperor intends to build a solid frontier here and we have legionary vexillations on their way to begin the building. But we need stability behind the lines before we can start work. You have just become settled here but you are the most mobile force we have." He paused, "Some of you are wondering why the Prefect is not leading you, well he will still be in command here but there is a Gallic mixed cohort who are coming to reinforce the frontier. When you return you will no longer be alone."

"When do we return sir?"

"Good question Rufius. The Decurion Princeps has orders to head east after he has been to Glanibanta. Once you have rejoined him and the threat is gone then we will send orders for you to return. You will not be taking wagons for you will need to be swift. You will use the remounts as pack horses and when you get to Morbium acquire more remounts from Cato."

The ala needed no urging to make good speed south. All of them had connections with the area around Morbium and the Dunum. Marcus and Macro's turmae had even stayed at the farm and had great affection for Gaius' family. The Legate stayed at Rocky Point to await the arrival of the mixed cohort and Rufius led them across country to save time. They picked up the main road well south of Coriosopitum.

Macro and Marcus were riding together, as was their habit in days past; "We should reach Morbium by nightfall."

"Brother it is not Morbium that worries me but home." Marcus had always been the strategist, the one to see the bigger picture. "If there are raiders at Stanwyck they have three directions to take, Eboracum, the farm or back to the west. The easiest option is the farm."

"But father would have seen the signs and left for the safety of the fort wouldn't he?"

"I hope so but he was behaving strangely the last time we had leave. Perhaps it was my imagination, I don't know but I will be happier when we ride through the gates and their smiling faces greet us."

There was still a pall of grey smoke to the south as they rode through the Porta Decumana at Morbium. Rufius halted the ala outside the walls for he knew they would not have accommodation within. He turned to the brothers, "Organise the camp and, when it is erected, join me at the Principia."

Macro was about to voice his objections when Marcus restrained him and shook his head. "Yes sir."

Rufius smiled his thanks. He was fond of the two brothers, regarding them as family rather than fellow warriors but he did not want emotion to rule their heads. The task of building a camp would take their minds off the bad news they might receive. Rufius knew that events might not have gone the family's way and he would have to assess the situation and then deal with the consequences, whatever they were.

As he walked through the gate he could see the signs of the conflict, wounded soldiers and men preparing to march. Admitted immediately to the Principia the Prefect greeted him warmly. Marius Arvina knew the ala well. "Rufius I am I glad to see you. Things are on a knife-edge." He glanced at the door. "Are the boys with you?" They both knew that Marcus and Macro were, 'the boys'.

"They are building the camp."

"Good. You will have some bad news to give them. The farm is destroyed and their father, Cato and their men dead."

"The family?"

"They are safe, within these walls. But there is more bad news, the Brigante have risen and attacked Eboracum."

Rufius was taken aback. "Have they taken it?" Everyone knew that, once Eboracum was taken the whole of the north of Britannia was vulnerable.

"No for the Sixth had a vexillation there and they destroyed them but it is imperative that you find these raiders and destroy them and then get to Eboracum and reinforce the Governor."

"It will have to be first light. We have travelled hard to get here."

"By first light, I will have men to support you. I need to know what the situation is just south of us. That will enable you and your ala to pursue these raiders."

"Do we know who they are?"

"My First Spear thought they were Hibernians."

"A long way from home but I smell a witch in all this."

"I pray to the Allfather that this is not so. The Governor is keeping us informed of the events in the city and I will send a despatch rider to inform him of your arrival. You were quicker than we had hoped."

"This is the home of the ala Prefect, our home in every sense. Gaius was our last link with Ulpius Felix and the time of Cartimandua. It will be a hard task to tell the boys." He sighed and then stiffened his shoulders. He was in command now, not Cassius, nor Metellus and he had to shoulder this unpleasant responsibility. "And now Prefect if I might see Ailis."

"Of course. They are using my quarters although Decius was keen to return and rebuild the farm."

"Just like his father."

Ailis threw her arms around Rufius. "My boys, they are safe? They are here?"

"Aye they will be entering the fort soon." He pulled back to see her face. "I feared the worst and I wanted time to prepare to tell them the bad news. I am glad that I did so for it will be a hard task."

She leaned up and kissed him on the cheek and then stepped back shaking her head. "You are a good man Rufius and a good officer but that is the task of a mother. I will tell the boys of their loss and then the three of them can share the grief and the honour."

"Not that I doubt it but it was an honourable death?"

"Cato and my husband held off a thousand warriors to enable the remnants of the cohort to make it here. His last action was as brave as his first and he died as he had lived, an honourable warrior."

Kissing her lightly on the cheek Rufius hugged her. "Your husband has gone Ailis but there are a thousand troopers who will defend you, your home and your children."

"I know."

As he left he saw Macro and Marcus almost running towards the Principia. When they saw Rufius, and aware that they were being watched by the garrison, they both halted and saluted. Rufius gestured them in to the Principia. "Your mother awaits."

Marcus said, "And father?"

"Go see your family and you may have some time with them. I will send for you when you are required, for we ride south before morning."

A grizzled and heavily bandaged centurion limped over to Rufius. "I am First Spear and I fought with the boys' father. He was a brave man and he saved my men. We have a debt of honour to repay."

Rufius shook his head. "Gaius would not wish you to be indebted. It was not his way. Who are these people? For we are charged with pursuit in the morning and I would know as much as I could about this new enemy."

"They are good warriors but wild. Some of my men thought that they were the Irish, Hibernians. Certainly, they are not a local tribe. They have little armour and used swords and axes. They have archers but I think not many."

"Horses?"

First Spear shrugged. "They were attacking us on foot so I do not know but if they do have mounts they are few." He looked south, "Would that I was leading the men tomorrow but with this wound, I would slow them up. I am to remain here and guard the fort."

Rufius put his hand on the veteran's arm. "From your wounds, First Spear, you have done your duty and your comrades will just be rebuilding. I fear our prey will be long gone."

"You are right. If they had had enough men then they would have attacked here."

The three brothers and their mother embraced in a tearful reunion. Marcus reproached his elder brother and his mother. "Why did you not tell us of this sickness? We did not get the chance to say goodbye."

"Only I knew, Marcus, and your father did not wish to burden you with thoughts of death. He said that you needed all your attention on survival not thinking about old men. He could not

92

abide sympathy and sentiment; he said it did no good. He died a good death, a warrior's death, as did faithful Sergeant Cato."

"Cato has gone too?" Marcus had been particularly close to the horse master.

"He died at your father's side."

"The last of the warriors falling together. We will return their bodies tomorrow for we ride to the farm."

"I will come with you."

Ailis looked at the determined face of Decius and nodded. "I will watch over your family until you return and now let us talk of your father and the good memories, for, that is what he would wish. He would not want us to be sad for he died a happy man with a sword in his hand and not coughing and wheezing in an old man's bed."

The Fist soon caught up with his comrades. The road they had chosen was well south of the area devastated by the raiders. The last thing that the deserters needed was to lose their hard-earned booty to barbarians from across the sea. They had selected the route because it was little travelled and yet not too arduous. It twisted and turned through deserted and little-used valleys bringing them well south of the land of the lakes. Although an area rich in farms there was no military presence and that suited those who had fled the Roman yoke. The Fist was not complacent. He had seen how Aelius Spartianus had taken too many risks and suffered as a result. The Fist and his companions were not as clever as the decurion but they had common sense and this route promised safety.

"What do we do when we reach the coast?"

The Fist nodded at the question. "An interesting situation presents itself. We have gold but not safety. Safety lies away from Rome but that means some danger from barbarians. We need to make contact with the Witch Queen of Manavia. Offer her gold and advice in return for sanctuary. Better to give away half of our gold and be safe rather than risk losing it all and our lives."

The other five lived in fear of the violence of The Fist but they also respected his native cunning which had seen him outlive those who had been, apparently, better equipped mentally. "Whatever you say boss. For me I am glad to be away from Rome."

Gaius and Antoninus Brutus also wished that they could be away from the powerful fingers of Imperial Rome. The revolution had failed but at least Gaius had emerged alive, unlike his followers who had been slaughtered to a man. The legion had been ruthlessly efficient at ridding Eboracum of those who would have rebelled. The Governor's decision to commandeer the shipping had proved to be crucial as the rebels who escaped, few though they were, ran like rats to try to board the ships. As they were moored midstream it had left them nowhere to run and they had died or drowned on the edge of the river.

Gaius and Antoninus now had a dilemma. Did they brazen it out or flee? If they fled they would have little with them for their gold had been used to fund the revolution. It had been a gamble which had failed. Father and son were still rich but it was in land and not gold. If they stood their ground they risked discovery and death. Antoninus looked fondly at his son. Better to escape with their lives and try to start again. From what he had heard the Roman garrisons would have their hands full with the raiders who had devastated the frontier.

"Come, my son. I believe it is time for a trading trip to Mamucium."

Gaius Brutus still had the same shocked look he had had when he had returned from the debacle which was the putative attempt at rebellion. "Trading trip?"

"Yes we will need to build up our finances again. The Romans will need more stone to strengthen their walls. We can supply it from our quarries but we will need more wagons to haul the material. Mamucium has good wagon makers and we can trade the jet I acquired." Closer to the coast were jet mines worked by Antoninus. He had cheated the owner out of the rights and allowed him to continue working for a pittance. "It will also keep us from the view of the Romans when they are looking for someone to blame."

Dully Gaius shrugged. His dream of being a Brigante prince was over for a while. It had not been as easy to defeat the Romans as he had expected.

Chapter 8

Faolan found nothing of worth in the farm but he did collect another twenty mounts from the fields around the farm. He and his bodyguard were now far more mobile; they had the means to escape any pursuers. He called the leaders of the warband together. "We have driven the Romans from this place and gathered much plunder. Already Conan will be nearing Manavia and when we return there we shall all share in the profits but we must move swiftly. The Romans will come. We will return the same way we came. We must move quicker than the behemoth which is the Roman army. Each warband will move as one. If we meet a large force we will disperse and meet further west. The boats will be off the coast and when we have all arrived we will embark."

Angus was sceptical. "And you, Prince Faolan, will you travel with us or will your horses speed you away from us, away from danger to our treasure?"

Loegaire's hand went to his sword and many of the chiefs began to mutter angrily. Faolan restrained his faithful retainer. "No Loegaire, Angus is right. It could be that I wish only the treasure and wish to abandon my men. However, Angus, you are forgetting that my prize is not the treasure. It is the throne and I will need all of you and all of your men to secure it. When we have done so we will raise an even bigger army and this time when we return to Britannia we will conquer it and we will stay!"

The warriors roared their approbation but Angus was not convinced. He would keep a close watch on the slippery Irish warrior. When he reported to Morwenna he would have much to tell her.

Cassius and Metellus found the decaying and decomposing bodies of the slaughtered garrison. The wild beasts had done their best to feast on them but there were so many that they would have eaten for a month had the troopers not arrived. Whilst it was important and urgent that they pursue these raiders Cassius also knew they had to bury their comrades. The rocky ground made a poor burial ground but with every trooper and officer working they took less than half a day to bury them under a mound of the plentiful stone lying along the shoreline. While Cassius and most of the vexillation searched the camp Metellus rode in a large circle to look for sign.

"It was a large band, Cassius. I estimate almost two thousand but, thankfully, mostly infantry. They cut a large swathe through the valley as they headed east."

Cassius nodded, his examination of the camp had revealed much the same information. "They left nothing of any use in the fort. Every piece of armour, useable wood, food, amphorae, all of it was taken. It is as though they came as scavengers."

"I could find nothing discarded on the trail. They are at least five days ahead of us."

"Then let us ride east and see who these mysterious scavengers are."

Rufius ensured that Macro and Marcus were both detailed to the flanks on their ride south, he needed his sharpest eyes and wits there. The troopers and the infantry were wary of attack and ambush although the carrion birds, picking at the dead lining the trail which marked the retreat of the Romans, indicated that there was no living human presence. The pall of smoke from the burning farm had dissipated but, walls without roofs and empty windows like eyeless skulls, gave the farm a dead feel.

The centurion in charge of the auxiliaries formed his men up into a large defensive square. Macro, Marcus, Spurius and Drusus took their turmae in a sweep around the fortified villa. Rufius entered, sword drawn through the broken and shattered gates. The raiders had removed their own bodies, the spiral of smoke on the nearby hillside showed where they had honoured their dead. The defenders lay where they had fallen, desecrated and mutilated to prevent them haunting their killers in the afterlife. It was obvious to Rufius that there was no danger and he waved the infantry and the rest of the ala forwards. The auxiliaries stacked their shields and spears to help them begin the grisly task of gathering the remains for a fit burial. Although Rufius wanted to honour Gaius and Cato, his two old comrades, he knew that that would have to wait. He ordered the ala forward and they headed down the lane towards Stanwyck. Here were more bodies, more badly ravaged by the animals for these were the soldiers who had fallen following First Spear to the sanctuary of the farm.

Drusus rode up at the head of his turma. "They headed east." He pointed along the line of the Dunum. "They had wagons and horses."

Spurius reined his horse in. "They buried their dead on that hill. I left my turma to look for sign."

Rufius now had a dilemma. Should he follow the raiders or secure the farm? He looked at the faces of his men; they were eager to follow and gain revenge for what was done at the farm. Inside the gates Rufius could see the auxiliaries still gathering the remains. He had not realised until that moment just how hard leadership was. As an Explorate and a decurion he had had much freedom but now he was responsible for almost a thousand men.

"Antoninus and Drusus put your men out as a picket line. The rest of you gather up these fallen and take them inside the farm. I will wait here for the others.

Marcus was the first to arrive with Macro close behind. "Sir the only signs of the enemy are the bodies burning on the hill and the trail east."

"Good. You two and Lucius take your turmae and follow the raiders. Find a suitable camp and begin to build it. I will follow hard on your heels with the rest of the ala."

Macro made to nudge his horse forward into the farm but Marcus restrained him. "No brother, if Decurion Rufius does not wish us to see our father it will be for a good reason." He looked at Rufius who nodded, sadly. Marcus leaned into Macro and said quietly, "We have trusted Rufius since he first let us ride with him. I trust him still." With tear-filled eyes Macro acknowledged that his brother was correct and they wheeled their horses, the three turmae setting off at a steady trot.

As they rode Macro said to Marcus, "I swear this brother. I will have revenge on those that did this."

Marcus felt the same but there was something in Macro's tone which worried him. They had been raised by the same parents but Macro had inherited much of his father's irrational and excitable nature, Macro too would be a hero of Rome, with all the danger that entailed.

The land through which they travelled was not difficult to traverse for it was rolling hills and gentle, shallow valleys but it was country which had the potential for ambushes. Macro was keen for an ambush as he wanted to get to grips with this savage enemy but Marcus, still the level headed one, insisted on sending out scouts. The trail was a wide one and they could see from the improvised burial mounds along the way that the defenders had wounded many who had perished on the escape. The line of retreat did not deviate other than to allow for the rise and fall of the hillside. The steeply rising land to the north meant that they were edging further south as they went.

As they rested their horses and ate some dried meat Marcus pointed south-west. "I think they are heading for Glanibanta. They will be trying to get back to Hibernia."

Macro looked up, darkly, "Or Manavia."

Sighing Marcus agreed, "Or Manavia. I think we could camp at the bridge over the Dunum."

The Dunum twisted and turned and passed through a narrow valley. It was a perfect place for an ambush but also a good place for a camp. Although but fifteen miles from the farm Marcus knew that they needed a solid camp with a thousand raiders on the loose. He turned to his two best scouts. "Ride to the Dunum and make sure there is no ambush. If the enemy is there then one of you return to tell us."

Rufius wasted no time at the farm. There were too many distressing memories to remain and become even more depressively morbid. The Centurion laid out the bodies ready for the family to bury them and they were cleaned up to give them a little more dignity. Already a rider had returned to Morbium to tell the Prefect that the family could return. Rufius had little problem persuading the centurion to leave a century of soldiers as a guard. After what the family had done for them the garrison would do all in its power to protect the family. Decius nodded his thanks to Rufius as he waited for the family to arrive and bury his father. Rufius could see the young man had become much older since he had seen the death and devastation of the happy family home. The family had a new paterfamilias, Decius Gaius Aurelius.

Rufius rode his men hard for he feared that his two young decurions would push on and try to come to grips with the enemy. Even with the whole ala chasing the warband it would not be a simple task to destroy such a large group but with two headstrong decurions set on revenge then it would be a death ride and Rufius cared too much for the young men to allow that to happen.

It was late afternoon by the time they crested the rise over the frail-looking bridge across the Dunum. Rufius was relieved to see that the men had obeyed his orders and a camp was already being erected. Harsh words had obviously been exchanged between Marcus and Macro for there was an uneasy atmosphere in the camp. Lucius looked to be embarrassed while Marcus was red-faced.

The best policy was just to get on with things as though the siblings had not a problem in the world. When they were ready it would be released, until then any interference would not be welcomed by either brother. Rufius sighed; Metellus or Cassius would have handled this better. Rufius was a warrior, more at home tracking and fighting than being a strategist.

"Well done decurions." The snort of derision from Macro told Rufius what the problem was; Macro had wanted to push on. "This is the perfect place for a camp. As I recall there is nowhere for another twenty miles, it is exposed moorland. We will make an early start tomorrow. With luck, we may be able to catch them within the day."

Marcus flashed a grateful look at Rufius. That was obviously the point he had made. "How far ahead do you think they are?"

Lucius, pleased to be able to speak, came forwards. "We found a fresh fire. They camped here yesterday. They have a few horses but they are largely afoot. They will be at Glanibanta the day after tomorrow."

Rufius rubbed his chin thoughtfully. "The Decurion Princeps and four turmae were there. Interesting. We have them between us. I hope that our comrades have their wits about them."

Macro nodded and added, sullenly. "They have Metellus, I am not worried, and he is the thinker in the ala. I owe my life to him. They will find a way to halt these killers of my father."

Marcus shrugged as Macro headed off to berate some troopers who were not adhering to his instructions. Rufius came over. "It is to be expected Marcus. Metellus told me of the horror at the hands of his mother, to have your father die so soon after…"

"I just wish he wasn't so impetuous."

"Then he would not be his father's son for Macro was the most impetuous warrior I ever knew. Brave as a lion and fearless but rarely thought with his head always his heart."

Thirty miles ahead, just where two knolls rose above a twisting river Faolan was in conference with his two advisers. Loegaire knew that the men's mood was worsening. "They expected more easy fights and they do not want to run from the Romans they have vanquished so easily."

Faolan laughed ironically. "Were it not for their first victory over the unsuspecting garrison, then they would have lost more men than the Romans." Faolan was learning that you needed more armour to fight these tough Roman warriors. Their discipline was superb; during the retreat to the farm, he had been amazed just how many times the red-crested leader had ordered and straightened his lines and repelled the brave but futile charges of warriors, intent on glory. "If they want plunder then they will need to bite back their pride and return with me when we are better trained."

Angus looked approvingly at Faolan who had grown during the campaign. He would make a good leader, a bad enemy but a sound leader. Angus would not trust the man but he did not need to. When they reached Manavia his role would be done and he could get back to training and honing his warband. "The Romans will follow us; you know that. Probably with whatever cavalry they have which means they will catch us before we can reach safety."

Loegaire had been silent; listening to the conversation and planning his own strategy. "This is a good place for an ambush. This side of the river has a steep bank and it has good cover."

Faolan looked at the site. Loegaire was right. Two hundred men could be hidden by the hedgerow and trees. Any force would then have to climb a steep slope; never an easy task against determined opposition. "Perhaps we can kill two birds with one stone here." The two men waited for Faolan's idea. "Angus, can you find me two hundred of the most vocal of our warriors, the ones who are moaning about the retreat and the ones who are keen to come to grips with the Romans."

"Aye, there should easily be a hundred, maybe more."

"All the better. We will see if they can ambush and destroy the Romans here."

Angus shook his head. "They might slow them up but they won't defeat them."

"It matters not for as long as they delay them it helps our escape and it will make our pursuers warier." Striding off Angus went to look for his foolhardiest warriors. Faolan took Loegaire to the bluff. "That was a good idea. We will need more ideas like that if we are to escape back to the land of the Ebdani."

"Stakes."

"Stakes?"

"Aye stakes like the Romans use in their ditches. If we put them in the river it will slow their advance and might make them easier targets."

"Good man. See to it."

"Sir. Found something interesting here."

"What is it, Metellus?"

"The tracks are heading west."

The four turmae had had an easy task following the raiders but they had been careful to check both sides of the line of march, in case some of the group had split off. So far their prey had been faithful to their course. The two officers trotted over to the trampled land. It was over two hundred paces south of their group. Cassius did not doubt Metellus' judgement, he was, after all, the best tracker they had but he knew that someone else's ideas helped to clarify one's own.

"This is a slightly different group. They have women and children. You can see from the footprints." In a bare patch of mud, the smaller footprints could be seen. "They also have more horses." He pointed to piles of horse manure which was of varying sizes and hue indicating that there were different types. "And this time they have a wagon, well at least one."

"The question is Metellus, is this the same group?"

"If it is then they have been thinned out a little. There are more women and children than men."

"Refugees? Fleeing the devastation."

"Could be. The other thing is that they are recent. They only passed through here the day before yesterday."

Metellus was glad that the decision Cassius would have to make was not his. He knew the Decurion Princeps well enough to see the thought processes at work. Did he risk losing the warband by tracking this new group? Or did he abandon these women and children to whatever fate the west had for them to follow his orders. Cassius smiled as he watched Metellus watching him. "One day Metellus you too will have to make these decisions."

"Hopefully not for a long while."

"Well here it is. I will continue to follow the first group. You take Cicero and identify the new one. They will be closer so if it is harmless then you can rejoin me whilst if it is something sinister you can send a rider for me."

"Sir!"

As Metellus led his fifty men west he wondered at the wisdom of the Decurion Princeps decision. "Come on Cicero we have many miles to go to catch these mysterious travellers."

Metellus was very familiar with the land, having explored it since his days as an Explorate. "Any idea where they are going, sir."

"It is Metellus when we are alone on patrol and yes I do. They are heading further south than the group we followed. They will have to either go back through Glanibanta or head south around the huge lake. Either route takes them to the coast but eventually, they will have to head north-west again."

Cicero looked at the steep hills which rose before them. "How does that help us sir er Metellus?"

"If we haven't caught up with them before the lake then we will ride towards Glanibanta, either we catch up with them there or we will be ahead of them near the high pass."

The lake on their left seemed almost overpowered by the high hills rising steeply to each side. For Metellus this was a good thing for it meant that his quarry had to follow the path and could not deviate. They pushed on hard knowing that the sooner they found them the sooner they could rejoin their comrades. Suddenly Marius, who was on point held up his hand. Immediately every trooper was on high alert with his javelin ready and his shield tucked tightly into his side. Signalling for Cicero to remain where he was Metellus trotted forwards. "There sir. I can see a hand sticking out from behind the bush."

"Good eyes, Marius." He peered closely at the hand and noticed the swarm of flies nearby. "Has it moved?"

"No sir."

"I think it is a dead man but let us go forwards carefully in case it is a live one."

As they emerged into the small clearing they could see that it was a dead man. The ripped throat told of how the man had died but not who had done it. "Looks to me like one of the Irish so perhaps this group is the raiding party we seek. He looks to be important from the number of amulets, bracelets and torcs but who did this to him?"

"Sir?"

Metellus whistled for Cicero to bring up the rest. "Oh just speculating son. Normally barbarians bury their dead. He was just left here and I wonder why."

When Cicero arrived Metellus said, "Give them a short break while I scout around."

Marius turned to Cicero. "He knew the man was dead even though we could only see his hand and the way he works things out..."

"Decurion Metellus is a very clever man Marius. You would do well to learn from him."

Metellus found where some kind of combat had taken place; there were broken branches and patches of blood. He stood and mounted his horse to get a better view. Peering towards the lake he saw what he sought, an unnatural pile of stones. He trotted towards it and began to move the stones. He knew what he would find but he wanted confirmation. As soon as he saw the face he knew he had his answer. It was an Irish chief with torc and tattoos. The bloody patch at his stomach told how he had died. Metellus hated having to do it but he took the torc from the body. "Forgive me, unknown warrior, forgive me Allfather. I will return this when I discover your name."

Cicero and Marius were mounted when Metellus reached them. They both looked expectantly at Metellus. "Oh, you want to know what happened? It looks like this is some of our raiders. Both dead men are Hibernians. I think the chief was killed by the warrior Marius and I found and the chief's men disposed of him. This is good because it means dissension is in the ranks and we can push on much harder and with great care. These are not friends ahead."

Creagth and the other fifty warriors left by Faolan to guard the high pass were bored. Already three had been slightly injured in stupid, drunken swordplay which had suddenly become serious. Unless the Prince returned soon then Creagth might find himself with but a handful of men. They had found the perfect place to defend; the path twisted and turned though sheer high walls and Creagth had chosen the place where it flattened out at the side between two old rock falls. The rock falls provided the building material for a primitive barrier, as high as a man with a firing step on the inside. As a punishment for fighting, four men had been sent down to the valley bottom to gather enough wood to make a primitive gate. That was days ago and now his men were, once again, bored.

"Someone coming!"

"To arms!" Action, any action was preferable to boredom. Creagth soon recognised Conan and his bodyguard. He was not prepared for the huge number of women and children who, tied together, trudged up the steep pass. The wagons which accompanied them were also struggling to get up the slope. "Open the gate and get those wagons up here."

He strode down the pass noticing, as he did so, the bandages on the chief and his limping gate. "Good to see you Creagth!"

"And you old friend." He gestured at the bandages. "I see that you have had some action at last."

"Aye, but it was not as easy as the old witch made out. These Romans are tough bastards. If you come against them don't think that because they are short and don't rush at you that they are afraid; they are not. I can vouch for that."

Creagth escorted the chief to the shelters they had constructed. "You had better stay the night here. It is but a day to the coast and I will send one of my men to summon the ships." He looked curiously at the scarred veteran. "I assume you are returning?"

"We are. These men," he waved a dismissive hand at the twenty men who were not members of his bodyguard, "are some of the wounded. Others died along the way. I had to slit the throat of that bastard Aed. He murdered my cousin Blarth and a few others wanted their way with the slaves."

"Was that a problem?" Creagth was eyeing up one or two of the young women, his loins aching already.

"Don't get any ideas. Faolan does not want them devalued and I gave my word."

Creagth held up his hands. Once your word was given then it was as though it was set in stone and inviolable. "And where is our young leader?"

"I left him trying to get the sword but he will be hot on our heels soon. I tell you old friend, I will be glad to get back to my glens and my women. I am getting too old for this sort of thing."

Chapter 9

"Sir. I have found them."

"Good man Marius. Where?"

They had seen the trail cross the stream close to Glanibanta and Metellus had sent scouts out along both sides of the stream in case they were splitting up. They knew that they were within a few hours of their quarry for the signs they had passed were fresher and fresher.

"It isn't good news sir. They are about ten miles up that pass. There are wagons and, as you thought, captives. They were easy to see climbing the pass. It looks like there was another warband there to meet them. I counted at least eighty warriors. Sorry, sir. I wanted to make sure I had counted them all."

"No Marius. Information is never wasted. Are they halting or moving on?"

"They have a wall across the pass. It would be a bugger to take sir but I think they are camping."

"Excellent. Get some food. Decurion Cicero." The keen young decurion trotted up eagerly anticipating some action; all the other scouts had returned earlier and they were ready to ride. "Send a rider to find the Decurion Princeps. We have caught up with the raiders. There are eighty of them and they have women and children with them."

Soon the two turmae were riding hard to cover the ten miles before dark. The messenger would have a harder and more dangerous task but Metellus couldn't worry about that. He had to come up with a plan which might see them rescue the captives or, equally likely, find themselves slaughtered on a remote hillside. He recognised the pass having travelled through it on a number of occasions. He knew that it led to Itunocelum and the sea, and thence, Manavia. He could almost see the place they had chosen and knew that a frontal assault was out of the question. They could see, from the glow of the firelight, where the camp was and leaving two men to watch, he and the others found a sheltered dell in which to work out a strategy. Rather than plan, tell Cicero and then have it repeated to the troopers Metellus decided that honesty and a frank explanation were called for and all of the troopers would find out at the same time.

"Right lads well here it is. We are between a rock and a shit hole!" They all laughed at the coarse humour. "Up there are Brigante captives. We don't know if they are from Eboracum, Morbium or one of the many settlements between here and home, but it doesn't matter for they have to be rescued." He knew he had their attention for many of them were native Brigante and the majority of those were from the lands around Gaius' farm. "A frontal assault would just get us all killed. The only alternative is to climb up there." He pointed at the dark and hidden hillside which rose like a tower behind them. "We would not be able to take our shields just swords and bows. When we get to the top we will be outnumbered and so we need to strike whilst it is dark and they are unaware of our numbers. If they realise how few we are then they will just climb up and pick us off at their leisure. Our only hope is to take out as many of their leaders as we can and hope that the barbarians take their wagons, horses and run. The measure of success will be that we get the captives safely back. Anything else will be a bonus."

There was a silence as the men took in the decurion's words. Cicero leaned over and said, under his breath, "Well at least you didn't sweeten it eh sir?"

"Well lads if anyone has a better suggestion, I am all ears, otherwise choose two of you to be horse holders while I go and tell the other two what we are about. Leave any spare equipment on your horses. If we have to leave in a hurry, we won't have the luxury of time to pack. When we get up there we fire two volleys and cheer and shout on the second then run to a new spot, two more arrows and retreat back up the slope to the ridgeline. Any dead men we leave. One last thing, smear mud on your faces and hands it will make us harder to see." Cicero looked dubious, "Trust me, boys, it is an old Explorate trick. If we had charcoal it would be even better!"

While the men checked their equipment Metellus told the two troopers watching the pass what their instructions were. Both were disappointed to be missing out on, what they saw as, an adventure but Metellus pointed out that they could be the only survivors and, as such, would have to follow the captives and then report to the ala. Sobered by the serious message the two young troopers addressed their role with much more enthusiasm.

"Cicero I shall lead off…"

"But sir I am younger!"

"Exactly and how would it look to the men if the oldest man, who happened to be the leader, was the last man up? No this is better for we will all reach the top with enough breath to fight. Bring up the rear and make sure they know not to make noise."

"What is your plan at the top sir… er Metellus?"

"That depends upon our enemy. If we can surprise them, shoot their leaders with arrows and make a lot of noise then they may retreat but if they stay then we keep the high ground and kill as many as we can. They can escape but not with all the captives."

Cicero looked appalled. "But sir that means some of our people may end as slaves?"

"True Cicero but it would take a miracle to save them all. If the Decurion Princeps was here we might have enough men to take them but there is still a huge warband out there. This way we save some…" He put his arm on the young officer's shoulder. "Get used to it, Cicero, the odds are always against us. We do what we can."

Using hand signals the two officers, who had left their shield and spears tied to their mounts, led the way up the steep bank. It was not sheer but it was difficult to ascend and the troopers were soon grateful that they had both hands free to pull and tug at rocks, bracken and branches as they took any help they could get. The wind was blowing, if not a gale then quite strongly, but that worked in their favour for it masked any noise they might have made. Metellus was feeling his age as his thighs began to burn and he found himself heaving. How did one get unfit? Then he realised, it was not a lack of fitness, he was just getting older, a foe it was difficult to fight.

Suddenly there was nothing looming above him and he dropped to all fours. His white eyes showed against his blackened face as he watched as his men scramble up. Cicero was the last man and he crawled over to Metellus. "One man injured sir, Agrippa he fell, and I think he has broken his wrist. I sent him down to the horse holders."

"A better result than we could have expected." He leaned over to look down into the encampment. There was neither order nor organisation. The barbarians had just put a few shelters up anywhere. Their fires, too, were dotted around but their glow helped the troopers to identify the sentries. From their perch, they could see that there were only guards on the gated barrier. Metellus held up six fingers confirming that there were six guards. He pointed at six men and signalled that, when the order was given, they would take out those guards. The rest began to slip slowly down the slope to get closer to the camp for they needed to see where the leaders were. Metellus assumed that they would have the best shelters, closest to the fires and the wagons. He saw a small group whose arms were covered with bracelets and honour bands. They were the leaders. He pointed to another twelve troopers and gave them the signal that the ten by the fire were theirs.

Cicero and the rest knew that they would just have to pick their targets as best they could. Metellus unslung his bow. He looked left and right to ensure that all were watching him. He drew back his bow as did every other trooper. Metellus' arrow hurtled towards the bearded warrior sleeping closest to the gate. Forty-four other arrows flew at the same time. They all reloaded but this time, as they shot they screamed and shouted.

The guards at the gate fell to the man but the leaders were luckier, only six of the arrows found their mark. As Metellus scampered to a rock higher up the slope he noticed that at least fifteen barbarians were down but now they were alerted and it was more difficult to hit them. "Choose your targets. Don't waste arrows; we have time on our side but not ammunition." Although he sounded confident, in reality Metellus was not too sure. Perhaps it would not be the ala riding to their aid. The huge warband who had destroyed Glanibanta might reach them first.

Down below Conan had taken charge. The early shock at being surprised had given way to anger that no-one had thought to put sentries on the high ground. "Creagth, they are on the slope. Take half your men and go down the trail, flank them. Have the other half try to get to them. I will take the wagons and as many of the captives as I can to the coast. Join me when they are dead."

Creagth almost spat his reply but wisely held his counsel. There could be a thousand men up the slope. He would do as ordered but if there were too many he would join Conan. This enterprise was not as glorious as he had hoped. Leading his best men he clambered over the dead guards. The two men behind him fell to deadly arrows fired from the hillside. Shit! They were sitting targets. "Get in the lee of the hill they can't see us there. You two crawl through the gate and try to get around the side."

Metellus could see what they were attempting but it did not worry him. If they tried to climb up, as he and the turmae had discovered, it required two hands and they would be easy targets while doing so. More problematic was the escape of the others. The barbarians were trying to drag the prisoners to their feet. "Shoot at the guards near the captives."

The captives kicked and struggled against their captors. When the barbarians trying to take them fell, they wriggled and squirmed away making it harder for the barbarians to reach them. Their leader, for Metellus recognised the torc of a chief, was busy helping his men harness their horses. He had ten of his men hold shields to protect them but in doing so it enabled the captives to begin to scramble up the slope. Conan roared his anger but the wagons began to roll west. Grabbing the nearest captives and throwing them across their saddles the thirty men of Conan's bodyguard followed the wagons out of sight behind the cliff edge and down the other side of the pass.

Creagth saw that he had been deserted. He was now in dire straits. He had been ordered by Faolan to defend the pass but now he did not have enough men. He chose to make a strategic withdrawal to the other side of the pass. The mysterious archers would have to come down to be able to hit them and then they could strike back. The huge Hibernian yelled out his orders and the remaining men, shields held above their heads ran back across the killing ground to safety. Over thirty of them made it but many others lay amongst the shambles of a camp.

"Cicero!" The decurion scrambled over to Metellus. "Take your turma down the slope, mount up and man their barrier from the other side, see if you can keep their heads down."

"Do you want us to attack them, sir? I think we outnumber them."

"We do but that is a narrow pass and we would lose too many men. I want you to keep their heads down so that I can get these captives to safety."

Cicero and his men scurried down the fell side. As dawn was breaking it was a far less hair raising journey and Metellus watched as they reached the horses. He switched his attention to the fifty or so captives cowering amongst the rocks. He could see some of them attempting to climb up the slope and he yelled down. "This is Decurion Metellus of the Second Sallustian Ala. Stay where you are! We will rescue you." One woman raised her hand in acknowledgement and he saw her mouthing instructions. The problem the Romans had was that, although they could not fire on the raiders, the barbarians could see the captives. Metellus could only assume that, like him, they had limited ammunition and for that he was grateful.

He heard the clatter of hooves and then saw the arrows begin to arc towards the hidden barbarians. He turned to his men. "Right. Down the slope and help the captives up here. Don't bring too many at once. You two," he pointed at two of the younger troopers, "you stay with me. Collect any spare arrows from the others. We will try to help Decurion Cicero."

The journey down was not as hazardous as it had appeared and they were safe from the barbarians until the last twenty or so paces. Metellus could see Cicero and he shouted, "Fire a volley," he paused, "now!" As the twenty arrows flew high Metellus and his men sprinted the last few paces.

The woman who had signalled took Metellus' hand and kissed it. "Thank you, sir."

"Thank me when you are safe. My men will get you up the slope in groups. Tell your people to be patient. We will get you all to safety." Leaving his men to their task he took his two archers and found a rock behind which they could hide. They could see the edge of the barbarian line but their leader had learned that the Romans were accurate and they had shields held up to protect them. "Don't waste arrows. If they fire, they will be shooting blind so just watch for a target and then fire."

It was a nerve-wracking duel. The raiders loosed arrows in the air but as they heard them clatter harmlessly on the rocks they soon stopped. One impatient warrior stood to get a better

shot but two arrows quickly impaled him and no-one else risked
that. The sun had reached its zenith before the last of the captives
was helped over the top. Metellus turned to his two archers.
"This is the hard part. We have to cover the killing ground to the
blind spot and then climb that slope." The two grinned. Metellus
had chosen the two because they were good archers but also they
were fast and he had known that this would be the difficult part.
Cicero had few arrows left and could not give them a volley.
Metellus and his men would have to rely on speed. "Go!"

The three of them raced and zig-zagged across the rock-
strewn floor. They had almost cleared the danger area when the
young trooper in front of Metellus stumbled. The decurion had to
stop to avoid falling himself. It was in that moment when the
barbarian behind the barrier risked lossing an arrow. The arrow
plunged into Metellus' left calf and he crashed to the ground.

Leaving the glory hunters at the river Faolan led his depleted
band west. He had hoped that he might have caught up with
Conan but so far there was no sign of him. Faolan was trying to
keep to the same route they had taken when travelling east. It had
been relatively easy and, more importantly, kept to the valley
bottoms affording cover. The cart containing the gold was being
driven just behind Faolan and his intimates. That was his future
and he wanted it closer to him than his clothes.

He turned to Angus, "How far to the coast?"

Angus looked at the line of warriors spread out along the
valley. "At this speed? Probably two more camps. If we pushed
it we might get to your men the day after tomorrow."

Faolan had asked the question for confirmation of his own
thoughts. He hoped that Creagth had, as ordered successfully
built a barrier. If his men could delay their pursuit at the river
and if they made the pass by the next day then they would have
escaped. He was certain that Creagth would not have been
bothered by Romans for the only ones on this side of the divide
had already been slaughtered. As there was still no alarm from
the river Faolan could only assume that their pursuers had not
reached them. It looked like Morwenna had worked her magic
with the gods, or Mother or whoever and they had returned
successfully from their foray. It was with a sinking heart that he

heard the sound he had not heard before he came to Britannia but which he now dreaded. It was the sound of the buccina. The Romans had found them.

"Sir." The excited trooper reined his horse next to Rufius.
"Yes trooper what is it?"
"We have found them sir. They are on the other side of the river just ahead." He was so excited that he carried on. "Decurion Marcus halted us and, even though they were hidden, he saw them." The hero worship dripped with every word.
Smiling Rufius acknowledged the report and turned to the column. "Enemy ahead, form a column of fours."
The troopers of the eight turmae all began to check their equipment, tightening chin straps and ensuring that their shields were tightly slung. At the rear Macro was cursing that it was his brother who had stumbled upon them and not he. He loosened his sword in its scabbard for soon he would be sword to sword with those who had destroyed his home. His troopers saw the angry face and wondered at the change in their decurion. Since he had returned from the north he had become more withdrawn, moodier and far less cheerful. They longed for the early days when he and Marcus had been the happy cheerful pair who could raise men's spirits in a heartbeat. Decurion Marcus appeared to have changed little but Decurion Macro had grown older very quickly.
Marcus met the column below the crown of the hill. "Well done decurion. How many do you estimate?"
"They are hidden by the bank on the other side but I would think there are more than a hundred and fifty."
"A rearguard then?"
Marcus shrugged, "Either that or an ambush."
Rufius looked at the ground around them and saw that it was not favourable for an ambush which meant that this was a rearguard operation intended to surprise and kill as many pursuers as possible whilst enabling the main party to escape. "So they want us to charge frontally across the river."
Marcus grinned, "It would appear so."
"Any crossings up or down stream."

"Plenty. You can tell that they are warriors on foot; it might be too deep to wade for a man but not a horse."

"Decurions, to me." The decurions galloped up and formed a half circle around Rufius. "There is an ambush ahead. They are expecting us to charge across the water and be surprised when we reach the other side. We will not be obliging them." The officers all laughed. "Macro, take Drusus and Calgus. Work downstream and cross the river. When you hear the buccina then you take them from the flank. Marcus you take Spurius and Lucius up stream and do the same. Antoninus your men are the best archers so you will be the bait for our own little trap; you will lead your men to the water and when you are midstream let your mounts drink. I will follow on with the other two turmae. If you are attacked then fire a volley and retreat otherwise I will sound the buccina for the attack and your turma will fire arrows whilst Graccus and I charge and throw javelins. Clear?"

At the river bank the Hibernians had finished off the last of the looted spirits from Stanwyck and the farm. They were ready to fight. They had heard the sounds of the horses in the distance and knew that the Romans were close. Their leader, Torin, was a huge bully of a warrior. He had been desperate to leave Faolan since Stanwyck and he had grasped this opportunity with both hands. His part of Hibernia was poor and boggy. He had joined this venture for rewards and having seen how poorly the locals fought he intended to stay here. He was pragmatic enough to know that he would have to defeat those following him before he could desert with this warband, kindly given to him by Faolan, and head south for the ripe plums he knew would be there for the picking. He had no intention of spending too long protecting Faolan's rear. As soon as they had driven off the first attack he and his men would depart. Had he not heard the horses he would have done it sooner but he knew that they could not outrun horses but this way they might even capture a couple of mounts for him and his fellows.

"Try to avoid hitting the horses, boys. Torin fancies taking it easy after this on the back of one of these Roman beasts." The men smiled, Torin was not the smallest of men and any horse would struggle to carry the weight. At that moment Antoninus and his turma stepped from the woods into the water. "Quiet now, here they come. Let them get a little closer." The weakness of their defence, in Torin's eyes was the lack of bows; they had slings and spears but arrows would have given them the edge. He saw the other horsemen come to the water. "This is it boys. On my command..."

Before he could utter another word the strident notes of the buccina echoed across the water. His men were ready for action and they loosed stones and javelins at the Romans barely forty paces from the bank. Before they could loose another attack they found themselves being assaulted by arrows and javelins. The hedgerow and trees dissipated the effect of the missiles and the Hibernian shields did the rest. Torin smiled as he saw the empty saddles. He could see at least fifty horses in front of him, when their owners were dead, they could ride away on the freshly acquired mounts. "Steady now boys. Keep your lines. Wait for them to get closer." He did not want to lose any of these notoriously reckless warriors now. Better to drive the cavalry off and then fight another day.

The last thing they were expecting was to be attacked from their flanks but, as he heard the cries of pain and turned he saw to his horror more than a hundred and fifty cavalry hurtling towards him. He was an astute enough leader and he knew that he had the hidden stakes to protect him from the river; this new threat was the more dangerous one, but he estimated that he still outnumbered them. "Turn lads. Come on you whore sons let us be about these horse shaggers!"

The Hibernians roared forwards. Once they left the security and safety of the trees then they became better targets for the cavalry javelins. Even though many of the barbarians used shields to protect themselves some, inevitably fell. Back in the middle of the river Rufius had ridden his men to the edge of the bank. He knew a charge would not work and, as he saw the hidden stakes, he thanked the Allfather for the protection he had afforded them. It would take time to negotiate the obstacle. "Antoninus see if your men can hit them with their arrows. We will have to get around these stakes."

While Antoninus and his men picked off the warriors they could see, the men led by Marcus and Macro were tearing into the raider's hastily deployed shield wall. Although the turmae were not in one line the troopers had managed to form smaller lines of five or six troopers. Their horses were trained in combat and, hurling their javelins at the last minute, their mounts reared to crash their hooves down on the barbarian shields. The Hibernians had not fought cavalry before and they became terrified by these beasts which fought like warriors. Suddenly they heard a roar of voices, "The Sword, follow the Sword of Cartimandua!"

Every barbarian heard it. This was the sword they had come to Britannia for, this was the mystical weapon which would capture a kingdom, this was the ultimate treasure. Torin saw the blade, gleaming from the red crested rider's hand and he turned to his men, "Wedge! I am going to have that sword, boys!"

The Hibernians launched themselves forward. This was how they won their battles at home, a wedge of warriors with the fiercest leading. In Hibernia no-one could stand in their way. What they had not met, however, was Marcus and his oath sworn. They too formed a wedge and Torin found himself facing tons of horseflesh and whirling steel. One of the Hibernians from the rear of the wedge had managed to consume more of the spirit than the others and, feeling emboldened yelled, "Fuck this!" and leapt forward, his double handed axe whirling above his head. Although pierced by two javelins and dead before he hit the ground , the momentum of the axe embedded itself in Marcus' horse's neck; killing the beast instantly.

Marcus flew over the dying beast. He had been taught how to fall by Cato and, as the horse master of the ala, was the best rider. He rolled easily to the side as his dead mount crashed into Torin and disrupted the whole wedge. Marcus shield strap had separated and he was left with just his sword. He sensed the warrior approaching from behind and whirled around, the blade slicing through the unprotected gut of the man, his intestines oozing out.

Torin was the first to react and he stood with his axe and shield searching for the mythical blade. As soon as he saw Marcus he leapt as him, as did two of his bodyguards. Slashing the blade in front of him, Marcus reached down to pick up the dead Hibernian's sword. Although not as good as Macro with two blades he was competent. The first of the bodyguards was too eager to gain the sword for himself and tried to duck below Marcus' blade. The Hibernian weapon in his left hand plunged into the unprotected neck and Marcus jumped backwards to avoid the falling body. Torin and the remaining guard were more wary and circled Marcus. They grinned in anticipation. No-one could fight front and back against two warriors. Marcus identified the bodyguard as the most dangerous as he had a sword; feinting to Torin with the Sword of Cartimandua, he rolled to the ground as the bodyguard's blade flew harmlessly over his head. Marcus, lying on the ground stabbed upwards between the man's legs and the blade sank deeply into the man's body. As he fell backwards the sword was torn from Marcus' hand leaving him with just the one, the Sword of Cartimandua. Infuriated, Torin swung the axe at the recumbent Marcus who rolled out of the way. He quickly stood and noticed that the huge chief was out of breath. The longer the contest went on the more chance of success Marcus would have. The contest ended suddenly when Macro's horse crashed into the back of the chief and he was speared to the floor by Macro's javelin.

Leaping from his horse he stood over the wounded chief. "Couldn't let you have all the fun brother could I?"

As the two brothers looked around they could see that the skirmish was over and the wounded were being despatched. Macro was about to finish off the mortally wounded chief when Rufius' voice roared, "Wait!" The two decurions stepped back. As Rufius dismounted he said, "Let us ask him a few questions first eh? Then we can send him to the Allfather."

They roughly turned him over to face them. His eyes widened when he saw the Sword of Cartimandua but his eyes burned black with hate. "Coward! You needed help to finish the mighty Torin." Marcus was about to mention the three to one odds but realised that it was pointless.

"So we know your name. We know you are Hibernian and we know you are heading for the coast for a boat back to Manavia." Rufius only knew some of that but when Torin did not contradict him he continued. "All we now need to know is who is your leader?"

"Why? So that you can kill him? Fool." His dying eyes scanned the scene. "Faolan has ten times the men you have and the Ebdani are proud warriors." Rufius nodded with satisfaction, he had the information he needed. "But do not worry Roman, for he is coming for that sword, and he will take it."

They all looked at the sword in Marcus' hand, dripping blood but still shining in the afternoon light. Coughing blood Torin grunted, "End it warrior. Kill Torin with the magical sword so that I may tell the tale in the hereafter." Rufius nodded and Marcus slid the sharp blade through the neck of the chief; killing him instantly.

Macro looked at Marcus as they both realised the implication of the dying man's words. "They came to the farm for the sword. Father died at this Faolan's hands for the sword. I swear brother that I will follow this Faolan to the ends of the earth and have my revenge."

"And I brother, will be at your side."

Rufius shook his head. They had just spoken of desertion in front of a fellow officer. He would have to talk to Livius at the earliest opportunity. He called over to Graccus. "Your men are freshest, decurion. Find the trail of the main band. They can only be a few miles ahead. Find them and then send me word." He turned to the others. "Roll call. Find out how many of us are left and how many cannot move." Although they had won it had been at some cost. He had seen many empty saddles and he could see trooper's bodies lying amongst the fallen barbarians.

At the furthest edge of the field lay Tearlach. He had been knocked over by a horse as Macro's men had charged in. He had lain, stunned until now, some way from the rest of his dead comrades. He slowly raised his head and saw, to his horror, only Romans remaining on the battlefield. There was little point in a glorious death when he might reach Faolan and gain some reward for his report. He had news that his leader would want. The Sword of Cartimandua was within touching distance and the Romans who guarded it were small in number. He crawled unseen over the ridgeline and then ran south west. Faolan would only be a short distance away. He could be making his fortune.

Chapter 10

Cassius and Decius were making slower going than they had hoped. The trail which Metellus had found kept crossing the larger trail. In the small valley bottom close to the rising uplands they made a tragic discovery, the bodies of three despoiled young women. The position of their bodies and their state of undress left the troopers in little doubt as to their fate and what had happened in the short time before they had been killed. Cassius looked westward, Metellus was following the captives but he still did not know if this was the main band or not. "Decius, get the bodies below ground. I am going to ride to the top of the ridge, see if I can make sense of this trail."

As he rode towards the vantage point which would let him see many miles to the east he wondered if he had made the right decision. In his heart he knew that the main band of barbarians was still somewhere to the west, probably closer to Eboracum but he could have stayed with Metellus and followed the captive band. His problem was he had too few men with him. This was a task for half the ala where they could cover a larger area. He was also acutely aware of the inexperience of many of his decurions. Decius was keen and hardworking but he had been an officer for less than half a year and he still needed the guidance of someone like Cassius. Metellus had the same issue with Cicero. It was ironical that Macro and Marcus, although young, were probably amongst the most experienced officers he had. Suddenly he heard the welcome sound of the buccina; it was ahead of them and not far away. It was the ala; and he idly wondered, as he waved his men forwards, what they were doing this far west.

They kicked their horses and crested the ridge, there, less than two miles away was an untidy mob of barbarians. Although spread out over a large area Cassius could see that there was some sort of order there with the horsemen to the front and those with helmets and armour at the rear. Decius' mouth dropped open and Cassius smiled. "Yes Decius there is the warband. Obviously, the ones Metellus is pursuing have the captives with them so, it would seem, that my decision has proved to be fortuitous."

"Fortuitous sir? Are we going to attack them?"

Aulus, one of the senior troopers guffawed, to be silenced by a look from Cassius. "No Decius for they outnumber us by almost ten to one." He pointed at their horsemen. "If their cavalry try to flee then we may well pursue them but otherwise this is a watch and wait situation. That buccina we heard sounds like a cavalry one. It may well be that the Prefect has brought the ala to reinforce us but whoever it is, they are Romans and, therefore, our friends." He turned to the column. "Eat in the saddle and rest alternate troopers. We may be here some time."

"Sir?"

"They have halted Decius and no longer moving so we will also rest and eat." He slid from the saddle and took out some dried venison and a piece of hard bread. He chewed contentedly. He had learned, as an Explorate, eat when you can.

"Halt!" Faolan cursed to himself; Romans behind him and Romans in front.

Loegaire nudged his horse next to his leader. "There is only a handful. We can sweep them before us."

Angus shook his head. "They will retreat before you. I recognise the standard. The sword you seek is in their ranks."

For the first time in many days Faolan showed excitement. Could it be that the witch had spoken true and the sword had sought him out? Truly it was both magical and mystical. Coming back to his present dilemma Faolan looked over his shoulder. "The most pressing problem is who is behind us? Is it more of the same?" As though answering him, Graccus and his turma appeared on the hillside two miles behind them.

Angus spat into the turf. "I think that answers your question."

"Loegaire, empty the cart of the gold, discreetly, and mount the two guards. Split the gold between the two pack horses, our bags and the two guards. We may have to leave the bulk of the army and make a run for the coast."

Angus shook his head. "That would be a mistake. The cavalry can run you down. These are nags we have. They have grain-fed, well trained cavalry mounts and they look after them. In a race, you would lose." He could see the indecision on Faolan's face. "At the moment the situation has not changed. We keep on heading west. If they attack us, and I hope they do, then we can

120

whittle them down and make it easier for us to escape. If we stay together we are too large a group for them to attack and there are no foot soldiers here. It just means that we will take a little longer to get home."

Faolan considered the information. It made sense. He still had almost a thousand men and they were in good fighting spirit. The problem would be in making them resist the urge to fight. "Angus, go around the chiefs and tell them to resist charging the Romans, no matter what they do."

"Sir! They are our lads. I recognise the standard."

"Well done trooper." Cassius could relax now. "Ride around the valley and tell them who we are. Return to me when you have discovered how many of our men are over there. Is it the one turma or more?" He added as the man had ridden off, to no one in particular. "Hopefully the Allfather has thought to send the ala and a cohort of auxiliaries."

The Roman dead had already been reverently placed on a wooden pyre, Spurius had found the buried stakes in the river and they had been improvised into the funeral pyre. The barbarian dead were thrown together and wood piled on the top on a separate mound. Altogether the ala had lost twenty troopers. The barbarians, fired by drink, had fought on beyond all reasonable hope of success. They had all wanted to die with their swords in their hands and it took many blows to kill them. The fact that over a hundred and fifty barbarians were slaughtered was small comfort to Rufius and his decurions who felt, somehow, as though they had let their men down. As Drusus lit the flames on the two fires each man said his own goodbyes to those he lost. Every thought was different, from the brother who had lost a brother to the decurion who had lost the youngest man in his turma. As the flames flickered and the fire began to take hold the only sound to be heard was the crackling of the fires. As the flames caught around the bodies and the smell of roasted meat began to fill the air, Rufius ordered the men to be mounted. They had lost more men than horses and had a string of remounts.

"Sir! Rider approaching." Before they even looked every trooper had a weapon in his hand.

"It's a rider from Decurion Graccus' turma."

The young trooper skidded to a halt on the wet grass. "Sir, Decurion reports we have seen some of our men about three miles away and we have found the barbarians."

"How many?"

The excitable youth shrugged, "Hundreds of the bastards, er sir."

Covering his smile with his hand Rufius asked. "I take it that we are both in front of them and also behind them?"

The trooper's face took on a strange expression as he tried to work out the question and then the answer. "Er yes sir."

"It looks like my first independent command, thank the Allfather, will soon be coming to an end. It sounds like the Decurion Princeps has rejoined us."

It took longer for Rufius' force to close with the barbarians as Faolan was moving them, as he had been advised, westwards. Cassius had feigned a couple of attacks to see if they slowed up but the behemoth kept its nerve and moved at the same pace it had done before the encounter. The Decurion Princeps felt the sun slipping behind the hills to the west and wondered if and when the enemy would camp. Once they did so then he would be able to contact the bulk of the ala and begin to make some plans. It had been almost ten days since he had left the Stanegate and he had no idea what had gone on in his absence. At least he would have enough men to send a turma to Metellus. Metellus' despatch rider had told him of the decurion's situation but he could do little about that until he had solved the problem of the beast which lay before him.

By the time night had fallen, the raiders and their hunters were exhausted and camped a few miles from the first of the long lakes. Angus had selected the site as the valley was narrow and easy to defend; with a lake on one side and the steep mountain on the other, they would not be surprised. Even though he was tired Cassius had ridden around the huge barbarian camp to meet with his decurions. The fare was basic as no-one had had time recently to gather any additional supplies and Cassius sensed a depressive air. He listened while Rufius explained all that had befallen them and his face creased with pain when they told him of the last stand of Ulpius Felix's companions, Gaius and Cato.

The Decurion Princeps looked from face to face. "Do not berate yourselves. You have all performed to the highest standard. The fact that this band raided and destroyed Stanwyck was not your fault. You reacted as quickly as you could and your performance has been exemplary." He paused and looked directly at Macro and Marcus, sat oddly, apart. "Gaius and Cato died as they would have wished, as I would wish. They had lived long lives and they died doing what they had done for the majority of their lives, defending Britannia." He shook himself, the evenings were becoming cooler. "That is the past. It is time for the present. There will be no reinforcements to help us; that is obvious so we are on our own. By my estimate, including those in the turmae of Metellus and Cicero, we have about four hundred troopers left. That is not enough to defeat this band. There are more barbarians in the high pass and Metellus is watching them." They all looked at each other when they heard the new intelligence. They had thought that the threat was contained within their circle of steel. Cassius pointed towards the long lake. "Many of us know this country well; the land ahead is difficult for us. The paths are narrow and a small band can hold up a large number however there are some places where we can ambush them." He was pleased to see the interest and enthusiasm fill their faces once more as they leaned forwards. "I intend to send my turma to reinforce Metellus. Rufius will take his turma, collect Decius and prepare an ambush close to the valley of the two lakes."

Rufius closed his eyes trying to recall the terrain. "Close to the burnt-out watchtower north of Glanibanta?"

"Well done Rufius, the very place. I assume that they will take that route as it affords few opportunities for us to attack. Should they take the route they first used, west of Glanibanta then we have the chance to attack them where the land opens out. The rest of us will dog their trail. When the opportunity arises, we will attack them but I notice that our supply of arrows is limited and it is unlikely that we will find a new source soon."

He paused to let his ideas sink in. Macro stood. "Sir. Why not let a couple of us sneak into the camp and kill this Faolan? A snake without a head can easily be killed."

"No Macro, for there are too many of them. I am sure there is more than Faolan driving this band. They have shown local knowledge that no Hibernian would know and besides it would be a suicide mission."

"But we would kill my father's killer and our honour would be intact!"

Marcus jerked his head around. This did not sound like the Macro he had grown up with. He was almost shouting at the Decurion Princeps. Cassius did not rebuke him. His eyes softened for Cassius knew the loss would be felt deeply by a young man whose birth father had also been slaughtered. "We are not about honour decurion; we are about doing our job and that is difficult enough. Any more questions?" Every head shook, while Macro's reddened. "Good. I will lead this vexillation." He turned to Rufius, "If you come with me I will give you my final instructions." Once they were away from prying ears and close to the horses he asked Rufius about Macro. "Macro seems changed."

"Aye, sir. He took his father's death badly. I fear my influence on him has waned and I would that Metellus were here for they bonded when they were in the land of the Votadini."

"I will watch him. Now when you reach Decius you will need to ride all night. I know that you are tired but you can rest up during the day. I think they will reach you at dusk."

"I will send a couple of men to Glanibanta in case they take that route."

"Good." He paternally put his arm around Rufius' shoulder. "You have done well in your first command. Now go and may the Allfather be with you."

Metellus lay in the lee of the ridge his leg still pulsing with pain. The arrow had missed the bone but gone straight through the muscle. His men had disobeyed his orders and returned for him after the rest had reached the ridge. Had they not done so then he would have been a corpse for he had lain exposed on the scree. The capsarius looked at the angry wound. He had taken the arrow out cleanly but not stitched the wound. "I have put some moss and lichen on it, sir. It will draw out any poison but it means that you cannot move the leg for a few days. Once it has done its work you will be able to walk and move. It will be a limp but you will still have a leg and still be mobile."

Metellus flashed an angry look at the capsarius. "Don't be ridiculous man! I have to know what is going on here."

The capsarius stood his ground. "Sir, with respect, you can still give all the orders but you do not need to fight this battle single-handed. We are a team, aren't we? At least I thought those were the words you used back at Rocky Point."

Metellus relented and sagged back. The capsarius was right. He turned to the troopers. "We are doing no good up here; we have no target to fire at. Get the captives down to the pass and then join the decurion. The capsarius will help me down."

The capsarius, Sextus, grinned. "Oh no, sir. It will take a couple of us. You wait here and we will come for you when we have escorted the captives."

Metellus lay back, defeated. He was facing east and he saw the sun creep over the peaks in the distance. He was about to turn around and risk a look over the ridge when he remembered his wound. He cursed. Looking down he could see that he had been lucky. The barb had plunged down at a steep angle. A little to the left and he would have had a broken leg and then been out of action for much longer. By the time his men returned for him, his leg had stiffened up and every jolt and rock jarred his body on the tortuous journey down. His men carried him as gently as they could but the slope, going down, was even more treacherous than when coming up.

Cicero was waiting for him at the bottom. Metellus noticed that he looked happier and more confident than hitherto. Perhaps, being on his own, and in charge for a few hours had made the difference. "Sir they are still on the other side. They have made no effort to attack but they have built a wall sir, with no gate this time." Metellus nodded and Cicero added, apologetically, "We could have slowed them down sir but we didn't have enough arrows."

"You did well decurion. Now the first thing to do is to get the captives organised and fed."

Sextus grinned. "I think that is done, sir. The woman who ordered them around at the rescue has already done that."

"Good. Cicero, divide the men into three groups. I want one watching the barbarians, one resting and the third group can hunt and improve the defences here."

Cicero looked confused. "Here sir? But they are behind the wall and we have a wall."

"Have you forgotten decurion? This is not the main band. The Decurion Princeps is chasing the main band. I can only assume this group was to make sure that the main war band would escape. We could have an unknown number of Hibernians coming from the east at any time now."

Shamefaced Cicero scuttled off. "Yes sir, sorry sir."

As Sextus fussed with the bandage he said, to no-one in particular. "Decurion Cicero is doing a grand job."

"I know Sextus. I know." The capsarius nodded, satisfied that Metellus understood.

The foragers returned at noon with some autumn berries and a couple of hares. Nanna, the organising Brigante woman quickly took charge and soon had the hares turning over the fire. She scurried around the dell and returned with wild thyme and garlic. The sentry guarding that side glanced over at Metellus and shrugged his apology, "I would have stopped her sir but she is scarier than a warband of Hibernians."

"I know trooper, just try to keep them safe. We don't want to lose them again." Metellus had counted thirty women and over twenty children in the group they had rescued. Sextus had told him that Nanna had asked him when they were going after the others, the sixty taken by the chief. At least they had a name for him now, Conan.

Cicero returned and slumped to the ground. "Rest decurion; with me wounded and incapacitated, the last thing we need is for you to be out of action too."

"Sorry, sir. I was checking the barrier."

"And?"

"And they have tried to rush across a couple of times but we discouraged them with arrows."

"Get any?"

"Not killed sir. They have learned to use shields but we need more arrows."

"I know. When the group resting awakes have half of them see if they can find any usable ones around here."

The smell of the food was making Metellus' hunger pangs even worse. He could see the band of women and children sniffing the cooking meat appreciatively. Nanna kept them all back. He watched her tug a leg from the hare and, using a dock leaf as a platter brought hare and berries for the decurion. "No feed the children first."

"You are wounded and you saved us."

"Feed the children and the women and it was my men who saved you, not me alone."

The woman handed the platter to one of the other women as they began to dole out the pitiful rations. "No Roman I watched you. It was you who gave the orders and you who had the wise plan. We are grateful."

"Tell me, Nanna. What happened at Stanwyck?"

"They came in the early morning. My husband and son were killed as they left our hut. I tried to fight them but they tied me up and I had to watch my uncles and brothers die before me. It was only when the Romans came that we had hope."

"Horses? Like us?"

"No these men fought on foot and they killed many of these savages. After that, we were marched by one of their wounded leaders, Conan. His men had no honour. They ravished some of the younger girls and they were killed. They even fought amongst themselves. We hoped that they might kill each other. When we arrived here all hope was gone for they had many more men here. And we could smell the sea. We knew that the slave market would not be far away and we would never see our homes again." She grasped Metellus' hands in her own, rough and red ones. "You must save them sir. There are many young children amongst them and girls I grew up with."

The pleading in her eyes moved Metellus but he was an honest man and he could not lie to this fine woman whose resolve had helped her people. "I will not lie to you Nanna, I believe that if they are not already across the sea, they soon will be but we will not rest until they are returned. Tell me how many men were there?"

"The band who brought us? About forty. Then there were slightly more here. Your men killed many."

"And do you know the name of their leader?" She had a confused look upon her face. "Then we know where to seek them should we cross the seas."

"The men said he was Faolan of the Ebdani and he would be a king but they said that we were bound for Manavia." She bit her lip. "They said we were going to the Witch Queen. Is that true?"

"It is and in that beast, there is both hope and despair for she styles herself Queen of the Brigante. She would change your women and your girls to become her servants and although they would live they would be changed and they would not be the people you knew."

She stood. "Thank you for your honesty sir and I know that you will return them to us."

Metellus hoped that he could but he wondered how the Prefect would view an invasion of Manavia to face the wrath of the Red Witch and her fanatical Hibernians? He was roused from his reverie by a shout from a sentry. "Sir, a rider coming in!"

To his relief, he saw that it was his despatch rider who slid from his mount and saluted in one movement. "Sir I found the Decurion Princeps. He has made contact with the barbarians. There are hundreds of the bastards sir and he has found the rest of the ala. He said he would send reinforcements as soon as he could."

"Thank you, trooper. Now rest. Cicero."

The decurion awoke quickly and looked around for danger. "Sir?"

"The Decurion Princeps is coming but so are the barbarians. I want a defensive line building there." He pointed to a point a hundred paces down where the pass narrowed slightly. "I know the men are tired but…"

"Don't worry sir. I think that the rescue of the women has given them a second wind. They all feel like heroes now."

As night fell the exhausted men dropped and slept where they stood. Cicero had collapsed asleep and Metellus found himself the one who was most alert. He knew it was the pain in his leg which throbbed and pulsed which kept him awake, but he was grateful. He had ten men on guard, five watching the top of the pass and five watching for the barbarians at the eastern end. His ears were fully attuned to the sounds of the night, his old Explorate training kicking in and it was he who recognised the noise. He hissed, "Stand to!"

Cicero and the rest of the troopers awoke in an instant. The couple of hours' sleep they had had were refreshing enough to make them alert. "What is it, sir?"

"I heard horses, coming from the east." Cicero listened and then looked sceptically at his leader whom he assumed was delirious with pain. Metellus smiled. "Trust me Cicero there are riders approaching. Put your ear to the ground and listen."

After a few moments, Cicero jumped up. "You are right sir. That is a handy little trick."

Suddenly they heard a horse neigh and the jingle of harness. "Prepare to receive cavalry!"

Chapter 11

The voice called from the dark. "Appius Calpurnius and the third turma coming in."

Cicero called out, "Watch them it may be a trick," and was gratified when Metellus nodded his approval.

They were all relieved when the reinforcements arrived. The chosen man dismounted and, recognising him, approached Metellus. "Decurion Princeps compliments sir. He is on his way with the ala." The trooper leaned and said a little more quietly. "He said to prepare yourself, things could get lively."

"Thank you, Appius. If your men are up to it could they relieve these guards? They have been on duty for a day and a half."

"Of course sir."

Metellus fell back into a deep sleep, the pain was suddenly gone. With reinforcements, they could survive, at least for a short time.

Julius saw the boat being rowed up the Tinea towards Coriosopitum. He and Hercules were standing at the stern of '*The Swan*' with Furax, grown considerably, intently listening. "So old friend, you made good time then?"

"Aye. I remembered that at this time of the year there are good winds from the south." He gestured at the rowing boat. "I think that one is from the three biremes we saw astern of us eh Furax."

"Yes. I can now tell a Roman ship from a pirate."

"His young eyes make up for my old ones."

"And the ship Hercules, it is sound?"

"We spent the winter re-caulking her and renewing the rigging. She is as good now as the day she was launched." He looked suspiciously at Julius, the owner of his ship. "Why have you something planned?"

"Let us just say that I will be taking a voyage with you but I will wait with the details until I have spoken with the Governor."

"The Governor?"

"Yes, Furax. He is the man in the stern of the rowing boat. I will see you later. If you could turn it around, we will be ready for a quick getaway."

Muttering under his breath the old men began to shout out orders. Since he had met Julius Demetrius his life was anything but dull.

Later, in the Prefect's quarters, the two Legates shared information. "The rebels were soon despatched by the legion and as I said I brought the vexillation up on the three ships of the Classis Britannica to make a start on the limes."

"And the ringleaders? Did you ascertain their identity?"

"Yes, my interrogators questioned the survivors." Julius shuddered, the interrogators were renowned for their cruel tortures. "It appears that the warrior who led them was the son of a trader, Antoninus Brutus. He was called Gaius Brutus. The two of them were last heard of heading southwest. I have sent Gaius Saturninus in pursuit. His regular cavalry will catch them. And there was a connection to here." Julius looked up in interest. "They were advised by an ex- trooper and some deserters. He was called The General but apparently, he was known as The Fist."

"That is a local connection. Livius will be interested in that news. The raiders were last seen heading west. The ala is in close pursuit and they appear to be making for the coast and Manavia."

"Can the ala destroy them?"

"Unlikely. There were almost two thousand of them originally and, even with losses, they will still seriously outnumber Cassius. No, they can only follow."

"Well good riddance and the sooner our defences are up the more secure I will feel."

"What do you mean, 'good riddance'?" Julius looked suspiciously at his old friend. "We have to get the captives back."

Falco looked bemused. "Why? They are women and children and…"

Julius did not give him the chance to finish. "If we do not do anything then it sends a message to the Brigante. It says that we do not care and their women and children are irrelevant. They have shown, in this failed rebellion, that they are unhappy. This might just be the catalyst to set them off. If we can return them safely then it will send a message to the Brigante and we will reap the benefit." He paused and allowed himself to calm down. He felt himself almost bursting and knew that his face was red and angry. "If these Hibernians get back and tell others how easy it is to raid Britannia then we will be opening up more problems than we can handle and the *limes* will not be enough. Already this coast is riddled with pirate raids, do you really want boat loads of Irish pirates coming to make their fortune at Rome's expense? We would need to build a wall all the way around the coast and not just across the country."

Pompeius held up his hands in mock surrender. "I give up and you are right but what can you do about it?"

Smiling slyly at the Governor, Julius said, "Give me two of your biremes and I will tell you."

Faolan saw the fort at Glanibanta loom up in the twilight and breathed a sigh of relief. The charred remnants would provide both shelter and defence. The presence of the cavalry was unnerving the warband even though they knew that they were safe from a major attack. Cassius had sent in small groups of troopers to harass the rearguard with javelins. The warriors there had all developed stiff necks from looking backwards over their shoulders. Although they had not lost many men it was a war of attrition and they were losing.

Loegaire and Angus huddled besides the fire eating the last of the increasingly rancid meat taken from Stanwyck. "It is straight across country now to the pass isn't it Angus?" Faolan was seeking confirmation because he remembered coming directly from the west. "We are less than a day from Creagth."

Picking a piece of indigestible gristle from between his teeth Angus pointed north. "If you go west then you are inviting trouble for the cavalry can spread out more and attack us from a number of sides at once."

Loegaire was tired of the retreat from this pitifully small band of soldiers. He wanted to fight. "If they attack us then we fight them, man to man on horses."

"And you would all die. You," he pointed at the two of them, "are not horsemen. You are men riding horses. They," he pointed east, "are horsemen and they could fight you three to one and still win."

Sullenly Faolan nodded; unpleasant though it was, Angus was speaking the truth. "What is your idea then?"

"Head north and then west. There is a trail bounded by the river and the bluffs, just like the country of the long lake. They could not attack us."

"But it would take longer."

"Yes, Loegaire it would take longer, about half a day."

"Suppose we divided the army." Both Angus and Loegaire looked at their leader in surprise. "Well Angus, as you pointed out we are just men on horses but we can move faster. If I take the horsemen towards the pass then some of the Romans will follow us. You could take the men on foot the safer way. For you it is no different to your plan but it means that, when I reach the pass I will have a hundred men to defend you and the rest as you brave the open ground before the pass."

Angus could see no flaw in the plan but he did not trust Faolan. "And you would wait for us at the pass?"

"How many times do I have to tell you that it is in my interests to bring as many warriors as I can to Manavia to support my attempt on the throne?"

"Very well but I need you and your horsemen to make a feint, as though you are going to charge the Romans first. That will give us a head start and, confuse them."

"That is a good plan. Until the morrow."

Cassius' pickets were suddenly surprised the following morning when there were fifty mounted Hibernians arrayed before them, armed to the teeth, looking ready for war. Racing back to the camp they alerted the Decurion Princeps who quickly ordered the ala to stand to. He and Marcus rode quickly to the picket line. "What in the Allfather's name are they doing?"

"It looks to me as though they are tired of being chased and intend to fight us."

Just then Faolan let out a roar and the line of barbarians hurtled towards the fifteen pickets. Cassius knew that they would be overwhelmed and he yelled, "Retreat!" The seventeen of them made a rapid retreat, through the trees to their camp, where Macro had taken charge and begun to dismantle the temporary refuge. When Cassius and the others raced into the partly dismantled camp Macro quickly ordered everyone to stand to.

They all stood, blades facing west, waiting for the onslaught; the onslaught which didn't materialise. "Where are they, Marcus? They were right behind us." Cassius peered into the west but could see nothing. Was this a trap? There was nothing for it but to face the beast head-on." Mount up!" As they trotted forwards Cassius decided that the dismantling of the camp could wait until they had found out what was going on. They rode gingerly forwards, every nerve end jangling as they waited for the rain of arrows or the crash of blade on flesh. When they reached the picket line they could see no sign of the enemy; it was deserted. Marcus ordered scouts out and Cassius sent Spurius back with his turma to complete the dismantling of the fort. When the scouts returned Cassius knew he had been outwitted.

"Sir the horses have headed due west and the main warband has headed north."

"I told you Marcus that this has someone behind it who knows the country. We will have to split up again. I do not like to do that but I have to. Which turmae have the maximum complement of troopers?"

"Graccus and Spurius. They have almost sixty men between them."

Cassius would have preferred to send either Macro or Marcus to follow as they had the most experience but Spurius was an older officer, not prone to stupid decisions and would follow any orders to the letter. "Very well. They can keep their swords in the backs of the men on the horses and we will close Rufius' trap with the majority of the ala."

"Sir!" Macro almost bellowed it as a challenge. "Let me go after them!"

Cassius looked curious, "Why Decurion Macro? The two officers are sound and they will only be following. It is we who will be fighting soon. I would have thought you would have relished that?"

"The man who killed our father is on a horse. Let me follow the horses. I do not want him out of my sight."

Marcus had a sudden intake of breath but Cassius put his hand out to restrain him and said coldly, "Decurion Macro this is not a private war. You are not here to revenge yourself. You are an officer in this ala and you will obey orders or I will have you placed under arrest. Is that clear?"

Sullenly Macro spat out, "Sir! Yes sir!" and rode off to rejoin his turma. Everyone had a look which was both shocked and embarrassed that they witnessed the outburst.

Cassius leaned over to Marcus. "He has been under stress lately but I will not tolerate outbursts like this again. Have a word with him."

"Sir I am as shocked as you. I will speak with him tonight."

Rufius' two scouts broke the news of the change in plan as soon as they reached him. "Well that has put the cat amongst the pigeons."

"What sir?"

"Oh nothing Decius, it is just that the Decurion Princeps and myself assumed that when we attacked the front of the warband, the rest of the ala could attack the rear but if they have split up will the Decurion Princeps have followed this band or the other?" Decius looked totally confused and Rufius smiled. "It matters not. We still perform our part. We are not trying to wipe them out but merely bloody their noses." He turned to the two turmae and pointed west. "They are heading for the high pass. When we withdraw, and boys we will withdraw, I will personally punish anyone who gets themselves killed here!" They all laughed. "We will withdraw west. Keep ourselves between them and their goal. Now get to your positions."

He had chosen the ambush point well. There was a bubbling stream which headed south from an old Roman watchtower to the north. It split into two just before the first lake and there was a ford across the shallow river. Further up the river could only be forded by swimming horses and Rufius' plan was simple. He and his men were waiting to the east for the column of men to pass. Just as they turned to cross the river he would attack with arrows and javelins. In the confusion, he hoped that some would drown and others run. Cassius' original plan had involved a simultaneous attack from the rear to cause even more confusion. The one part of the change which suited Rufius was that he would now be attacking infantry and not the horsemen who could have chased him down.

They heard the noisy warband long before they saw them. Their leader, who was easily identified by his shock of red hair, urged his men on at a half run. They had not been travelling far and even the most unfit were managing. Angus was looking for the stones. He did not mind his men getting wet but it sapped their energy and the wily old warrior was certain that the Romans would purse him and he wanted to be on the trail with a steep slope at his side when that happened. Metellus waited until the leader was in the water and then ordered his men to charge. They did so silently and, with the noise of the stream and the noise made by the barbarians their approach was undetected. Metellus waited until they were twenty paces from the warband and shouted, "Loose!" Almost immediately every trooper who had one took his bow and began shooting at the targets who were at point blank range.

As soon as the angry warband saw how few there were they launched themselves at the turmae. "Retreat!" His men needed no further urging as two hundred warriors chased them. The turmae headed north towards the deeper river. At the rear Cassius launched his attack as soon as he saw the warband hurrying to their comrade's aid. With more men than Rufius he caused even more casualties but he too withdrew in good time.

By the time Angus had reorganised his men he saw that over sixty men had died and many others were wounded. Those too wounded to walk were despatched by their comrades and the warband trudged westwards, once more flicking their eyes behind them for the phantom horsemen.

Faolan had a rude shock as he and his horses reined in and looked up at the pass for they could see the red crests which identified the defenders not as the men of the warband but Romans. Loegaire sent four of the younger warriors forward. "They have better eyes. They can count the enemy."

Faolan shook his head. "We chose the path because it could be defended by a small number of men. That works as well for the Romans as us."

"Then how did Creagth manage to become dislodged?"

"I am learning, Loegaire, that these Romans are neither as effete nor as rigid as we were led to believe. They are resourceful, clever and brave. I think our men will report thirty warriors holding the pass."

Loegaire made the sign against evil. "Are you bewitched, do you have second sight?"

Faolan laughed. "No I am using one of the tricks of the Red Witch, I am using my mind. There are thirty men in each group of horsemen. In that the Romans are predictable."

The returning scouts confirmed Faolan's judgement. He had a problem now for his local knowledge was with his warriors far to the east. He knew that there would be another pass to the coast, either north or south of the present one but he could not risk wasting time finding out. "We will have to see if we can dislodge them ourselves. Do you notice Loegaire that they are facing west? They are there not to stop us leaving but to face an enemy we cannot see."

"Creagth!"

"Exactly. And hopefully, he will have some of Conan's men with him."

"Not all of them?"

"No, for Conan would have obeyed orders. I told him to get the captives and plunder to Manavia and he will have done that but I can hope that he has left some men there."

"Let us ride closer and see what they do. I have seen that they can shoot arrows from long distances but we should be able to get closer to them." They nervously trotted forwards. They knew that there were about fifty men trailing them, keeping a judicious distance away. Faolan did not want to be caught between the pursuing cavalry and those on the pass but he did not want to lose lives needlessly when he was so close that he could actually smell the sea. The steep path twisted and turned but the defenders had chosen a site from which they could see a long way down.

Up on the pass Creagth had also seen his leader. He had the same number of men as the Romans but he knew that, in a combat situation, they would be hampered by the captives. He turned to his men. "When the Roman warrior's attention is on Prince Faolan I want one last charge, let us see if we can dislodge them from their rocky perch." His men were eager for battle, still smarting from not having come to close combat with this elusive enemy who liked to fight from a distance.

As Faolan came closer to the Roman lines, so the tired sentries nervously looked over their shoulders at the advancing line. Creagth judged the time right and yelled his battle cry. The sixty warriors raced the fifty paces to the crude stone barrier fired up by the desire to sink their blades into enemy flesh and knowing that their oath-sworn prince was but a few paces away. Faolan heard the cry and yelled, "It is Creagth! Charge!"

The men at the wall were attacked from two sides simultaneously. They were between a rock and an even bigger rock. On the hillside, Metellus was waiting with his reserve turma, their horses and the captives having been moved further along the ridge to a safer location. But should Metellus lose then the brave women would once again be in Faolan's clutches. His only hope was the two turmae he could see in the distance who were now galloping to attack the dismounted warriors; if they could reach the skirmish in time then the women at least might be saved. Faolan's horse holders had seen the danger and were racing their mounts in support of the prince. Faolan saw his men following and knew that his time had come; this was the moment for a last push to escape the Roman trap. "Ebdani warriors, let us drive them off this pass!"

As the beleaguered Roman defenders fought two enemies, Metellus led his men to crash into the sides of the warband. For the first time Faolan had the advantage; until the two pursuing turmae arrived he would outnumber the Romans and he urged his men on. They stabbed and fought as only men who are fighting for a cause greater than themselves can fight; they were fighting for the prince to whom they had sworn their allegiance and given their blood oath. Faolan too, fought harder than he had ever fought before his blood fired up as trooper after trooper fell to his blade.

Suddenly as he hacked a final trooper in the thigh, he found himself face to face with Creagth. Faolan had no time for words but he nodded his thanks. "Hold them as long as you can and then follow us. Do not lose too many men in the retreat, the rest of the warband's warriors are coming."

Creagth and his men formed a shield wall as Faolan and his last thirty warriors mounted their horses, with their precious cargo still tightly tied on their saddles and kicked on over the pass, Metellus cursed the lack of arrows for, with but a quiver of them, he could have killed the leaders as they fled. When Spurius and Graccus arrived with their two turmae the barbarian defenders began to slowly retreat west. They had taken heavy casualties and were few in number. It seemed that they would die in the pass when Creagth saw the remaining horses left by Faolan and he ordered those still standing to mount. Those too injured to mount lurched forwards to hold off the tired troopers and enable their comrades to flee.

Spurius reined in but Metellus roared at him. "Follow them! Stop them getting aboard a boat!" As the two turmae hurtled off Metellus looked around at the remains of his command. Out of three turmae, there were barely twenty men still on their feet and he could see brave Cicero lying with a half severed head, sword in hand and defending the pass as ordered. The troopers left looked shocked and shattered but Metellus knew that this was no time for rest. The larger warband was coming and, although Metellus knew that he would not be able to hold them he would have to die trying.

He looked around and saw that Sextus, although wounded himself in the leg, was still alive. "Sextus, take the wounded and use them to guard the captives and the horses on the ridge. If… when we fall try to save them."

Sextus looked as though he was going to object but, as the capsarius glanced around at the devastation in the pass, he knew that the Decurion was right. The next attack would sweep over the last defenders. He saluted and limped away.

Metellus turned to the survivors who were walking around dazed. He could see that many of them had slight wounds as he had but it mattered not. "Half of you move our dead over there and we will honour them when we can. The rest of you come with me. We have a new defence to create." He took the men to the destroyed wall. As one or two went to lift the stones Metellus shook his head. "First we have another wall to build, a different wall which might deter our foes more effectively." He picked up a barbarian body and laid it in front of the wall. "I want every barbarian laid here as a barrier. When that is done we will rebuild the stone wall."

It was a grisly task but the troopers soon saw that the barrier they were creating would be a hard one to negotiate as there would be less purchase on the bodies soft and slippery with congealing blood and gore. By the time they had finished, the bodies formed a wall eight paces wide before a wall which was as high as a man. Satisfied Metellus turned to look at the pile of trooper's bodies. There would be no time to burn them as there was little wood in the high pass. Tired though the men were he knew they had no other option. "Let us honour our dead and build them a tomb." The one thing in plentiful supply was stones and they laid a line around the perimeter of bodies and then built a low wall up. Once that was completed, they began to fill in the middle. As soon as the last face was covered Metellus stood to order them to rest but he saw that the men continued to work. One of them saw his confusion and said, "Let us make a monument that we can remember and hope that our friends do the same for us." By the time they had finished, there was a dome over the grave of those who had given their lives defending the last pass.

By the time Angus halted his warband, it was already dark. The barbarians put out a thin line of warriors and, exhausted fell into an immediate deep sleep. That would have been the perfect opportunity for Cassius to launch an attack but his men were also totally exhausted. A series of sudden attacks on the flanks and rear of the column had killed thirty barbarians but his men and their mounts could fight no longer. In addition, he feared an attack on the diminished ranks of the ala and had to use a turma as guards. Rufius and his ambush party had rejoined the main group as the ala was so depleted that Cassius needed numbers now. His ruse had worked and the barbarians had taken to using their own scouts to watch for further ambushes. Another sneak attack would be difficult to pull off.

When the ala slumbered Marcus sought out Macro, remembering Cassius' words. As he expected Macro was not sleeping but standing looking westwards. "Brother you should sleep."

"As should you."

"But you appear troubled and that concerns me. I cannot sleep knowing that your mind is filled with serpents."

Macro spun round his face angry although his voice was a whisper. "You do not know my mind brother! You do not know me!"

Shocked, Marcus recoiled. "Macro what has come over you? You are not the man who was trained, as I was by Gaelwyn; who was taught the way of the ala by Rufius and taught by our father to obey orders."

Macro's shoulders sagged. "You are right Marcus and I am sorry to take my anger out on you but we are not real brothers and it has taken the death of Gaius to make me realise that. My father, Macro, died saving my life and yet the first thing my mother did when she met me was to try to kill me. Those raiders who took Gaius' life came from Manavia; they came from my mother. I cannot rest until she has died at my hands. That means I must kill this Faolan first."

Marcus was appalled. Morwenna was a witch but she was his mother. How could someone live knowing that they had killed their own mother? "She will be protected and she will be guarded. It will be impossible. You will be killed before you can reach her."

"Then I will die trying but that will be better than the living death I have now, knowing that she wants me dead and one of her acolytes could poison me or one of her men could sneak up at night and murder me." He looked terrified. "I have not slept well since she had me in her clutches and I saw the hate in her eyes. She is a witch and she wants me dead. I am a dead man walking." His eyes softened and he put his arm around his brother. "Sleep now Marcus. You can tell Cassius that you spoke to me and I will be a dutiful soldier once more. But when we reach the coast..."

Chapter 12

The Fist and his band of deserters made good time as they travelled through the empty lands which lay well south of the heavily contested part of Brigantia. Their horses were fresh and for all his cruelty towards his fellow troopers, The Fist knew how to care for horses. So they came down at last from the barren moorland to a fast-flowing river. They kept to the north bank and the river turned north-west. They were no longer in a hurry for there had been no pursuit. The initial worry for the deserters was that the Romans would send cavalry after the survivors and now that it had not occurred they could take the trail at their leisure. They were also trying to grow out their hair and develop facial hair. They had looked too Roman and now, after a few days on the trail, they looked more like the barbarians or at least natives of Britannia. As the river turned west they found a road of sorts which headed north-west in a more direct line. It seemed likely that it would lead to the sea and that was their ultimate destination. When they struck the next river, they kept to the western bank and were rewarded one sunny afternoon with the port of the Setantii. They had played the part of traders seeking a port as they had travelled through the country and discovered that the small tribe who lived in the region existed through fishing and a little commerce. Seeing little evidence of Rome and its influence they ventured into the small settlement which did not even have a substantial wall, merely a wooden palisade which would have stopped no-one.

"This looks like a likely place." The Fist looked out at the port which had a small jetty and a few small ships and boats lying at anchor. "We keep a low profile and just ask for passage on a ship." He glared at his small band. "We pay for everything and we cause no trouble! The last thing we need is for them to remember us. Once we get away from this island we will be safe. Until then we are peaceful."

The port had one tavern which had a stable in which both their horses and they could be housed. Occasional visitors from the passing ships often stayed overnight but there was curiosity as to why they had not used one of the bigger ports further south or even Itunocelum, north.

The Fist would have made a good actor as he leaned in to confide in the headman. "Have you not heard of the trouble? The Brigante revolted and the Irish invaded. North of here is dangerous. No, we came here because we heard you were a fair people and we would be able to take passage."

The headman beamed at the compliment whilst worrying about the two conflicts his guest had mentioned. The last thing the Setantii needed was war. And they could do without the Romans taking an interest in them and taxing them. They plied their trade with both Hibernia and Manavia both of which left them alone but if raiders came or rebels, then that would upset their economic success story.

"Where would you like passage to?"

This was the part which had the deserters the most worried for they had no idea of the relationship between Manavia and Setantii. "We had heard there were good opportunities for trade in Manavia."

They were all relieved when the headman nodded. "Indeed they are good people and we have many boats which trade with them. I believe there is one going there on the morning tide. I can arrange a passage," he paused as he weighed up the potential purses of these travellers, "for a fee. In gold."

The Fist smiled, "That will be agreeable."

The headman was delighted to have made such an easy profit for the boat in question was his and he would make double money as he would charge them twice over. "Yes, there is a cargo of shackles going over. They are expecting a consignment of slaves. When the new moon rises there will be a huge slave auction. Traders will be travelling from all over Britannia and Hibernia. You will be well placed to do some deals in...?"

The Fist was too crafty to fall for that trick. "Oh, we trade in all sorts of commodities from people to services. We just need a new market. You know?"

The headman had them summed up now. They were fleeing Britannia and he mentally upped the price he would charge. "You are wise to travel to Manavia then for they have a very liberal view of trade. There are two ports one in the south and the larger one in the north. The ship on the morrow is going to the southern port but it is but half a day's ride to the northern one. "

"That will suit us for we would like to see the whole island before choosing our base."

"You will have to go to the northern port eventually then for you will have to ask the council's permission to stay." He leaned forward, "They are druids you know."

"That doesn't worry us."

"Good. Well until the morrow. I will meet you at the jetty and we can settle up then."

Spurius and Graccus whipped their mounts as hard as they could along the trail desperately trying to catch up with the remnants of Creagth's command. The advantage they had was that they had not fought earlier and their mounts were fresher than those they pursued. When they reached more open parts Spurius could see that some of those before them sported wounds. Their disadvantage was that they did not know what they were riding into. The trail they followed was the packhorse trail to the port of Itunocelum and was well worn. The fact that it was downhill helped the barbarians before them for the Roman armour made their burdens greater. Spurius turned to Graccus, "You have better eyes than I; can you see the other band?"

"Yes, Spurius. They are about a mile ahead."

"That means that when we catch up with them we will be outnumbered. We need to hold them until the ala can catch up. We must prevent them from boarding their ships at all costs." Just at that moment one of the barbarian's horses jinked to avoid a rock and the warrior, unused to riding, slipped from the saddle. His companions glanced around and saw the pursuing Romans. As the hapless raider was speared by a trooper's javelin the shout went up. "Romans! Behind us!" Urged on by the danger the barbarians kicked even harder and soon began to catch up with Faolan and his men who had slowed up believing that their comrades were still holding the pass.

Faolan heard the sound of horses and turned to see a handful of his warriors, led by Creagth, his arm bleeding heavily and a column of fifty Roman troopers bearing down upon them. "Can you see the sea yet, Loegaire?"

"No but I can smell it and there are gulls. It is not far now."

"As soon as we reach it dismount and prepare to receive cavalry. I do not want to be picked off as we try to get to the ships and, Loegaire, you must make sure that our gold is safely secured. I do not want to lose it this close to safety."

Angus was a hard taskmaster. "Come on you sons of whores. We have but a few miles to go and we will reach the safety of the pass."

Ceol was a huge bully of a warrior and he had had enough of being ordered around by Morwenna's pet thug. He came from the north-west of Hibernia and he had seen most of his friends die. Now there was just himself and three others left from the original group. He had come to Britannia for glory and plunder and, apart from one or two occasions, it had been retreat and disgrace that they had endured. He had had enough and he knew that many of the others had had enough.

"No! I say we fight the Romans here. We run no more!"

Angus heard the murmurings from some of the others who were disaffected and knew that this had all the hallmarks of a revolt. He nodded and walked over to Ceol. They were about the same height but Angus was older, the first wisps of grey flecking his beard. "So you would fight horsemen. On foot?"

Ceol laughed. "There are trees and forests where the Romans cannot ride but I can run. I am not an old man who is afeared."

Approaching him Angus too laughed. "It is true that I am older than you Ceol but in that I have wisdom and unfortunately for you, I do not have that other trait which is patience." In one well-practised move, he took his two-handed sword from its scabbard over his back and took off the head of Ceol who was already forming his reply. He saw the two men behind the dead Ceol begin to reach for their weapons and with two strokes they lay dead.

"Now does anyone else wish to challenge this old man or will you obey me?" There was a sullen silence. Ceol had been a fierce warrior but he had been killed as easily as a helpless child. "We will fight today, believe me, but we will fight where it suits us. When we reach the pass, the Romans will be at a disadvantage and we can turn on them and kill many of them.

Then we will travel to the coast and, after a rest at my home of
Manavia, you will all travel home to Hibernia, rich men." Even
the most truculent of rebels realised that their goal had always
been to kill Romans and become richer. They could achieve that
with Angus and they banged their weapons on their shields to
show they agreed.

"Sounds like they are happy about something?"
"Yes, Marcus but I wonder what? You take the point today
and keep your blade in their backs. We reach the pass this
morning and I hope that Metellus is still there." Cassius was
worried by the lack of news from the pass. He had asked his
friend to do an impossible task. The cunning of his enemy had
thrown the Decurion Princeps' plans into disarray and he did not
know what he would find at the pass. "Did you speak with your
brother?"
Marcus looked away, unable to meet Cassius' stare. "I did
and he will now follow orders. There will be no more outbursts I
can promise you." He shrugged apologetically, "I think he just
wants to fight."
"Well today he will get his wish. Believe me." He pointed
west. "The land begins to rise and there are no trees. We will be
able to use our speed there. Keep pushing."
Once the warband saw the pass, rising like a scar in the
distance, their spirits too rose. They could see the barrier created
by Creagth and felt relief. Soon they would turn like a cornered
wild boar and tear these dogs to shreds. Angus had been right
they just had to be patient.
High in the pass Metellus spirits fell just as quickly as his
enemies rose. He did not have enough men to defend the pass.
There were hundreds of warriors approaching. They were like a
black cloud moving across the land. Behind them, he could see
the distinctive shapes of the ala but he knew that there could only
be seven turmae there and they would not be at full strength. The
best he could hope was that he could slow them down and
whittle their numbers to enable Cassius to catch them. "Take
every weapon you can and withdraw up the hill." He could see
the disappointment in their faces but it was more important to
protect what they had saved so far and not risk all in a glorious

but, ultimately useless sacrifice. The twenty-two of them limped up to the rock-filled hillside; each trooper working with another and hiding behind whatever cover they could find. "The ala is coming but it will do them no good to find our corpses and those of our charges littering the hillside. Our task is to slow them down and thin them out. If I fall then withdraw slowly to the captives. They are our prime concern!"

The grim-faced troopers glanced up the hill; those women could be their sisters and mothers. They knew that their comrades' sacrifice would have been in vain if they fell into the raiders' hands once more. One of the older hands shouted anonymously, "We'll not let you down sir!"

As the warband approached the foot of the pass Cassius became uneasy. There was a wise head guiding these warriors for they did not race up the steep slope to the improvised barrier but they halted and two hundred men turned to face the ala, now five hundred paces away, and formed a shield wall. Lucius rode next to Cassius, "What are they doing sir? Are they going to charge us?"

"No Lucius. Unless I miss my guess they are stopping us from charging but the question is why? We have made no attempt to do so yet. Tell me, Lucius, can you see our men on the barrier?"

Lucius scanned the stone-built blockage. "No sir, there are men lying down in… no sir there are bodies in front of the barrier."

"Ours?" Trepidation oozed from that one word.

"No sir, barbarians. There sir. On the hillside, I can see some red crests, but there are only a few of them."

"That is why they have halted then Lucius. The bulk of the army will dispose of the wall and the others will stop us from attacking them."

"But they will get away sir!" Even Lucius could see that, once the band passed the col, they would be safe.

"I know son, which is why we have to get rid of these warriors." He turned to the ala. It was much depleted. With a notional roll call of seven turmae, he should have been able to field over two hundred troopers. With the casualties they had taken, he had less than a hundred and eighty fit men available.

Their route was lined with wounded men awaiting their successful return. "Men, I know that you are tired and we have ridden far in the past days but we need to dislodge those warriors from the entrance to the pass. We have not the time, nor the ammunition to whittle them down with javelins and arrows so we will have to use cunning. I will lead an attack on the centre, Lucius and Antoninus will support. We will try to draw their fire first. When I give the signal then we will retreat. I believe they will try to follow us and when they do then, Rufius and Calgus, you can take your men and harass the left of their line but do not commit. Macro and Marcus, you have the harder task. I want you to attack their right when the centre surges forward. It is where they are the weakest and you are the best swordsmen. You will need to dismount and fight afoot. Rufius when you see them shift to their right then go in harder and I will swing around to support Macro and Marcus." All of the troopers banged their shields making the rearguard look upon them with a little more interest. "You two," he addressed the two brothers directly but looked particularly at Macro, "fight hard but not recklessly. We still have to defeat the bulk of the warband on the pass and I need every trooper I have."

It was Marcus who answered for the two of them. "We will sir. We have a nephew we would like to see on our next leave and tell him the tale of how we destroyed an Irish Warband and rescued the Brigante slaves!"

The warband was led by an Ebdani called Carn. He was proud to have been chosen by Angus for this task. Unlike many of his tribe he respected the older warrior. He knew that he had done exceptionally well to get so many warriors here in the face of this determined Roman opposition. He had placed himself at the centre of the wall with his oath brothers around him. He had no doubt about the fidelity of the rest but he wanted the reassurance that those around him would give their lives defending the line. He watched as the steady line of Romans approached. He noticed with interest that it appeared to be a wedge formation with the red-crested leader and the standard-bearer in front of a double line of twelve troopers, behind which was a double line that appeared to be twice as long as the first. He nodded, pleased. He would have the honour of taking the first blow. He roared out, "Lock shields and every warrior interlocked his shield with his neighbour, keeping his weapon above the shield wall to strike any unarmoured place. Behind them were the men with double-handed axes, their shields slung over their backs. They would sweep over the heads of those in front, all of whom would drop to their knees on Carn's command.

Some of those in the front rank began to tremble slightly as the ground shook with the thunder of the horses. Out of the corner of his eye, Carn could see the rest of the cavalry moving forwards a little slower. He smiled to himself, the brave ones were in the middle and the others would flee once their leader was down; it would fall to him to kill the leader. "Brace and prepare to drop!" The horses were thirty paces away. When they were but twenty away he roared, "Drop!" and the line fell to its knees. At exactly the same time the line of horses stopped and a volley of javelins fell amongst the men with axes who were about to decapitate the horses. Carn cursed the dishonour of warriors who would not fight man to man. "Up!" The second lines approached and did the same but this time their javelins thudded into shields and not flesh. Carn noticed that the rest of the Romans had stopped to watch. Cowards. As the Romans in front of him reformed, the line braced itself. An idea came into his head. When the Romans threw their javelins and turned, they were vulnerable. He turned to his oath brothers. "When they turn this time, we charge them and kill their leader."

The angry axe men who had lost some of their fellows heard his instructions and roared, "We're behind you."

This time the line threw fewer javelins and, as they turned the line suddenly bulged as the Hibernians chased after Cassius and his troopers. The speed of the warriors took the Decurion Princeps by surprise and he had to kick his mount on quickly to avoid being caught. The turmae of Antoninus and Lucius were also surprised by the unexpected charge and three of the horses were hacked by the axemen with the wickedly sharp double-handed blades. The troopers were despatched ruthlessly. The feigned retreat became real as the two turmae raced away from the vicious blades.

On the flanks, the waiting barbarians took heart from this easy victory and relaxed. Their shields were no longer locked as they waited for their chance to charge. Suddenly they saw the two turmae approaching and knew what to expect. They did not drop to their knees but they all raised their shields slightly to protect more of their thin line. Macro and Marcus' turmae flew steeply into the air as they jumped the waiting warriors and they fell, almost vertically amongst the second and third ranks. Then, most surprising of all, half the troopers before them jumped from their mounts and charged on foot. Many of the raiders in the front ranks who had survived still had shields about their faces and the first that they knew of an attack was when their bellies were ripped open. On the Hibernian left, they watched the two lines of troopers approaching them and they braced for a volley of javelins. Instead, Rufius' and Calgus' turmae unslung their bows and began to pick off men in the centre of the line, striking their unarmoured backs.

When Carn realised he had been deceived he shouted, "Back in line! Lock shields." The men in the centre and the left did so easily, presenting a solid wall of wood and iron but, on the right, their cohesion had gone and the line began to crumble from the side assaulted by the turmae. Those mounted troopers, still holding their companion's horses began hurling javelins at the warriors who were fighting Macro and Marcus.

The blood lust was on the brothers as they felt the line crumbling and Marcus chose his moment well. "Forward! The Sword of Cartimandua!" With a roar, the two turmae charged even more fiercely and the barbarians were dismayed as they heard the name of the blade roared.

Carn could see that the integrity of the shield wall was compromised and he shouted, "Fall back!"

Rufius and Cassius charged with their turmae hurling javelins as the disorganised barbarians tried to avoid the horses' hooves and make it up the ever-narrowing pass. Those who tried to scramble over the fellside were easy targets for Rufius' archers whilst Macro and Marcus were still rolling up the line as they faced men on their unarmoured side. The rearguard was haemorrhaging and bleeding warriors.

Angus looked admiringly at the barrier erected by the Romans; it showed a cunning mind for the barbarians were infuriated when they saw their dead friends and comrades' ravaged bodies piled up like the carcasses of animals. "Pull down the barrier!" They looked at him in horror as though he had asked them to do something horrendously sacrilegious. When they hesitated, he pointed down the pass, "Your brothers are dying down there so that we can escape this trap!" Spurred on they began to tumble the bodies down the steep sides of the pass. Suddenly those at the front were plucked from the top as Metellus' archers picked them off. Angus was becoming increasingly impressed with the stubborn defenders but enough was enough.

"You men! Protect the workers with your shields. You twenty get up the slopes and dislodge these archers." They hesitated again." Fools there cannot be more than a handful. Go!" Angus glanced over his shoulder; he could see Carn's fighting retreat and he could also see the trail of bodies which marked their passage.

On the slopes, Metellus had begun to hope that they might, against the odds, actually get out of this alive. He had watched in admiration as the ala had destroyed the shield wall and taken so few casualties; now as he heard the tumble of rocks he knew that they were the next target. "One in each pair, take the arrows and keep firing; the other prepare to defend against swordsmen." He gave his quiver to the trooper next to him and hefted his sword. His leg was still stiff and, if he moved too much, then it would burst open making not only Sextus but also Nanna, very unhappy. They did have the advantage of height and he replaced his sword in its scabbard and took instead one of the spears they had recovered from the barbarian camp.

The warrior making his way up the slope saw the bandage on Metellus' leg and grinned. His first kill would be an easy one and he moved towards the decurion. It would have been easy for Metellus to throw the spear and kill the man but then he would have lost his weapon so he allowed the man to come closer. The barbarian swung his sword at Metellus' good leg and, hopping over the scything blade Metellus plunged the spear into the man's unprotected neck. The dead man soundlessly fell and then his body rolled down the steep slope gaining speed as it did so. The dead man killed one of his comrades when his body took the man's legs from under him and he crashed over those destroying the barrier and tumbled to a rocky death.

The barrier of bodies was no more and Angus began to order his men to demolish the stones. The rearguard was now less than forty paces away but the Roman progress had been slowed by the narrowness of the pass. At the point where the two forces met was a deadly conflict between Carn and his oath brothers and Marcus and Macro and the oathsworn of the sword. The brothers were finding it more difficult as the barbarians had the high ground but their superior weapons and armour gave them the edge. Ironically it was the axemen with the superior reach who were the raiders downfall for, once swung, the momentum left them open for an upwards stab of the blade. The Roman helmets also saved many lives as blows from swords, to the head, merely stunned them and there was always another Roman to take his place. Cassius could see however that the front rank was tiring and he gave a command which he knew Macro would hate but he hoped he would obey.

"Ready Rufius?"

"Sir!"

"Front rank rotate!"

Instantly obeying the front rank disengaged and stepped backwards as Rufius' men replaced them. Carn yelled, "Cowards!" but none of Macro's men spoke Gaelic and merely walked back to the rear of the line. Macro shot a dirty look at Cassius but he obeyed.

The change had an instant effect. Some of Rufius' men still had javelins and the extra length proved effective. Carn was screaming in rage. These Romans had no honour and would not fight as men. He swore that when this was over he would return one day to wreak his revenge on these Romans.

Further up the pass Angus had finally succeeded in breaking through the wall but it was not wide enough for all of them. He shouted to the men who had dismantled it, "Get through and build a defence over there. We will be through soon!" To the rest he shouted, "We are nearly through. I want this barrier gone! Now!" The men redoubled their efforts as they saw how close they were to success and, in a shorter time than one would have expected the barrier was gone. Angus grabbed his horn and blew an enormous blast upon it. Every warrior knew that it meant retreat and they disengaged and ran as fast as they could through the gap. One or two of Carn's men, their bloodlust up kept fighting, enabling more of their colleagues to flee but it was in vain as they were cut down. When Cassius reached the site of the wall he looked up and saw a bloodied Metellus waving to him. They had the job half done; now it was time to complete it.

Both sides were bloodied and exhausted. They had fought all day and the sun was already beginning to set giving the air an even cooler feel than it had in the valleys. Cassius ordered Calgus' turma to form a defensive line while the rest began to build a crude wall in lieu of the traditional wooden camp. "Rufius check our casualties and set up a station for the capsarii beneath that rocky overhang. Marcus set up a picket line for the horses and see to their feed." Marcus gave him a quizzical look; where would he get feed? Cassius shrugged.

When they felt the scurry of rocks tumbling from above, every man's hand went to his weapons but they smiled with relief when they saw that it was Metellus and his men leading their horses and the captives down the treacherous slope. Cassius turned to Rufius, "It looks as though the expedition has not been a total disaster."

"You do yourself a disservice old friend. Neither the Governor nor the Legate could have expected you to do more."

Cassius shook his head. "It shows that we need better planning and support."

"How do you mean?"

"If we had had more arrows and javelins then we could have whittled them down. They had no missile weapons. We might have been able to stop them earlier."

"You may be right but that is the future. You did… we did well here and we should be proud."

"I am proud but I am also sad for the losses we suffered." He pointed to the tomb erected by Metellus and his men, the pile of stones topped by a solitary shield and javelin.

Chapter 13

The horses of the two turmae were flecked with sweat and the poor beasts were labouring when Spurius halted the column above the small port of Itunocelum. To call it a port was a little grandiose for it was little more than a fishing village with a jetty, a jetty constructed under the watchful eyes of the druids of Manavia to act as a supply base for their sanctuary. It was built upon an estuary and the port was on the northern bank. The estuary was wide enough for ships to turn around and Spurius could see that it had been well chosen. Spurius could see that they had arrived before Faolan could escape but unfortunately there were other barbarians there along with captives. Spurius assumed that they were the ones who had fled first. Whoever they were it meant that he could do nothing for they were behind the solid walls and wooden ramparts of the town. It would take ballistae and scorpions to breach them. From the small number of ships, the decurion could see that not all of the barbarians could easily be extracted in the near future which gave him more time.

The younger officer, Graccus, turned to his superior. "What do we do now sir?"

"Good question." He scanned the land around. "I think I will leave a couple of scouts to watch the port here and then the rest of us will head back to help Metellus deal with the rest of the barbarians."

"Perhaps the rest of the ala will be there?"

"Perhaps but I have learned never to count on anything before the event," he grinned, a disconcerting sight as he had lost many of his teeth over the years, "it saves disappointment."

"We sent for the ships as soon as we arrived, Prince."

"Then why are they not here?" It was a rhetorical question and Conan made no attempt to answer it. "Let us make the best of a bad job. Strengthen the defences and then feed the men. They have had short rations long enough." He looked again at the empty harbour. "There are no boats here?"

"The fishing fleet was at sea and I sent Angus' man in that. I hope he made it, it didn't look very seaworthy." Faolan shrugged, the man's survival was irrelevant so long as he sent for his ships. "Damn that witch. She should have had boats waiting for us. If she has played me false…"

"I think not lord for we have not been away as long as she might have expected. We had great success." He waved a hand around the huddled captives and captured gold."

"But I did not get the sword!"

"You might yet," Conan stroked his beard. "One of the captives heard my men talk of it and she boasted of its powers. She said that the man who wielded it lived on the farm we destroyed and she knew he would come for you."

Faolan snorted, "I will believe it when I see it but at least I have the gold to buy my throne and depose my cousin. This time next year we will have conquered the whole island."

While Loegaire whooped his agreement, Conan was not sure. He had not seen enough skill from his leader to warrant such a claim. The auxiliaries they had met had proved more than a match for Conan's men and he did not doubt, for a moment, the courage and the skill of his men but their enemy had had something they had not, discipline.

At the high pass that very discipline was in evidence as Cassius and the ala worked long after exhaustion had set in. Food was collected, shelters built, defences enlarged and watch kept on the enemy. Cassius and Rufius were amused by the attentions of the strong-minded Nanna who fussed and fretted around Metellus, much to his embarrassment. Even Sextus, the capsarius found the strength to smile as, for the tenth time, she checked his bandage.

"I think our old friend has an admirer, Cassius."

"Now don't tease Rufius, I think they make a lovely couple."

Snorting her displeasure Nanna stormed off to see to a couple of the younger captives who were crying. "You two are shameless. She is just a kind woman. If it were not for her strength we might not have recaptured them, think on that."

"We are only having a little fun, Metellus. In truth we have had little to laugh about lately for this has not gone the way we hoped."

Metellus' face became serious. "There are more captives on the way to Itunocelum. I sent Spurius after them but I am not sure he will have been in a position to do anything."

"This is just like all those years ago when we chased the Witch Queen and her men."

Cassius' face darkened at the memory and at the name of Morwenna for she cast a shadow over the ala, even more so since the attempt on Macro's life. "I know Rufius. If only we had a naval base on this coast we could close the door on her." He looked eastwards, as though to Rome. "Perhaps this new Emperor will get around to it when he has built his frontier."

Metellus looked incredulous. "Built the frontier? We will be old men before that is done. Besides would it have stopped this? I think not." He looked around at the camp. "This would make a perfect site for a fort. A couple of centuries of auxiliaries here and a cohort at Glanibanta would make sure this never happens again."

Cassius looked, seemingly for the first time at the flattened area almost at the top of the pass. Metellus was correct although it would have to be built from stone as the ground was solid rock. He inclined his head as he visualised the structure. That would make it even stronger. "I will mention it to Julius the next time we see him. he appears to have the ear of the Emperor."

Metellus nodded his head at Macro who was still walking around with an angry sulky look upon his face. "What is the matter with our young decurion?"

"He wanted to fight the Irish leader by himself. He is angry... well he is just angry, Gaius dying, you know?"

"Marcus was his son but he is not angry."

The three of them looked to where Marcus was laughing and joking with his troopers as they built up a wall. Rufius lowered his voice although with the noise of the work in the camp they could not be overheard. "Marcus is Gaius' son and is very much like his father whereas Macro is the son of Macro, and, remember how unpredictable he could be?"

There was a pause and Metellus spoke the unspoken words, "And his mother was not Ailis but Morwenna. There is no dark side to Ailis but Morwenna..."

"Keep an eye on him will you, Metellus? You, of all people know him best. And let us get our people some rest for tomorrow we need to dislodge these barbarians and then try to save the other captives."

The barbarians under the wily Angus had not been idle. They were all tired but they had not been ordered to build up their defences for Angus had no intention of staying there to be destroyed piecemeal. He had his men find the bodies of those slain earlier, Creagth's men. At first, they were reluctant to do so but Angus explained his idea and they eventually agreed. The dead were placed, with weapons showing along the defences. The six of seven badly wounded warriors who would normally have been given a merciful death were left to sacrifice themselves when the Romans made their inevitable assault. They were all happy to be given the chance of a glorious death and a verse in the song which would be composed of their last stand. As soon as the preparations were completed, and as the Romans slept, the warband slipped silently away. The Roman sentries saw nothing for the pass went downhill after the barbarian barrier and they saw the warriors still, apparently, on guard. They saw what they expected to see.

It was a weary Roman force which awoke the next morning in the half-light of early dawn. The first rays were peeking from behind them, illuminating the barbarian's stone barrier whilst leaving them in the dark. It was sharp-eyed Rufius who saw that something was amiss. "Metellus. Look at those barbarians. They look to be in the same position they were last night."

Metellus peered over. "Perhaps they have found a comfortable spot or," he peered closer, "perhaps they are asleep." He turned to the sentries. "Have you heard anything?"

The sentry looked worried as though he had done something wrong but the reassuring nod from Metellus gave him the answer. "We heard them talking in the night. I think we even heard them laughing, which we found strange."

Rufius saw one guard, at least, moving. "But not all of them. Still it may be something."

They quickly woke Cassius and the other decurions. "Some of them are asleep. We still have arrows. If we shoot the ones we can see are awake then we can rush them."

157

Macro spoke up. "But we will have to be swift for the sun is rising."

"Metellus get your archers, Rufius wake the turmae. We use Marcus, Macro, Antoninus and Rufius' men to storm their wall. When you have breached it we will all fall upon them. With the Allfather's help, we may surprise them."

With no horses to prepare, the men were ready in moments and they waited, crouched in the hollow before their wall. As Cassius dropped his sword twenty arrows flew true and the assault party silently sped across the open ground, each man dreading the sound of alarm which would precede the spears and death. Macro was the first to leap over the wall and as he landed his sword was ready to dispose of any attacker. Instead, he found a badly wounded man, lying with his back to the rock face, his comrades at the wall slain by arrows.

"We have cheated you Roman as you cheated us by not having the courage to fight us man to man. They have left for you are not worthy enemies."

Macro was about to plunge his sword into the man when he was restrained by Marcus. "Let the Decurion Princeps ask him questions first and then you can kill him." Macro's eyes narrowed in anger but he nodded his head.

As soon as Cassius saw the scene he understood the barbarian mind. "They have outwitted us and have had the whole night. They will now be in Itunocelum."

The barbarian coughed up some blood. "Angus has more wits than you Romans."

Cassius wandered over to the man. "You are a brave warrior waiting here to die, making us believe that your comrades were still here."

"Aye we spent the night telling the tale we will never hear but our families will and the saga of the wounded warriors will be told around campfires long after you are dead, Roman."

"And you deserve the honour. We are warriors and we salute you."

"Pah! You are not warriors. Warriors do not hide behind arrows they face a man and look him in the eyes."

Macro hissed, "Believe me I shall look you in the eye when I finish you off."

Cassius restrained Macro with his arm. "But you will not share in the plunder and captives this Faolan has taken."

"It matters not for my brothers are with him and when the captives are sold on Manavia they will have my share and they will join Faolan as he becomes king of the Ebdani."

Cassius nodded; satisfied that he had all the information he was going to get from the brave barbarian. "Go to the Allfather and your comrades." He took his arm from Macro who plunged his sword downwards into the raider's neck. "Metellus you stay here with your turma and the wounded to guard the captives. Send a rider north to Luguvalium with a message for the Prefect. Tell him what has transpired. Send another to Eboracum with the same message. We will go to Itunocelum and see if we are in time."

Rufius' frowned, "I am worried about Spurius and Graccus. They should have returned by now or else they will be caught between over a thousand barbarians."

"That is on my mind too but there is little that we can do about that. Let us worry about getting there speedily."

The ala quickly mounted and trotted down the pass. The sight before them was a shock for those who had not travelled the road before. The land was green and verdant with farmsteads and small settlements dotted around. Had they not been under the protection of the druids it would have been a ruin from slave raiders and other predators but the wise priests had decided that a compliant population was better than a dead one and they managed to get information and trade from the crafty people who lived there. The Roman bureaucracy was too far away to affect them for good or ill and they managed the best they could. They were the last free remnants of the Carvetii and they had never been friends of Rome.

They found the remnants of the two turmae when they were halfway along the road. Forty troopers were gathered around a pile of bodies, tending to their wounded. Cassius saw that Graccus was wounded but of Spurius he could not see a sign. He turned to Antoninus. Take your turma and form a picket line down the trail. Capsarii, help the wounded."

Cassius and Rufius dismounted and went to Graccus. "You met the warband?"

Graccus had a bad wound to his left arm which made his face contort with pain as the capsarius tended to it but his eyes flashed anger as he replied. "Aye. We were heading for the pass when we came upon them. They had made not a sound and the noise of our mounts disguised any sound they did make, it was a well-planned ambush. They were upon us before we knew it. Spurius was killed instantly. I led the survivors up to that knoll," he pointed to the only high point they could see, "but they didn't follow. I was going to trail them when we had seen to the wounded." He shrugged, "We could have done little for they outnumbered us."

"You did well Decurion Graccus. When your men have had their wounds tended form the rearguard."

With Antoninus at the point, they trotted forwards. Every trooper knew that there was a warband ahead and their prey had proved to be both elusive and crafty; an ambush was likely. As they crested the ridge above the port they saw that they were going to be too late. Lying next to the jetty and in the small estuary there were many ships of all sizes and they could see them being boarded, some were already pulling away, out to sea. As soon as Cassius was informed, he knew they had one throw of the dice left. "Ride as hard as you can column of fours."

With less than two miles to go there was little point in saving their horses and they galloped quickly down the inclined trail. As they rode Cassius considered his options. They might not be able to stop the embarkation but they would at least make the Hibernians remember their visit to Britannia and he still had a vain hope that they might save some of the captives. Metellus had done well but the majority of captives were still in the hands of the slavers. He suddenly turned to Rufius, "When you were taken off the shore by Hercules, what were the problems you encountered?"

Rufius looked puzzled and then Cassius' intention became clear. "It is slow-moving in water and you cannot turn easily. Also, ships and boats do not move as swiftly as horses and we can do much damage whilst they are close to shore."

"Good. As soon as we can I will form lines and we will charge those who have not embarked, you take every man with a bow and kill as many in the sea as you can. The one advantage we have is that whoever is their rearguard will be outnumbered by us. If we can stop any of the captives being taken…"

Both Rufius and Cassius knew that it was unlikely that they would capture any captives for they were worth far more than the warrior's lives. They, and their plunder, would have been the first to be embarked but, until the ala saw the captives sail away they would do all in their power to stop them.

Macro was close to the front and he was determined to kill as many of the chiefs as possible. He had a mad idea that he could actually board the ship and kill all on board. He had inherited from his father, not only a rare skill with all weapons but also a total belief in his own skill compared with any other warrior. The idea of being defeated by a foe, no matter how numerous, never entered his head; there was no man yet born who could kill him.

Faolan had made sure, once the fleet arrived, that he was the first onboard, along with the gold and the captives. He left Loegaire to supervise the embarkation. He was delighted when the rearguard led by Angus tramped into the port. He had worried that he would have to buy additional soldiers for his attempt on the throne. He had been pleased with the way his warriors had performed. They had acquitted themselves well against the Romans and he knew that, with lessons learned, they would sweep through his own island. He would pay for mercenary archers having seen, at first hand, the devastation they could inflict. He would also make sure that his bodyguard, at least, had armour. As he stood at the stern of the large trader, he was feeling happy. The only cloud on the horizon was Idwal whom Morwenna had sent to supervise the embarkation. The two warriors had taken an instant dislike to each other on the occasion of their first meeting and, not for the first time, Faolan was glad that it had been Angus who had accompanied him on his raid into Britannia. Unfortunately, the Manavian warrior was in Itunocelum paying off the chiefs there to ensure their continued support for Morwenna, and Faolan would have to suffer that particular cloud.

Suddenly all his pleasure was shattered when he heard the wail which went up from the outskirts of the town. He could see, from the elevated stern, the Roman standard which told him that his pursuers had finally caught up with him. He roared out,

"Angus, Loegaire, get the men aboard now! I want to lose no more men."

Loegaire looked at the string of horses which were about to be boarded. "What about these? They are too valuable to leave."

"Leave them! The warriors are more valuable." Thankful that he had boarded the captives first he turned to the captain, "Are we ready to sail?"

The captain shook his head. "We have to raise the anchor and hoist the sail and besides you still have men we could board."

"Just make your preparations if they are not aboard by the time you are ready they can take another of the boats."

The captain shook his head at the cynicism of the prince. He could see that the warriors had given all for him and he was callously abandoning them. However, Morwenna was paying him and she had made it quite clear that this prince was important to her, he would have to obey this heartless leader. The captain knew that many warriors would die needlessly as his ship, the largest, had been tied to the jetty where embarkation was easy. Most of the others were lying in the river on the opposite side waiting to come in and pick up the warriors. The men would have to wade out to them. He was glad that it was not his decision. He shouted down to his crew, "Cast off forrard, cast off aft. Raise the anchor and hoist the sail." Although he had tied up to the jetty the currents were notoriously dangerous and the anchor was an element of safety he now regretted.

The first line of troopers had smashed into the thin picket line of warriors, their speed down the trail had taken them by surprise. Idwal and Angus raced to organise the others for, despite what Faolan had said, they needed to embark in an orderly fashion or they would lose many more men than they needed. Loegaire had released the horses, his men smashing their swords against the beast's rumps to make them stampede. The frightened herd had galloped towards safety, running through the lines of the ala and disrupting their cohesion.

"Shield wall!"

A hundred warriors, the closest to the charging horsemen locked shields with Angus, Idwal and Loegaire at the rear. Angus glanced over his shoulder where warriors were still wading out to the boats and running along the jetty. Already

Faolan's ship was moving slowly away from the jetty and those warriors close enough leapt to grab the sides. At first, they were successful but the further it drifted the fewer actually made it and many fell into the sea which claimed their lives mercilessly. Idwal turned to two of his men. "Go to the Eagle and let no one but us aboard." The Eagle was the other ship tied to the jetty. The Manavian turned to Angus. "I'll be damned if I will be abandoned by that coward." Loegaire's eyes flared with anger but he held his counsel. They needed each other but there would come a time for such a reckoning.

The first of Cassius' troopers to hit the enemy hurled their javelins at the shield wall. Both sides knew that they would hit few men but the javelins would weigh the shields down and make them ungainly and difficult to control. At the same time, Rufius' men were firing their arrows at those men on the beach and the jetty, the missiles striking unprotected backs and limbs. Angus turned to Idwal. "We need to fall back. Make them turn their arrows to us." When Idwal shot him a questioning look the wily warrior said, "We have shields and protection."

Macro had the blood lust upon him and he had dismounted to attack the shield wall with his two blades. No-one could stand in his way but Marcus could see that warriors were running to kill this hero of Roman; by killing him they would gain much honour. Marcus could not allow his brother to die alone and, hurling his spear to kill the warrior about to hit Macro's unprotected back he leapt from his horse roaring, "The Sword of Cartimandua." The oathsworn heard it and they dismounted echoing his shout.

Across the water, Faolan heard the shout. The witch had been correct; the sword had come to him and he said to the captain. "Stop the ship!"

"How? This isn't a horse I…"

Faolan's sword was at his throat in an instant. "Stop this fucking ship or you die!"

"Lower the sail!"

The crew looked confused until Faolan shouted, "Do it or your captain dies!" As they rushed to obey Faolan went to the rail and yelled, "Loegaire, the sword! I want it!"

Idwal looked astonished, "Is he mad?"

"He is, above all, my Prince, and we obey. Ebdani, wedge!"

The Ebdani warriors quickly left the shield wall to form behind Loegaire. The disruption of the wall allowed many of Antoninus' men to get amongst them and soon the line became a series of individual battles and melees while Loegaire and his wedge pushed their way towards the Roman formation led by Macro and Marcus. Loegaire hit the left side of the Roman wedge and the trooper behind Marcus took a blow to the shield which broke his upper arm. His shout of pain alerted Macro who yelled, "Turn!"

The well-trained troopers wheeled as one and Loegaire found himself facing Macro. He saw a tall trooper who was as broad as any warrior he had ever seen. His chestnut hair framed an angry face but the most intimidating feature was his eyes for they were a green he had not seen since… since Morwenna! His eyes widened as he realised that this was Morwenna's son and as their blades clashed he knew that this would be the day he would die for the man before him had his mother's power and that would be his doom. Even though Loegaire knew he would die he was blood sworn to obey Faolan and the Prince wanted the sword which was but a man away. He hacked and chopped in a vain attempt to get through the auxiliary's defence.

Macro knew that he had a chief and that this chief was a skilful warrior. He coldly analysed the man and saw his weakness, the man used the shield as defence, and Macro would show him how to use it as an offensive weapon. Just as he was about to punch the shield into Loegaire's face the warrior to Loegaire's left saw the bare flesh of Macro's leg and he thrust his sword towards it. Suddenly the Sword of Cartimandua flashed down to shatter the blade and then upwards to gut the man. Within moments the two brothers were side by side.

"You want this sword? Then take it!" The sight of the blade and the momentary loss of concentration cost the bodyguard his life as Macro punched him in the face with the boss of his shield and then, in one practised motion chopped off the head which rolled to the edge of the jetty, the lifeless eyes of the faithful retainer staring up at Faolan who saw the sword slip from his grasp once more.

As he saw the rest of Loegaire's men fall to the swords of the Romans, he turned to the captain and said dully, "You may hoist your sail now. There is nothing left for me here."

The captain bit back the reply which might have cost him his life and quickly ordered his men to hoist sail before they were wrecked on the shore. Idwal and Angus had taken advantage of the focus on the battle for the sword and withdrawn their men the Eagle which was trying to pull away with the last few warriors alive on the jetty attempting a leap for life.

"Rufius! Kill those barbarians on those ships, let the others drown."

Rufius switched his volleys from the men in the water to the men on the Eagle and soon the survivors were forced to shelter beneath shields as the deadly arrows swept the decks. Eventually, the only ones remaining were the dead and the wounded. Macro watched, in satisfaction, as those who were in the water finally succumbed to the body filled estuary and drowned.

"Gather up the prisoners. Capsarii, see to the wounded. Rufius, we failed again and our foe has escaped."

Rufius swept a hand around the body littered beach. "More of the barbarians lie in Britannia than will make it back to their haven in Manavia."

"Yes Rufius and the men have done well but there are Brigante women now who are slaves and in that I failed." He turned to Macro and Marcus. "You two did well but I hope that the defence of that sword will not become a regular feature of our battles."

Marcus smiled sheepishly, "No sir. It's just that when it is in your hand it takes over and seems to control you."

"Then perhaps you might consider leaving it somewhere safe?" The look of horror on the face of those who had sworn an oath to it almost made Cassius smile but instead he shook his head and said, "Get your oath sworn to make crosses. We are going to make a statement here."

By the time that the wounded had been attended, the dead placed on byres, the forty crosses were ready. The timber had been found in a large hut, as Rufius had surmised, "Obviously intended for Manavia. I wonder what they would have built?" It had seemed appropriate to punish the villagers who had to have been complicit in the evacuation and the loss of revenue would hurt them.

Every barbarian who had not died was crucified, their hands and ankles broken by hammers and their sides pierced by blades. The troopers ignored the pleas for a warrior's death as they remembered the pitiful cries of the captive children and their dead comrades. Those younger troopers who had never witnessed a crucifixion were horrified by the sight. Sextus looked at the faces and said," It is a slow and inevitable death. Some will take four or five days to die. Look and remember."

One of them had a quizzical expression, "Why has the Decurion Princeps done this? Why not just kill them as we did before?"

"He is letting the village know that this is the punishment for rebellion and it will be a sign to those from Manavia that this is their reward. They will see the crosses and the corpses and they will remember."

The troopers of the oathsworn were gathered around Macro and Marcus who were helping the capsarii tend to their wounded comrades. One of the younger troopers went up to Macro to look at his two swords. "Are you never afraid sir? You seem to have a charmed life and you don't even have the Sword."

Macro smiled, "I do not need the Sword. There has never been a warrior who can defeat me." The words were spoken with neither bravado nor arrogance. "I will never be killed by a warrior, I know that and it makes fighting simpler."

Marcus snorted, "Not for a brother who is not privy to this remarkable knowledge."

Macro laughed, "Perhaps that is why a warrior will never kill me for I know that my brother and the famous Sword are there to protect me." He glanced at the oathsworn who were taking in every word. "And of course, the oathsworn."

They all shouted, "The Sword!" making Rufius glance over in irritation.

"What now sir?" Antoninus had grown up in this campaign and seemed to ooze confidence. Cassius smiled at the enthusiasm.

"Why Antoninus? What would you have us do now? Cross to Hibernia and fight the island or go north and defeat the Pictii?"

"Sorry, sir I just…"

"No son. I am just teasing. Don't lose the enthusiasm. You have done well."

"Ships coming in!"

Antoninus looked around in shock. "Are they coming back?" It was only half a day since the barbarians had departed.

Rufius peered out to sea and then laughed, "Well bugger me! That is '*The Swan*' and two biremes of the Classis Britannica. What in Hades are they doing here?"

"I don't know Rufius but perhaps Antoninus' desire for action has prompted the Allfather and the Parcae to provide it!"

Chapter 14

The decurions all gathered around the jetty as the small flotilla edged its way in. The two biremes of the classic Britannica dropped anchor half a mile off the shore but Hercules nudged and tacked his way to the jetty. "Julius Demetrius! Sir!"

As Hercules' men were hurling lines for the decurions to catch the Legate leaned over the rail. "I can see that we were too late. Sorry."

"How on earth…?" Cassius shook his head, this was not a conversation to be shouted, "I'll wait until you are ashore."

Rufius tied the bow rope off and grinned up at Hercules. "I thought I had seen the last of you, you old pirate."

Before the captain could answer Furax jumped the two paces from the side of the ship to the jetty. "Rufius!"

"Furax! You are a long way from Rome. Are you a sailor yet?"

The erstwhile street urchin and thief grinned cheekily at Hercules. "Getting there but I have to wait until he is asleep to steer the ship."

"Little bugger!" Hercules wandered off muttering but Rufius could see the twinkle in his eye.

"You have grown. The last time I saw you, you were half the size."

"Hercules says it is down to a life at sea and the better food we eat."

"I take it you had an interesting voyage?"

The boy's eyes widened. "We sailed all the way around the coast." He dropped his voice and leaned in to speak conspiratorially, "I thought we were going to sail off the edge of the world and so did Hercules but the senator, well he was confident and kept saying, '*Agricola did it and so can we.*' The cliffs were higher than at Surrentum and the waves so big that I thought we would be swallowed whole." He looked seriously at Rufius, "The thing is Rufius; we didn't see a single person from leaving Coriosopitum to landing here. No-one, not a single ship of any description. It is as though no-one lives up there." He shuddered, "I didn't like it. I prefer people!"

"Come on, let's go and find Macro and Marcus. I am sure they will be delighted to see you."

Cassius nodded as the two went off. "He has grown and seems a much happier youth."

"He and Hercules are good for each other. The old man dotes on him and he will be master of '*The Swan*' eventually." Julius scanned the detritus of the battlefield. "It looks as though you had a hard time."

"One of the hardest we have endured and I am sorry, Legate, for I have let you down."

"Let me down? How/"

"The Irish have fled to Manavia with Brigante captives. We were only able to save some; at least Metellus was responsible for saving some."

"Your humility does you justice Cassius but you were given an impossible task; the Governor knows it as do I. That is why I am here. The assignment is not over. We are going to Manavia, we are going to recapture the captives and let this Red Queen know that raids can go two ways. She feels inviolate in her little rocky empire. She is in for a hard lesson, no-one steals from Rome and gets away with it."

Cassius glanced out at the ships in the bay. "Is that why you have brought the ships? They have more troops aboard?"

"No Cassius, the frontier is not secure enough yet, it is up to you and your men I am afraid. There is no rest for you. Come on board, I have some wine and we can discuss my plan, and Cassius, I am not sending you to do what I will not, I am coming with you."

Macro's face lit up for the first time in months when he saw the irascible Furax. "What in Hades' name is Hercules feeding you? Sea monsters?"

"No just fish and hardtack," his face became serious, "but we did see sea monsters when we rounded the northern coast."

The decurions all became attentive. "Really?" asked Rufius, "genuine sea monsters?"

"Yes, they were huge beasts, bigger than a horse. They had two enormous teeth as long as a legionary sword, huge whiskers but no arms and they lay on the rocks and roared at us."

Rufius looked sceptical. "Have you been at the spirits?"

"No he is speaking the truth," one of the sailors who had been tying up the ship came over. "He isn't exaggerating either. I was sure that they were the guardians of the edge of the world, like Cerberus at Hades, you know, but the Senator he was calm as you like. *'We will not sail off the edge of the world'* he says *'but they are fine monsters, perhaps we will come one day and hunt them, captain'.*" He shuddered, "He can hunt them without me. They looked like they could bite a man in two and chew him up.'

"I apologise for doubting you young Furax. You have, indeed, had quite an adventure."

Furax had a happy, confident look. "I wasn't sure, after meeting Sergeant Macro if I wanted to be a horseman or a sailor but I am sorry Sergeant, I have chosen the sea. It is much more interesting."

"No need to apologise Furax and now it is Decurion Macro, but I quite envy you and I will come with the Legate when he hunts this beastie."

"The Legate?" Furax looked confused.

Rufius ruffled his hair, "The Senator but he has been promoted by the Emperor and is now our general, our Legate."

Just then Cassius came on deck. "Decurions if you could drag yourself away from the young mariner the Legate and I would like to discuss our next moves."

As they went aboard Macro shouted over his shoulder, "And I want to hear more about these monsters and your sea adventures."

Hercules had arranged sacks around the quarter deck for them to sit upon whilst Cassius stood, like a schoolmaster lecturing his students. "We have a new task, gentlemen. Some of you are going to become marines." If he had grown another body part he could not have surprised them more. Even Rufius' jaw dropped. Cassius smiled. "We are going to Manavia and we are going to rescue the Brigante captives."

He glanced over at his brother. He had felt the surge of excitement through his body and when he looked at his eyes he saw that they were actually gleaming in anticipation. He hoped that this was not another of the Parcae tricks.

Cassius continued once the initial murmurings had ceased. "Now not all of you will be going. One of you will have to remain behind with the wounded, the horses and to await the arrival of Metellus and his charges. The rest of you and your men will sail in the three ships here, to be landed as close to the slave pens as we can and when the guards are asleep, slip ashore and rescue them."

There was a silence and a smile played around the lips of the Legate and Cassius as they wondered who would have the courage to ask the inevitable questions. They knew it would not be Macro for he would go into a fire without regard for himself. He did not need to ask questions; he just had to be given a task. Sensible, cautious Rufius was the one who stepped forwards. "Firstly sir, how do we know where the slave pens are and secondly aren't there at least a thousand barbarians who would love to get us on their turf and spend six months killing us?"

"Good questions. To answer your first question Hercules and those on '*The Swan'* will find out where the slave pens are by sailing into the port and asking. Secondly, we are not going there to start a war, we are too few." Macro's snort of disappointment made everyone turn and look at him. "For we are too few. But we will make sure that we let them know we have landed and retaken their prize. Any further questions?" There was an embarrassed silence. "Oh, surely there is one hanging on your lips?" Again silence. "Surely you want to know who is staying behind?"

"Every decurion's face showed the same expression and made the same plea, '*not me, please not me'*.

"I will put you out of your misery. It will, I am afraid, have to be you, Graccus. Your wounds make it impossible for you to move quickly." Seeing the wisdom of the decision but cursing the barbarian who deprived him of the task, he nodded. "Gather your men together but do not tell them anything. We do not know yet who we can trust in this nest of vipers. We will tell them when we are on board. As with Decurion Graccus bring no-one who is wounded. Make sure your men all have sound equipment for this will be the most difficult task the ala has ever performed."

There were one hundred and fifty troopers aboard the three ships. Cassius, Decius and Calgus boarded one of the biremes whilst Rufius, Antoninus and Lucius boarded the second. They all had the largest turmae and '*The Swan*' was the one at the greatest risk and Julius, sensibly, decided not to put the largest force aboard her. Marcus, Macro and Drusus joined the Legate aboard the cramped trader. They would not have the luxury of being able to walk around the open deck as their companions for they were sailing into the heart of the druidic domain whilst the biremes would remain hidden from view.

The port to which they were heading was on the northeastern shore of the island. The sullen villagers at Itunocelum had been questioned about the geography and the currents around the remote island. When Julius pointed out that he was leaving troops in their town with orders to kill the headman should they not return then they became sulkily cooperative. They had told the Legate that there were three main settlements; one in the west, one in the south-east and the main one in a large bay at the northeastern end of the island. They also found out that it was close to the druidic centre and Morwenna making it doubly dangerous. Cassius had tried to persuade Julius not to give Macro the opportunity to desert and gain revenge upon his mother but Julius was confident that, having been promised by Macro that he had no such intentions he would be better placed aboard '*The Swan*'. Cassius had to agree that Macro and Marcus were excellent Explorates and if they needed someone to sneak ashore and scout out the lie of the land they were the best two but Macro's behaviour of late had led Cassius to doubt the boy who had changed in the last two years.

All of that was forgotten as the two biremes heaved to, north of the island to await the return of '*The Swan*' with news of the location of the slave pens. The small ship suddenly felt very lonely to the Legate as he went below decks to the dark and somewhat pungent heart of the ship. The three decurions and the one turma were huddled together in the cramped space. They had no concept of place and speed just the rise and fall of the boat in the northerly swells. The troopers of the turma had all emptied their stomachs and the smell of the vomit was adding to the general smell of decay. The Legate hoped that they would have recovered by the time they went ashore or they would be useless for the task in hand. Everything now depended upon the old man who was now steering the ship.

Up on deck, glad to be away from the smells which occasionally wafted to him, Hercules was going over in his head the story he and Julius had concocted. He called over Furax. "Now have you got this story straight?"

Furax sighed, for the first time since joining the legate and the captain, Furax would be using his old skills of the Lupanar, deception and trickery. "Of course. We were going to the land of the Pictii to buy slaves when we were hit by a storm and driven south. We went to Itunocelum to buy spares for the ship but they had none and they told us of Manavia." He spread his hands like a market magician who has just deceived his audience.

"Well done but don't get cocky. This is a dangerous game we play." He shouted so that all the crew could hear. "No-one goes ashore but me and the lad and no-one, get that, no-one comes aboard. If they realise we have Romans aboard we are all doomed."

The crew needed no further urging and they all made the sign against evil. The Red Witch's reputation terrified them all. Furax was the only one who was curious about this woman. He had heard so much from everyone and they all seemed to fear and respect her in the same breath. He wondered what she was really like.

"Land ho!"

"Right boys this is it, lower the mainsail, we'll take her in on the foresail. Be ready to luff when we see the lie of the land."

When Hercules saw the island, it reminded him of Capreae but bigger. There was a large hill as at Capreae, too small to be called a mountain, in the middle which seemed to divide it up. He could see the cluster of buildings around the small wooden jetty and then a ribbon of dwellings leading up to a natural mound where there was a palisade suggesting a fortress or citadel of some kind. He made a note of all this to relay to the senator. There appeared to be a large number of ships and boats of all shapes and sizes. Hercules presumed this was the fleet which had rescued the raiders. He just hoped that they had left the vicinity of the port; they might just want to ask some awkward questions and, even worse, wish to board.

Judging the distance and the wind was a skill which Hercules had acquired over many years and Furax watched in admiration as the old man looked at the sail, the wake and the land to decide the most opportune time to give his orders. "Lower sail!" The sailors quickly furled the foresail and the ship visibly slowed. She still had seaway and gently turned to touch the jetty. As she moved away from the wooden jetty the sailors threw coils of ropes over the side to act as buffers whilst two of the nimbler crewmen leapt to the mooring posts with the two main hawsers in their hand. '*The Swan*' was securely tied to the jetty within moments of arrival and the usual hangers-on nodded their approval.

If this had been a Roman port then some wizened official would have scurried up with a list of demands and taxes. Hercules wondered what the equivalent was here. His curiosity was soon satisfied as two druids, identifiable by their uncut hair and beards and the garlands of herbs and mistletoe around their necks walked up to the ship, assessing its worth as they did so. "Well judged captain. Many others would have damaged both their ship and our jetty. We are two of the leaders of the village. May we ask your business?"

Although politely put there was an air of a threat about their words and Hercules noticed the small gang of armed men who were within twenty paces. "We were heading for a port north of the Roman frontier to pick up some slaves when we hit a bad storm which drove us all the way to Itunocelum. We had hoped to buy some spares there for many of our ropes were damaged and the foremast weakened. They had none but they told us that you might be able to supply our needs."

The answer seemed to satisfy the druids but the second one asked. "Did you see Romans there?"

"No, but the villagers told us that the Romans had been there and there had been a battle of sorts. We did see crosses on the hillside." The Senator had impressed upon Hercules to keep as close to the truth as he could. "I was just glad we had missed them." He tapped his nose. "The Romans and I don't always see eye to eye. They want too much tax."

Now fully satisfied the hint of a smile appeared on the two men's faces. "Then you are welcome here. We charge no taxes merely berthing fees. It is one gold piece for every seven days berthing."

"But I only need one day and then I will be off again!"
Hercules managed to put the expected indignation into his voice.
It was an exorbitant fee but the Senator was paying.

Openly grinning now, the first druid said. "Those are our
terms. And we expect payment up front." He held out his hand.
They might be religious men but Hercules could see that they
were businessmen as well. He tossed the coin down which they
bit to test it. "Now you are welcome and you will find what you
need in the settlement and if you want slaves then we have a new
batch just in. They will be put up for auction with the new moon.
Do you wish to view them?"

This was working out even better than they had planned.
"Well if it will save me a trip," he turned to Furax and winked,
"Shall we go and view the slaves then?"

"Oh yes, grandfather!" Furax played the part well.

As they left the ship Hercules said, to the two druids but
loudly enough for the armed gang to hear, "No-one allowed on
board. Understand me. I think one gold piece should guarantee
privacy."

The two druids looked at each other, the point having been
well made, they nodded to the armed gang who slouched off,
disappointed that they would have no fun that day.

Below decks, the Legate's party breathed a collective sigh of
relief. They were safe, at least for the time being. They now had
to wait in the increasingly stuffy and smelly hold, helpless to
affect the course of action and securely in the hands of an old
man and a young boy.

Furax was really enjoying the day. The port was different
from anything he had ever seen. It was the first place outside of
the Roman world and everything was made of wood. There were
no roads merely tracks which the boy assumed would become a
muddy morass once the rains came. He wondered how wheeled
vehicles would get up the slope they were climbing to, what they
both assumed, would be the slave pens. Hercules was also
interested but he was becoming worried when he saw the number
of guards and armed warriors who seemed to be camped around
the lower hillsides. Evidence of the recent conflict could be seen
as druids attended to the wounds of the warriors. He could now
see where the pens were for there was a plateau below the fort. It

looked as though the guards and the ramparts would have a direct view of the insides of the pens. Hercules was glad that the problem was the Senator's and not his.

When they reached the pens Furax and Hercules initiated part two of the plan. "Grandfather, can I have a look around?"

"Yes but don't get lost and don't get into trouble." As the boy raced away Hercules said, sadly to the druids. "His mother and father were killed when the Romans invaded his village. He hid amongst the dead." The look the druids exchanged told Hercules that they had bought the story.

"A fine set of slaves are they not? Mainly Brigante, women and children but we have some men slaves as well. The Brigante are fresh meat but we have others who have been captives for longer. They are kept on another part of the island. They will be brought here for the sale. These are just the new ones. What is it you seek?"

Hercules pointed at the women and children who sat abjectly well away from the men. "The prices in Aquitania are too high. It is a peaceful province and we need wars to make slaves. I am hoping for bargains and a quick profit. We need house servants and children who can be specifically trained to perform particular tasks. When did you say the auction will be?"

"The new moon."

"Good for I will have the chance to sail north and look at these Pictii slaves." He wrinkled his nose. "The trouble with the Pictii are the tattoos. Many fine homes will not entertain them but they are cheap and they are plentiful. Well thank you for your help. When I find the boy we will buy the masts and ropes and set sail on the morning tide."

Furax's job was to check the defences of the fortress. He wandered up the steep trail. He noticed that it turned sharply right and he knew enough from talking to the troopers that this was a good defensive strategy as it allowed arrows to be poured at the side of an attacking force. He saw that there were only two towers by the gate but they were manned. He quickly counted twenty sentries. One of the guards noticed his interest and wandered over. "What do you want then young 'un?"

"I have never seen a fort before. Are all the guards as tough as you?"

The guard took the flattery as genuine praise and puffed his chest up. "I am one of the tougher ones believe me. Where are you from?"

Furax pointed innocently down to the harbour. "That ship there. We are getting spares but we have to leave soon. I would love to look inside the fort."

"Sorry son. There is a big meeting going on in there, Princes, Druids, Chiefs, there are even some Roman deserters in there."

Furax glanced through the open gate and his heart almost rose into his mouth. "Oh, maybe next time. Thank you for being so kind sir."

"No problem son." As Furax raced away to rejoin Hercules the guard turned to his companion. "What a polite young lad. Makes me almost want to have a son myself."

His companion sniffed. "More like you fancy a fuck, you horny old bastard!"

"Ah there you are grandson, where have you been?"

"Exploring!" Furax then added under his breath, "We need to get out of here fast!"

Hercules trusted the boy enough to believe him. As they passed by the ship's chandlers Hercules went in and made a couple of unnecessary purchases for the ship in case the druids checked up on them and then the two of them made it back to the ship as quickly as possible. As they went on board Hercules turned to the first mate. "Get ready for sea we may need to leave in a hurry. Furax saw something."

Once in the hold, Furax explained what he had seen. "I saw some of the men who were in the ala. The deserters who fled."

Julius looked doubtful. "How can you be sure? It was some time ago." He peered at the boy to see if this was some story he had told to impress them.

"The guard said that they had Roman deserters meeting with the Prince and the Witch and when I looked in I recognised one; the big one who didn't like anyone at the fort and was always frowning. He had a funny name like, the hand or..."

"The Fist!"

"Yes that is it, The Fist. I saw him."

"Well that complicates things. Did he see you Furax?"

"No I saw him from the side and then I ran away."

"Well we are in the clear then. We just stay on board."

"Not quite so easy Macro. If the druids start talking about a ship and a young lad then The Fist might remember Furax."

There was a silence as they all considered what the options were. "If we leave too early it will look suspicious."

"I have told the crew to be ready to leave quickly. The trouble is the tide won't be perfect until the morning. We could get out tonight but it would look strange. No ship would risk unknown waters at night."

"We will have to bluff it out then but be ready to cast off if anyone approaches the ship." Julius looked around. "I am just not certain that I can stay cooped up here all night."

Hercules smiled, "As soon as it is dark you and your men can sneak up on deck and sleep in the open. To be honest you are all stinking my ship out."

One of the troopers said indignantly, "We are stinking it out! I have been in better-smelling latrines!"

Chapter 15

The council which was meeting was more of a war cabinet than anything else. Faolan, Angus and Creagth were reporting the success of their raid whilst, at the same time, The Fist and his men were asking for sanctuary on the island. Morwenna and the three senior druids had convened the meeting as it seemed everyone would have something to contribute. Morwenna was not as disappointed as Faolan that the raid had not resulted in more destruction. She had learned in the years of her long battle with Rome that small victories could sometimes result in better outcomes rather than one cataclysmic slaughter. In her experience, Rome had an inexhaustible supply of men from her vast Empire and her aim was to make Britannia untenable and not worth the effort to save. The problem, as Morwenna had come to realise, was that it was a rich province. The wheat which they farmed in the southern half of the province was a supplement to the sometimes problematic Egyptian harvest; the copper and tin further south was also invaluable for a nation so reliant on weapons of war. The gold of Wyddfa was also a very attractive lure. It was in the north where the Romans lacked riches and that was Morwenna's hope. If she could make the loss of Roman lives too expensive then they might move south with a line from Deva to Lindum and she could return as Queen of the Brigantes.

She looked again at the motley and disparate group of men gathered before her. The plainly dressed Roman deserters led by the huge brute called, The Fist, and she could see why he was called that were in complete contrast to the gaudily arrayed warriors around Faolan. For the first time, she had access to someone who knew the Roman war machine. When she had fought alongside Decius Sallustius it had not been the same for he knew of Roman Britannia but he had never served in the army and that was the subtle difference. The Mother had, once again, delivered to her all the elements which would contribute to Rome's downfall. This time she had to harness them all effectively and not waste the good fortune which had come her way.

Faolan's sulky face showed his feelings quite clearly and Morwenna thought that he needed someone to guide him to help him become a great leader. That was not her but she wondered about her daughters. Angus had told her that Faolan was not one of the normal Hibernians who were totally immersed in honour and glory; she now knew that this Prince was more political than any she had met. That could be used but he would need to mask his feelings more. She knew from whence came his impatience; he had expected to be the centre of attention and the arrival of the deserters had detracted from that. She would have to take charge and energise the gathering or risk losing the support of all of the players who were gathered before her.

"We have introduced ourselves and we can now move on to the next, most important discussion, where do we go from here?"

Faolan leapt to his feet. "I do not see why we have to discuss my business and the business of my people with a Roman, and a Roman deserter at that!"

If he hoped to rile The Fist into action he failed for the ex-trooper sat with an impassive face drinking the wine before him. "Prince Faolan we are here to discuss the island business. This Roman wishes to settle amongst us and receive sanctuary. That is important and there is a price." The Fist's hooded eyes flickered as they took in her statement. Here it was the huge fee he would have to pay for safety. "The price may not be gold, although gold is always welcome, but knowledge, information and advice." When the Roman visibly relaxed Morwenna knew that she had read him right. "You, Prince Faolan, wish to return home to take from your cousin your lands and become king. Is that not so?"

Flashing a filthy look at the Romans he snarled, "It is and how does their presence help me?"

Sighing at his apparent naivety and his lack of vision the Red Witch explained, as though to a child. "We will hold the sale of the captives soon and when that has taken place we will all be richer. You will then be able to hire more mercenaries and more weapons." She paused. "When you fought the Romans did you see their war machines?"

"We did when we burned their fort why?"

"You did not see them used?"

Faolan and Creagth laughed, "No for the soldiers who would have used them were dead."

"Angus, tell the Prince of these weapons and their effect."

The Fist smiled. He knew that she had not asked him because Faolan would have dismissed it as lies but the Hibernian appeared to respect the red-haired warrior. "It works like a huge bow and the men operating it wind it back and fire a bolt. I have seen them used and they go through not just one man but a line of ten and every man dies. The Roman legions have one for every hundred men. If we had attacked a fort frontally then we would have been slaughtered."

Faolan looked thoughtful. "So?"

"Has your cousin seen Roman soldiers and met Roman weapons?"

"Of course not."

Sighing again for the obtuse man so hated Romans that he could not see where he was being led. "So if you had some Roman war machines, some Roman armour, weapons and tactics do you think it would help you and your warband to seize the throne?"

Understanding lit up his face and his mouth opened slightly as he, finally, linked the ideas. "And this Roman could do that?"

The Fist spoke for the first time. "This Roman could do that. I could find men like us," he looked darkly into Faolan's eyes, "deserters and I could help you to buy the machines and weapons. You would not have to dishonour yourself by fighting alongside, deserters, but we would train the men you would use; your archers, your cavalry and your artillery."

Morwenna gave a subtle nod to the Roman to show that he had said the right thing in the right way. She could use this Roman. She liked a man who was only interested in money for they were more careful than glory hunters.

"Given those terms then how can I refuse?"

"However, Faolan, there is more to this bargain. When you have conquered your lands I would have this army fight for us to retake Britannia."

"You want my army? Ridiculous!"

"You intend to pay for an army to sit on your land and milk you dry of gold or will you get more gold and riches from Hibernia?"

Her comment was not lost on Faolan. He had had to go to Britannia to get the finance to take back his kingdom. He could not afford to pay for a huge army of warriors. Perhaps there was a way for him to benefit and keep his throne. "If you used my army then I would want a share of the profits."

Morwenna's look of triumph became s smile which lit up the room. "We will all share in the profits, Manavia, Hibernia and our new Roman adviser." They all raised their beakers to celebrate the union. The deserters with The Fist were not certain what the work would entail for them but their leader was happy and so were they.

Morwenna held up her hand for silence. "We will not have gold for a while but, Roman, where would you get these weapons and men?"

"Not near the frontier but further away perhaps Camulodunum. That is the largest city in the province and we are more likely to find disillusioned men there. It is also the place through which the weapons arrive from Rome and so we would have more chance of acquiring them."

"You would need a ship then?"

"It would save us crossing a country fired up by revolt and rebellion where every soldier is on the lookout for trouble."

"We will meet again on the morrow at the port and find a suitable ship for your journey."

One of the druids spoke for the first time. "It had better be early then for the tide turns in the night and some of the ships we used to bring the men back from the raid will have sailed."

"Then we will meet before dawn breaks."

As the crew of '*The Swan*' and the troopers enjoyed the fresh air Hercules peered intently at the citadel. He had been watching lights flicker, brighten and then observed a line of them descending the trail he and Furax had taken the previous day. Someone was coming. He went to the seaward side and glanced out to the black murky waters. The tide was not perfect but it was getting better. Eastwards there was just the hint of a glimmer of dawn. Although no other ships were stirring Hercules could feel in his bones that they ought to move. He woke Julius and his first mate. "I think we should sail."

The First Mate looked at the blackness with a perplexed expression, not helped by being woken from a deep sleep. "Has the tide turned?"

Hercules pointed to the line of torches making its way down to the jetty. "I think someone is up and about. Better we look keen than get caught with Roman soldiers on board. Senator, get your men below. Wake the crew!"

The troopers had been only half-asleep for sleep in an enemy stronghold was not easy and quickly descended to the hold. As the crew began to get the ship ready for sea, Hercules nodded to Furax. "Up the mainmast, you can see who this is and then help to guide us out."

The agile boy leapt up the ropes and scampered to the top of the mainmast. "There are about ten of them and one is a woman."

Hercules worst fears were confirmed, it was Morwenna. "Cast off forrard. Get the foresail up." Lying in the lee of the island Hercules knew that it would take some time to tack away from the jetty. The first dim rays of the sun lit up the eastern horizon and gave Hercules hope that they might just be seen as being keen to sail north. The torches were now only two hundred paces away and the captain could now see Morwenna, some Hibernian warriors and the unmistakeable hulk that was The Fist. The boy had been right and had he not told them then all of their plans might have ended in bloodshed on the Manavian beach. As it was they were not safe yet but Hercules could see a gap between them and the jetty. "Hoist the mainsail!" As the sail unfurled and they moved a little further out of the lee of the island '*The Swan*' leapt forward as though eager to be away from the land.

"Rocks to port!" Furax's shrill voice made the captain stick the rudder over. The last thing they needed was to be wrecked on the rocks.

Morwenna frowned as she saw the small trader tacking away. "He is leaving a little early is he not?"

One of the druids nodded, "He is a slaver. He came yesterday for repairs and he is going to return for the auction. I think he is sailing for the land of the Pictii to buy some from them."

"A pity his ship would have been perfect for the Roman to use."

The Fist shrugged, he knew nothing of boats or water. "It matters not to me. I just need a ship to get where I need to go and for a captain who will obey me."

The druid who had spoken to Hercules pointed at the departing Swan. "That one would not have suited. I got the impression that the old man was a careful businessman who looked after himself and his grandson."

"An old man and a boy?"

"Aye why?"

"I am not sure but it sparks a memory. It will come to me eventually. I will leave it to you to choose the ship. For you will be paying," he wanted them to know that he would do as they wished but he would be paid for his services. He wondered why he had not thought of this before; it was better pay than the army that was for certain and safer. He thanked the Allfather for the day Gaius Brutus had walked into his life.

Faolan was cold and he was tired. He didn't know why he had to be on this cold jetty, on this unbelievably fresh morning. He glanced at the departing ship. "That one is certainly fast. We could do with one as quick ourselves."

The druid nodded. "If he could have got his spares at Itunocelum he would not have come here. Fortunately, they had none there."

Morwenna's interest was piqued. "He came from Itunocelum? Did you see him there?"

Angus shook his head. "When we left there were no ships and only the wounded we left."

"Aye well, they were crucified."

They all looked at the druid. "How do you know?"

"The captain said he saw the crosses on the beach."

"Did he see the Romans?"

"No, he said they had gone."

"Then he was lying!" They all looked at The Fist. "The commander of those troops would have made sure that you did not come back and that those on the crosses were not rescued. They would stay there for a few days, at least. What did they do when they landed?"

"Bought a mast and rope. The old man and the boy went to the slave pens and then the boy had a look at the citadel."

"The boy was he cheerful, always smiling?"

"Yes, why…"

"They are Roman spies. I saw them at Coriosopitum before I left the service of Rome. That is why they have fled."

Morwenna looked at the other ships on the jetty. "We need to get after them."

Faolan shook his head; he had been watching the departing ship as it sped into the darkness to the north. "You will never catch them and you do not know in which direction they went. They could have changed course as soon as they were out of sight. The question we ought to ask is why they were here?"

They all looked at each other until The Fist pointed a finger at Morwenna. "They were looking for you." He turned to Angus. "Did you say that the Sword of Cartimandua was wielded by these warriors?" Angus nodded. "And was there a warrior who was a fearsome fighter with red hair and eyes like," he pointed at Morwenna, "those."

When Angus nodded, Morwenna said, "Macro."

"Macro indeed. Your son is hunting you, my queen."

Rather than being discomfited by the comment, Morwenna seemed elated. "The Mother is all-powerful for she brings the sword to the island for you my Prince and my son to me so that I may rid the earth of his stain for once and for all. We keep a watch for the return of the ship and we lay a trap. I do not want to scare them off. I think, Roman, that we will delay your departure for I can see that the Mother brought you to us for a purpose and you are too valuable for us to lose. When they return we will all win."

Hercules made the rendezvous with the two biremes well to the west of the island. If there had been a pursuit then Julius knew they would head north and the west would be the last place they would look. The captains from the ships and the decurions all met aboard '*The Swan*'. "We now know where the pens are and we know that we have got seven days to get them out."

One of the bireme captains said, "Plenty of time."

Julius shook his head, "Not so. Our departure was not the one we had planned and we may have been compromised."

"You mean they know what we intend?"

"I don't know Cassius but I think they will be looking for this ship so we cannot do as we planned and sail back into the harbour. Whilst we were sailing to this meeting I had the captain sail in closer to the island. There is a flat plain with a high area to the south. If we land the troops in the west then they can make their way the seven or so miles to the pens. We will sail around the island and await a signal. They have no warships in the harbour and the ballistae on board will help the evacuation."

"Signal?"

"Yes, Rufius. If you fire the fort then we should see that!"

"Fire the fort?"

"Yes. This is how we will have to do it. They will be watching the front of the fort and the pens more carefully than the rear. You kill the guards at the rear of the fort, work your way around the ramparts killing the other sentries. Once you have done that then the rest can free the prisoners and make their way to the jetty. You then fire the fort and come down to the jetty. They will have to put the fire out, which we can see, and should give you the time to escape."

Cassius was not convinced. "How quickly can you get inshore and protect our retreat?"

Hercules spat over the side. "We can wait just a mile offshore. The biremes have oars and they can be at the jetty before the captives are down the slope. It will take me longer but it is the biremes you need."

"It will work Cassius. I am not sending you on a suicide mission. They will not be expecting trouble from the south. The hard part is scaling the walls and getting rid of the sentries."

"Sir." Furax's voice sounded very small.

"Yes, Furax?"

"The walls are only as high as a man if two men stood together they could help one over."

"Or use their shields as a ladder."

"Even better Rufius."

"No time like the present then Legate. Land us tonight!"

As the three ships edged in they used the four small skiffs to ferry the one hundred and twenty troopers who would be undertaking the mission. A turma was kept aboard the first bireme to act as relief should there be problems whilst trying to escape. Julius came ashore with Cassius. "We will stand off the shore tonight and await your signal."

Cassius said soberly, "If there is no signal sir then we have failed."

"You will not fail me."

They had checked that there were no dwellings on the beach they had chosen for their landing and the first skiff had contained Rufius, Macro and Marcus who had quickly spread out with eight of their men to act as scouts and to ensure that the rest of the landing was unopposed. As they watched Julius sail back to the ships the troopers felt very isolated and lonely. Only Rufius had operated outside of Britannia and he knew that everyone they met would be a potential enemy. "Right, no time like the present. Decurion Macro you take point and I will bring up the rear."

They moved swiftly up the gentle slope to the escarpment which stretched away westwards. There were stands of trees and hedgerows to provide some cover but the line of the hills edged in and out making Macro's job even harder. He had to be the first to see an enemy and then warn the rest. He had deigned to bring a shield as he did not want to be encumbered and, like most of the other troopers, he had left his helmet aboard '*The Swan*' for he wanted to be as mobile as possible. If it came to a standard battle and combat then they would have lost. Their only hope lay in subterfuge and stealth. With less equipment, the ala made good time travelling through the empty western lands. Macro halted the column three miles from the citadel. He could see it in the distance which meant that eagle-eyed sentries could see them.

"Well done Macro. Right men find some cover and get some rest." Cassius detailed four men to act as sentries whilst the rest rolled themselves in their brown cloaks and found whatever shelter they could. They had all eaten well aboard the ships and would not need food again. Fortunately Macro had chosen a place to hide which had a spring and everyone filled his waterskin. The night attack was something none had attempted before and everyone was nervous.

Macro and Marcus lay in a dell beneath an elder bush. "You will be careful, brother? No heroics and no reckless tactics. Our mother wants to see us both." Despite the apparent change in Macro, Marcus sensed that all was not well with his brother. There was nothing that you could put a finger on and both Cassius and Rufius felt that they had the old Macro back but Marcus knew better.

"Of course brother, besides you are the one with a sword that seems to attract attacks!" Marcus knew that Macro was correct; as soon as the sword was unsheathed every barbarian seemed to be willing to give their lives to try and take it.

"Nonetheless I will be happier when we are both aboard '*The Swan*'."

"In that, we are agreed. Now sleep!"

Chapter 16

The sentries on the walls had been warned that Roman soldiers might attack them and they had to ensure that the captives remained safe. It was impressed upon them to keep a vigilant watch for any strange ships entering their waters, especially Roman. All day they had scanned the horizon and been kept on high alert. As the guards changed in mid-afternoon, the old watch passed on their fears to the new one. "Watch out for the dusk, that is when I would attack."

The new watch had nodded their agreement, worrying about this enemy who was threatening their base. Rumours abounded about who it was from Morwenna's son to a band of gladiators. Manavia was a safe and sound stronghold, it had never been invaded; the druids stopped enemies from attacking but these godless Romans feared no-one. The guards stared intently out to sea each one desperate to be the one to see the ships and thwart the attack. They could see the Hibernian warband hidden in the huts and buildings close to the jetty. The sentries could see that their leaders had thought their strategy out well. When the ships returned, probably during the hours of darkness, the Romans would come up the trail to release the captives. Once away from their ships they would be slaughtered, caught between the citadel and the warband. The guards all knew that they would all gain much plunder from these Romans who were all so rich that even the ordinary ones could afford a sword, armour and a helmet; rich indeed. Until then they would huddle in their cloaks against the chill night air and watch for the flash of sail which would be their sign.

Rufius, Macro and Marcus were with Marcus' turma, crouching in the bushes forty paces from the wall. Macro could not believe how lax the Manavians were. The undergrowth should have been cleared for at least a hundred paces and there were no ditches! All that the thirty troopers were waiting for was the sign that the rest of the ala was in position, ready to fall upon the slave pens. Cassius and his men had further to go and they risked observation for they would have to be close to the front of the fortress.

The messenger silently appeared at their side and nodded. The turma went into action, with no need for words. In groups of threes, they bellied up to the wall, their faces and arms blackened and their brown cloaks wrapped around their bodies. To a watcher on the walls, had they been staring intently, all they would have seen was a shadow slowly moving across the ground. Once at the wall two men stood with a shield between them whilst the third awaited the signal. They had counted the guards and they knew that they had overkill, there were two jumpers to every guard, but they needed to be sure and to be silent. Rufius held up his hand and, as he dropped it, ten troopers ran up to the shield held by two of their comrades and jumped on it. In one motion the two men hurled it in the air so that the troopers appeared to fly over the ramparts. One sentry actually saw a trooper land next to him but he was so shocked and surprised at the sight of a man flying through the air that he did nothing, not daring to believe his eyes. He died with a sword thrust to the neck. All five sentries died as swiftly and their bodies dropped over the side. Once the other twenty troopers were helped up they split into two groups and made their way around the walls. There were ten more guards to be dealt with. The first on each side was taken quickly which left one on the other sides and the difficult ones, the final eight at the front. Rufius signalled for troopers to stand where the guards had and while the rest hid in the dark shadows near to the wooden walls, Macro and Marcus each walked casually along the rampart. They were both seen by the lone guard who assumed it was their comrade; the mistake cost him his life.

They had almost succeeded but the last part would be the most difficult. Rufius and ten of the troopers slipped from the ramparts and went to the gates and the ladders which led to the two towers. Leaving two men to guard the gate the others followed Rufius up to the towers. There were three men in each tower and they would have to use weight of numbers to overcome them. Macro and Marcus watched them ascend and then, nodding to each other they took out the last guards as the ones in the tower were killed. One was thrown over the tower where he landed with what seemed to the turma, a noisy crunch and they all froze as they waited for the sound of alarm. There was none. Rufius went to the tower and gave the Explorate whistle. The rest of the ala quickly killed the guards at the pens who, like those in the citadel were watching for a seaborne assault.

Rufius turned to Marcus, "You open the gate and get the fire going. Macro, take half the turma and deal with anyone who comes out of the barracks. I'll go and help Cassius." Controlling the captives would be difficult as they had to remain silent.

Marcus and his half of the turma quickly piled wood around the two open gates. There was plenty. One of the troopers found some hay which they added and finally one of them found an amphora containing lighting oil which they threw on. Taking out his flint Marcus chipped with his steel. Sparks flew but the fire did not catch. He tried again but the wood was just a little too damp. One of the troopers suddenly took a knife and cut off a hunk of his own hair. He shrugged and handed it to Marcus who tried again. This time the hair sizzled and there was a glow. Marcus blew gently on to the feeble flame, his hands cupped around the outside. First one flame and then two leapt to the oil and suddenly the whole thing erupted. "Bring more wood, feed it!"

Rufius came racing in through the now much narrower opening. "We have trouble there is a warband at the jetty. We have the captives but we will need to force the passage until the ships can make it. As soon as the fire has caught bring Macro's men. You are the rearguard."

Marcus turned to his chosen man. "Keep the flames going and I will fetch the others."

Those in the barracks had heard nothing for the only noise was the faint crackle of wood. "Macro. There is a warband we have to leave; we are to form the rearguard."

"You take the men and I will follow." Marcus looked at him suspiciously. "I can run faster if I am not slowed up by others and I can make sure the fire is well lit. Now go!"

Reluctantly and with a heavy heart filled with dread Marcus left. The mission was to rescue the captives and he put his fears about his brother's state of mind to one side. He turned to the turma, "Take burning brands from the fire and set the fort on fire. We need to delay the garrison when they pursue us." The troopers needed no urging and they spread out to set the old timbers alight. As Marcus turned around to shout to Macro again he saw that two sleepy warriors who had emerged from the warrior's hall, probably to relieve themselves, stood lit by the glare of the inferno. Even as they turned to shout Marcus saw Macro race towards them, both blades drawn to silence them. He succeeded in killing them but not before they had shouted and men began to erupt from the hall. Macro fell back into the shadows and waved Marcus away. With a sinking heart, Marcus knew that his brother would have to make his own way out of the citadel. Even as he turned Marcus and his troopers could see the walls well alight. "Come on through the gate or it will be too late."

The last of the turma crashed through the narrowing opening and Marcus could feel his hair burning as they burst through. The ones who were anxiously waiting put out the spots of fire and ash on their comrades and Marcus formed them up.

"The decurion sir?"

"Don't worry Aelius he will climb over the rear of the walls and rejoin us."

The rescue appeared to be going better than they had hoped. Marcus could see the warriors making their way from the jetty and he could also see Cassius and two turmae forming a shield wall. The captives were just below Marcus and Rufius was busily organising them. When he saw Marcus he came to join him. "Well done, that will slow down the garrison." He glanced around, "Macro?"

"Coming over the back wall." Marcus almost believed the lie he had told his friend.

"The ships are here," Rufius pointed out to the bay where the two biremes were racing in and Marcus wondered if they would be able to stop. "Keep your turma as close to the captives as you can. When we reach the jetty, you will have to hold them off while we get these aboard the ships." He stared into Marcus' eyes. "That is when you will need your strength and iron. Do not throw it away before then." Marcus nodded; they both knew what Rufius really meant.

The column of troopers and captives moved slowly down the slope. The barbarians moved confidently knowing that the garrison would soon close the jaws of the trap. They did not know of the extent of the fire nor did they fully understand the tactics Cassius would employ. Marcus could see that Cassius had three lines of troopers with javelins and shields whilst the fourth were archers. As soon as the barbarians were in range flight after flight of arrows plunged down upon them. Bravely they pushed on urged by the prayers of the druids who chanted from within their ranks. As soon as they reached the line of troopers they found themselves outranged by the longer javelins and they furiously tried to force their way through.

Suddenly, from the bireme, came the sound of a buccina. To the barbarian's amazement, the leader of the Romans suddenly shouted, "Down, everyone down and lie on the floor!" The captives had been warned and the first forty captives dropped like stones. Before the barbarians could react to this, the visible effect of their druid's prayers, the bolts from the biremes bolt throwers sliced and scythed through the ranks of barbarians. Those in the front ranks, anticipating slaughtering the Romans watched in horror as their comrades were hurled forward, impaled by the deadly steel-tipped harbingers of death. A second buccina sounded and Cassius shouted, "Up!" Before the barbarians could react the bolt throwers changed their target to aim at the barbarians closer to the jetty. There the slaughter was even greater as the range was less than a hundred paces. As the jetty was cleared the reserved turma leapt ashore to finish off any who still showed the willingness to fight.

"Wedge!" Cassius and his vanguard bowled through the shocked and shattered ranks of warriors. The troopers along the sides killed any of the wounded there whilst the captives took their revenge on the unfortunates who lay in their path.

From his high vantage point, Marcus could see that the jetty had been cleared and the bolt throwers were now still, fearing to hit their own. There was a roar behind him and he saw, a hundred paces up the hill, the first of the garrison to escape the inferno. "About face!" His men obeyed instantly. "Appius keep walking down and warn us of the turns. We are going to retreat down to the jetty."

Before the barbarians reached the thin line of troopers someone on the biremes had shifted targets and, although at long range, the bolts began to hurl warriors back who had charged down the hill confident that they would wreak revenge on these Roman raiders. The one or two who made it through were easily slain.

"Sharp turn sir."

With an internal sigh of relief Marcus knew that they were almost at the jetty. As soon as he felt the wood beneath his feet he roared, "Halt!" This would be the test for the rearguard. Armed only with swords and lacking shields they would have to hold off the barbarians long enough for the captives to be boarded, not an easy task on warships designed to keep people off and not let them aboard. As Rufius and the other decurions joined him with their turmae Marcus felt a little easier for shields appeared and Marcus felt, for the first time, that they might just escape with their lives.

The bolt throwers were less effective now and the emboldened barbarians began to form up in a shield wall. Marcus recognised the red-haired warrior who had managed to thwart them so many times on the retreat. He marked him out for one day he would have to kill him. He noticed now that the man acted more as a general, directing his men to where he saw the weaker parts of the line. The warriors who came at them were enraged that they had been attacked in their homeland and they fought with a fury and a passion fired by the zealous druids whose chanting had been raised a notch at the arrival of the ships. The troopers, in contrast, met their passion with cold efficiency. They needed no druids to fire them up for they were protecting the innocent women and children. They didn't need the evocation of white-haired priests for they had the Sword of Cartimandua and an oath which bound them all together as a band of brothers.

Slowly the rearguard edged backwards. Like a mother giving birth, they allowed the barbarians to fall upon them and then withdrew a step until they could almost feel the sea a few paces behind them. Marcus allowed himself a moment to think that they would, after all, survive and then he peered up at the inferno that had been the citadel. He half-turned his head and his eyes met those of Rufius, almost like brothers themselves, they were both thinking the same thought, what had happened to Macro?

When Macro watched his brother and the turma escape the fiery gate he was calm. He had not intended to be left behind but he had, secretly, wanted to find the man who was responsible for Gaius' death, Faolan. He had imprinted his face on his mind when he had seen him on the beach at Itunocelum. Now that he was here in the citadel he wondered just how he would find him. As he crouched against the wall he saw warriors erupt from the barracks. There was confusion as the only chief in the citadel had been killed on the wall. They looked around for a leader and, luckily for Macro, their attention was focussed on the gate. Suddenly an idea came to him. He looked very similar to the warriors, his hair was shorter and he had mail armour but so did some of the warriors, courtesy of the garrison at Glanibanta. What did mark him as different was his lack of bracelets, armbands and religious tokens. He quietly slipped around to the rear of the barracks building and sought out the bodies of the sentries who had been slain earlier. He quickly removed as many items as he could and arrayed himself in them. Smearing mud on his face also made him look less like a Roman. By the time he had returned to the front of the building the warriors had formed themselves up and someone had taken charge.

Some of the words were unfamiliar to Macro as the dialect was unusual but he picked enough up to gather that they were going out of a small gate at the side. Passing through it Macro wondered how they had missed it. He placed himself in the middle of the band and jogged along with them. Dawn had finally broken and as they emerged on the bluff above the slave pens Macro could see that the battle was in full swing and his ala looked perilously outnumbered. He resisted a smile as he watched the bolt throwers decimate the ranks but, as the ala closed with the ships the good feelings changed to fear as the bolts began to hit those warriors around him.

Taking advantage of the confusion as the warriors took cover Macro raced down the trail keeping to the side away from the ships. He did not want the ignominy of being killed by his own men. The warriors from the garrison only saw a brave young warrior eager to close with the Romans and some followed him. Cursing his misfortune, he had no alternative but to continue down the sloping path. He could see Marcus at the front of the rearguard and it gave him hope but then he saw that there were a hundred men between him and safety. Off to the left, he saw some huts; behind them lay a low hill. He could just see the beach below the hill and spied a boat pulled up on the sand. Macro decided that he would make for the hill and, as the ships sailed away he would row out to them. The odds on getting through the massed warriors, even for someone as skilled Macro were slim. He also had, at the back of his mind, the thought that he would kill Faolan; he had not given up on a final act of heroism but so far his elusive prey was hidden from him. Revenge preyed heavily on his mind rather than the self-preservation which might have influenced another man.

Rufius glanced over his shoulder. Many of the captives were now aboard and one of the biremes was backing out. Rather than worrying why Rufius smiled for the next phase of the Legate's plan would begin. The bireme did not go out to sea but instead methodically rowed offshore and then came in again to ram and sink all the larger ships in the port. As they passed the smaller boats the marines hurled in pots of Greek Fire which set up a conflagration amongst the moored Manavian fleet. Rufius could see Julius Demetrius urging the captives aboard whilst Cassius directed the fire of the archers at those places where the thin line of troopers appeared to be in danger. The weight of their opposition and their exhaustion began to take its toll and the line was pressed further and further back. Finally, they heard the sound they had longed for, the buccina signalling 'withdraw'. The troopers already knew what to do; in pairs, one man lunged forward to make the enemy withdraw and then they ran back to the ship. The remaining troopers closed ranks with Marcus and Rufius as the point of the wedge. In the original plan, it would have been Macro but he was no longer an option.

Rufius nudged Marcus in the side and pointed to the knoll overlooking the jetty; too far away for a missile it, nonetheless, afforded the group there a fine view of the battle. Marcus saw the figure that Rufius had seen, there next to Faolan was The Fist. The deserter and his fellows were spectators with the barbarian leader. The ex-trooper saw them and ironically raised his blade in salute. Rufius murmured, "There will come a reckoning and I will see you crucified yet."

They heard Cassius' voice cry, "Down!" and as they dived to the floor they saw a barrage of arrows and javelins punch the barbarians back. "Now! On board! As quickly as you can!" They needed no further urging and they turned, suddenly surprised to see *'The Swan'* four paces away. They all leapt to the side and were unceremoniously hauled on board.

Glancing at the jetty, which was now burning at one end, Marcus could see that none of their comrades were moving but there were mercifully few of them. He heard Hercules shout, "Cast off!" and as he turned to see him he saw that most of the dead had been brought along with them. The barbarians would have only a handful of bodies to mutilate. Marcus just hoped that his brother was not amongst them.

The warriors following Macro hurled themselves to the ground as the volley of bolts flew at them. Macro judged his jump and leapt behind the huts. As he lay there, gathering his breath, he suddenly saw one of the raiders. It was not Faolan, but the warrior standing guard outside the large hut with garlands of mistletoe had been at the pass; could it be that Faolan, his enemy was inside the hut? The warrior was certainly on guard, and he was a chief. Macro slipped his pugeo into his left hand and walked around the far side of the hut. He could hear nothing from within but the sounds of the battle were such that it would have been difficult to hear even a raging row.

Creagth resented having to be on sentry duty but Faolan had insisted that the ordinary warriors were needed for the fray and he was guarding a more important treasure. The warrior looked enviously as he saw his comrades gaining honour as they fought man to man with the Romans. This was not the fight he had had at the pass, avoiding arrows, this was the way a warrior fought and he dearly wished he were there. He flicked his eyes to the right where he saw Faolan and the other chiefs directing the fight. A real warrior would not be watching, he would be fighting. In the last moments before Macro ended his life the warrior decided that, after the battle, he would leave Faolan and form his own warband.

Macro's razor-sharp blade sliced through Creagth's neck as though it was butter. The decurion lowered the dead body to the ground and scanned the area to see if he had been observed. When he felt secure he slipped inside the huge hut which was lit with just a fire in the middle. He peered around in the gloom for Faolan but the perfumed smell told him that it was not a warrior but a woman. The figure by the fire turned around and he saw that it was Morwenna, it was his mother.

As soon as the last trooper scrambled aboard, Hercules began to tack the boat away from the jetty where the flames had now taken a firm hold. There would be no ships leaving the port until they had built a new one. The two biremes had finished demolishing the boats and, under oars acted as a rear-guard for *'The Swan'*. Aboard the ships of the Classis Britannica the archers picked off any target which raised its head. The crews of the bolt throwers looked for an opportunity to eliminate larger numbers but the barbarians had decided that the artillery had no honour and were not worth risking their lives for. The captives were gone and, barring a sudden, cataclysmic change in the weather the three Roman ships would escape.

On the knoll, Faolan was seething with rage. A large portion of his army had been either wounded or killed and the captives, his fund for the future, had been snatched away. The druids busily laid curses on the departing ships making Faolan roll his eyes heavenward. He had had his doubts about the power of this religion before but if these druids could not even protect their sacred home then they were not worth listening to.

The Fist also smiled grimly. The druids had not prevented the Roman legionaries from sacking and desecrating the holy groves of Mona and they had failed again here. For himself little had changed. He still had his plunder and he might be in an even better position as the locals had suddenly become poorer. He could not see them being able to afford more weapons but perhaps the Witch Queen had secret funds.

On *'The Swan'*, Julius came over to Marcus to ask the question no-one else dared ask. "Where is Macro?"

"We were separated in the citadel and cut off by the fire. I didn't see him but he will have escaped. You know Macro, there is no man on earth who can hurt him. It was dark and there was confusion. I believe he will have escaped."

"If he wanted to."

Marcus looked in anguish at the Legate who had voiced his own fears. "No, he wanted to live, if only to kill him." Marcus pointed at the leaders who had kept well out of bolt range. "If he were still on the island then we would see him for he would be trying to kill Faolan. He will come to us."

Hercules, who was standing nearby with an arm around a tearful Furax, looked up at the sails. "We can potter around here for an hour or so." He pointed at the shore. "They can't hurt us and the gentle wind will just keep us steady. When the tide turns then so will the wind and we will have to leave. I can give your brother an hour or two."

Marcus' face filled with gratitude. "Thank you, Hercules."

Julius shrugged in surrender. "I had better go and tell our companions that we are going to potter around here for a while." He shook his head in wonder. "I cannot believe that potter is a nautical term."

Sniffing Hercules said, "Does the job doesn't it?"

The three ships sailed across the bay from east to west and back again. The barbarians who lined the shore wondered why? Did it presage a new and larger invasion? Were the ships coming back? On board the three ships there was an unbearable atmosphere as the tension could almost be seen and touched. All wanted Macro to return to the ala but none could, realistically, see him being able to do so. The only ones who really thought that he might return were Furax and Marcus. The others who knew him well, Julius, Cassius and Rufius thought that he had had the death wish and was now with the Allfather.

"Captain, can I go up the mast? I'll be able to see further."

As Hercules nodded Marcus whispered his silent gratitude. The slippery climber quickly made the top and, with his legs wrapped around the cross braces, peered earnestly to the shore. He had not been there long when he shouted, "I can see him! Marcus, he is there! He is heading for a boat and there are men chasing him!"

Without needing a word Hercules threw the helm over and then looked up to see if Furax had held on. Rufius and Marcus grabbed their bows as did the others. The two biremes saw them head inshore and by backing one bank and rowing with the other, turned in their own length and headed back in to give the unarmed trader much needed support. The first bolt flew over the surprised head of the first warrior but the second scored a hit. It was now a race to see who had the nerve and the will to get to Macro first.

"So, my son. I might have known that you would have had a hand in this. As always you and your father both have an unhappy knack of spoiling my plans but this time the Mother has led you to me, here where I rule, not Rome and here you shall die."

Holding his sword before him he advanced towards his mother. She was framed by the fire and her whole body seemed to glow with the blue and red flames dancing around her silhouetted body. Perhaps she had put something in the fire to burn that way but the effect was eerie. He kept his dagger in his left hand as he approached her for he knew that she was like a snake and could strike in many ways. He did not fear her magic but he feared the animal cunning of the woman who had borne him. He had faced many men in combat but his mother had a calmness about her which was disconcerting. She did not seem afraid and yet Macro knew that, even if she moved to escape he could throw his knife and kill her instantly for they were barely five paces apart. Every part of him was tense as he edged forward.

"Your men killed Gaius, my father, and you will die here in your sanctuary and then I will kill the leader of those men, Faolan, and finally I will rid the world of others such as you, wicked evil women who do not deserve to live."

"What a confident little cockerel you are and what a pity that you will not see the face of the one who slays you."

Macro caught a tiny movement in Morwenna's eye and knew that there was someone behind him. He reversed his dagger and stabbed it upwards feeling the crunch as it slid through bones to strike a vulnerable part of someone's body.

"Brynna!"

Just then he felt a sharp prick in his back and he half-turned to see Morwenna's daughter sliding dead to the floor and the dagger sticking in his thigh. He sensed movement and turned as Morwenna, eyes wide and snarling like a wild beast launched herself at him, her long nails like talons seeking his eyes. The pain in his thigh was bearable and, as he swivelled to the side he plunged his sword upwards ripping open his mother's stomach. She gave an ethereal scream which echoed throughout the settlement and fell backwards, her hands desperately trying to put her entrails back inside. She was in a pain such as she had never borne and she could not believe that the beast she had spawned had killed her. Her eyes lit up as she saw him standing over her and she gave a smile. "You are your mother's son and you have killed not only your mother but your half-sister, will the Allfather welcome you now?"

Taking the knife from his wound and sticking it into his belt with his own, Macro went a little closer. "I am not ready to meet the Allfather yet for I have other monsters to kill."

The smile was now even more cruel than it had been, "But you are dying. Come kiss your mother and we will die together."

Sickened by her twisted words and fearing her poison both literal and metaphorical he took his sword and crying, "Rot in Hades, you evil witch." With a mighty two-handed blow from his sword, he chopped off her head and ran from the hut. When he emerged, he saw that the cries had been heard by others and men were running from the knoll and the jetty towards him. Despite the sharp pain in his leg, he was able to run faster than they and he sprinted towards the beach and the boat. His heart soared as he saw '*The Swan*' and the biremes. He had not been abandoned. He glanced over his shoulder and noticed that they were closing. Neither of his legs seemed to want to run. He could feel himself sweating and he suddenly felt sick. He tightened his grip on his sword and ran as hard as he could. The boat was but ten paces away. He was aware of bolts and arrows flying above him and he felt, in a detached sort of way, that he had trained all those men to be so accurate. He threw himself and his mother's decapitated head into the boat, his weight and the momentum carrying it into the surf. He found that he couldn't move very well and he put his arms over the prow to paddle. As darkness descended upon him he heard a voice, seemingly far away, shouting, "Macro!"

Chapter 17

When Macro opened his eyes he found himself staring up at his brother, Furax and Rufius. "You gave us a scare, are you wounded?"

"Aye, the daughter of the bitch Morwenna stabbed me in the leg with a knife. It is just a scratch but I must be more tired than I thought for it is hard to lift my arms and my eyes feel heavy."

Marcus looked in terror at Rufius who turned and shouted, "Sextus!" The capsarius came with his bag of tools and herbs. "Stabbed in the leg but he feels sleepy and finds it hard to move."

"Roll him over." Sextus could see where the blade had entered and he took his knife and cut the cloth completely open to reveal the bare leg. "It looks like a shallow wound." He put a handful of spider's webs on it and doused it with vinegar. "This will stop the bleeding and stop the wound becoming dirty." Macro barely murmured. Sextus turned him over. "Who did this to you?"

Macro was about to ask why the stupid question when Rufius restrained him. "The witch's daughter with …." He feebly tried to take the sharp blade from his belt but could not.

It was easily recognisable as being alien to Macro and Sextus pulled it carefully from the belt. He sniffed it and then recoiled. Putting it on the deck he said, "No-one is to touch it. Furax, fetch some water." The water appeared as though by magic. Pouring a small amount in his beaker the capsarius added some charcoal and mixed it well. He lifted Macro's head and said, "Drink." Macro opened his eyes and looked confused. Sextus said, sadly and slowly, "You have been poisoned. The blade was covered in it." Macro drank. He coughed and he spluttered but he kept most of it down. As Sextus rose he caught the eye of Marcus and shook his head. Knowing the capsarius to be the best in the ala Marcus did not doubt his judgement but, as he fought back the tears he hoped that he was wrong. The charcoal would not be an antidote but would slow down the effects, the brothers would have time for a goodbye, that was all.

Macro opened his eyes. "I always said that there was no man who could ever defeat me. Perhaps I should have avoided women." He attempted a laugh but it came out as a mirthless grin.

"Sextus might be wrong, brother. The charcoal might work. It did when Marcus was poisoned by the witch."

"No, I can feel the life force leaving me. Tell our brother that I am sorry I was not able to see our nephew grow into a warrior and tell Ailis... tell Mother that I love her and I am sorry that I was not able to avenge our father."

The two brothers hugged and Rufius looked away. Furax, tears streaming down his face, hugged Hercules as tightly as he could.

"You will be with him soon and the Allfather. Here is your sword."

Macro shook his head. "No brother, I have killed my mother and my half-sister. I will not be welcome in the hall of the Allfather until I have atoned. I will become a death shadow and watch over you brother until I can save your life until then I will wander the wind."

"No Macro! Take your sword. You have done many fine deeds and the Allfather will welcome you."

They could all see the life force leaving the brave trooper but he forced his eyes open and whispered, "But I am not ready yet to meet the Allfather and my fathers. I will be the spirit of the sword and when you fight I will be there with you. Take out the blade."

Almost mesmerised by the words Marcus slid out the Sword of Cartimandua. Macro grabbed hold of the razor-sharp blade so tightly that he sliced through his fingers and blood gushed down the blade of the mystical sword then with a sigh and a smile he lay back on the bloodstained deck and died.

The only sounds which could be heard for a while were the crack of canvas, the surge of water at the bow and the almost silent sobs of Furax. Almost everyone jumped when the hawk, miles away from its home gave a cry as it plunged down on to the petrel. Everyone but Marcus and Julius gave the sign against evil, but the brother and the mentor were in no doubt that Macro's spirit was but a little way above their heads. They had all witnessed the most damning and tying of blood oaths, the oath of the death shadow.

The headless corpse of the Witch Queen and her daughter terrified both the druids and the warriors. It was unheard of for two of the high priestesses to be slaughtered in such a way and, for the head to be taken, was an outrage which demanded revenge. Morwenna could not join the Mother until her body was whole. Someone would have to fetch it back. They all knew that it had been taken aboard the Roman ship for the hunters had watched as it was taken with the body of the killer. The ship was identified and would help them to find those responsible for this outrage.

Faolan felt at a total loss. He had, selfishly, counted on the money from Morwenna to finance his coup. Although never stated openly he had felt there was an agreement. He might just as well have stayed at home and had Corentine murdered. He had lost most of his oathsworn and was left with mercenaries and fortune hunters. As they all stood around the body wondering who would take charge the door of the hut was thrown open and there, in the light of the sunset, framed in red stood a red-headed younger version of Morwenna.

The druids almost fell to their knees in relief. "Caronwyn!"

Her eyes narrowed as she fixed a glare of unbelievable hate upon all those in the room. Each one quailed before it. The Fist was the one who held her look the longest before he too looked away. "My Mother came here for protection and yet you, her warriors, her priests and her protectors could not save her from one warrior." She looked down at her sister's body and felt a shiver of anger run through her body. "Do you, at least, have the killer?"

They all looked at the floor in silence. The only one with the courage of words was The Fist. "It was her son, Macro, but I think your sister hurt him."

Suddenly animated she rounded on the deserter. "What makes you say that?"

"When we pursued him he was not running well and he was unable to raise his head in the boat. He had to be carried aboard the ship."

"Where is my sister's knife?"

They all looked for it, grateful to be able to do something and avoid the recriminations of the new Witch Queen. When they could not find it they feared another outburst but were shocked to see her smile. "Then her killer is dead for my sister, as we all did, carried a blade tipped with a deadly poison to which there is no antidote. He will have died a slow and painful death and for that I am glad." As she moved her eyes across the hut she seemed to see, as though for the first time, that her mother was without a head. Her eyes wide and angry she launched herself at the chief druid, grabbing him unceremoniously by the shoulders and shaking him, "Where is my mother's head?"

"They took it on the Roman ship."

"Then sail after them and return it!"

"We cannot, the Romans burned all our boats."

"Then send a rider to bring one." She seized Faolan by the arm. "You, Hibernian, your captives are gone and you are without gold. If you fetch me my mother's head I will give you the money you need for your army!"

Faolan's face lit up. Perhaps there was something to this religion, he had had no hope and now he had his crown within his grasp again. "As soon as we have a ship I will follow them and return with that which you seek."

Coldly, and hissing like a venomous snake, the girl who had, in a heartbeat become a grown woman said, "If you fail to do so then do not return here or I will kill you, slowly."

Metellus had organised Itunocelum well. The captives had all been housed under the watchful eye of Nanna. Metellus had thought that she would make a perfect quartermaster; such was her organisational and logistic skills. They had created a hospital under canvas close to the beach. The capsarii had said that the sea air would clear away the risk of disease and so it had proved for they had not lost a man since the fleet had departed. Metellus and two other troopers had undertaken a patrol to ensure that there were no other barbarian survivors to be added to the line of crosses. There were still one or two of the stronger barbarians left alive and Metellus had to admire their spirit. The lack of water had meant that they had no voice but the glares and stares as the Romans passed by left them under no illusion about the feelings of the barbarians.

"Sir, the ships they are back."

Metellus breathed a sigh of relief for the first time in days. To beard a lion in his den was a dangerous feat and Metellus had wondered if he would every see his friends again. He shielded his eyes from the sun. They had seen the fishing ships arriving back over the last couple of days and Metellus was confident in the time it took them to dock. He estimated that he would have at least an hour and decided to check on the horses. They had recovered well from their ordeal but now would have to travel back across country, almost a hundred miles and autumn was rapidly approaching.

As he passed Nanna she came over to him. "Have you eaten today?" The question had an accusing tone to it for Nanna was convinced that Metellus was wasting away.

"Yes, Nanna. I ate with the men." She fell into step with him, obviously wanting to talk. "The ships are back which means that soon you and your people will be home."

She humphed, "Home? I have a home no longer. My husband and sons are dead. There is nothing in Stanwyck left for me but memories."

Metellus was surprised. He had thought that she would be delighted to get back to the familiar. "But these people they look to you..."

"They look to me because I can make decisions and they were the ones whose husbands told them what to do. They were unable to think. Once they get home do you think I want to look after them again? No it was my duty as the wife of a headman to help them but when we return? No thank you."

They had reached the horses and Metellus went along the tethered line checking legs and heads. "But what will you do?" There was a silence and Metellus knew that she was looking at him. "Have you no relatives? Somewhere you could stay?"

"You live among us and you fight for us Roman but you do not know us."

"I am not Roman, I am from Britannia although not a Brigante."

"I did not know that. It explains then why you are taller than the other Romans. In our tribe, we live as a family with close family around us. My husband and his father had been the headmen of Stanwyck. Now that they are dead, as all the men are dead then other people will come to Stanwyck for it is a good settlement and those women," she pointed dismissively, "will take new husbands and go back to their way of life. That I cannot do. She slowly stroked the horse. When I was younger I loved horses and when my husband chose me I was glad for he was a smith and I got to work with horses. I think I will go and raise horses for they are kinder than people."

Metellus stood and looked at her, seeing the sadness in her face and finally, understanding the true effect of these raids. It not only killed the innocent, it robbed the survivors of their lives. "What would you like to do?" He emphasised the word you. Looking after horses alone was an unrealistic dream and he thought that she knew it. He could also see the tears close to the eyes telling him that she had more to say, if he let her. He gave her a shrewd look for he thought he understood her words.

"What I would do? If I, a mere woman, had a choice?"

"Men and women all make the same choices Nanna."

She snorted, "How long have you been a soldier?"

"Most of my life, ever since I was no longer a boy."

"Then you have lived your life in a world ruled by men. When you were on leave you chose where and what you ate and drank. If you wished to buy something then you chose it. If you wanted a woman then you chose her and paid for her no doubt. She did not choose you. When I was a young woman then I was chosen. The house in which I lived, it was chosen and built by my husband and the men. When I went to the market it was when my husband chose. When we bought anything, food, clothes, animals, even the jewellery I wore, then my husband chose not I." She paused, almost out of breath at the torrent which had emerged from her mouth. "So how do we have the same choices?"

They began to walk back to the shore, the ships now much closer and almost ready to dock. Metellus felt he was getting closer to her and went on quietly, "Then let us suppose that you had the same choices that a man has, what would you choose?"

"I would choose to live quietly in a home close to neighbours but out of sight. I would choose a home with a stream and a wood. I would choose to keep and raise horses and to ride them when I chose." She paused and stared intently at the tall decurion. "I would choose a kind thoughtful man with whom to live; an intelligent man with whom I could talk as equals." She sighed and then said, simply, "I would choose you, Metellus."

Taken aback Metellus stopped. "But why me? I have nothing. I am a decurion of the auxiliary and I have lived more than thirty-five summers. Already the first snows are falling on my head and I have nothing."

She laughed and it was a tinkling happy laugh like a mountain stream and her eyes lit up. "You are a fine and noble man; I have seen you and seen the respect you have from your men. They do not give that to anyone. You have nothing? You have wit and intelligence I have rarely witnessed; besides I have gold." He stopped, his mouth dropping open. "The barbarians did not get the gold and savings of my family. When we return I will dig them up. You said, think as a man and make a man's choices. I choose you. Will you have me?"

Metellus was stunned and, as he stood looking at this woman, he had spent every waking hour with for the last ten days, he knew that he did. "Yes," he said weakly, "I will."

The journey of Gaius and Antoninus Brutus had been fraught with danger and uncertainty. Deigning guards and companions, to keep a low profile, they had made their way across the desolated highland which separated the lands of the eastern Brigante from the western clans. Mamucium was as far as they could travel and yet still remain in the land of the Brigante. They hoped that news of their flight would not have reached the garrison at Deva or all their attempts to save their lives would have been futile.

Gaius was largely silent on the journey across. The wonderful helmet his father had bought for him was buried close to the high part of the hills for they needed as little evidence of their involvement in the failed rebellion as possible. Since he had buried that symbol of his failure Gaius had barely uttered a word. It was as though he had buried his hopes and dreams with the shining helm. Antoninus had tried to cheer him, telling him that they would not find him quickly and, once they had done their business in Mamucium they would return as though they knew nothing of the revolt which had culminated in disaster. It was not that Gaius did not believe him, although he did not, he just did not care any more. For a brief moment in time, he had had real power. He had had thousands of men who did his bidding and he had controlled an army. He had felt alive and, for the first time, like a real man. He found it hard to look at his father who had chosen a life of trade over a life of war. Had his father chosen to lead his people rather than making profit then who knows how Gaius' life might have been different?

As they approached the vicus at Mamucium, Antoninus reined in their weary mounts. "We will need to be as inconspicuous as possible. I have contacts who will give us shelter from prying eyes." His greedy eyes flickered to the two pack horses laden with the black jet; a commodity more valuable to some than gold and his hope for a return to better fortunes. Once the jet was sold he could buy the wagons needed for the stone, hire the drivers and return home as though they had missed the whole revolution. A canny businessman he had ensured that both of them each had a belt into which were sown gold pieces. If things went awry then they could flee. Antoninus looked fondly at his son. "We will emerge stronger Gaius, believe me."

"How? " Anger flamed in his eyes. "Will we buy a new army? Where? The only warriors who would fight now litter the streets of Eboracum."

As they made their way down the gentle slope to the gates of the vicus Antoninus tried to give him a glimmer of hope. "There are Brigante who are dissatisfied with Rome and there are tribes," he pointed west, "across the sea who would follow a brave leader. You at least showed your bravery."

"But my face was hidden, no-one knows. And if they did I would be a hunted man." There was his dilemma; to cash in on his limited success he needed to leave Britannia but at least he now knew that there was hope and there was a change in the young man for a while and his father was pleased with his own wisdom which, it appeared, had helped his son to turn a corner.

The man Antoninus sought was more of a criminal than a businessman. He had made his money robbing travellers crossing the high land and then, when the Romans began to patrol more, changed to become a trader himself with armed guards preventing others from doing what he had done. He had expanded his empire so that he now produced wagons as well. Before the arrival of the Roman roads, wagons were of limited use but now they enabled men like Antoninus to convey larger and heavier cargoes. For Gnaeus Vedius saw an opportunity to expand his empire to the east. He knew that Antoninus had quarries in the east and Rome was voraciously devouring stone in their huge road-building programme. The desire for Roman villas also fuelled the need for quality stone and that was what Antoninus had.

Gnaeus had a fine fortified house between Mamucium and Deva but it suited his purpose to have a home in the vicus, an anonymous though well-apportioned dwelling where he could do his business close to the busy Forum. He greeted Antoninus and his son like old friends even though he had only met the Brigante trader once.

"Welcome old friend to my home. A good journey?"

"A tiring one."

"I will have your horses stabled at once."

"Before you do that could your man bring in the cargo? It is valuable."

Gnaeus' eyes widened as he sent his slaves to the horses. "Gold?"

Tapping his nose Antoninus said, "Better. It is jet which is lighter and, around here, more valuable."

Gnaeus could see that he had, potentially, a good ally. Around Wyddfa and Mona, jet was prized by the druids and priests who still hid in the secret caves and forests which proliferated in the high places and there was an increasing market in Camulodunum where the rich and noble had it fashioned into fine jewellery. "How much?"

In answer, Antoninus pointed to the four bags which the slaves deposited with a reassuring thud to the floor. "An Emperor's ransom." Gnaeus was impressed. "I believe I know a man who will buy it all. Shall I arrange it?"

Antoninus became the businessman again and Gaius
wandered out into the street not wishing to be part of the sordid
business. The father frowned and then thought better of it. He
would conclude his business first and then sort out his son. "Ten
percent?"

"I was thinking more of thirty. You do not know where to sell
it but I do."

"I am sure that if I went to the Forum and said that I had jet I
would sell it easily."

"Yes but not in one deal. Twenty."

"I am in no hurry, I can bide my time for the right price."

"Fifteen then."

Antoninus gave the hint of a smile. "Give me a good deal on
the wagons and you can have your fifteen."

Gnaeus could already see how he would charge the buyer a
fee and he would make money all around. "It is a deal."

Gaius Saturninus and his weary turma reported to the Prefect
at the fort. It was merely a courtesy for Gaius was on the
business of the Governor but he knew that the Prefect could
hinder his investigations unless he was kept informed. "So the
Brigante revolted?"

"As revolts go it was a skirmish. The Irish raiders did more
damage but the Governor wants to make an example of the
leaders. Apparently, they are a trader, Antoninus Brutus and his
son Gaius who led the uprising. Their trail has led us here. They
had two pack horses with them."

The Prefect checked his daily reports. "They did not come
into the fort which means that, if they did venture here, they
would have visited the vicus."

Gaius did not want to say that the Prefect's judgements were
obvious so he just nodded. "And who would they go to in the
vicus?" The rather slow Prefect, whose face reminded the
Decurion of an ass, looked blankly at the legionary Decurion.
"Which traders are happy to work outside the law?"

"All of them!"

"Which would you say was the most important?" Gaius
Saturninus tried one last question; another blank look and he
would ask one of the sentries.

"Ah, that would be Gnaeus Vedius. A nasty piece of work. He keeps armed guards at his villa and his fingers are in every pie."

The Decurion could sense that this was his man. "Where would I find him?"

"He has the largest house in the vicus, close to the inn called The Saddle. You will see two thugs outside with cudgels."

"Thank you. If I apprehend my men have you somewhere, I could hold them until we return to Eboracum?"

"Yes, we have a cell here."

Gaius went into the tavern to buy himself some wine. He felt he needed to drown his sorrows. The Saddle, which was nearby was owned by a one-armed ex-soldier called Horse. A garrulous man he happily chatted away to Gaius for it was a quiet afternoon. "Here on business eh?"

Gaius ignored the question, having seen the shield and crossed spears on the wall behind the bar. "You were a soldier?"

"Aye, Marcus' Horse. Fought in the north. A grand life. Do you fancy being a soldier?"

"Perhaps."

"They are recruiting at Deva for horsemen. There was a revolt up north and they need auxiliaries. You ought to try it. You look like you can handle yourself."

Gaius was flattered and he liked this happy, fat, one armed ex-soldier. "So you just turn up and say you want to join?"

"That's all there is to it."

"Thank you for that, I might just do that." He slid a denari across and The Horse smiled. A good tip; it paid to be pleasant.

As Gaius stepped out he found himself behind a line of Imperial cavalry tramping down the street. The hairs on the back of his neck stood up. He somehow knew who they were seeking. He slid into one of the alleys which marked the edges of the closely built huts.

"You four, guard this end of the street, you four the other. You six, round the back." Gaius glanced out and could see that the officer was looking towards Gnaeus' domus and the two guards on the door were looking nervously at the heavily armed soldiers. "Remember we are looking for a father and a son.

Anyone who fits that description just grab them. I want too many rather than too few."

As soon as he heard the words Gaius knew that his time in Britannia was up. He ran down the alley desperately trying to get his bearings. He remembered that, at the entrance to the vicus, there had been a stable. He made his way there as swiftly as he could and then entered casually. He wandered down the stalls eyeing the mounts while the owner greedily assessed the purse of this potential customer. Gaius saw one black mount he fancied but carried on to the next one which was a chestnut.

"How much for this chestnut?"

"Five denarii!"

"Five?" I want a horse, not your business. Two!"

"Four and I will throw in a saddle."

"What about the black in the next stall, is he cheaper?"

"No sir, he is the best horse I have. I could not let him go for less than six."

"I will give you four and I will buy a saddle or ride bareback."

The owner shrugged. He had hoped to fleece the young man but he knew how to haggle. "A deal."

As Gaius kicked his horse on heading for Deva he reflected that he would never see his father again but then rationalised his betrayal. His father stood more chance of survival if his son was not with him and he knew that his father would want him to live. He would head for Deva but not to enlist, he would not fight for Rome but he would fight against. He would take ship and sail west.

Antoninus felt his bowels shift as the huge Decurion burst in through the door. The two thugs on the door lay in the street oblivious to all. Gnaeus Vedius wondered what Antoninus could have done to warrant the attention of an Imperial officer.

The Decurion grabbed hold of Antoninus. "You are Antoninus Brutus?" He was so petrified that his wits failed him. If he had said no then he might have gained some time. His silence was answer enough. "Where is your son? The traitor Gaius Brutus."

"He is not here."

"I can see that you dozy old bugger! That's why I asked you where is he?"

Antoninus suddenly decided to brazen this out, unaware that Gnaeus could see where this was going and was backing gently away. "Now look here. I am an honest business man. My son is also a trader. I don't know who you think we are but you are mistaken and I will take this up with higher authorities."

The self-satisfied look which appeared on the officer's face should have warned Antoninus but he failed to recognise it. "Higher authority eh? Like, say, the Governor?"

"Precisely! I knew the old Governor and..."

"And the new Governor has issued a warrant for your arrest for financing the rebellion led by your son."

At that point, Gnaeus wondered how he could keep his hands on the valuable black jet which lay at Antoninus' feet, for one thing, was certain the Brigante trader would not need it. Antoninus tried to bluff it out a little longer. "I don't know what you are talking about."

"I am afraid, my little tubby trader that the survivors of your pathetic rebellion and their parents gave you up. Your lands have been confiscated," he looked down, suddenly seeing the bags of jet at his feet, "as will, this booty. We will return to Eboracum where you will be tried. Now, where is your son?"

Even though it was all up and he knew it Antoninus showed, at last, the kind of courage his grandfather had shown. "I do not know!"

"Very well bring him with us, and the jet and the slimy bugger trying to slip out of the back."

Gnaeus blustered, "I am a businessman and I..."

"And you are harbouring an enemy of the state." He turned to his optio, "Take some men and ask around, see if anyone has noticed him."

The Prefect was amazed at the speed with which Gaius had found his man and delighted to finally have something on Gnaeus Vedius. "We'll be getting back soon. Just have to go to Deva. Apparently, he said he might enlist. I can't see it myself but if he has gone to Deva and not joined up then he may have already left. A pity, but at least we have the man who financed the rebellion and from what I hear his son was a waste of time as a general anyway."

Chapter 18

The funeral pyre had been built upon the beach facing the west. Macro was laid upon it in full armour with his weapons about him. Protruding from the top was a spear topped with the head of Morwenna and in the teeth of the dead queen was placed the blade which had ended the Decurion's life. The whole of the ala was gathered around in a hollow square along with the sailors from the ships and they, in turn, were surrounded by the captives.

Julius had made it a formal occasion for a number of reasons, firstly it was a ceremony to mark the death of a great warrior, secondly it mourned and celebrated all the dead of the ala who had perished in the campaign and, finally, it celebrated the death of an enemy of Rome. He was acutely aware of the attentions of the villagers. He knew that they had sympathies which lay, not with Rome, but with Manavia and he wanted a message sending to them. The last of the crucified barbarians had died in the night and as the crows and magpies feasted on the dead bodies it provided a sombre message for the wider community. Fight Rome and this is your fate.

Marcus took the burning brand from Julius Demetrius, Legate of Rome and walked slowly towards the byre. He knew his dead brother would wish him to do this but he found himself oddly reluctant to do so. It was as though by setting fire to his brother he was confirming that he was, indeed, dead and Marcus still expected him to leap up and be alive once more. Over the hills he glimpsed the hunting hawk and knew that it was a message from the afterlife that Macro was watching. He thrust the torch into the kindling at the base of the byre and stepped back. It was a well-made pyre and soon the flames were licking around the warrior's body. The armour and the leather slowed down the effects of the flames and instead the spear caught fire and its bright tongues ate their way to the grinning skull of the dead queen. The dry red hair, now duller in death suddenly erupted making a corona of flame around her head. The flesh began to melt and drip from her face and white bone briefly flashed before being wreathed in smoke. As the spear finally crumbled the skull fell crashing to the ground, the knife still fixed in the dead teeth and the mouth in a rictus grin. At that moment the flames finally consumed Macro and the decurion of the Second Sallustian Ala of Pannonians passed over to the half-life.

Later, when the assembly had dispersed Julius called a meeting of the ship's officers, the decurions and Hercules. "I propose that the wounded be taken by '*The Swan*' back to Eboracum. The Classis Britannica can return to its duties on the east and we will return the captives to their home."

Cassius looked unhappy. "Could the captives not sail back in the biremes for the journey over land will be hard?"

Hercules sucked in his cheeks, "Bad luck to have a woman aboard, let alone a whole gaggle of 'em."

Although they smiled Julius could see that the two bireme captains agreed. It would be too crowded and, having sailed around this island, not as safe as the land journey."

"We can make wagons. There are more horses here than we will need."

"But Metellus, there are no roads. The wagons would not last more than a few miles. Remember there is no road to Stanwyck."

Grinning slyly Metellus said, "No, but there is one to Luguvalium and thence along the Stanegate to Dere Street."

Cassius put his hands up in exasperation. "Well that is even better then; let us take them to the frontier where the Selgovae are flexing their muscles."

"Metellus is right, Decurion Princeps. This way we have protection all the way from Luguvalium to the fort Vindolanda and thence to Coriosopitum. I think that is an excellent suggestion."

Still mumbling his complaints Cassius moaned, "It will take a week longer to do it that way." He did not notice the smile exchanged between Metellus and the captive called Nanna.

By the time Faolan had managed to get a boat and sail to Itunocelum with the fifty warriors chosen by him and Caronwyn to find her mother's head, the ala had been gone from the port for three days. The crosses still marked the ridge above the houses, the circling carrion feeders still flocking and squawking for the right to feast. The frightened villagers had not dared to

218

touch the pile of ashes which marked Macro's end and the queen's skull still looked skywards. The ship's captain sailed up and down the beach for a while as the warriors looked for a sign of an ambush.

Angus took the decision for his leader. "I will go ashore with ten men. If it is a trap, then be prepared to pick us up quickly." He no longer trusted the Hibernian Prince since he had abandoned his men on the beach on their last visit. The captain took them to the jetty and Angus and his men sprang ashore, weapons ready. The only sounds were the carrion crows fighting over the bodies and the Manavian wedge moved towards the blackened patch of the beach. As soon as Angus saw the skull he knew that the Romans had, as he suspected left. "You eight, scout out the settlement, bring me the headman. Tuarch, tell his majesty that it is safe and I have found the Queen."

The old warrior reached down to tenderly pick up the blackened skull. It was clearly Morwenna for not all of her hair had burnt and her features were still recognisable. He felt sad, like a father who has lost a daughter. For all her cruelty to others she had always shown kindness to Angus and he had been her bondsman for the last ten years. He still regretted that it had been Creagth who was watching over her and not him. Had he been the guard then he was convinced that she would still be alive. He would have to do something to make up for his error. Perhaps he would offer his services to Caronwyn for she was the double of her mother.

He was still gently cradling the skull when Faolan appeared at his side, his nose wrinkled in disgust at the sight and the smell. He looked at the knife with a puzzled expression on his face. "Why would they do that?"

"A sign for the afterlife showing what the Queen had done." Angus pointed at the pile of ash. "This was the funeral pyre for the warrior who killed her and this," he held up the skull," was the trophy he had won. The knife represented the other one he killed, Brynna."

The headman appeared between two of the warriors. He was shaking with fear. Seeing that Faolan was about to snap out something which might reduce the man to abject terror, Angus spoke quietly. "When did the Romans leave?"

"Yesterday after they had …" unable to say the words he pointed at the skull.

"And you did not move it because…"

The man fell to his knees. "Lord, we did not want you to think we did it! We were helpless, there were many Romans and we were afraid and besides that…"

"She was already dead. Stand for you have done no wrong. How did they leave?"

"Some went on the three ships and they built wagons for the women. They travelled east."

"Good, now take your people and cut down our warriors. Then take the crosses and build them into a pyre. We will say goodbye to our dead now." The man looked in fear at the dead bodies. "They cannot hurt you and their spirits will honour you for this kindness." The man still hesitated and Angus said quietly, "If you do not take them down then their spirits will wander this shore forever. Do you want that?" Shaking his head, the man ran away.

Faolan seemed disinterested in his men and was peering eastwards. "If they left yesterday, we could catch them and recapture the prisoners."

Angus looked at him with an expression which was a mixture of disgust and disbelief. "You were not able to fight these Romans off with a thousand men. What makes you think you can defeat them with fifty?"

Faolan bit back his reply. He had been insulted but he knew that he needed Angus. "At least Caronwyn will be happy for we have the head."

Angus strode up the beach anxious to be away from this man he wanted to kill. "If you think she will be happy to receive *this*, then you are an even bigger fool than I took you for. I have better things to do with my time like burying brave warriors who were abandoned to their doom."

Livius was not impressed by the Second Gallic Cohort. It was his first contact with a mixed cohort and he had expected to see a different version of his own ala but they seemed a very slovenly bunch. Perhaps his judgment was coloured and tainted, after his meeting with the Senior Decurion, Catuvolcus. It was obvious that he had become used to running the cohort in the short time since the Prefect's death and bridled at the decision of the Governor to place him under the control of Livius. He was both surly and arrogant. Livius wondered if it was a sign of his advancing years that he did not like the fact that the man retained his Gallic name when the convention was to change to a Roman one once they enlisted. He also still affected all the accoutrements of a Gallic chief, with the long moustaches and hair, arms covered in bracelets. Livius still recalled the stories from Cassius about the ponytailed auxiliaries who had started a war and caused the deaths of his friends in the Ninth. Finally, there was his insistence on the title of Decurion Princeps when he was, patently, still just a decurion. It had been that difference of opinion which had caused their first rift.

"When I am satisfied that you can perform as a Decurion Princeps then I will promote you and you will receive the appropriate pay. Until then you are just the senior decurion, my conduit to the other officers and if you do not like it I will appoint someone else." Later Livius realised how pompous he had sounded but there was something about the man which brought it out in him. His counterpart in the cohort, Vibius Hostilius, seemed a much more reasonable man. Older than the decurion and shorter he looked every uncia a Centurion, and a Roman Centurion at that. He seemed happy to let the Decurion claim the title of Decurion Princeps for it did not impinge upon his world. He was in charge of the infantry element and that suited him. In fact, he also did not get on with Catuvolcus which also brought Livius and Vibius closer together.

Livius had allowed the cohort to have a few days at Rocky Point to become used to the harsh conditions although the fort was rather overcrowded. He called a meeting of the eight decurions and six centurions to explain how they would be used.

"Welcome gentlemen and you have come at a very appropriate time." It was at the first meeting that Livius detected the air of bored compliance, especially from the decurions. Perhaps he was used to the keen and hardworking decurions of his own ala. The centurions all had the fixed inscrutable stare which seemed to come with the vine staff. "The ala which is based here has been detached to put down a rebellion further south and until they return we will be the force which has to react to problems." If he thought the cavalrymen would be impressed with his news he was wrong. The horse element will be based in four of the seven camps my ala built north of here. The infantry element will be based here at Rocky Point." He pointed to the map on the wall at the four camps. "Our only eyes on the Selgovae and the Votadini will be the eight turmae. You will each need to patrol every day until the return of the ala."

"And who will guard these camps while we are patrolling?"

The question was the moment that Livius knew he and Catuvolcus were not going to get along, it was not the question, which seemed very reasonable, it was the tone and the attitude which went with it."

"You have thirty men in a turma, I would suggest that you leave six in the camp to guard it and prepare your food. When the ala returns then you will be in pairs in these camps and have more men available."

"Pah! We have women to cook our food."

"Not up here you don't. There are no women other than the barbarians and, until the *limes* are built we avoid contact with them."

The decurions all sat bolt upright, almost as a man. Catuvolcus stood, "But we always take slaves and they work for us."

Smiling Livius gestured for him to sit. "Not here, not on this frontier." He leaned forward, "It is the Legate's order."

"Where is this Legate? I will speak to him myself. We must have slaves, it is our right."

"At the moment Legate Julius Demetrius is with the ala but he will be returning soon." He lowered his voice and his eyes bored into those of the Gaul. "I will inform him of your unhappiness and I am sure he will wish to hear from you personally."

The Gaul wondered at the relationship between the Legate and this Prefect but, in his experience, once you were away from the Prefect you could do as you liked.

Vibius spoke up, "And the infantry?"

"You have a far harder task. We have vexillations from three legions coming north to build the *limes*. One will be based at

Coriosopitum and your job will be to protect them while they build."

"And we will be based here."

Livius spread his hands, "If you wish it, then yes but I am happy for you to build another fort closer to the workings if you think it necessary."

Vibius nodded, satisfied, "We will walk to the workings each day for a while this will help us get a feel of the land, if it becomes necessary then we will build our own camp."

"One last thing, we do not want to antagonise the tribes. We have too few men to deal with a full-scale revolt. We watch and we defend. We do not attack."

This was too much for Catuvolcus who, once again, stood up. "But we are warriors. Attack is what we do."

"No, you are Roman soldiers and here, you obey orders, that is what you do and do not underestimate these tribes. They are effective at ambush and they know the land far better than you. Avoid the forests they are horse killers."

When the officers left Livius turned to Julius the clerk. "Well, how do you think that went?"

"I am pleased with the infantry cohort for it will give us better protection than the fort guards but I, for one, will be glad when the ala returns for I fear the horsemen will not follow your orders."

Prophetically and sadly it proved to be true. Catuvolcus took his turma out on a patrol and headed north to the distant smoke they could see on the horizon. The twisting trail took them through the thick forests but they were lucky for they met no Votadini. Catuvolcus was keen, despite the admonitions of the Prefect, to acquire some women. They not only needed feeding they had other wants and desires which needed satisfying. The Prefect was safe in his fort miles away and the Gaul was certain that he could take some women, and, no doubt, plunder without the Prefect being any the wiser.

They came through a shallow valley and saw, in a clearing further up, a party of charcoal burners unfortunately men and boys. Heedless of the warnings from Livius, they charged into the camp, confident that they could overcome their victims. Before they had even reached the camp they heard the strident notes of an animal horn but they continued their charge, spearing four men and scooping up two young boys who were, unceremoniously slung over saddles. Catuvolcus was no fool and he knew the horn would bring others. They had their pleasures for the night and he led his men back to the undefended fort.

As they joked along the trail, the two boys silenced with a sword pommel, they talked of the pleasures they would have with the boys before they ended their lives. They were Gallic horsemen, the finest riders in the western half of the Empire and no painted barbarian could catch them afoot.

The ambush when it came was simplicity itself. The forest warbands were dotted around the edge of the forests. Their summer had been a barren one for the Romans had kept away but their king had told them to keep up the waiting, it would pay dividends. So it proved on this early autumnal day as Catuvolcus and his turma trotted towards their camp. Two small warbands had converged to the trail they had identified as the point of entry. Ten of the men covered themselves in bracken and lay alarmingly close to the trail. Ten of the others had positioned themselves at the head of the trail while the other twenty waited for the last man to pass.

The Gauls had no idea they were being ambushed until the huge warrior charged the scout and, with a single blow decapitated the horse. As the rider plunged to the ground he was hacked to death by two younger warriors with short, Roman swords. When the trap closed behind them Catuvolcus knew that they were in trouble and yelled, "Charge through them!" An excellent rider he charged his mount at the axeman in the middle of the trail and, as he swung his axe the decurion hurled his javelin to spear him. At that moment the hidden barbarians leapt to their feet and dragged the hapless Gauls from their saddles. The ones with the two boys were the target of especial violence and they were captured alive.

By the time they emerged from the forest Catuvolcus had but eight men left and two of those were wounded. His second in command was dead and the standard had been captured. His men looked to him with terror-filled eyes. They had never been so roughly handled before and two-thirds of them were dead or captured. "I have had enough of this, boys, let's go to one of the other forts. We cannot defend one by ourselves." The depleted turma made its way to the next fort along, the one formerly occupied by Marcus and Livius. The decurion in charge was shocked at the arrival of the turma but was grateful that he now had a quarter more defenders.

The next morning, when they awoke, the night sentries reported hearing strange noises emanating from close to the fort. As dawn broke they saw the grisly origin of the noises. One of the captured Gauls was nailed to a tree on the edge of the forest. He was naked and had been badly cut. Catuvolcus took ten men out in skirmish order, ready to race back to the safety of the fort at the first sign of another ambush. As they drew closer some of the troopers gagged for his penis and testicles had been hacked off and pushed into his mouth which had been roughly sewn closed to prevent him getting rid of them. They could see from his legs that he had been hamstrung but they wondered why he was standing on his toes. As they came within ten paces they could see that he was almost seated on a sharpened stake; if he lowered his feet he would be impaled.

"Cut him down but be careful." The decurion did not think that the man could live but having had the opportunity to end his own life he had chosen to live; it was the least the Gaul could do.

Once freed they quickly took him to the fort where the capsarius cut the stitches from his lips and took out his genitalia. As his wounds were tended to the man tried to speak but they could see that his tongue had been cut out. The exertion proved too much and, with a sigh, the tortured trooper died.

As the column moved north Cassius had to agree that it was a better way to travel for the roads were good and they moved at a brisk pace rather than the funereal one with tired captives. He was still worried about the Stanegate remembering the uneasy peace they had encountered. If the rest of the province was in turmoil then it stood to reason that the Votadini and Selgovae would use it to their advantage.

A newly philosophical Metellus merely shrugged at Cassius' concerns. "Take it one day at a time. There is no point in worrying about what may happen. The road is safe until

Luguvalium. There the Prefect will apprise us of the state of the road further on."

"You have changed Metellus. That is sound advice, not that I am saying you did not give sound advice before, but you are different now. What has changed you?"

"Perhaps Macro's death…"

Cassius looked at him shrewdly, "That has affected all of us and you as much as any but there is something else, a peace about you that was not there before."

Metellus shrugged. "I feel the same but I think I worry less. Macro was like a son to us all and it does not do a man good to have his son die before him. Perhaps I am making my peace."

"That I don't believe but I will discover what it is, believe me."

The fortress of Luguvalium was a welcome sight for it meant no camp building and some hot food. While the captives and troopers were made comfortable Julius and Cassius visited the Prefect.

"Am I glad to see you and I know that Prefect Livius will be as well."

His tone suggested something serious. "What has happened?"

"The mixed cohort arrived and the cavalry decurion managed to get almost a whole turma massacred and make the Votadini rise up along the whole frontier. The Selgovae have joined them and it looks as though they are going to attack us in force soon."

"You are saying that the Stanegate is not a safe route at the moment and we should wait?"

"Leave the captives here you mean? They cannot stay, for this is a war zone. You need to get them south as soon as you can."

"Back the way we have just come? I don't think so. Is the Stanegate still safe?"

"Safer than staying here."

"That settles it then, we will leave early in the morning before day has broken. If we ride all day then we can be at Coriosopitum before dark."

"But the captives will be exhausted!"

"Cassius, which is better, exhausted or dead?"

Reluctantly he had to agree. "Rufius send our best rider to Rocky Point. Tell the Decurion Princeps of our predicament. We can only hope that he can aid us."

Chapter 19

The legionary vexillation was a welcome sight for Livius. They were regular troops and the Prefect thought that they might just be the mortar to hold the crumbling frontier together. The ships had sailed all the way from Eboracum, having been sent by the Emperor himself. The interlude with the rebels had just honed their skills a little more. The Second Cohort was commanded by Quintus Licinius Brocchus, a twenty-year veteran whom Livius immediately took to. As soon as he stepped from the transport he had organised his men and made their way to Rocky Point.

Livius was surprised to see him and his column of veterans. "That was quick Centurion; I only just received the message that you had landed. We may be cramped but I believe we can accommodate you."

"No, thank you Prefect, a kind offer, but the sooner we get our own camp built the sooner we will be finished. I came here to get an escort to the site of the *limes*." He peered around. Is the Legate not here?"

"No we had problems further south and he was dealing with it and the Governor is on his way from Eboracum with the vexillation from the Second Augusta. They will be building further west."

"I am in your hands then."

Livius summoned Julius Frontinus, the clerk. "Julius here has been making maps for you and your engineers. They should be accurate."

The clerk snorted, "They are as accurate as I could make them from your trooper's measurements." He handed them over and then stomped back to his office.

Quintus laughed. "It is good to see that clerks are the same the Empire over." He opened the calfskin documents and nodded approvingly. "These are well made and will help us. While we head for the first site would you be good enough to fill me in on the situation."

"I will indeed." With the remaining members of the ala, all twenty of them mounted as scouts and Quintus on the largest horse they had remaining in the fort, they set off eastwards. "The tribes were at peace but the auxiliary unit which arrived a short time ago have managed to stir them up. I am afraid that, until my ala returns from a punitive raid, the only effective defence for your force will be the infantry of the Second Gallic Cohort."

Quintus nodded, "Well at least their infantry is more disciplined than their horse."

There was an unspoken question in the silence which followed and one which Livius fully understood. "The ala which is stationed here, my ala was raised in the province and they are all experienced at fighting the Votadini and the Selgovae."

"I did not mean to imply…"

"Do not worry about offending me Centurion, I have found it is better to be honest and avoid confusion which might otherwise interfere with efficiency."

"Good. These tribes, how do they fight?"

"Well. These were the ones who ended the Ninth when they ventured into their homeland."

"Ah, that tribe. The Ninth was a good legion. Some of their officers transferred to us and they told us of the disaster. They mentioned two young Explorates who bravely defended the eagle. Do you know them?"

Livius' face lit up, "Aye, Macro and Marcus are both decurions in my ala. You will meet them soon."

"I am happy already then for if all your officers are of that quality then we will be safer."

"The tribes love to ambush, my men will always be close by, but your men will need to keep their weapons to hand."

"Where is the first site?"

"I would suggest close to the river crossing. It is a logical place to start and your camp can be defended a little easier by the river."

"Building materials?"

"There is a quarry nearby but we will send to Morbium for some stone which is already quarried. It can be here within a couple of days."

"Good that gives us time to build our camp and lay the groundwork."

King Tole met with King Lugubelenus at the junction of their kingdoms, close to the upper Tinea. An uneasy truce existed between the kings but neither trusted the other. They were a political alliance working on the principle that the enemy of my enemies is my friend. The incursions by the Gallic horse and the sudden proliferation of the Roman camps had them both worried, initiating this meeting.

The two sets of bodyguards fingered their weapons and looked suspiciously at each other as they stood in the circle in the clearing. It was a tense time for one false move would result in a bloodbath. The two kings were well aware of this and knew that the alliance was on a knife-edge. They strode up to each other with open arms and embraced. The atmosphere became visibly more relaxed as hands left hilts and eyes looked less aggressively at potential enemies.

"We hear that the Romans have begun to attack your charcoal burners?"

"They did but they left more of their men than they killed. We have mobilised our warriors. As soon as the whole harvest is collected then we will drive them back beyond the Tinea. And you brother?"

"They have just built camps at the moment but my men are eager to gain revenge for past hurts. I have summoned the warbands and we will attack their roads now."

Lugubelenus remembered how aggressive young King Tole was. When they had planned a joint invasion of Britannia it had been King Tole's impetuosity which had worried the older king.

"Are your men ready?"

"I believe they are but, more importantly, I believe that the Romans are unprepared. There are no legionaries and we have heard that the feared cavalry with the sword have departed to be replaced by long-haired horsemen."

"Yes, they were the ones we defeated." The intelligence was new to Lugubelenus and he now understood why the Selgovae were taking advantage. "Thank you for that information. We will also attack now for I did not know the cavalry had departed," he gave an apologetic smile. "I thought they were not close to my land because they were attacking yours."

King Tole also smiled. "I thought the same until we captured a despatch rider who told us the true story before he died."

"We must keep each other informed about our actions."

"I will do so. Perhaps we could use a red arrow with the messenger to show that the message comes from us."

"A good idea. Might I suggest that we meet again at Yule?"

"Bring your wife to my capital and I will repay your hospitality."

So, the alliance of the Selgovae and the Votadini was cemented on the fast-flowing banks of the Tinea and hell was about to be unleashed on the frontier.

It was a weary, although considerably happier Prefect who rode through the gates of Rocky Point. The worried-looking clerk Julius Frontinus raced to him as soon as he dismounted. "Trouble Prefect."

"Not the Gauls again?"

"Not this time. A rider came, in the ala is returning along the Stanegate with the rescued captives but the Prefect at Luguvalium cannot guarantee their safety for the tribes are restless. The Legate asks if you can do anything?"

"Where is the rider?"

The weary trooper stepped up. "Gaius Spurius sir, eight turma."

"That is Decurion Macro's turma is it not?"

The young trooper's face fell and he said quietly, "It was sir but the decurion is dead sir; killed in Manavia."

"Macro dead?" Livius could not believe it, first Gaius and then his adopted son. He had thought that the finest warrior was invincible. He desperately wanted to know the details but that was not the priority. "How are they travelling?"

"Sir, we have wagons but there are many captives and the ala has been knocked about a bit sir."

Livius knew understatement when he heard it. "Never mind son we will get you all home. Now when did they leave?"

"They will be leaving Luguvalium before dawn tomorrow."

"That gives us a chance then." He turned to his chosen man. "Agrippa, ride to the nearest forts and ask the decurions and Centurion Vibius to join me. Trooper, get some rest for you will be returning with me I am afraid."

The young warrior's face lit up. "Suits me, sir, I want to get back to the lads, I am one of the oathsworn."

As he raced off Julius tutted, "Ridiculous allegiance to a piece of metal. Not logical at all."

"No, and you are right but sometimes the heart is stronger than logic. Now get me the maps of the Stanegate. I need to work out where they are likely to strike, where I would strike if I were a barbarian."

When the Gauls arrived Livius noticed once again the difference in attitude and demeanour between the arrogant and lacklustre decurions and the calm and dependable Vibius. "Gentlemen, first the good news, the vexillation from the Sixth legion has arrived and the ala is finally returning. Now the bad news, we believe that the Selgovae will attack the ala as it is guarding captives which will prevent it reacting to the attacks. Centurion I want your full cohort ready to march in an hour. We will go to their aid. Decurions you will ride east and provide a screen for the Sixth."

Livius was pleased to see Vibius nod and begin to rise but Catuvolcus and his cronies just sat there. "Decurions?"

"It is late and we will ride in the morning."

"*It is* late and you will ride now. The Legion is vulnerable until it has begun the defences, now is the time for you to protect them."

"You want us to stay out all night?"

Sighing with exasperation and seeing the sympathetic glance from Vibius, Livius put his hands on his desk. "Decurions. Soon I will have my ala returned to me. There are many excellent officers and chosen men amongst them. Unless you have begun to impress me as officers I will return you to the ranks and replace you with my men. Is that clear?"

"You cannot do that sir. That can only be done by an Imperial Legate!"

"Do not worry Decurion, the Legate will do that."

Realising that they were beaten the decurions stormed out. "I am glad that someone has finally stood up to them sir. The Prefect, well I know you don't speak ill of the dead, but he was a soft bugger who let them do as they liked."

Livius smiled as the Centurion's words and tone suddenly reminded him of Decius Brutus. "Come along then Vibius let us go to rescue my men."

The children were carried by their mothers, still asleep, to the waiting wagons. The troopers, by contrast, were on high alert for they knew the dangers they faced. The Stanegate, which had formerly been a bastion against the barbarians and the safest way to traverse the country, was now an unknown quantity. The Prefect had told Julius Demetrius of the many despatch riders they had lost in the past weeks. "I just hope your man gets through."

The Legate had smiled. "I know the boy looked young but believe me he has seen more battles and negotiated tighter spots than this one. This ala can smell a barbarian."

The Prefect had looked intently at Julius. "Tell me sir, will the Emperor send more men?"

"Even as we speak Prefect a vexillation of the Sixth is on its way to build a frontier *limes* from the west. And the Second Augusta is heading for Vindolanda. It is just unfortunate that this hornet's nest has been stirred up at this juncture and now that the Second Sallustian is back things should become safer."

The Prefect gestured at the depleted ranks, "There are not as many as there were."

"True we have littered our trail with our dead but the enemy lost many more and we have many wounded who will return to the ranks. It is the lot of the auxiliary cavalryman to suffer higher casualties."

"Probably why they pay you more!" The disparity in pay was a sore point amongst the infantry elements of the auxilia but Julius could tell that it was not meant that way.

"Take care Prefect may the Allfather be with you."

"I fear you will need him more than I for there are many eyes out there watching you and as soon as you leave messages will be sent."

"I know and I just hope that Prefect Livius received our message and, more importantly, is in a position to help." He turned to Cassius. "Right Decurion Princeps, lead them out."

The Selgovae scout was mounted on a small hill pony and the noise of the wagons being loaded had woken him from his shallow sleep. He was pleased that his chief had not found him that way or he would have been punished. That did not matter now for he could tell his chief that a juicy target was moving along the Stanegate, women and children!"

Moray, his chief, had brought his warband far from his home by the sea, for while many of the other warbands were still collecting in their harvests his clan lived by the fruits of the seas and the old men and boys could continue their harvest. His men were lean, keen, hardy fisher folk and he was looking forward to some plunder. Although only small in number, there were less than fifty of them, they were sound fighters. When the scout gave him the news he knew that he could not work alone, the numbers of the dreaded horsemen decided that but with help from King Tole he could and before that he could slow them down. "Find the king, he is camped close to here, and tell him that there is a rich prize nearby. I will slow it down and await his further instructions." The boy galloped off, excited to be part of such a grand enterprise.

It felt good to be in the saddle again. He had insisted that Vibius ride for, although the Centurion looked uncomfortable on the back of the horse, Livius did not want to speak down to him and it was important that they understood each other. "Where did you do your fighting then Vibius?"

"Mainly Germania. Mad buggers they are and fucking cruel. Pardon my bluntness sir."

"I told you before Vibius be yourself and speak your mind and we will get along. As you will when you meet the Legate."

Vibius looked across at the cavalryman who looked young to be a Prefect. "Do you know the Legate well then sir?"

Livius laughed, "He was my commanding officer for a while and then last year he and I did a mission for the Emperor and he was returned here as a legate. He began life as a trooper in Marcus' Horse."

Vibius nodded and said, almost to himself, "So we have a Legate who has actually fought at the sharp end that makes a change." Realising he had spoken out of turn he reddened, "Sorry about that sir. Me and my big mouth..."

"You are probably right Vibius but he has fought and all across this frontier and in that I have hope also he brings my ala and they are the best horsemen you have ever seen. But if they are tied to wagons then they cannot fight as they should."

"Which is why you need us footsloggers."

"Well put Vibius. Now these barbarians will attack from ambush. The best place from which to do so is close to the cliffs and the lake for they will have the advantage of height on the northern side and woods on the southern side. How are your men at open order fighting?"

Vibius grinned. "When you fight the Germans that is the only way to fight. The legions would stand in their squares outside the forests and we would have to go in after the buggers. Man for man I will back them against anyone."

"These Selgovae are also cunning and the masters of stealth and hiding. They will let your men walk by them and then leap up and slit their throats. Their concept of honour is not necessarily the same as other tribes."

"Good tip sir, I'll bear it in mind. So a double line in the forests might be the trick?"

"Triple if you can. That is why I brought all seven hundred of you. It might be overkill but we cannot afford to lose. If we can best them then they might decide to go home for the winter and return in spring. We need to buy the vexillations time."

"Well my lads'll do that. Once winter comes we can get down to controlling the frontier and I can start brewing my beer."

Livius was reminded of other auxiliary Prefects he had served alongside, Batavians and they, too, had liked their food and drink. "You are a brewer then?"

"I will be honest prefect, I probably like my beer more than I should but it keeps the mind occupied and the lads seem to like it. The waters around here look perfect for making beer. All I need is some wheat, for the hops we have."

Smiling Livius said, "I look forward to tasting some."

"Just wait a month or so sir. By Yule we will have enough for a serious session."

Livius had brought ten of his ala with him and he turned to them. "Two of you get down the Stanegate and tell the Legate we are coming but be careful there will be ambushes and I would hate to deprive the chef of his helpers." The two men rode off grinning. Although fighting troopers they doubled as the assistant cooks in the camp working with the skilful Septimus. "The rest of you spread out north and south of the road, find the enemy and then report back to us."

Vibius smiled to himself. This Prefect knew what he was doing. Perhaps it was no bad thing that the former Prefect or 'useless tosser' as Vibius had called him had departed this life.

Decurion Lucius was on point when Moray launched his first attack. The Stanegate crested a rise and then dropped sharply; Moray was a cunning warrior and knew that the horsemen would be concentrating on their footing, no matter how alert they were. As soon as the first riders crested the rise they were met by a barrage of slingshot, fortunately just stones and not the lead balls used by the Romans for they were far more accurate and deadly. Lucius immediately went into a defensive posture. "Shields!"

The first ten men came into a solid line with their shields defending their bodies. The missiles were still striking their mounts but the leather headpieces protected their most vulnerable parts and they were trained well enough not to rear and buck.

"Next ten, winkle them out!"

The next ten troopers took off, lashing their mounts into the forest from whence the attack had come. Their speed took Moray's men by surprise and they ran swiftly through the woods confident that they could outrun the horses which had to twist and turn through the trees. One warrior slipped to be speared like a salmon as he lay prostrate on the ground. Eagerly the troopers looked for new targets when they heard the disappointing notes of the recall.

Cassius rode to the head of the column as the scouts returned. "Casualties?"

"A couple of troopers and their mounts were hit by slingshots but nothing that will stop us."

"I think this will be the pattern for a while. They will make these quick attacks to keep us on the edge. I will relieve you in an hour."

"We are doing alright sir." The young decurion sounded offended

"I know Lucius and I do not doubt your ability but we need you to be totally alert and we have other turmae."

So, as dawn broke and the new day arrived, the pattern was set. Barbarians would attack, sometimes from the north and sometimes from the south, once from both sides of the road, using hit and run. Each time they injured troopers although none seriously but each time the column was slowed up and, unknown to the ala, King Tole and his retinue drew closer and closer.

Chapter 20

The King himself came with the two hundred warriors he had available. Others were making their way from further afield. Once he knew that the famous ala was isolated he knew he had to risk an attack, despite the disparity in numbers. The additional incentive was the large number of slaves they could capture. It was rumoured that they had been snatched from the Witch Queen herself and King Tole knew that he could gain much credit by taking them from the Romans.

Moray bowed when the king arrived. "You have done well my chief and slowed them down."

Moray scowled in the direction of the Stanegate. "But it has cost me four warriors and we have yet to kill one of theirs."

"Patience Moray, for soon they will bleed their lifeblood on this stone trail which they have built. He turned to his men, pointing at one of his lieutenants. "Take one hundred men and ride ahead of the column; hide in the woods to the south of their road close by the deep lake, when you hear my horn, then attack." The men jogged off quickly. "Moray, you and your men wait here. When the last men are passing then attack them."

"How long for?" Moray knew that his band was becoming smaller by the mile.

"Until they move and then keep harrying them. Do not risk your men but you will be able to kill some for your slingshots will begin to tell. I want them looking over their shoulders." Moray nodded and led his men back through the woods. Tole turned to the rest of the warband, ten of whom were mounted. "We will get to the lake and use the high ground. Today we take Roman heads."

Rufius was at the point when the major attack began. His men were pelted by stones and badly thrown spears from the rocks to his left and he wheeled his men to face the new enemy. Even as he moved forward Rufius noticed that this was a heavier attack and there were more missiles coming his way. His archers, all five of them, were already notching arrows and seeking targets. They brought down three warriors who erroneously thought that they were well hidden. Suddenly a horn sound in front of Rufius and he wondered what it prefaced; nothing good, of that he was certain. "Fall back!"

Just as his men began to back their horses to the head of the column he heard a roar and the trooper next to him crashed to the ground with a throwing axe embedded in his back. They were being attacked on two sides. His men were falling from their mounts as the two warbands closed in on the vanguard. He looked around, desperately, for support and saw that the wagons had closed up on him. On the left side, Metellus was racing forwards with his turma whilst on the southern side he heard the roar of "The Sword!" and knew that Marcus and his double turma was on the way.

Rufius spied hope. "Defend yourselves, help is on the way!" Warriors had closed with the ala and were hacking their swords at the legs of their mounts. Troopers thrust their javelins at the men on foot in a desperate attempt to save their mounts. Once on the floor other Selgovae raced in to finish off the dismounted and vulnerable troopers. Enraged Rufius rode his mount at the three warriors who were surrounding a wounded trooper, his sword slashed down, savagely splitting open the head of one, his mount trampled a second and his shield punched the third in the head rendering him unconscious. The grateful trooper grabbed the pommel horn of Rufius' saddle as his horse backed away from the enemy.

Marcus' voice rang out, "Rufius fall back and we will cover you!"

Rufius yelled, "Fall back!" as Marcus' men hurled their javelins to slow down the advancing barbarians. Suddenly the tribesmen disappeared back into the woods and the rocks.

Cassius rode up, blood streaming from a wound on his arm. "They have attacked the rear and a wagon is isolated. Metellus, you and Rufius hold them here. Marcus, take your turma and retrieve the wagon."

Marcus' men rode down the column. As he did so Marcus noticed that the Legate had ordered the men to dismount and defend the captives with their shields. From the dense woods and rocks, a barrage of stones, arrows and missiles rained down on the wagons hence the need for protection. Approaching the solitary last isolated wagon Marcus could see that there were only ten or so troopers left to defend it. He saw Decurion Graccus lying in the open space between the lonely wagon and the rest, a spear in his dead chest. One of the troopers, lying under the penultimate wagon, tried to run to help the beleaguered troopers but was cut down before he got there.

Marcus' mind was working overtime and he shouted to his men. "We can't clear the north of the road; let's relieve the pressure to the south. The Sword!"

With a collective roar of defiance from the whole turma of troopers, they wheeled from column into two open lines and crashed ferociously into the woods heedless of the missiles heading their way. The confident Selgovae were stunned when the troopers, fired up by a campaign of ambushes and shield walls, hacked and slashed at the unarmoured bodies of these barbarians who had strayed within the length of a sword. When twenty lay dead the rest decided that discretion was needed and they fled. Marcus knew they had no time to pursue; the wagon was still under threat from the northern side. "Back to the column!"

When they reached the trail, they saw that it was hand to hand combat amongst the surviving wagon guards and there were but five troopers still on their feet. One of the women, Marcus knew her as Nanna, was wielding an axe as she swept it before her to keep the tribesmen from mounting the wagon and making off with it.

"Charge!" The troopers galloped at the wagon and Marcus reared his horse to fell one warrior who had hold of Nanna's legs and was trying to pull her over the side. He leapt from his horse and stabbed a half naked, heavily tattooed warrior in his back. As he punched another one in the face with his shield, he saw that the rest had fled.

Nanna leaned over, "Well done but next time could you get here a little quicker! I did not fancy a stay amongst the Hibernians and these barbarians are just as unpleasant."

Laughing Marcus shouted, "Sorry my dear, I'll do better next time. Back to the wagon, put the wounded inside. Ten of you, form the rearguard, ten get on this side and ten on the other. The rest ride with me."

One of Marcus' men who had been unhorsed took the reins of the last wagon and it gradually closed the gap to the rest of the column. A cheer rippled down the line as they saw the rescue unfold.

Marcus led his small group of troopers through the rearguard. "We are going to be an extra rearguard. We don't wait for them to attack we look for them and attack them first so keep your eyes peeled!"

Tole was relieved when another fifty warriors jogged through the woods from the north. "Take these men to the rocks which are closest to the road." Tole pointed to a knoll which rose close to the Stanegate. Behind it, the cliff rose steeply; it was a perfect place from which to launch an attack on a column already weakened by the gnat-like bites of the barbarians. They trotted off and Tole gathered around him a hundred warriors. "We will cross the road and attack from the woods to the south when the head of the column is halted and we will hit the soft middle." He pointed at the turma of Marcus which was just passing their hiding place. "They have placed their best troops at the rear, that is good. Let them watch for the attack which will not come."

Cassius decided to lead at the front. Although wounded it was not fair on his decurions to ask them to endure and blunt all the barbarian assaults. The easy road was proving anything but easy. The wagons were moving faster than they would have done over the land but the horses were not draught horses and they were going slower than a man could walk. Just when his spirits were at their lowest and he was considering making a fortress of the wagons, a trooper yelled, "Rider coming in!"

Every trooper's hand went to his weapons as he anticipated another barbarian attack but was relieved when the young despatch rider from Rocky Point reined in his lathered horse. "Sir, message from the Prefect. He received your message and he is coming to get you. He has a cohort of Gauls with him."

"When did he leave?"

"He will be a couple of hours behind me sir, they were on foot."

"Good. Ride down the line until you see the Legate and report to him." There was some hope then. He turned and shouted to those around him, "The Prefect is coming! Pass it on!" The news spread down the column and the resolve of the defenders, which had been weakened by the attacks now hardened. Cassius glanced ahead. Once they had reached the knoll which was ahead they would have a difficult stretch of the road to negotiate for it was a mile or two where the road passed closest to good ambush sites. The Decurion Princeps was torn between going slower so that the relief column would be able to aid them and going faster to reach the relief column quicker. The decision was taken from him as the arrow flew from the knoll and struck him in his thigh. He grimaced but held on to his reins.

Sextus was in the first wagon, tending to the wounded and he leapt from the moving vehicle and helped Cassius to the ground. He turned to the troopers who were nearby. "Help me get the Decurion Princeps to the wagon!"

Although well-meaning the decision was a disastrous one for the whole column halted just as the men on the knoll attacked. As the dismounted troopers struggled to help Cassius to the wagon, the remainder formed a thin shield wall to protect their vulnerable comrades on the ground. At the same time, they all heard the wail from the middle of the line of wagons as King Tole led his warriors to attack the centre of the column. Amidst it all, they heard the voice of the Legate shout, "Dismount and fight on foot!" The column was totally surrounded and under heavy attack from Selgovae who had the advantage of both numbers and cover.

Livius and Vibius were discovering that the barbarians were not the only dangers in the northern woods. They were being eaten alive by midges. Little red blotches erupted all over their bodies as the greedy bloodsuckers feasted on fresh flesh. Livius kept them moving through the woods anxious to reach the wagons quickly but keen to avoid detection. They had left the road an hour since when Livius deemed that they were close enough for Selgovae scouts.

Vibius suddenly looked at Livius and held up his hand. The auxiliaries halted and they listened. In the distance they could hear the clamour of iron on metal and the screams of death. Vibius turned. "Right lads, somewhere up ahead, is a column of Brigante women and some barbarian bastards who want their

way with them. Let's show them that the Gauls are here! Open
order, half centuries." Without waiting to see his order carried
out the two officers led their men forwards quickly through the
woods. Now that they were no longer in column they moved
much more quickly.

Suddenly some horses appeared from the woods to the front,
before Vibius could order a defensive position Livius restrained
him. "It's our men."

The heaving troopers saluted Livius. "Sir they have the
wagons trapped, about a mile up the trail. They are held up by
some warriors in the rocks and they are being attacked on this
side by a large warband." The trooper looked pained. "They are
suffering sir. Things don't look good."

"Take the scouts and dislodge the men from the rocks." They
turned and crossed the road. "Right, Vibius we have a mile. Can
we get there in time?"

"Piece of piss sir! Come on ladies, let's kill some fucking
barbarians."

This time they set off at a healthy jog, and, even though they
were not in one line, they all retained the same rhythm of well-
trained soldiers. Livius and Vibius led them deeper into the
woods to enable them to have a broader front for their superior
numbers. Livius saw a lightening ahead and knew that they were
close. He was relieved to see the rear of the barbarians as they
pressed closer to the wagons. The Gauls hit them silently which
proved more effective than sounding a charge for the first thirty
warriors fell without knowing why as they waited their turn for
battle at the rear of the line. The half-centuries opened to full
centuries and gradually overlapped the Selgovae lines.

The deception could not last long and it was King Tole, sat
upon his horse at the front of the onslaught who, turning to urge
his men on, saw the waves of Romans slaughtering his men.
They were outnumbered and were between the wagons and the
swords, there was but one option, retreat. "Fall back! We are
surrounded!" The men turned and, seeing the Romans charging
fled west.

"After them!" Vibius led his victorious auxiliaries through the
forests following the speeding Selgovae. Livius turned his horse
to go to the aid of the column.

Marcus was frustrated at the rear. His men could hear the conflict ahead but they were the rearguard and no-one was there for them to fight. He was sensible enough to realise that, the minute he left his post then the barbarians would attack the vulnerable rear and, despite his misgivings, he kept to his post. In the end, it proved to be vital as the warband fled south and west, gradually outrunning the armoured auxiliaries. The first of the Selgovae to emerge were the men on horses led by King Tole and Marcus led his turma straight at him. "The Sword!"

King Tole was stunned as the line of steel rode straight at him. His nine bodyguards edged ahead of him to form a protective phalanx of bodies around their anointed king. Marcus deflected the first warrior's sword on his shield and slashed the sword across the neck of the warrior, his headless corpse riding ghoulishly into the woods. King Tole suddenly found himself facing the mighty Sword of Cartimandua; the king was a brave man but there seemed something almost palpably magical about the weapon which sliced towards his head. He held his shield above his helmet only to have it shattered by the blow from the blade. His momentum carried him through the line and he kicked his horse on. Marcus spun his mount and launched himself after the king. Tole hunched down and kicked on. Marcus' horse had charged a number of times already and was slowing. "Come on! One last spurt!" Marcus, the horse whisperer nuzzled its mane with his sword hand. Up above a hunting hawk shrieked and Marcus horse leapt forward and took him within a sword's length of King Tole. He slashed down with his blade, it slid from the armoured shoulder down the slide of the king to cut his leg open to the bone. The last effort was all that Marcus mount could manage and King Tole and the last of his warriors escaped. Marcus reined his mount in. "Well done!" Glancing up at the hawk still circling above he said, "And thank you, my brother!"

Catuvolcus was not enjoying his night time sentry duty and he was seething with resentment. In their past incarnation, in Germania, they had enjoyed the luxury of a fort and simple patrols. This night time work was just that, hard work. He had been angered by the sudden arrival of the centurion from the

Sixth, Quintus Broccus who had been there to ensure that he did have some protection.

The veteran had assessed Catuvolcus the moment he had seen him. Prefect Livius was an example of the new breed of auxilia, adaptive and yet conforming to the disciplines of the army. Catuvolcus was the old fashioned auxilia, clinging to their idiosyncratic dress rather than the efficient uniform and arms of the Roman army. That attitude transmitted itself to tactics and Quintus worried that the Gauls might take it into their heads to charge off after a hare!

"Glad to see you Decurion. The Prefect told me you had the picket duty. Have you seen anything?"

"There is nothing to see. These barbarians are safe in their huts while we freeze in this forsaken land."

"Such is the lot of the Roman Army on the frontier." Against his better judgement, Quintus offered an olive branch. "When dawn breaks, if you would like to come to our camp we will have some hot food for you."

"Bread and porridge? Thank you for the offer but we will forage ourselves."

It was an ungracious answer but at least the centurion had made the offer. "Do not stray too close to the barbarians. We want peace here while we build." The Gaul did not say a word but his expression told Quintus that the Decurion cared little for the peace of the Sixth. Quintus left without a goodbye. If they wanted such coldness then so be it. The Sixth could manage just as well alone.

The night darkened and it grew colder. His line of pickets began chuntering and mumbling to themselves. Catuvolcus sympathised with each and every moan. As the moon rose and the temperature dropped even more their spirits sank even lower. One of the outlying guards came in to speak to Catuvolcus, a greedy and lascivious look on his face. "There is a hut in the woods. They have a fire and they have food."

Remembering the debacle at the charcoal burners Catuvolcus was cautious. "Any sign of warriors?"

"None. I scouted around for half a mile."

His second in command leaned over, "We could say we heard the noise of warriors and had to investigate. If this is a lonely hut then no-one will know."

That convinced Catuvolcus, it seemed eminently plausible and he led the fifteen-man patrol as they followed the scout. He was now a cautious Gaul and the Decurion had his men ride all the way around the hut to ensure that it was isolated. Leaving five men to guard the horses and keep watch the others approached the hut. The latent heat from the hut warmed them even as they approached and hardened their resolve. They would take whatever these people had, including the women.

Inside the hut were the woodcutter, his wife and his two daughters. His son, Aed, was away with the king, training to be a warrior and the two girls had had to take on much of the work of their older brother. The result was that all four were sound asleep as the Gauls slipped in through the wattle entrance. They had not seen the old dog which slept by the fire and as they crept in, it growled. Alert in an instant, the woodcutter leapt to his feet. A powerful man he took up his axe and, seeing figures in the hut hacked at them. The first trooper looked down at his entrails as they oozed on to the floor and he dropped, silently dead. A second Gaul saw the blow coming which split his skull open like a melon but could not react. Catuvolcus ended the brave woodcutter's defence with a sword to the throat. The women did not scream, or cry or flee, they were hard Votadini women and they would fight for their land. They fell upon the remaining troopers, biting and scratching, kicking and gouging. The younger girl pulled a knife from beneath her pallet and slashed at the face of the Gaul who was trying to subdue her. With a mighty punch, he rendered her unconscious. The remaining two women were overpowered by the remaining Gauls who looked at the three helpless women. Without a word, the Gallic troopers spread the legs of the victims and ruthlessly raped them, including the young girl who lay unconscious. With their lust satisfied Catuvolcus nodded and the throats of the three of them were cut.

"Get whatever food there is and then we get out." He nodded to the scout who had found the hut. "When we are out, burn it."

The man looked at him with an uncomprehending expression. "We leave no evidence!"

As dawn was breaking they rode away from the burning hut, a glow in the dark and dim forest. They were leading the two mounts of the dead troopers whose bodies now burned with their victims. Catuvolcus turned to his men. "Remember we were attacked by a large band of barbarians. But we fought bravely and escaped with our lives." The Gauls nodded. "We go back to our picket line and then return to our fort when the sun rises. No-one will know of this."

Someone did know for Aed arrived soon after dawn. His warband was camped close by and he wanted the opportunity to see his family and show them his new sword and shield. When he saw the thick pall of smoke he began to worry and as he closed he began to fear. Finally, he ran as hard as he could to the home which was now a charred shell. He quickly found the bodies of his family and then started when he saw the other two bodies. The uniforms were still recognisable, Romans.

When the column of wagons finally reached Rocky Point, the troopers were at the point of exhaustion. Their mounts would need a long period of rest and recuperation to be back to their fighting best. As Livius sat, with Vibius and Julius at his side, watching the weary troopers trudge in to the fort he just hoped that the barbarians would give them a breathing space over the winter. They needed time to enlist both men and horses.

He turned to the Legate. "Well, sir at least we know that we have sent King Tole home with his tail between his legs."

"As long as King Lugubelenus and the Votadini are quiet then I shan't complain. Did you say that the Sixth was here already?"

"Yes sir, I met their Centurion. He seems sound. They have begun their camp and we are hoping to start the limes in the next few days."

"That should give us time to send the women and children back to Morbium and use the wagons to return with some stone. I know that it is a hard question to ask but can you escort the wagons?"

Looking at the troopers and their horses he was not sure. "If the frontier is quiet then we may get away with two turma, perhaps Macro and..."

"Metellus!"

The Legate was so quick with his suggestion that Livius looked at him askance. "Why Metellus, if you don't mind me asking?"

Julius had a cheeky smile playing about the corners of his mouth. "Let us just say that romance may be in the air." He nodded to the wagon containing Nanna which had just entered the fort, Metellus was helping her down and, even at thirty paces distance Livius could see the flirting. "I have learned, as I get older, to keep quiet and to watch. You learn much more that way." He looked as Marcus came into the fort, saluting them. "I agree with you about Marcus, he will need to see his mother and brother and then they can grieve properly."

Vibius had noticed the warrior and his sword. "He is a game 'un though isn't he? I am glad he is on our side and those men of his. How does he get them all so fired up?"

"You see that sword? They all swore a blood oath to it."

Vibius' eyes opened at that. "I haven't heard of a blood oath since..."

Julius finished it for him, "Since you left Gaul and joined up."

"Yes sir. It is good to know that the traditions haven't died out. That explains a great deal."

"And as for being a game warrior. If you had known his brother Macro then you would have seen someone who could outdo Marcus."

"Is he the one your lads were talking about? The one who was killed..."

"By his sister, just after he had killed their mother? Yes."

"Interesting people you meet up here on the frontier. I can see that my life will become far less dull in the future. And if you will excuse me, sir, I would like to get my lads back to the camp, it is nearly finished, but not quite. I would hate to get caught out if the Votadini start anything."

While the stocky Gaul stomped off, relieved to be off his horse Julius dismounted. "What is he like?"

"He is the opposite of his mounted counterpart. He'll be fine. Let us put it this way, I think he will be reliable and sound. You can ask for little more."

"The next thing we need here Livius is a bathhouse."

"You could always ride down to Coriosopitum, sir?"

"The last thing I want is to see the back of a horse for a while. No, a little food and a good sleep and then a few days to organise the *limes* and then I will see about riding again."

As the gates slammed shut Livius was glad that they had emerged from the latest trauma so well. Little did he know that an even bigger disaster was about to unfold as the Votadini came south, south for revenge.

Chapter 21

The wagons were streaming down the Stanegate with the two turmae of Marcus and Metellus as escorts. As Marcus had a double turma, having incorporated Macro's men, they were a formidable-looking force. Metellus was not taking any chances and he had procured as many bows and arrows as he could for the defence of the caravan. It might only take them a long day to reach Morbium but their experiences in the west had taught them all to take nothing for granted.

"Remember to get as much stone as you can from the quarries near Morbium and, while it is being readied try to get arrows from the Prefect. Oh, and horses you had better call in and see…" The words froze on his mouth as he recalled that Sergeant Cato would be supplying no more mounts.

Marcus put his arm on Livius' arm, we will get the horses, sir and do not worry, and we will be back as soon as we can. Perhaps when we return these women to their homes we may find more recruits for we shall need them."

"Sir a message from Centurion Vibius." The despatch rider had been patiently waiting for the prefect to say his goodbyes. "He says to tell you he has finished the fort and he is taking half the cohort to relieve the decurion."

"Tell the Centurion I thank him for his prompt action." He was not looking forward to meeting the Decurion again but he would have to. He needed to garrison the forts with the ala, however, depleted it was. "Cassius. I know it is cruel of me but we had better distribute the turmae once again to their allocated forts. We will rearrange the ala into eight turmae. There is no point my having one. Julius has the new rosters. You Marcus, Metellus and Decius will garrison the three to the west. The Gauls the two either side of here."

"To keep an eye on them?" Cassius raised an eyebrow.

"When you have met them then you can judge. Let us put it this way, I am glad we have Vibius and his men. Calgus, Lucius, Drusus, Rufius and Antoninus can garrison the two forts closest to the Sixth. I think they will be busiest. When we get more recruits I will send them your way."

"Right sir. I'll get the western turmae sorted."

"And I will get the Legate; he is leaving us to bunk with the Sixth."

Julius Frontinus sighed as the last of the horses left the fort and he was alone once more with the century of guards and the cooks. This posting was certainly livelier and more interesting than his job in Eboracum, checking invoices of goods which arrived and left. The trouble was, when the young warriors weren't there he missed their banter and their humour. He even enjoyed the gentle ribbing he received but now many of those young men would no longer be there to mock him, Spurius, Graccus, Cicero and, of course, Macro. He was not a superstitious man but there had always been something about that likeable young man which smelled of death. He rubbed his hands to take away the chill and he went back to the Principia to write out the requests for more men, horses, arrows, javelins and spears. He and the Quartermaster would have a long morning's work and then the requisitions would have to be taken to Coriosopitum to be sent to Eboracum; it was not easy getting supplied on the frontier.

Livius felt something was wrong when he rode up to the fort occupied by Catuvolcus. Firstly he was not ignored and secondly, he noticed fewer men in the fort and many men sporting wounds to their faces. He introduced the Legate and smiled when the complaints Catuvolcus had promised did not materialise. "You and your turmae will occupy the two forts either side of Rocky Point. That should make life easier."

"Thank you for that sir."

"If you send a rider back to Rocky Point and tell my clerk what supplies you require he will deal with that. Have you had some trouble decurion?"

"We ran into some Votadini last night. We ran them off but we lost two men."

Livius looked at him sharply. "Make sure you write a report and send that to my clerk. Were you on the picket line when it happened?"

Livius couldn't tell if the hesitation was a sign of guilt or indifference but the Gaul replied. "Yes sir but they didn't get through to the Sixth."

"Good. Well I will call and see you later. We need to push on to the building work."

Leaving Calgus and Lucius to settle in to their fort Livius and Julius led the last two turmae to the Sixth's camp. "I have to agree with you Livius about that man, I didn't like the look of him."

"I know Legate. Neither did I when I first met him and I am afraid that he does not grow on you. Perhaps we might change him."

Julius looked dubious, "But you don't think so."

"I don't think so." The newly built fort of the Gauls was close by and Julius was pleased to see that it had double ditches and towers on each gate. "Your centurion friend has worked well."

"As I said earlier; he is the opposite of Catuvolcus and for that I am grateful." When they neared the fort of Rufius and Antoninus only Antoninus took his turma inside. "We will keep you with us Rufius. This close to the Votadini it would not do to lose a Legate."

Julius laughed," After what Rufius and I have been through lately, this is easy."

The half-empty legionary fort also looked formidable and the two officers began to breathe easier. As they crested the rise above the river they could see both the Gauls and the legionaries busily digging the vallum. The two centurions, Quintus and Vibius had taken their helmets off to get on with the work and were labouring alongside their men.

"You have done well. "Julius looked admiringly at the progress and then he glanced at the horizon. "But you have guards out I assume?"

"Yes, sir I have two centuries on the picket line north of the river. We will have advanced warning, believe me."

"Rufius, just take your turma north and scout the edge of the forest." In the distance the first of the great northern forest stood like a sentinel to the northern badlands, it loomed some way beyond the red-crested sentries of the Gauls. Rufius led his men, glad to be back, once more, in familiar country and familiar enemies.

Quintus came up the bank to survey the scene with Julius and Livius. "We will build the vallum first for that will give us waste with which to build the wall. Tomorrow we will begin to dig the defensive ditch and that will allow us more spoil for the top." He looked searchingly at the Legate. "And the stone?"

"I have sent the wagons to Morbium. I would estimate perhaps four days for the first consignment."

"Good. There is some stone close by we can use but we will need bigger ones soon."

"You are closely following the Emperor's plans?"

Quintus quickly glanced to see if there was an implied criticism from the Legate but seeing none he nodded, "Yes sir. It will be four paces wide and six paces high. As soon as we have the first section in place then we can begin construction of the first fortlet. I assume our Gallic friends will be the garrison."

Vibius looked up grinning. "Well if it gets us out of work then we will rough it in a nice stone fort with a bathhouse and a hypocaust."

Quintus laughed, "Who said we were giving you a hypocaust. You Gauls are supposed to be tough aren't you?"

The banter was ended when the sound of thundering hooves could be heard from across the river and Rufius and his turma came hurtling over the northern bank. They heard him shout something and, as he and the turma reined in and turned, the two centuries of auxiliaries came racing down the bank towards the wooden bridge.

Vibius and Quintus both quickly donned their helmets. Vibius ran to the bank while Quintus shouted, "Stand to! Prepare for an attack!"

The legionaries calmly laid down their trenching tools and began to put on their armour. The pickets were climbing up the bank as Rufius thundered across the bridge the hooves of the turma shaking the temporary structure as though it would shatter with the vibration.

Livius, Quintus and Julius waited patiently for Rufius to arrive and report. He slid from his horse. "Votadini sir, hundreds of them and they are armed and bloody angry."

They all looked at each other and then back at Rufius. Julius said, "Why?"

Rufius had a wry smile, "I didn't stop to ask, sir. They were screaming that they wanted my bollocks as a war trophy so I knew they weren't friends."

"Sorry, Rufius it's just that they have been quiet for a while."

"Perhaps the wall?"

"Perhaps. Time to worry about that later. For now, we need a defence. Vibius, form a skirmish line this side of the bridge, try to slow them down. Quintus, form your men at the top of the ridge. When Vibius falls back we will have six ranks of javelins to face them. Let's see if we can discourage them. Rufius, send a rider to fetch Antoninus. A few more horsemen would not go amiss. Then place your turma on the ridge to the right of Vibius, your men are fairly accurate I believe." He looked up at the sun to estimate the time. "It took half a day! Slightly quicker than I thought."

"Half a day for what sir?"

"For the shit to hit the ceiling Livius."

Rufius led his men along the ridge. "Centurion we have a good day for it."

"It's always a good day to be slaughtering half-arse barbarians who just charge at you."

Rufius dismounted. "Don't expect these to be so obliging. They are sneaky. They will charge if they have to and they will do it regardless of danger but their king is a canny young bird and he likes to make the enemy bleed where he can. He doesn't know you nor does he know the Sixth so expect him to do something to test you."

Vibius was intrigued. "Like what?"

"If I knew that Centurion then I would be teaching at the military schools in Rome and not sitting up here at the wrong end of the Empire trying to save my manhood."

A silence fell over the battlefield and some of the auxiliaries glanced over their shoulders at Rufius wondering if he had made a mistake. Rufius saw their looks and said, sotto voce, to Vibius. "See, he holds his men in check making yours worry and fret about what he will do."

Suddenly there was a roar and, almost magically, a long line of Votadini stood along the other ridge just out of arrow range.

Julius turned to Quintus. "Perhaps a few bolt throwers along the wall might deter them."

"My thoughts exactly sir. Sorry I should have thought of it."

"No, we are all learning as we go along. It is early days yet."

The line of barbarians parted and two warriors astride hill ponies rode forwards dragging something. When they reached the end of the bridge two more warriors ran down the gentle slope and lifted up the object. It was one of Vibius' auxiliaries. The Gallic Centurion said to Rufius without turning his head. "Drusus, a twenty-year man. He was already planning his retirement." The words were spoken in a matter of fact tone as though the man was already dead.

The unfortunate Drusus was brought to the end of the bridge where his arms and legs were tightly tied to the bridge stanchions. Rufius noticed that the man was naked. Even from that distance, they could see that he had been wounded and marked; he bore the marks of many punches and blows with cudgels and sticks. One of the warriors took a knife and, in one motion, removed his genitalia. As Drusus opened his mouth to scream the second man took his tongue and sliced it off. The genitalia were shoved into his bleeding mouth. The soldier could not fall for he was tied and some of the auxiliaries began to murmur.

"Silence!" Vibius' voice roared out and then he added, quieter, "He can see us and he knows we watch. Let him die with dignity and do not let these bastards win." He looked up at Rufius. "I am told that you are an accurate and skilful archer." He pointed at the bow.

"So I am led to believe."

Vibius nodded, "End it and we will be beholden to you."

"I will do it gladly, as a friend." Rufius took out his straightest arrow as the warrior behind Drusus dropped his breeks and began to rub animal oil on his penis. He roared as he prepared to enter the doomed man. Rufius' arrow flew true and hit the auxiliary in the centre of the head. His whole body sagged and as he did so Rufius next arrow took the man with his breeks around his ankles, splitting his head open and, as the other three fled back to the safety of their lines his third struck a rider in the back.

The whole cohort turned to thank Rufius as a man, Vibius roared, "Eyes front. It isn't over yet", and then to Rufius, "better than fair I would say. We owe you."

"You owe no-one Centurion, we are all in this together." Having failed to rouse the auxiliaries into reacting the Votadini slid down the slope. Those close to the bridge held huge man-sized shields, large enough for two men to cower behind. The rest spread out along the bank and, holding bags of hay before them jumped into the water to swim up and downstream. The archers began to fire but the shields and the speed of the water made a hit unlikely. Once ashore the warriors began to crawl up the two banks on the flanks of the legionaries and auxiliaries.

"Very clever. We have to realign and, when we do, they will attack across the bridge. And there is also a blind spot on each side where we cannot see them."

"Are you going to oblige then sir and realign?"

"No Quintus. I am going to upset them. Keep your men facing the bridge. Vibius echelon right. Rufius, do something about these barbarians on our left."

As Vibius began to offset his line so that he was diagonally facing both foes Rufius and his men galloped away from the bridge, south an apparently cowardly action which the Votadini jeered. Their leader, seeing the movement of the Gauls and the flight of the cavalry ordered his men across the bridge. Led by the huge shields the arrows of the auxiliaries were largely ineffective. Once they closed to javelin range then they had more success and warriors fell to the swiftly flowing river, struck by javelins which penetrated the wood. Others took their places and soon there was a warband of at least a hundred, south of the river and closing with the Gauls. The men in the third ranks of the warband began to hurl their mighty war hammers at the Gallic front line. The huge weapons smashed through metal, armour and bone causing huge holes to be created in the auxiliaries' lines. Smaller, nimbler warriors leapt over their comrades' backs to take advantage of the gaps and they darted below the spears to stab upwards in an attempt to hamstring the soldiers.

"Cunning little bastards." Vibius could see that defence was not an option and he roared, "Lock shields. Third and fourth ranks, let's push these blue painted sheep shaggers into that fucking river." The burly centurion launched himself forwards and, using the momentum of the slope the Gauls pushed down. As soon as they hit the Votadini line the barbarians behind could not get the space to throw and the front ranks became a melee of slashing swords, daggers and the crash of war hammers on metal.

Quintus glanced to his left where the unseen enemy were still crawling his way. He was desperate to order his men to turn to face the new enemy but the Legate seemed to know what he was doing.

Julius turned to him. "Now Centurion. Take half your men and support the Gauls, we should be able to push them into the river." Quintus glanced to his left. "Don't worry Centurion, Rufius will deal with those and I can command the half who remain."

The remaining centurions looked nervously to their left. At least they would have shields with which to defend against this attack. Suddenly the warband rose and charged the Roman lines. Julius said, quite calmly, "Third Century face enemy."

The centurion muttered, as his men turned quickly to their left, "About bloody time too."

The Votadini were but forty paces away when they began to fall, hit by unseen arrows and then, just as swiftly, thirty of Rufius' troopers hit them in a loose line. The tribesmen stood no chance and were speared, trampled and slashed, the survivors running and diving into the Tinea.

The Centurion of the Third Century nodded his admiration and was then surprised to hear a quiet voice over his shoulder. "It's all in the timing." The Legate walked over to the bridge to see the rout of the last of the attackers.

Rufius rode back from the river and halted next to the Third Century. The Centurion nodded at Julius' back. "He's a cool customer."

"He's had a lot of practice. Sorry, we were a little late. They had more men up the trail trying to get around our rear. I left my colleague dealing with them."

The Centurion of the Third Century looked up as another thirty troopers appeared with two bound captives. "Good man

Antoninus. Now we might be able to find out why they were so pissed off."

By the time the wounded had been dealt with and the bodies cleared, Rufius had finished questioning their captives. The two bodies were thrown in the river, already dark with blood and bodies. Rufius' face too was dark, but with anger. "Well, sir he said to the bevvy of officers who gathered around him. "It seems our Gallic friends have been up to their usual tricks. Not you Vibius but your horse. Seems they found a hut last night and killed the man and raped the women. They burnt it down afterwards."

"How are you certain it was Catuvolcus?"

"I am not certain it was him but I am certain it was his men." He held up a Gallic amulet. "It seems the ones in the hut killed two of the attackers and our friends found their bodies. They won't rest now until they have had revenge and they don't differentiate. We are all Romans and all guilty. We now have a blood feud."

Julius' shoulders sagged. "Livius I think we shall have to have a trial and an investigation."

"We don't have time for that sir."

"What then?"

Livius' face became grim. "Rufius and I are still frumentarii and we still have the Emperor's authorisation. We will find the truth and execute the punishment." He turned to Vibius. "You are more than welcome to be present Centurion. It is your cohort."

"Just let me know when you have done with him. If I get near him…" He looked across the river at the forlorn body of Drusus. "Drusus was a good soldier, worth ten of him." The sad centurion went off to see to his wounded.

Julius examined the start of the wall and the detritus of battle. "Centurion we have made a start and none too soon. Livius you will need to patrol the north bank. If they attack too often then destroy the bridge." They looked at him, appalled. He shrugged. "We can always rebuild and in stone but we will need a fort over there. We will have to take our time gentlemen. This will not be built in a year, nor even five years for we will have to fight for every single uncia of it no thanks to one man and his men."

Catuvolcus was not worried when he was summoned to the Principia for there was but the Prefect and one solitary Decurion, no Legate and no board of fellow officers. He was going to get a telling off. He slouched in arrogantly, sneering at the ala clerk who gave him a mysteriously sad look as he passed him. The two guards on the door stamped their feet and rapped their spears on to the floor which sounded ominously to the Decurion like the lid on a tomb rattling shut.

"Decurion Catuvolcus, you are here for a serious offence. You disobeyed orders and put the lives of all those who defend the frontier, in peril."

He shrugged, "What did I do?"

"You left your picket line." Livius was a fair man and he waited for the Gaul to deny it but annoyingly the Gaul just smiled, "You went to a woodman's hut where you killed his family and raped his wife and children." Again, Livius paused and again there was no denial. "What I need to know is this, were you instrumental in this or did you just go along with it? Or did you, indeed, try to stop it?"

"Try to stop it? Stop what? They are animals and my men and I needed a woman." He pointed accusingly at Livius, "You would not let us have slaves. Those deaths are on you!"

Rufius began to rise but Livius restrained him. "Answer the question. Were you in charge?"

"Of course I was in charge. They are my men. They do as I say. Now I am tired and I would like to get back to my men."

"You are going nowhere Catuvolcus."

The use of his name seemed somehow sinister and, for the first time since entering the room he felt fear. "You can do nothing to me without a trial. I know my rights."

In answer, Rufius threw a leather packet on the desk. "You can read, I know that. Open the document and read it." As the Gaul read it all colour drained from his face. "You know what that is, don't you? You have heard of the frumentarii. You know that they answer only to the Emperor and we have this as well." Livius tossed over the document used, years earlier and signed by Emperor Trajan giving them the Emperor's authority to act as they saw fit to protect the Empire. The Gaul's shoulders sagged.

"We have rarely had to use these but the Legate agrees with us, for the good of morale you will disappear. Your turma will be split up and watched and we will try to rectify your misdeeds."

"How will it be done?" He asked dully.

"Despite what you believe we are neither cruel nor vindictive. We will give you a warrior's death. You will be taken from here to the forest and given a sword. I will then cut your throat."

All fight left Catuvolcus and he was not the same arrogant man who had swaggered into the Principia. Later when Rufius and Livius returned to the fort, the dead body already being picked over by foxes and the carrion of the night, they looked north to the forests stretching to the lands of the Pictii. "But for that man Rufius we might have built this wall safely, a barrier which the Votadini would have accepted and would have protected us but because an Irish prince wanted slaves and a Brigante trader wanted power we had to allow that creature free rein and the result will be a longer war and many deaths."

Rufius looked up at the skies. "Yes sir but we both know that the Parcae and the Allfather give us tests to see if we are worthy; we just keep proving that we are."

Marcus found himself smiling as they road down the road towards Morbium. The resilient woman from the last wagon, Nanna, and Metellus appeared to be a couple for Metellus rode next to her wagon and spent the whole journey talking and laughing. When they stopped to rest their horses Metellus sought out Marcus who was discreet enough not to impose himself on his friend.

"Marcus, Nanna has told me how you saved her on the Stanegate. I am eternally grateful to you."

The decurion looked down modestly, he did not like compliments. "It is what we do. She is a brave woman Metellus; she was keeping huge Selgovae warriors away with a war axe."

Metellus laughed. "I will remember not to get the wrong side of her."

They both watched as Nanna played happily with two of the orphaned captives. "She is a fine woman." Marcus paused, not certain how to phrase his next question; Metellus was like

Cassius, one of the older mentors whom Macro and Marcus had looked up to. "Will you be marrying her?"

Metellus' face reddened. "I do not know. How could I leave her alone while I soldiered? The frontier will be even less safe now. Besides I would have to ask Livius' permission."

Marcus laughed. "By the Allfather! Do you think Livius would refuse you? And as for living alone, my brother has a large farm with many buildings. You know that he would let you have one and then she would be protected by the family."

"She is a proud, independent woman. I am not sure."

Suddenly the young man was the one offering sage advice to the older man. "Life is short Metellus. Look at Macro, he was a candle which burned brightly but was snuffed out too soon. You have a chance of happiness, do not spurn it. Take it by the hands. The Parcae have thrown you two together for a purpose, do not waste their bounty. You will have happiness and should the Allfather and the Parcae end that happiness then you will still have the memory of that time." His face was effused with passion and sadness. "My mother and my father neither regretted their union nor their meeting which was equally traumatic. Do not regret yours."

"You have grown young Marcus. Today I see the man and a great man. Thank you for your advice."

Epilogue

Caronwyn's face was white when Faolan and Angus finally returned with their grisly prize. The storms which had raged for four days had kept them penned in Itunocelum. The delay had not helped Caronwyn's humour. Now, aided by her younger sister Eilwen she had seized control of the Druidic council and energetically organised the rebuilding of the jetty and the citadel which was now much improved. Her envoys had gone to Hibernia to recruit more warriors but nothing could be initiated until her mother was laid to rest. She remembered how her mother and the others of the cult had been angry that the body of Fainch, the greatest of the priestesses had not been given back to the Mother. Caronwyn and her sister were adamant that the same would not happen with Morwenna and already the burial mound had been prepared, the body laid amongst the grave goods and all they awaited was the final part of their mother.

When the ship finally made the newly built jetty, its shredded sails a testament to the storms it had had to endure, the two sisters waited there eagerly on the new jetty for the return of their mother's remains. Angus had, tactfully, wrapped his cloak around the head. Faolan ensured that it was he who handed it over to the new Witch Queen for he wanted his reward. Angus' opinion of this self-centred man, was dipping lower and lower as each day passed.

"I promised you I would return your mother's head and here it is." He proudly held it out.

Angus stepped forward and said, quietly and thoughtfully, his voice with the true sincerity of one who cares. "Lady, it is burned and it may upset you."

Caronwyn smiled at the fierce warrior who was showing all the gentleness of a grandfather. She smiled and touched his cheek. "Thank you, Angus. I know that you cared for my mother and I know that, had you been on watch she would still be alive. Would you take charge of my bodyguards for I will feel safer?"

"It will be an honour, my queen." The title was presumptuous for she had not yet been crowned but Caronwyn nodded as did her sister.

"As for the state of my mother's remains, I expected the Romans to desecrate her for she fought them all of her life. Give her to me." Faolan finally handed over the cloaked remains. Caronwyn opened it. Eilwen and she kept a stony face but those around gasped in horror at the blackened skull which blindly stared at them. "This merely serves to make my resolve greater. We will bury my mother and then we will give you your army, Hibernian Prince and hope that you can do better with it this time." She turned to The Fist, "And you, deserter, will earn your place here which my mother granted you. You will buy us weapons and recruit mercenaries to carry this war to Rome. This is not the end, this is the beginning of the revenge we will have."

Gaius Brutus stepped off the boat at the jetty of the only port left on Manavia. He had been surprised how easy it had been to gain passage and at a reasonable price. He did not know that, since the Romans had devastated the island and its forces, Faolan and Caronwyn were desperate for men and the ships they had sent out had actively sought young warriors. The captain of Gaius' ship had been delighted to make a little extra profit from the gullible young warrior. Gaius would not have cared anyway; he had a new sword, some fine armour and he was convinced that he was a great warrior who would lead the rebellion which would rid his land of the Romans. Once he trekked up to the heartland and met their leaders they would welcome him with open arms.

The wagons had been left at the fort ready to be sent to collect the newly quarried stone. Marcus' turma escorted the captives, now strong enough to walk, down the road to Stanwyck. For many of them, this would be a difficult time for they were returning, for the first time, to the place of slaughter. A place which was now a memory of the dead. As they neared Decius' farm Marcus turned to Gnaeus, his chosen man. "Take the captives to whichever settlement they choose. When they are all settled then return to the farm." Shouting and waving their thanks the captives trudged down the road to their home. Marcus and Metellus led the orphans and Nanna along the track to the farm.

Nanna looked dubiously at Marcus. "Are you sure your mother will want to be bothered with these orphans?" The five children were all under the age of five and had clung to Nanna since their return from Manavia.

Metellus answered. "You do not know Ailis; she was herself a captive and slave for many years. In this," he nodded at Marcus, "as in many things Marcus is right."

Guards had been watching and the gates opened as they approached. Decius and Ailis rushed out to meet Marcus and the three of them threw their arms around each other. For the first time, Metellus saw Marcus' face filled with tears as he sobbed on his mother's shoulder; the emotion of all the deaths finally getting to him.

Ailis held him at arm's length. "Do not cry Marcus for your father died the death he wished." She leaned in. "He had the coughing sickness and would not have lasted the winter. He wanted to save us."

Marcus nodded and coughed to enable him to speak the news he dreaded giving both of them. "Then prepare yourself, mother, brother for brother Macro is dead. He was killed in Manavia by his half-sister. He killed Morwenna. The witch is dead."

Decius, his elder brother could not believe it; Macro had been the ultimate warrior, how could he die? "Did he die well?"

"A poisoned blade. Not a warrior's blade." Marcus smiled, "He always said no man would ever defeat him, he was right."

Ailis shook herself. "Thank the Allfather that she is dead, she has hurt us enough. "She suddenly saw Metellus, Nanna and the orphans for the first time. "And who are these?"

"You know Metellus and this is Nanna, the woman he loves and he wishes to marry."

Nanna blushed and Metellus punched Marcus' arm. "I take it back what I said. How could you…"

In answer, Nanna put her arm around him and, kissing Marcus on the cheek said, "Thank you again Decurion. Once again you have saved me just in time."

"You are welcome and these, mother, are orphans from Stanwyck. We knew not what to do with them and…"

Like a mother hen with her chicks, Ailis folded the five into her arms. "Come with me we have more than enough room for such as you."

Decius looked at Metellus. "Congratulations and where will you live?"

Metellus looked at the ground and Nanna said defiantly, "I have money I will buy somewhere."

Marcus interjected. "Decius, I told Metellus that his wife needed to be close to protection. Is there no building we could give," Nanna snorted and Marcus went on hurriedly, "which they could buy?"

Decius grinned, "I have better. Sergeant Cato left me his horse farm when he died. I am spending too long travelling each week to supervise the men. If Nanna would live there and manage it for me then I would be grateful."

"A horse farm! Then all my prayers to the Mother have been answered, I have my man and I have my dream." She impulsively kissed Decius. "Thank you I will take the farm."

They walked through the gates and as they did so a hawk screeched and plunged behind the trees. They all looked up, Marcus nodded and murmured, "Macro approves."

Emperor Hadrian stepped ashore at Eboracum. The garrison had turned out on the jetty and Governor Falco was there ready to receive him. The keen-eyed Praetorians glared at the hangers-on and idlers watching from the wharves. This was a momentous occasion, the first time since Claudius that an Emperor had set foot in Britannia and the first time ever that one had visited the frontier.

"Ah, Pompeius. How goes the *limes*? And has the trouble been dealt with?"

"The rebels are punished. You will see their crosses as we head north. Their lands have been confiscated and sold; the profits have funded another cohort of auxiliaries. The Irish raiders have been destroyed and the captives returned."

"Excellent. You have done well."

The modest governor shook his head, "The Legate and the ala have done well but the barbarians north of the frontier have now risen. They do not like the idea of us building a frontier defence."

"Then the sooner I get north, the sooner my wall will be built. Come Pompeius I am anxious to see where Rome will build its final frontier."

The End

Author's Note

Si an Bhru is a World Heritage Site on the Boyne. Built before the Pyramids of Giza and the Greek and Roman wonders, its origins are definitely pre-history. There are the remains of the dead there and it has had many functions during its long life. It suited my purposes to involve the Mother cult. Most of Ireland or Hibernia as it was known to the Romans is also shrouded in mystery. Tacitus talks of Agricola going to Ireland but there is no archaeological evidence for this. There is no extant writing and the Roman writers just write of legends and myths. Again, this suits a writer of fiction.

Although the wall is credited with being started by Hadrian during his visit of 122 A.D. there is evidence that the turf element was already being constructed as were some of the main forts along its length before that date. There were many attacks from across the sea during Hadrian's reign and this may be why he secured both ends of his wall at defensible sea forts. The wall itself was built over a six-year period by vexillations from three legions. The legions built their own camps but were defended, whilst they worked by the auxiliaries. The wall was, indeed, started in the east, close to Corbridge. In the east, up to the River Irthing it was ten feet wide and, in places twelve feet high, faced with stone. West of the Irthing it was made of turf and only eight feet wide. I visit the wall as often as possible to give the novel as much realism as I can. I have had to speculate in many areas as rivers have changed courses over time and, in some cases, become less navigable. There are quarries near Morbium as well as close to the wall but I assumed that, to start things off, they would have brought in stone rather than quarrying new quarries. There is much archaeological evidence of temporary camps north of the wall and these are the ones I have ascribed to the ala. It made sense to me that they would have kept a screen of soldiers between the builders and those trying to stop them building.

The mixing of blood with a blade was a Celtic custom. Some smiths were reputed to have put some of their own blood into the steel to make it more powerful. The idea that Macro might become some kind of spirit until he had atoned for a misdeed goes all the way back to the Egyptians and was very common in the pan-Celtic tradition. Putting one's enemies head on a spear was a practice familiar to every army other than the Roman army. The Huns, Scythians and Pannonians would have ridden with felled foes' skulls on their saddles.

The series will continue, if for no other reason than I want to know what happens to these hardy warriors and I am enjoying discovering more about these great builders. Caronwyn and her like will ally with Faolan and Gaius Brutus to continue to cause mayhem. I will be travelling over to Hardknott Pass in the Lakes to visit the fort they built there to control the road to Ravenglass; as for the rest of the storyline- that is in the hands of my characters for it is they who determine where my novels end up-not me!

Griff Hosker September 2012

People and places in the book

Fictitious characters and places are in italics.

Name   Description
Ailis   Gaius' wife
Alavna Ardoch in Perthshire
Angus   Votadini bodyguard
Antoninus Brutus   Brigante chief
Appius Sabinus Quartermaster of the ala
aureus (plural aurei)   A gold coin worth 25 denarii
bairns   children
Bodotria Fluvium   Forth River
breeks   Brigante trousers
Bremenium   High Rochester Northumberland
Brocavum   Brougham
Brynna daughter of Morwenna
Burdach   King of the Dumnonii
Capreae   Capri
capsarius   medical orderly
Caronwyn   daughter of Morwenna
Cassius Decurion Princeps
Castra Vetera   Fortress of the 1st Germanica in Germany
Catuvolcus   Gallic Decurion
Clota Fluvium   River Clyde
Coriosopitum (Corio)   Corbridge
corvus   beak- a ramp which was lowered from a Roman ship
Danum Doncaster
Decius Lucullus Sallustius   Brother of Livius Sallustius
Decius Macro Culleo   Decurion
Derventio   Malton
Deva   Chester
Din Eidyn   Edinburgh
dominus   The master of a house
Drusus Graccus Decurion
Dumnonnii   A tribe from the west lowlands of Scotland
Dunum Fluvius River Tees

Eboracum   York
Eilwen daughter of Morwenna
First Spear   The senior centurion in any unit
frumentarii   Roman Secret Service
Furax   Street urchin
Gaius Brutus   Son of Antoninus
Gaius Metellus AureliusDecurion
Gaius Saturninus   Regular Roman Decurion
Glanibanta   Ambleside
Gnaeus Turpius Camp Prefect Corio
Gnaeus Vedius Criminal in Mamucium
groma   surveying equipment
Gwynfor   One of Morwenna's chiefs
Habitancum   Risingham Northumberland
HadrianRoman Emperor
Hen Waliau   Caernarfon
Hercules   Captain of *The Swan*
Idwal   One of Morwenna's chiefs
Itunocelum   Ravenglass
Julius Demetrius   Senator
Julius Longinus   ala clerk
Keltoi   Irish tribes
Liburnian   small Roman ship, normally a bireme
limes   Roman frontier defences
Livius Lucullus Sallustius   Prefect of the ala
Lucius   A deserter
Luguvalium   Carlisle
Lupanar   The red light district
Maban Morwenna's acolyte
Macro   Son of Macro and weapon trainer
Mamucium   Manchester
Manavia   Isle of Man
Marcus Gaius Aurelius Decurion
Marius Arvina Camp Prefect Morbium.
Mediobogdum Hardknott Fort
Metellus   Explorate
Mona   Anglesey
Moray Selgovae Chieftain
Morbium   Piercebridge

Morwenna   Fainch's daughter
Neapolis   Naples
Octavius Saturninus   Camp Prefect Eboracum
oppidum   hill fort
Parcae   Roman Fates
Petroc   Votadini warrior
phalerae   Roman award for bravery
Pompeia Plotina   The wife of Trajan
Porta Decumana   The rear gate of a fort or camp
Portus Santonum   An old port south of La Rochelle
promagistrate   Local official in charge of a vicus
pugeo   Roman soldier's dagger
Quintus Licinius Brocchus   Centurion Vexillation of the 6th
Quintus Pompeius Falco   Governor of Britannia
Quintus Arreius Verecundo   Captain of the *Hercules*
Radha   Queen of the Votadini
Rufius   Decurion
Sceanbh   High priestess at Si an Bhru
Scipius Porcius Prefect at Eboracum
Selinus The place in Cilicia where Trajan died
Setantii The tribe living near Fleetwood.
Seteia Fluvius   River Mersey
Si an Bhru   Sacred Iron age site in Eastern Ireland
Sicera   Cider
Surrentum   Sorrento
Taus   River Solway
Tava   River Tay
Tearlach   Hibernian chief
The Fist   Former cavalryman and mercenary
Tinea   River Tyne
Tole   Son of the King of the Selgovae
Traprain Law   Capital of the Votadini
uncia   Roman inch
Vedra   River Wear
Vibius Hostilius   Centurion Second Gallic Cohort
vicus (plural-vici)   the settlement outside a fort
Vindomora   Ebchester, County Durham
Vindonnus   Celtic god of hunting
VinoviaBinchester, County Durham

Viroconium   Wroxeter
WyddfaSnowdon

Other books by Griff Hosker

If you enjoyed reading this book, then why not read another one by the author?

Ancient History

The Sword of Cartimandua Series
(Germania and Britannia 50 A.D. – 128 A.D.)
Ulpius Felix- Roman Warrior (prequel)
The Sword of Cartimandua
The Horse Warriors
Invasion Caledonia
Roman Retreat
Revolt of the Red Witch
Druid's Gold
Trajan's Hunters
The Last Frontier
Hero of Rome
Roman Hawk
Roman Treachery
Roman Wall
Roman Courage

The Wolf Warrior series
(Britain in the late 6th Century)
Saxon Dawn
Saxon Revenge
Saxon England
Saxon Blood
Saxon Slayer
Saxon Slaughter
Saxon Bane
Saxon Fall: Rise of the Warlord
Saxon Throne
Saxon Sword

Medieval History

The Dragon Heart Series
Viking Slave
Viking Warrior
Viking Jarl
Viking Kingdom
Viking Wolf
Viking War
Viking Sword
Viking Wrath
Viking Raid
Viking Legend
Viking Vengeance
Viking Dragon
Viking Treasure
Viking Enemy
Viking Witch
Viking Blood
Viking Weregeld
Viking Storm
Viking Warband
Viking Shadow
Viking Legacy
Viking Clan
Viking Bravery

The Norman Genesis Series
Hrolf the Viking
Horseman
The Battle for a Home
Revenge of the Franks
The Land of the Northmen
Ragnvald Hrolfsson
Brothers in Blood
Lord of Rouen
Drekar in the Seine
Duke of Normandy
The Duke and the King

New World Series
Blood on the Blade
Across the Seas
The Savage Wilderness
The Bear and the Wolf

The Vengeance Trail

The Reconquista Chronicles
Castilian Knight
El Campeador
The Lord of Valencia

The Aelfraed Series
(Britain and Byzantium 1050 A.D. - 1085 A.D.)
Housecarl
Outlaw
Varangian

**The Anarchy Series England
1120-1180**
English Knight
Knight of the Empress
Northern Knight
Baron of the North
Earl
King Henry's Champion
The King is Dead
Warlord of the North
Enemy at the Gate
The Fallen Crown
Warlord's War
Kingmaker
Henry II
Crusader
The Welsh Marches
Irish War
Poisonous Plots

The Princes' Revolt
Earl Marshal

**Border Knight
1182-1300**
Sword for Hire
Return of the Knight
Baron's War
Magna Carta
Welsh Wars
Henry III
The Bloody Border
Baron's Crusade
Sentinel of the North
War in the West

**Sir John Hawkwood Series
France and Italy 1339- 1387**
Crécy: The Age of the Archer

Lord Edward's Archer
Lord Edward's Archer
King in Waiting
An Archer's Crusade (November 2020)

**Struggle for a Crown
1360- 1485**
Blood on the Crown
To Murder A King
The Throne
King Henry IV
The Road to Agincourt
St Crispin's Day

Tales from the Sword

Modern History

The Napoleonic Horseman Series

Chasseur à Cheval
Napoleon's Guard
British Light Dragoon
Soldier Spy
1808: The Road to Coruña
Talavera
The Lines of Torres Vedras
Bloody Badajoz
The Road to France

The Lucky Jack American Civil War series
Rebel Raiders
Confederate Rangers
The Road to Gettysburg

The British Ace Series
1914
1915 Fokker Scourge
1916 Angels over the Somme
1917 Eagles Fall
1918 We will remember them
From Arctic Snow to Desert Sand
Wings over Persia

Combined Operations series
1940-1945
Commando
Raider
Behind Enemy Lines
Dieppe
Toehold in Europe
Sword Beach
Breakout
The Battle for Antwerp
King Tiger
Beyond the Rhine
Korea
Korean Winter

Other Books

Great Granny's Ghost (Aimed at 9-14-year-old young people)

For more information on all of the books then please visit the author's web site at www.griffhosker.com where there is a link to contact him or visit his Facebook page: GriffHosker at Sword Books

Made in United States
Orlando, FL
22 March 2022

16056157R00168